THE
PROFESSOR

THE
PROFESSOR

ROBERT BAILEY

THOMAS & MERCER

Published by Thomas & Mercer, Seattle

www.apub.com

Amazon, the Amazon logo, and Thomas & Mercer are trademarks of Amazon.com Inc. or its affiliates.

ISBN-13: 9781503945548
ISBN-10: 1503945545

Cover design by Brian Zimmerman

Printed in the United States of America

In loving memory of my grandmother, Rene Graham Bailey

PROLOGUE

Tuscaloosa, Alabama, 1969

The Man had said to be at the Waysider at 5:30 in the morning. Tom arrived at 5:20, knowing that it was a bad idea to be late for a meeting set up by the Man. He hoped he would arrive first, maybe drink some water and gather his thoughts, but the Man was already there. Sitting at a table in the corner of the café, Coach Paul "Bear" Bryant read the Birmingham News *and drank coffee. Tom waded through the other tables and approached the Man, who hadn't moved since the jingle of the front door had announced Tom's arrival. Reaching the table, Tom cleared his throat.*

"Hey, Coach."

The Man looked up from his paper but didn't speak or smile. After two or three seconds, his mouth curved into a grin and he extended his hand.

"Well, you're still a scrawny sack a shit. Ain't that woman of yours feeding you?"

Tom smiled, relieved that the Man had broken the ice. As they shook hands and Tom sat down, a waitress came over to take their orders. The Man ordered two eggs, bacon, grits, biscuits, and more coffee. Tom said he'd have the same, knowing his stomach couldn't handle that much food, but too nervous to ask for a menu.

As the waitress shuffled off, the Man took a sip of coffee and leaned toward Tom.

"So, how are things in Birmingham?"

"Great, Coach," Tom said, trying to keep his voice steady. "I'm with a small insurance defense firm. Getting in the courtroom a little."

"So I hear. Three jury trials and three wins in four years, right?"

Tom nodded, flattered but not surprised. The Man had so many judicial contacts, he could have made one phone call to learn Tom's trial record. "Yes, sir, I've been lucky. George McDuff is a great partner, and he—"

"Lucky my ass," the Man said, squinting at Tom. "The guy I spoke to said McDuff lets you run the show. He may help pick the jury, but then it's your ball game."

Tom's face flushed with pride. The Man had done his homework. But why? The Man had not explained the purpose of this meeting when he had called yesterday. He had just said he needed to talk about something important.

"Tom," the Man said, looking down to light a cigarette. "Jim Heacock came by my office Tuesday morning. You know Jim?"

Tom wrinkled his eyebrows. "Dean Heacock?"

The Man nodded, blowing smoke to his side. "Jim said his Evidence professor quit last week and he needs to fill that spot. He also wants someone to start a trial program and field a team to compete against other law schools. Jim really wants some new blood. Some talent. He said there weren't any good candidates in the teaching ranks and asked me if I knew of any lawyers in the state who I thought would make a good professor." The Man paused, tapping his cigarette into an ashtray on the table. "The first name that came to me was yours."

"Mine?" Tom asked, dumbfounded. He had never given teaching a second thought. He wanted to be a trial lawyer. Just last week Lawrence Butler of the Jones & Butler firm had wanted to discuss Tom's future with him over lunch. Although an offer had not been made, Tom was confident he'd get one soon, if not from Jones & Butler then from one of the other big firms.

"Yours," the Man repeated. "Salary is fifteen thousand a year." The Man set his cigarette on the ashtray and took a sip of coffee. "Tom, it's real simple. If you want the job, I'll tell Jim to hire you."

Tom gazed down at the smoldering cigarette. Fifteen thousand dollars a year? That was a little more than what he was making now, but what about the future? What about being a trial lawyer?

"Coach, I . . . uh . . . I don't know. I've never thought about teaching. I'll need to talk with Julie. When do you need to know something?"

"Just get back to me in a week. I agree you should talk with your wife. But I want you to think about something." The Man paused, taking one last pull on the cigarette before crushing it out in the ashtray. "Tom, I've always believed in giving something back to the people and institutions that gave to you. The University of Alabama has given me a lot. It's where I played football and learned I wanted to be a coach. It's where I got my degree and met my wife. I've never regretted coming home." Then, forming a tent with his hands, he added, "You won't regret it either."

Tom met the Man's eye and couldn't help but think of that moment ten years earlier when the Man had sat at another table, flanked not just by Tom, but by Tom's momma and daddy. He could still remember the Man's words. "Son, you'll never regret choosing to play for me and choosing to attend school at Alabama." Turning to Tom's momma, the Man had said, "Ma'am, I think your son's a great football player and, more than that, a great kid. We'll make him a man. We'll make him go to class and get his degree." Looking at Tom's daddy, the Man had said, "And if he gets out of line, we'll get *him back in line, even if we have to lean on him a little." Tom's daddy had smiled at the last statement and met the Man's gaze. The Man concluded by saying, "Folks, if you send your boy to Alabama, he'll come out of it a winner. We'll teach him success on the football field, and that success will carry over into every part of his life." The Man had gone away without an answer that night, but Tom had known. He was sold, just like his parents, on Alabama football and Coach Paul Bryant.*

A few minutes later the waitress brought their food, and the talk turned to the past, of the '61 team and whether Tom kept up with any of the boys. The Man ate his breakfast quickly and looked at his watch every so often. He had done what he had come to do and now it was on to the next job at hand. When they were finished, the Man picked up the tab, and the two men walked together to Tom's car.

"Think about what I said, son," the Man said, squeezing Tom's shoulder. "I'd love for you to come home."

"OK, Coach, I . . ." But the Man was already walking away, passing out of earshot before Tom could get the words out. Through the glare of the sun, the Man's six-foot-four-inch body cast a shadow over half the parking lot. Tom smiled and opened his car door.

He would talk to Julie. He would speak with George McDuff. He might even write out the costs and benefits of becoming a law professor. But by the time he was halfway to Birmingham, Tom knew. Just as he had known those many years ago.

The Man had called. And he knew he must answer.

PART ONE

PART ONE

1

At 10:30 a.m. on Tuesday, September 2, 2009, Rose Batson stepped out of the Texaco gas station that she managed to grab a smoke. None of the four self-serve pumps were in use, and Rose spat on the ground after blowing out her first puff. "Ain't makin' no money today," she said to herself, taking a long drag on her Camel unfiltered cigarette. Of course, it made no difference to Rose. She was on salary. But customers helped make the day pass. Yesterday had been crazy, what with all the beachgoers coming home. There hadn't been a time from 10:00 a.m. to 8:00 p.m. when at least one of her pumps wasn't in use. Rose herself had only been to the beach once. Back in the summer of '67, when she was a teenager. Panama City for a long weekend. Rose smiled to herself, thinking of the long-ago trip that marked the first, second, and third times she had ever been laid.

"Old Rosie could throw that leg," she said out loud, laughing at the memory of her lost virginity.

Rose Batson had run the Texaco station at the intersection of Highway 82 and Limestone Bottom Road for over thirty-five years.

Raised by her grandmother after her mother and father perished in a house fire, Rose was hired on by Tom Sloan at Sloan's Bait and Beer Store in 1972. When Sloan sold the store to Texaco in 1990, Rose stayed on to manage the place. There wasn't anybody in Henshaw or Henshaw County that Rose Batson didn't know or at least claim she knew. She had seen a lot of things too. One night ten years earlier she had seen Rodney Carver shoot Henry Dawson with a twelve-gauge shotgun right outside her store window. Henry—or Hal the Pal as folks in Henshaw called him— had been too close a pal to Rodney's wife, and Rodney had taken offense. Henshaw County style.

Rose stretched her arms over her head and her back creaked loudly. She coughed and some phlegm gathered in her throat, which she violently spat out.

"Fallin' apart, old woman. You just fallin' apart," she growled to herself. Rose tossed the cigarette on the ground and stomped it out with her foot. Looking to her right, she thought she saw an object in the distance. Squinting, she noticed that the object was a car and it was approaching the station. She watched in silence as the car continued its ascent and smiled when its left-turn signal came on.

"Back in bidness," she said, turning to walk back into the store. As she opened the door, she saw out of the corner of her eye another vehicle approaching from the opposite direction. As it began to hit a slight dip in Highway 82, Rose felt her stomach tighten. It was an eighteen-wheeler, and judging from the cylinder shape of its trailer, it was hauling some sort of fuel. She took two slow steps back toward the pumps and watched. As the eighteen-wheeler arose out of the dip and came into view, Rose Batson looked back at the stoplight and saw the red Honda Accord beginning its turn.

Oh my God, she thought as her hands instinctively went to her cheeks and she held her breath.

2

Dewey Newton was hungover and running late. *Not good*, he knew. The goddamn dispatcher had said the rig would be ready by nine but it hadn't been. *Not my fault.* He shook his head. *It won't make a damn. Jack will blame my ass anyway.* Dewey had made the Tuscaloosa-to-Montgomery run a couple of times before, and it was no big deal. Straight shot on Highway 82—an hour-and-a-half drive by the speed limit, an hour-and-twenty if you drove a few miles over.

But when you don't hit the road till ten and you've got to be there by eleven . . .

Dewey squeezed the wheel and began fumbling with the radio, trying to find a station that played country music—not the new hip-hop country that Dewey couldn't stand but good old George Jones/Merle Haggard country. Up ahead he saw a Texaco station and a stoplight. As he passed a faded green "Henshaw City Limits" sign, Dewey glanced down at the clock on the dash.

10:35 a.m.

From experience, Dewey knew that Henshaw was the halfway point of the trip. He had made up some time, but he was still fifteen minutes behind where he needed to be.

Dewey scratched his stubble and wiped sweat from his forehead, thinking about his boss. Seeing the son of a bitch in his mind. Jack Daniel Willistone. Walking the yard, cigarette dangling from his mouth. His face red from exertion, his work shirt damp with sweat. His eyes mean. Unforgiving . . .

"We work longer, we work faster, and we work smarter." That was Jack's mantra, and Dewey knew only too well what it meant. Drivers were expected to drive more than the eleven hours a day allowed by DOT regulations and fix their driver's logs to show compliance. Drivers were also expected to push the envelope on the road. If a load typically took an hour, Jack wanted it done in fifty minutes.

That was the deal, and every man on the yard abided by it. And Dewey knew things were only going to get worse. There were rumors that Jack was talking merger with several of the big dogs up east, and the deal could be worth hundreds of millions. To get the price he wanted, Jack needed two things. More revenue and more customers.

Which means my crazy-ass schedule is only going to get crazier.

Dewey gritted his teeth, wishing that he could just quit. He had two girls at home. A wife. *I'm missing it*, he knew. *I'm missing their whole life.* But if he quit he'd have to go back to seven-dollar-an-hour gigs, moving from job to job, town to town, without any chance of a future. He and Wilma had talked about it a million times. Jack Willistone was a son of a bitch, but he paid almost double what Dewey could make working anywhere else. After the last speeding ticket, Dewey had wanted to quit. He had even filled out his notice. But Wilma wouldn't let him hand it in. "My girls are going to college. They ain't going to be waiting tables like me. We're going to do whatever we have to do to make that happen."

I can't quit, Dewey knew, glancing again at the clock. 10:36 a.m.

George Strait's "Amarillo by Morning" burst out of the speakers of the radio and Dewey whispered, "Finally," in approval of the DJ's choice. He took a deep breath and tried to relax. The highway had dipped a little, but he could still see the top of the gas station and the green of the stoplight.

Stay green, baby . . .

The speed limit was sixty-five miles per hour. Pressing the accelerator down until he reached eighty, Dewey Newton began to come out of the dip on Highway 82.

—

Bob Bradshaw hated Highway 82. But there was no quicker or more direct route from Montgomery to Tuscaloosa. *And I need this to be quick*, he thought, knowing that the word "quick"—or rather, the concept of a "quick visit"—was foreign to his mother-in-law. Bob shook his head, thinking of Richard T. McMurphy, his partner and boss, who would be riding him hard when he returned to the office tomorrow after eight days at the beach.

"Cows!" Nicole screamed from the backseat, jarring Bob from his fit of worry.

He glanced to his left and saw that they were passing a cattle farm. He could see it and, a few seconds later, could smell the evidence. *Ah, manure. Perfect*, Bob thought, wondering if his mood was going to improve any time soon.

"That's right, honey. You're a smart girl. How do cows go?" Jeannie Bradshaw, Nicole's mother, asked.

"Mooooo!" Nicole answered, smiling.

Bob smiled too. If anything could lift his spirits, it was his little girl. Nicole was really coming along, and her new trick was yelling out things she recognized while riding in the backseat.

"Can you believe she'll be three in a couple of months?" Bob asked, one hand on the wheel and the other pushing the stop button on the CD player.

"I can't even believe she's two," Jeannie said, sighing. "Seems like just yesterday . . ." But she didn't complete her thought and she didn't have to. Bob knew. *It seems like just yesterday we were bringing her home from the hospital.* Life was moving fast, and with any luck, Nicole would have a brother or sister in a year or so.

"Sign!" Nicole yelled from the back as they passed a green sign indicating "Tuscaloosa 50 Miles." Bob looked at his watch. 10:30 a.m.

"Making good time," he said, more to himself than to Jeannie, who just nodded. They had gotten an early start that morning and might make it home by 6:00 p.m. Bob grimaced, thinking about all the piles of paper that undoubtedly lay on top of his desk. And again about McMurphy. Lawyers needed vacations just like everyone else. *But it's a bitch coming back.*

Bob sighed and glanced at the gas gauge, which was getting perilously close to "E."

"Christ," Bob said, again more to himself.

"Gas?" Jeannie asked, reading his mind.

"Yeah." And Bob again wondered whether this detour was worth it. He really needed to get back, and Tuscaloosa was not on the way. Ruth Ann would probably be coming to Huntsville soon anyway.

"She's really excited about seeing us," Jeannie said. After nine years of marriage, Jeannie had become an expert at telling what Bob was thinking.

"I know, hon. It's just . . ."

"You'll get it all done, you always do. But Mom's been going through a tough time since Dad died, and we promised."

"OK," Bob said. He had already lost this battle a couple of weeks ago and there was no use pouting. Besides, he had planned around it. They would visit with Ruth Ann for a while, eat lunch, and try to get back on the road by 2:30 or 3:00 p.m., which would put them in Huntsville by 6:00 p.m. *A quick visit.*

Like that's going to happen, Bob thought now, feeling discouraged and a little foolish. When Jeannie and her mother got together, the best made plans usually got thrown out the window. It had been over a month since Ruth Ann had seen Jeannie and Nicole. After lunch, presents, girl talk, and God knows what else, they'd be lucky to get out of there by dark. The plan would fail. *Trying to plan around a bunch of women . . .* He stopped the thought. There was a gas station up ahead.

"Here we go," Jeannie said, and Bob knew she was talking about the Texaco sign.

"We told Ruth Ann noon, right?" Bob asked. There was a stoplight next to the station, but he couldn't tell yet if he should go past it to get to the Texaco or turn at the light and come in the back door.

"Yeah"—Jeannie glanced at her watch—"but it looks like we're gonna beat that. Maybe I should call her."

Jeannie reached for her cell phone as Bob put his blinker on and began slowing down.

Bob Bradshaw entered the intersection of Highway 82 with Limestone Bottom Road and his instincts said, *Turn at the light.* He glanced up ahead, saw nothing coming, and turned the wheel.

"Hello, Mom," Jeannie said into the cell phone. "It looks like . . . Bob!"

"Truck!" Nicole yelled from the backseat.

—

That motherfucker is not going to . . . But the red Honda *was* turning. Coming out of the dip, Dewey had seen the red Honda enter the intersection. It had been going very slow, as if the driver was unsure of what he wanted to do.

Now he's turning. The motherfucker is turning right in front of me.

Dewey hit the brakes.

"Oh, fuck!"

He was fishtailing, the trailer moving left.

Come on, move it.

But the red Honda was stuck in the intersection.

We're gonna hit.

—

Bob Bradshaw saw the eighteen-wheeler at the same time his wife and daughter screamed.

Where did that truck . . . ?

He pressed the accelerator all the way to the floor, and his tires spun. *No!* Jeannie undid her seat belt and lunged for the back, trying to cover Nicole. The Honda lurched forward.

Please make it, Bob begged, hearing the roar of the tractor trailer. *Please . . .*

3

Rose Batson opened her eyes and tried to get up. *How long have I been out?* She rolled onto her side, her neck aching, and saw the trailer. It was in the field across from the station. Burning. "Ultron" was printed on its side. *Ultron . . . Gasoline. Oh God.* She pulled herself up, limped inside the store, and grabbed the phone by the cash register.

"Jimmy. Hey, this is Rose down at Texaco." Her voice was hoarse and her words came out just above a whisper. "Got us a bad wreck. Real bad. A car and a tractor trailer hauling gasoline. Need an ambulance . . ." Rose stopped to catch her breath. Her ribs hurt when she talked.

"Ms. Rose, are you—?"

"I'll make it, Jimmy, but I doubt these people will." She coughed, and the pain in her ribs made her double over. "Call an ambulance, all right? And get Lou and the fire department out here on the double. Trailer's burning bad and the fire may spread."

"Will do, Ms. Rose."

Rose hung up the phone and staggered back outside. *Lord, have mercy.* The Honda lay on its back in a ditch about fifty yards up. It was also in flames. When they hit, the rig had taken the Honda about ten yards down 82 before the Honda had spun off and begun flipping. Rose had seen it all and started running toward the wreckage. She may have taken five or six steps. Then *boom!* Everything had gone black.

Trailer exploding must've knocked me out, she thought, eyeing the burning cylinder across the road. She rubbed her ribs, which she figured were either broken or badly bruised, and walked as fast as she could down the shoulder of Highway 82. She came to the rig first and opened the passenger-side door.

"You all right?" she yelled into the cab. The truck driver was slumped over the steering wheel, his head bleeding badly. Rose stepped up into the cab and grabbed the man's arm.

"Hey!" Rose yelled into the man's ear. Nothing. Rose smelled fuel and knew the rig could blow any second. *Move your ass, old woman.* She wrapped her arms around the man's midsection and pulled him toward her, dragging him to the edge of the cab. Then she looked down and sucked in her breath. *This is gonna hurt.* Rose planted her left foot on the bottom step and leapt backwards with all her strength, still holding the man around his waist. They landed in a pile on the ground, and Rose felt stabbing pain all over.

"Ahhh, Jesus!" she screamed, pushing the man off her and rolling to her side. *Move, woman, move.* She forced herself to her feet and dragged the man's body ten yards down the shoulder. When she thought she was far enough away, she leaned over him, her hands and arms now covered in his blood.

"Are you OK?" she screamed. "Are you—?"

But her words were drowned out by another explosion. Rose looked up and saw that the rig was now in flames. The door that she had just crawled out of was gone. She could see the steering wheel melting away, and then it was engulfed in a sea of orange.

Ten more seconds, she thought, her hands trembling. *If I had waited ten more seconds . . .*

"Help."

Rose turned at the sound of the voice and saw a figure on the ground near the Honda. Rose tried to run, stumbled, then fell. Her ribs exploded in pain, but she got to her feet. Walking now, she made it to the figure—a woman—and knelt beside her.

"Ma'am, are you—?"

"My baby . . . my baby . . ." The woman was whimpering and trying to move. Trying to crawl *toward* the burning car. "Please help . . . my baby," she said, her eyes glazed over but focused enough to make contact with Rose's.

"Ma'am, it's burning. I can't—"

"Yes . . . you . . . can . . ." The woman had moved a few inches, and Rose stopped her, feeling heat on her neck from the blazing car.

"No . . . please. My baby . . ."

Sirens sounded in the background, and Rose turned to see Sheriff Jimmy Ballard's patrol car coming toward them. An ambulance was behind him. *Thank God.*

"Please . . ." The woman's voice was softer. *She's fading*, Rose thought.

"Hang on, ma'am. There's help coming. You're gonna—"

"My . . . baby . . . is . . . in . . . there," she gasped, trying again to move, her finger pointing at the blazing car. "My baby is . . ."

"Ms. Rose!" Sheriff Ballard was running toward her, a couple of medics right behind him.

Rose Batson stepped back as the medics rushed in to assist the woman. Sheriff Ballard grabbed her arm.

"Ms. Rose. Are there any more?"

She was crying now. Rose Batson was crying, biting her lip hard enough to bring blood. There was a baby in that car. *A baby. Burning up in that car.*

Rose impulsively took two steps toward the Honda. *No. No. No.*

"Ms. Rose!" Sheriff Ballard grabbed Rose around the waist, but Rose kept moving, and he finally had to take her to the ground.

"No, Jimmy! That woman's baby's in there. I should've—"

"Ms. Rose, we can't help anyone in that car. Is there anyone else?"

Rose struggled for a couple of seconds, then stopped. *Snap out of it, old woman.*

"The truck driver . . . down the shoulder," she said, pointing and holding her ribs.

Sheriff Ballard stood and barked instructions to an approaching deputy. Had Rose looked back toward the store, she would've seen that another patrol car had arrived. And the volunteer fire department. But she didn't look back.

Rose sat on the grass, clutching her ribs and staring at the Honda. *No. No. No.*

4

As the phone rang in the work trailer, Jack Willistone leaned over his desk and grimaced at the words "Ultron Gasoline" flickering across the caller ID. He knew he would have to handle this call with care. Dispatch had already told him about the accident, and he had two messages to call the local television station for comment. *First things first*, he thought as the phone rang a second time. Then a third. Jack coughed and lit a cigarette, glancing down at his metal desk, where the signed merger agreement still lay open to the section entitled "Terms of the Agreement." After close to a year of negotiations, Fleet Atlantic, the largest trucking company in North America, had agreed to buy out Willistone Trucking Company, the biggest freight hauler in the South. The sum to be paid Willistone was marked with a yellow highlighter, and Jack gazed at it with satisfaction and pride.

Two hundred million dollars.

Four rings.

The deal was not yet forty-eight hours old, the ink on the signatures almost wet enough to smear. It was set to close in six months. *That is if nothing fucks it up,* Jack thought, fixing his eyes on the phone and feeling a pang of anxiety as he thought of the accident.

Five rings.

Finally, Jack answered the phone.

"Yeah," Jack said, leaning back in his chair and propping his feet on the desk.

"Jack, I assume you've heard." The voice of Buck Bulyard, manager of the Ultron Gasoline plant in Tuscaloosa, blared into the receiver, hoarse and tired.

"Accidents are like shit, Buck. They happen. I'm sure this isn't Ultron's first rodeo."

"It's not, Jack, but we got a problem. Newton didn't leave the plant until 10:00 a.m. We got two employees that remember it and a bill of lading that has the time stamped on it. Nine goddamn fifty-seven. Due at the first filling station by eleven. There's no way your boy can make it to Montgomery by eleven without speeding."

Silence filled the line as Jack waited for more.

"It's a bad accident, Jack," Buck continued, his voice high and panicky. "Real bad. Young family. The press will be all over it, and the Alabama Bureau of Investigation has already called, wanting a meeting."

Jack closed his eyes, knowing that the Alabama Bureau of Investigation investigated all traffic fatalities. "When do the ABI boys want to meet?" he asked.

"I didn't have a choice," Buck said. "They'll be here at eight in the morning. Jack, what if they—?"

"Just hold on to your panties, Buck," Jack interrupted, opening his eyes. "What are the names of the two employees?"

"Willard Carmichael and Dick Morris. Dick goes by 'Mule.' They loaded the trailer, so they would know."

"Anybody talk to 'em besides you?"

"Hell no. You think I was born yesterday?"

Jack forced himself to laugh. "You sure there's no one or nothing else?" Jack asked, his tone serious again.

"That's it. All we got is the bill of lading and what Willard and Mule remember. But, Jack, you know as well as I do that this has been going on for a while. If the ABI folks start digging tomorrow—"

"What?" Jack asked, his skin turning cold. "Buck, surely to God you don't stamp the fucking time on all your bills?"

"We have to, Jack. Our corporate office requires it," Buck said, the words hitting Jack like a slap in the face. "All bills contain the time of pickup and the time the gas is supposed to be delivered to the station."

"Are you fucking kidding me?" Jack asked. "Buck, you know how we operate. We make more deliveries, so your customers are happy, but there is a way we do it, and you know damn well what it is. Are you telling me you have created a *fucking paper trail*? Hell, man, if the ABI boys compare those bills to my driver's logs, we could all go to jail for a long time."

"I don't have any idea what you're talking about, Jack," Buck said, but his voice shook with fear. "If—"

"Don't play dumb with me, Buck," Jack interrupted. "You know what we do and you know how we do it. And you damn well know what's at stake here."

There was silence as Buck didn't respond. Jack took a drag from his cigarette and pressed his fingers into his temples, working the problem in his mind.

When the ABI investigators came to Buck's office in the morning, they would see the bills of lading, which would show that Jack put his drivers on a schedule that forced them to speed—a violation of the federal motor carrier regulations. Worse, if they compared the bills to Jack's driver's logs, the documents would not match. The logs would inevitably show a Willistone driver certifying that he was in the sleeper berth or off duty when one of Ultron's bills would show, for the same day and time, that driver making a delivery for Ultron. The ABI would alert the Office of Inspector General of the United States Department of Transportation, and the Office of Inspector General would have grounds to launch a full-scale investigation of Willistone Trucking Company and Ultron, Inc. The US Attorney's Office might then prosecute Jack and all Willistone drivers for falsification of driver's logs, a felony carrying a penalty of up to five years in prison per violation. Ultron, and specifically Buck Bulyard, could be charged, along with Jack, for conspiracy to violate federal motor carrier regulations, also a felony. Though the relationship with Ultron was fairly young, Willistone had still probably made hundreds of deliveries for Ultron. Which meant hundreds of possible violations, and hundreds of possible counts in the various indictments. Which collectively meant . . .

We could all go to jail for the rest of our lives, Jack knew.

Then there was the merger. Jack's eyes shot down to the terms of the agreement. He flipped over to the section entitled "Termination" and furiously read the words, pausing on the last line of the paragraph, which was printed in bold and underlined:

<u>If, at any time prior to closing, Willistone Trucking Company comes under any type of investigation for violating federal motor carrier regulations or if a lawsuit is filed against it that could leave the company insolvent, Fleet Atlantic can terminate or stay the agreement pending the conclusion of the investigation or lawsuit.</u>

"Shit," Jack whispered. *This could ruin everything,* he knew. *Everything I've worked for my whole life . . .*

"Jack, what—?"

"Shut up, Buck," Jack said, slowly looking up from the contract. He took a last drag on the cigarette and crushed it out, knowing there was only one way to handle this mess.

"Buck, if someone were to start digging, where would the gold be?" he asked.

"Here," Buck said.

"And where is 'here'?"

"The office. You know, the same place we signed the contract."

"You mean you're still in that old warehouse?"

"Yeah. Faith keeps the current documents—the last six months or so—in a filing cabinet in her office and the rest are in a storage room down the hall. Jack, what should—?"

"I assume the warehouse is insured in case of certain catastrophes," Jack interrupted. "Like—I don't know—wind, rain . . . fire?"

"Of course," Buck said. "Why do you . . . ?" Then Buck got it. "Jack, oh God, no. That's crazy. We can't—"

"Good."

"Jack—"

"Buck, just keep your mouth shut. Don't talk to anyone, especially not the press. I'll deal with them. And . . . I'd stay away from the office tonight if I were you."

"Jack, you can't. This is your problem, not mine. Your truck and your driver."

"Wrong, Buck. If the ABI ever gets wind of those bills, you'll probably end up in the jail cell next to mine. This is *our* problem. But don't you worry. I'm gonna handle it."

"The hell you are. You can't—"

"I can and I will. And if you ever breathe a word of this to anyone, Faith and the boys are gonna find out what you like to do in your spare time." Jack paused. "Michael's bar on Saturday nights. I know all about it, Buck. I even know what kind of K-Y Jelly you like to lube up with, so don't fuck with me."

"Whh . . . whhhat?" Buck said, barely getting the words out. "How could . . . how could you possibly . . . ?"

"Money talks, Buck. I don't ever go into a deal without covering my ass. I got video. I got photographs. I got you sucking cock and whistling Dixie at the same time." Jack paused. "This conversation never happened, do you understand?"

Nothing but heavy breathing on the other end of the line.

"Say you understand," Jack ordered.

More silence.

"Say you understand, Buck, or everyone in Tuscaloosa is gonna know you bat for the other team."

"I understand," Buck finally said, his voice just above a whisper.

"Good," Jack said, hanging up the phone.

—

Buck Bulyard felt his bladder give and the warmth spread down his leg. As the phone clicked dead, he dropped it, unable to steady his shaking hand. He looked at the pictures on his desk. Faith, his wife of twenty years. Sons, Buck Jr. and Danny. *What have I done?* Buck sat down, his backside damp. The smell of urine permeated the room, but Buck barely noticed, thinking of his last trip to Michael's and the young man he'd spent an hour with afterwards.

The accident. His job. Dealing with the press and the ABI. All were an afterthought now.

"What have I done?" he said out loud, gazing straight ahead but not seeing anything.

5

Ruth Ann Wilcox sat in the waiting room of the ER. *Jeannie is a fighter*, she kept telling herself. When her mind drifted toward Nicole and Bob, she forced it back to Jeannie. *Jeannie is still alive. She will fight . . . she will not . . .* The two double doors opened in front of her and a woman on a gurney was pushed to the back. Coming out of the doors toward Ruth Ann was a small man holding a chart. *The doctor.* Ruth Ann wanted to get up but she felt paralyzed. *She's alive right now. I believe she's alive. If he tells me . . .*

"Ms. Wilcox?" He was standing over her now. He wore green scrubs and was taking latex gloves off his hands.

"Yes." Her voice was soft, and her eyes pleaded with the doctor's. *Let her be OK. Let her make it.*

"Please come with me." He turned and she followed. She had to remind herself to breathe.

She followed him through the two double doors and then he stopped.

"Ms. Wilcox, I'm Dr. Merth. Your daughter suffered massive internal injuries in the crash. We tried to stabilize her, but . . ."

He must've seen the look in Ruth Ann's eyes because he stopped himself.

"I'm a big girl, Doc." She held his gaze, trying to steel herself for what came next.

"I'm so very sorry."

6

God forgive me, Buck Bulyard prayed as he parked in front of the burning warehouse. He had driven up and down McFarland Boulevard all night, knowing what was about to happen. When he saw the smoke begin to rise over the warehouse, he turned into the lot and cut his lights. He knew there was only one way out. Jack Willistone would never let him off the hook. If Buck threatened to pull the contract, Jack would come back with the same threats: *If you ever breathe a word of this to anyone, Faith and the boys are gonna find out what you like to do in your spare time.*

Buck sighed. If it were just Faith, he could probably live with it. *But the boys . . .*

Junior was sixteen and Danny was fourteen. They both played ball, had girlfriends, and were popular at school. *It would destroy them.* Kids that age were mean. Vicious. The taunting would never end. *Your daddy's a queer, a cocksucker, a faggot.*

Buck shook his head and wiped his eyes. *I won't put them through that. Better dead than that.*

Buck got out of the car on shaky legs and looked at the inferno in front of him. He grabbed his cell phone and dialed 911.

"Nine-one-one emergency."

"Yeah, this is Buck Bulyard, president of Ultron Gas!" Buck screamed, trying to sound hysterical. "Our office is on fire. Need a fire truck out here on the double. I've got an extinguisher. I'm going in to see if I can stop it."

"Mr. Bulyard, no. Don't—"

But Buck had already pressed the End button. He took out the fire extinguisher and looked one last time at the pictures of Danny and Junior that he had always kept next to the odometer behind the steering wheel, placing his hand on both photographs. *I'm so sorry, boys.*

Buck moaned, forcing himself to move away from the car and leaving the door open for show. Then, closing his eyes and gripping the fire extinguisher tight, he barreled into the blaze.

7

Jack Willistone could see the flames from his house overlooking McFarland. "You covered your tracks?" Jack asked, turning to the man standing beside him at the window.

"Like a bloodhound," the man said.

"I'm not fucking around, Bone. Are you sure?"

"One hundred percent sure, boss."

"Bone, when I was twelve years old I whacked off for the first time. After I did it, I was a hundred percent sure I'd do it again. I ain't been a hundred percent sure of anything since. You're telling me you covered your tracks?"

"As sure as the gizz on your twelve-year-old hand. Yes, sir. The Bone knows how to start a fire and make it look like an accident."

Jack glared at him, taking a slow sip of his bourbon and water. Then he bared his teeth, smiling. "You get the files?"

"Right here." He handed over two manila folders, one labeled "Willard Carmichael" and the other "Dick Morris."

Jack took the folders and flipped through them quickly. "They on the team yet?"

"Oh, yeah. They took the deal in a heartbeat. Five thousand dollars cash to each and instant amnesia. They can't remember jack shit. Just a routine morning. No hiccups, no rush, just your average everyday pickup. Easy as pie."

Jack put the folders down on the table behind him and pulled out two cigars from his jacket pocket.

"So no one will ever know," Jack said. A statement, not a question.

"Not a soul."

They lit their cigars and turned back to the window. As the warehouse next to the Ultron Gasoline plant burned below, along with all the documents inside, Jack felt relief wash over him. *Money talks and bullshit walks.* It was one of the two rules he lived by, the other one being just as simple. *Always cover your ass.* Watching as the smoke rose above McFarland Boulevard, Jack Willistone was confident he had done so.

No one will ever know.

PART TWO

PART TWO

8

As they filed in, he sat on the table in front of the whiteboard with his back to them. The first day of the second semester had arrived and many of these second-year students had never had him, only heard the rumors from those that had gone before them. As they tried to find a seat among the rows that sloped upwards until reaching the back of the room, some peered over the man's shoulder and saw the words on the board. Those who knew smiled to themselves with quiet assurance. For most of those who didn't know, the words had no effect. But there was a small contingent of the unknowing who felt as if they should know and already had doubts, though the man had yet to utter a word. On the board were five words written side by side in capital letters: MATERIALITY, RELEVANCE, HEARSAY, AUTHENTICATION, and PRIVILEGE. McMurtrie's five columns, to those who knew. Today was the first day of Evidence. And their teacher was Thomas Jackson McMurtrie. The Professor. He who wrote the book, literally, on evidence in Alabama.

As he turned to them, Tom smiled to himself, taking in the different looks he always saw when addressing such a large group of mostly young faces. Fear. Apprehension. Arrogance. And the one he hated—apathy. Tom could put up with hard but scared workers. He could put up with assholes that thought they knew more than he did. But he could not—*would not*—stand for those who did not care. It was his mission to work those people until they quit. To rid the team of the turds, as the Man would have said.

"All right, my name is Tom McMurtrie and this is Evidence. My goal in this endeavor is simple and twofold. First, I want you people, each and every one of you, to walk out of this classroom in May as five-column lawyers. And second, for those that aren't willing to work and pay the price to be a five-column lawyer, I want to make you quit before you quit on your client one day." Tom paused to let the words sink in. He saw a pained expression on a young woman's face in the front row. He looked down at his class directory, or "face book" as the students called it, which contained a photograph of every student in the class. The young woman's name was Dawn Murphy. Twenty-six years old. Elba, Alabama.

"Ms. Murphy," Tom bellowed, loud enough for the turds sitting in the top row to hear without leaning forward. The young woman, who was probably quite attractive when she didn't have the fear of God plastered on her face, raised her hand off the yellow notebook she had been furiously writing on and extended it to about shoulder level.

With her hand in the air, she stammered, "Uhh . . . Yes, sir?"

"You are Ms. Dawn Murphy?" Tom asked.

"Yes, sir," Ms. Murphy said, and Tom was convinced that, other than her two colleagues on the front row, none of the ninety-five students in the class had heard a word.

"Ms. Murphy, you're gonna have to speak up. Your esteemed colleagues who have chosen to make their first impression from a distance no doubt did not hear you."

"Yes, sir." A better effort that probably reached about half-way up.

"Ms. Murphy, you are from Elba, are you not?" A few snickers in the crowd. Elba was one of the smaller towns in Alabama. For some reason, Tom always picked the small-town students. Elba. Opp. Hamilton. Maybe it was because he himself was from the small town of Hazel Green in North Alabama. Or maybe these people, over the years, just seemed to be more interesting.

"Yes, sir. Born and raised."

Yes, just as Tom had thought. You were unlikely to get the "born and raised" part from the Birmingham folks or the Mobile blue bloods. But a sweet young thing from Elba. *Born and raised, by God.* Tom smiled at Ms. Murphy, hoping to make this cross-examination a little easier on a student that had already managed to impress him.

"Ms. Murphy, when you walk out of this classroom in May, are you"—Tom paused for effect, scanning the other faces in the crowd—"gonna be a five-column lawyer?" Trick question, Tom knew. Answer yes and the rest of the class will wonder who this girl thinks she is. Answer no and show weakness in front of the enemy.

"Yes, sir, I hope to be. By the grace of God, I hope to be," she said with a smile, invoking nervous laughter around the class-room. *That a girl,* Tom thought. *By the grace of God.* Gotta love those small towns.

"Me too, Ms. Murphy. Me too. It's my job to make that happen. Now let's get started." Tom scanned the faces in the back row, look-ing for the example. The sacrificial lamb. In the top row, the second to last seat from the upstairs exit, Tom found his victim. Blond, shaggy hair. Three-day growth of beard. Nothing in front of him. No books. *Haven't had time to hit the bookstore yet, huh, champ?* No notebook. Not even a damn pen. This was going to be fun.

Scanning the face book, he found the name he was looking for. Jonathon Tinsel. Twenty-five years old. Birmingham, Alabama.

"Mr. Tinsel," Tom said, loud enough to shake the foundation of the building. "Where is Jonathon Tinsel from the magic city of Birmingham?"

The shaggy, unshaven man on the back row raised his hand and, with a glazed look in his eyes, said, "Up here."

"Up there. Why all the way up there, Mr. Tinsel? Are you trying to hurt my feelings?" Without allowing an answer, Tom continued, "Mr. Tinsel, in the case of *Richardson v. Callahan*, give me a brief description of the facts and the court's holding." Tom knew what the answer would be but was looking forward to hearing this kid's version of "I didn't give a shit enough to get my books and schedule from the bookstore."

"I, uh—well, I haven't actually read that case yet. I'm sorry," Jonathon Tinsel said, chomping on a piece of gum that Tom had not previously noticed.

"I'm sorry too, Mr. Tinsel. Well, let's move ahead to a case you have read, shall we? Tell you what. You pick any of the cases I assigned as mandatory reading before the first class and give me the facts of the case and the court's holding."

"Sir, I haven't had a chance to pick up my materials yet. I'm sorry but I won't be able to help you today." The bastard even smiled at the end of the statement.

"Well, Mr. Tinsel, I'm afraid I won't be able to help you either. You are dismissed from today's class. For your sake, I hope you find the bookstore between now and tomorrow morning." Not waiting to see Tinsel's reaction, Tom moved on, scanning the faces for another victim. As he was about to call out the name of Vanessa Yearout, a petite black woman about halfway up, Tom noticed that Tinsel had remained glued to his seat.

"Tinsel, what part of 'dismissed' did you not understand? I mean it. Get the hell out of my classroom," Tom said, burning a hole through Tinsel's eyes with the ferocity of his gaze.

As Tinsel shuffled out of the upstairs exit, Tom transferred his gaze to the rest of the class, trying to make eye contact with as many of them as he could, telling each of them without words that *this is the way it is gonna be. It's my way or the highway. Any of you turds who don't understand can follow Tinsel out the door.*

After what must have been a five-second pause, Tom took a deep, audible breath and turned his eyes back toward his face sheet.

"All right now . . . Ms. Yearout," Tom began, speaking in a calmer voice. The storm had passed, and Tom saw the results he had expected. Almost every student was leaning forward in his or her seat, pen pressed to paper, eyes focused right on Tom, readying themselves for the call that might be coming. The Socratic method in all its glory.

Tom called on several more students, including young Ms. Dawn Murphy from Elba again, before the clock read 9:50 and it was time for the entire class to join Tinsel on the outside. The first day of McMurtrie's Evidence class was over. Those like Tinsel who had failed to read breathed a sigh of relief and made their way to the bookstore. Dawn Murphy crossed off Evidence from her to-do list and headed to the library to begin her Evidence outline. Tom stood by the board and waited for them all to leave.

Forty years of this shit, Tom thought, smiling. *And the first day is still pretty fun.*

—

An hour later, as he sat behind his desk in his third-floor office, the fun had worn off. The fifth edition of *McMurtrie's Evidence*—or, as his students were fond of calling it, the Bible—was supposed to go to press in two months, and Tom was struggling to meet the deadline. Tom had always loved the teaching aspect of his job. Trying to get that light to flicker in a kid's head was what made the whole experience worthwhile. But the publishing aspect was a different story. Since he had walked in the door some three weeks after accepting the Man's offer, every dean—Heacock, Jackson, and now Lambert—had pushed the faculty to publish. The first edition of *McMurtrie's Evidence* was published in 1973. To this day it had been the highest-selling hornbook for any faculty member, past or present, in the history of the Alabama School of Law. Every year Tom wrote a supplement to go in the back of the book containing any recent case law that affected his prior summary. And every five to seven years he published a new edition. But although it was a nice boost to his income, Tom hated it. Every damn bit of it. A knock on the door mercifully interrupted Tom's misery.

"Come in," Tom said, a little louder than necessary. He rubbed his eyes and tried to wake up.

The door opened only a crack, and the face of Dawn Murphy emerged behind it.

"Professor, do you have a minute?" Ms. Murphy looked nervous but not scared. Tom could see the strain of struggle on her face.

"Of course. Ms. Murphy, right?" Tom smiled and gestured toward a chair in front of his desk. Dawn Murphy wore black pants and a white blouse, but her plain-Jane manner of dress did not disguise her beauty. She had brown hair, cropped off at about shoulder level, and brown eyes that looked tired but pretty nonetheless. She smiled at Tom and held her hands together on her lap.

"Professor, I was wondering if you needed a student assistant." Her face blushed red and she looked down, squeezing her hands together. "I am a single mother. My daughter is five years old, just started kindergarten. Well, my mom and I are living together over in Riverview Apartments. Mom has a job waiting tables at the City Café from five in the morning till one thirty. I take Julie to school, and Mom picks her up and looks after her in the afternoon. Financial aid has helped a great deal, but Julie's a growing girl and I really need some extra money. The lady at Student Services said that some of the professors hire student assistants for the semester. Well, I, uh . . . you've probably already hired your assistant, but if not . . . well . . . I was just wondering if maybe—"

"You're hired," Tom said, not waiting for Dawn Murphy to finish. "Ten bucks an hour, twelve bucks an hour for weekend work. I expect you to work around your class schedule and to work weekends when I tell you to." Tom did not smile and turned his eyes to his draft of the new edition of *McMurtrie's Evidence*. He looked up when he felt a hand touch his own. Ms. Murphy had moved around the desk and gripped his right hand with both of hers.

"Thank you, Professor, I . . . thank you so much," she managed, shaking Tom's hand, her voice cracking with emotion as a tear began to run down her cheek. "This will help out so much."

"You're welcome," he said, smiling at her and putting his hand over hers to stop the shaking. "Now, let's talk about—"

"Uh, Professor," a male voice interrupted, causing both Tom and Dawn to turn toward the door.

Dean Richard Lambert peeked his head around the corner of the door, which Dawn must have left cracked when she entered.

"Sorry to . . . interrupt," the dean said, looking at Tom. "But I need to speak with you about Friday's board meeting."

"OK," Tom said, turning back to Dawn Murphy, whose face had gone beet red. "Ms. Murphy, here's your first assignment. Read the section in my book on the *Daubert* standard for the admissibility of expert testimony. Then research all Alabama state cases decided within the last year on that subject. I want to see what you've found by next Friday. If you have any questions, my office hours are ten to twelve in the morning or two to three thirty in the afternoon Monday, Wednesday, and Thursday."

"Yes, sir." She smiled, her face still red, and walked past the dean out the door. Tom smiled after her. There was nothing he enjoyed more than an eager, hungry student. However, his smile faded as he met the gaze of Dean Richard Lambert.

"So what's this about on Friday?" Tom asked once the dean had shut the door.

As much as Tom had liked Deans Heacock and Jackson, he felt the opposite about Lambert. There was something about Lambert's brown eyes and nasal voice that turned him off. As a trial lawyer and then a trial team coach for forty years, Tom had always been able to identify the genuine article. And whereas Dawn Murphy from Elba, Alabama, was as genuine as homemade peach cobbler, Richard Lambert came boxed and packaged, as artificial as the turf at the old Astrodome. There was also the fact that, in the eighteen months since Lambert's hire, four of Tom's longtime colleagues had either quit or been forced to resign. Lambert clearly wanted new blood, and he seemed to have a way of getting rid of folks who didn't fit his vision.

"Tom, the board has a number of things it wants to discuss with you on Friday," the dean said, not looking at him but out the window. He paused. "The first of which is the incident at nationals."

Tom glared at the dean. *I should've known.* "It's been nine months, Dick. How long is the board gonna beat that dead horse? It was just an unfortunate incident that happened in the heat of the moment. It wasn't anyone's fault."

"I know . . ." The dean paused, looking down. "I know you think that, Tom, but you put your hands on the kid. You were the instigator. There's video of it. The damn thing's on YouTube, and the title of the clip is 'Alabama professor assaults student and gets payback.' I think it's had over fifty thousand hits."

Tom squinted at the dean. "Assault?"

"That's what it says. People watch that stuff, Tom. They form opinions, and it reflects badly on the school. Look . . ." Dean

Lambert sat down and pushed a piece of paper across Tom's desk. "The board has drafted an apology for you to sign. Something we can release to the media. Just sign the thing, OK?"

Tom looked down at the document and his eyes scanned the words on the page. The apology had him accepting all of the blame for the incident and apologizing for his "lapse in judgment" and for the "inappropriate manner in which he had touched Rick Drake."

"Dick, if the school needs me to apologize, then let me do it in my own words. This is too much. I mean, I regret very much that the altercation with Rick happened, but I don't think I acted inappropriately by grabbing his arm."

Dean Lambert crossed his arms. "We need you to sign it, Tom. And . . . there are some other things."

"What 'other things'?"

"We've been getting complaints about *McMurtrie's Evidence*. A lot of the students think it's too hard to read. Students have called it the Bible for a long time, but now I'm hearing them complain that it's just as long and as hard to read as the Bible. The board wants to know whether there's any way you can make it more user-friendly."

Tom didn't say anything, just continued to glare at his boss.

"And you can't be kicking kids out of your class anymore, Tom. I know all about what happened with Jonathon Tinsel. With this Drake thing on YouTube still on everyone's minds, you just can't be doing stuff like that."

"He wasn't prepared for class," Tom said. "I've always handled kids that way. What if they show up to court unprepared after they get out of here?"

"We just can't have it, Tom. Not in the world we live in. Some might view that as abusive."

"Abusive? Are you—?"

"Tom, the board is worried that you might . . ." The dean stopped, looking down at the carpet.

"Worried that I might what?" Tom asked. He could feel the heat on his face.

The dean raised his eyes. "That you might have a Woody Hayes or a Bobby Knight incident. If you'll grab a kid by the arm, what's next?"

Tom crossed his arms and squinted at the dean. "That's bullshit, Dick, and you know it. I've been here for forty years and I've never hit a student. I've never done anything but lay it on the line for this university."

The dean didn't say anything for several seconds. Then he slowly rose from his seat and walked to the door. Before he closed it, he leaned his head back in.

"Times are changing, Tom. We need you to change with them." He paused, then added, "See you on Friday."

9

Tom arrived home at seven thirty. After storming out of the law school and grabbing some lunch, he'd returned to coach the trial team through its first practice of the semester. He was still pissed about his talk with the dean, but there was nothing he could do about it. Like it or not, Dick Lambert was his boss. He would go to the board meeting and see what happened. Though the makeup of the board had changed a lot in the last two years, there were still members whom Tom had known for over twenty years. Tom doubted Dick was really talking about a majority of the board's concerns. *But it's obvious he wants me out*, Tom thought, remembering his four fallen colleagues.

He grabbed a Michelob Light from the fridge and walked into the den to find Musso sprawled out on the couch. A sixty-five-pound solid white English bulldog, Johnny Musso McMurtrie was a little big to be left alone in the den and, for that matter, a little hairy and messy—can you say slobber?—to be left on the couch. But Julie was gone, and Tom really didn't give a damn about a little hair and slobber.

"How's my big boy?"

At the sound of Tom's voice, Musso was off the couch in the blink of an eye and nearly knocked Tom down in his excitement. Standing and shaking in front of his master, Musso licked his dry mouth and made a loud throat-clearing noise that shook the house. Tom grabbed him behind his ears and petted him, then stroked his back a couple of times, making Musso's hind leg jerk repetitively, until Tom stopped.

"You need to go out, big boy?"

Behind the couch were two french doors that opened to a porch that looked out over a fenced-in backyard. Tom walked past the couch, and Musso followed right on his heels. As Tom opened the door, Musso tore out of it, barking loudly to announce his presence to any would-be critters or animals that had dared to set foot in the backyard of Musso McMurtrie. Tom sat down in one of the two rocking chairs on the porch and watched his dog scamper around. He took a long sip of beer, and his eyes drifted to the third finger of his left hand, where he still wore the wedding ring that Julie had slipped on his finger forty-five years ago next month. He ran his thumb over the ring and closed his eyes.

It had been almost three years since Julie died. On a Saturday morning three Januarys ago, they had taken a shower together after a long walk, and Julie asked him to feel her right breast. Tom made a smart-ass sexual comment before realizing that Julie was being serious. When he felt the breast, the lump was unmistakable. One office visit and a laundry list of tests later and Julie was diagnosed with breast cancer. She went through two months of treatment—medication, radiation, the works. But on April 17, 2007, at 3:42 p.m. on a beautiful sunny afternoon, Julie McMurtrie died.

Tom would not—*could not*—forget that moment. He had been holding her hand. He did not cry or break down—at least, not then. He leaned over and whispered "I love you" into Julie's ear, gently closed her eyes, and walked out of the room to tell their son.

Tommy had tried to be stoic like his father, but it was no use. He cried and they hugged for what must have been ten minutes, Tom stroking the back of his son's head as the tears fell. A thirty-five-year-old doctor who lived in Nashville with his wife, Nancy, and two children, Jackson and Jenny, Tommy had been a momma's boy from the day he was born. And his mother's death hit him and his family hard. They had all stayed for a week after her death, helped Tom with the funeral arrangements, and in general tried to be a comfort. But Tom couldn't let it go. Not in front of his boy. He knew that if Tommy saw him cry it would make his son cry some more. Nancy would cry, the kids would cry, everyone would cry, and Tom didn't want any more of that. Julie would not have wanted that.

After they had all left, Tom got on McFarland Boulevard and stopped at the first convenience store he came to. He bought a twelve-pack of Michelob Light, came back home, and spent the rest of the day on the porch. Crying. Crying like he had never cried in his life. He cried for Julie and he cried for himself and he cried for his son and he cried for his grandchildren, who would never get to know the greatest woman that ever walked the face of God's earth. He had woken up that night around midnight, five or six empty beer bottles scattered all over the porch. He had picked up the trash and gone to bed. But since that day he tried to spend as much time on this porch as he could. Julie had loved rocking on the porch, and Tom could *feel* her presence when he was out there, her beautiful blue eyes looking down from what must be the highest point in heaven. And it felt good.

Tom's right hand felt moist and, peering down, he saw Musso licking it and nuzzling his wet nose against it. He picked Musso's paws up off the floor and placed them on his knees, looking his dog in the eyes.

"What are we gonna do, big boy? You miss Momma, don't you?" He took a deep breath, and Musso leaned over and licked him on the face. Wiping almost-dry tears from his eyes, Tom rose from the chair, whispering under his breath, "I miss Momma too."

He walked back into the house, opened the freezer, and scanned its contents. The beer, now empty, had made him hungrier than when he had walked in the door. What he really wanted was a cheeseburger and fries and maybe a couple more beers, but he instead chose a Healthy Choice frozen dinner.

As his food was being nuked in the microwave, the phone rang.

Tom tensed, looking down at the tile floor. He wasn't in the mood for another talk with the dean. He walked over to the phone, but the caller ID showed a number he didn't recognize, so he picked it up.

"Hello?" Tom asked.

"Hello, uh, Tom?" A female voice that sounded oddly familiar.

"Yes."

"Tom, I probably shouldn't be calling you at home, but, well, it's important and I didn't know who else to call and—"

"Ma'am, what's your name?" Tom interrupted. The voice on the other end of the line sounded frustrated and now distinctly familiar.

"Tom, this is Ruth Ann."

10

They decided to meet for lunch. Tom's office was tough to find in the maze of the law school, and besides, you gotta eat, right? Tom had actually used those words. *"You gotta eat, right?"* He shook his head, cringing at how awkward he must have sounded as he went over the previous night's phone call in his mind. Ruth Ann Mitchell, now Wilcox, needed some legal advice. She hated to bother him at home, but it was important that she speak to him. Could they meet tomorrow? That was it. No small talk. No "How you doing?" Or "What's been going on?" Or "What's up?" She was either nervous and forgot about such pleasantries or was on a mission of some kind that would not allow for such distractions. In any event, Tom recovered enough from the shock of the call to mention lunch at 15th Street Diner, so here he was.

As he sipped from a glass of sweet tea, Tom guessed he had always been curious as to how Ruth Ann had turned out. They had dated for three years in college, and back then Tom had thought he would marry Ruth Ann. But after his senior year he took a graduate assistant job at Vanderbilt without discussing it with her first, and she broke things off. She said she couldn't do a long-distance relationship and couldn't trust a man who would make such a big decision without consulting her. *Probably my fault*, Tom had always thought. But he had no regrets. If they hadn't broken things off, he would never have met Julie.

Tom heard a jingle at the front door announcing the next customer, and he noticed her right off. Same green eyes, long legs, and narrow waist, although her strawberry-blond hair had now turned a shade of gray. Tom, who was seated in a booth along the far wall of the restaurant, waved his hand, and Ruth Ann smiled, walking over.

"Hey, there," she said. Tom had stood to greet her—not sure if he should hug her, kiss her on the cheek, or what. Ruth Ann extended her hand, and Tom shook it gently. Still a beautiful woman, he thought, as she sat down.

"You look great," Tom said.

"Well, aren't you nice to say so?" Ruth Ann replied, smiling, but the smile quickly faded and she looked down at the table. "I wish I felt great," she said without looking up to meet his gaze, which had never left her face. "Tom, I . . ."

"There's nothing wrong, I mean, with you . . . I mean, you're not sick, are you? I . . ." Tom stopped, realizing he'd interrupted her. "I'm sorry. Go ahead."

Ruth Ann laughed nervously, placing her hand on his. "It's OK, Tom. No, I'm not sick. I . . . I have a problem. A legal problem." She paused. "A few months ago my daughter and her husband were in a car accident out on Highway 82 around Henshaw. You know, just before you get to the road that takes you to Faunsdale?"

Tom nodded. He and Julie had gone to the Crawfish Festival a couple of times in Faunsdale. He remembered seeing signs for the small town of Henshaw. But there was something else about hearing the name of this town. Henshaw. A memory that he couldn't quite place.

"Well, anyway, they hit a tractor-trailer truck head-on there at the light and . . ." She paused to take a sip of tea, some of which spilled down her chin. She grabbed her napkin, and the silverware jangled as it fell out. "Damnit, I'm sorry." She looked at him. "Still all thumbs, huh," she said, forcing a smile as a couple of tears began to fall down her cheeks. Her hands were shaking. Tom didn't know what to say, so he didn't say anything.

"My granddaughter . . . Nicole . . . she . . ." Ruth Ann looked down, and Tom could tell by the red color of her hands that she was squeezing them tight. "She was in the car too . . . She died. They all died. Even the trucker. Everyone dead." She put her head in her hands and began sobbing.

Tom remembered reading about the wreck in the paper but had not made the connection.

"Ruth Ann, I'm so sorry. That's terrible. I . . ." But he stopped. He knew he should just shut up and let her continue when she was ready.

After about thirty seconds, Ruth Ann looked up and smiled through her tears.

"I'm sorry, Tom. I . . ." She took a deep breath. "Anyway, after the funerals I ordered a copy of the police report." She reached into her purse and pulled out a packet of four or five pages. She scooted the report across the table.

Tom picked up the pages, the first of which had the words "Henshaw County Accident Report" at the top of it. He glanced briefly at the report as Ruth Ann continued.

"The police report has the driver of the truck going eighty in a sixty-five. It also lists his employer, which is a trucking company here in Tuscaloosa. Willistone. I think it's over on McFarland. Anyway, there's also a statement in the report from a gas station clerk, who saw the accident and said that my son-in-law turned in front of the rig." She paused, sighing. "But that just can't be right. Bob would not have just turned in front of an eighteen-wheeler. I just think this guy—Newton or whatever—was running late and was speeding to catch up, and Bob didn't see him before starting to turn. And the whole thing just . . . it pisses me off." She said this last bit through clenched teeth, and Tom saw the fire in her eyes, a fire that he had seen before—both in anger and in passion—many moons ago.

"Ruth Ann, I—"

"Tom, I've never filed a lawsuit against anyone in my life. But . . ." She paused and looked briefly out the window before turning back to Tom. "I just didn't know who else to call. I'd like your opinion on what I should do."

"Well, you know, Ruth Ann, I haven't tried a case in many years. You ought to take this to someone who's in active practice. I—"

"Oh, stop it, *Professor*," Ruth Ann said, smirking and then turning it into a smile. "I've heard about you and how they treat you down at the law school. Calling you the Professor, as if you're the only one. Treating you like you're the Coach Bryant of the law school. I read the newspaper too. You know, the good old *Tuscaloosa News* with its articles about your trial teams winning championships. So don't give me any mess about not knowing what you're doing."

Tom laughed, thinking that Ruth Ann had to be the most direct woman he had ever known. He started to say something but stopped when Ruth Ann grabbed his hand.

"Please, Tom. Just look at it. I trust your opinion. If you think there's something there, then maybe you can tell me what to do or who I should go to. I feel like I have to do something. I have to know why this happened to my family." Her eyes, always beautiful and active, were pleading with him. She looked like she might cry again.

"OK," Tom said. "I'll take a look. But as I tried to say earlier, I'm not a practicing—"

"Thank you, Tom. Oh, thank you so much." She was out of her side of the booth, placing her arms around his neck and a kiss on his cheek. "Thank you," she said, this time whispering, her breath the pleasant smell of sweet tea and lemon.

When she returned to her side of the booth, the talk turned to old friends. But Tom wasn't paying attention. A sense of excitement and guilt gripped him. He had felt something when Ruth Ann had hugged him, something absent in his life for a long time. The tingle. That tingle a man feels deep in his loins when he is attracted to a woman. He was excited to feel the tingle again, but as his eyes shifted to the ring on his left finger, guilt stabbed at him like a knife. *What the hell is wrong with you?*

But that wasn't the only thing that drowned out Ruth Ann's words. Tom had remembered something. That thing that he couldn't quite place about Henshaw.

Rick Drake was from Henshaw.

11

Richard Drake, Esq., he of the law firm of Richard Drake, Esq., sat in the back of the Waysider restaurant in Tuscaloosa, drinking coffee and thinking about how to increase his caseload. Richard—Rick to his family and friends—had by his count eaten at the Waysider at least once a week since hanging up his shingle. He had also eaten once a week at the City Café in Northport. Getting out and about and being noticed. Keeping his ear to the ground in the hopes of landing the home-run case. That was the name of the game. The life of the plaintiff's lawyer. The Waysider had been an institution in Tuscaloosa since opening its doors in 1951. An old clapboard house that was converted to a restaurant, it was a regular hangout for the locals. Back in the day, people said that Bear Bryant himself drank coffee and read the paper at five thirty every morning at the Waysider. And like all places in Tuscaloosa, the Waysider had plenty of pictures of Coach Bryant and those that played for him adorning its walls, even in the bathroom.

The jingle of the front door announced another customer, and Rick looked up from his paper to see Ambrose Powell Conrad, the youngest assistant DA in the Tuscaloosa County District Attorney's office, heading his way.

"What's going on?" Powell asked, grabbing a seat and placing both elbows on the table. Powell was about six feet tall, stocky, with thin dirty-blond hair. He was no doubt the loudest person Rick had ever met, and his entry into the Waysider had, as usual, caused everyone in the place to look up.

"Oh, not a whole lot. Just trying to decide which ambulance to chase today and waiting to get my breakfast fix," Rick said. "How about yourself?"

"Going over to that neighborhood behind Dreamland Ribs today. Guy selling crack out there got capped by a guy who wasn't pleased with his purchase. When I talked to the defendant's wife, who just happened to be screwing the dead drug dealer, two names popped up. Hopefully, one of them saw the shooting. Anyway, it gives me a good excuse to eat a slab for lunch." Powell put on his best shit-eating grin. "God, I love my job."

And Rick knew, despite the grin, that Powell was not exaggerating. The man was born to be a prosecutor. He thrived in the courtroom, where most young lawyers cowered. Rick and Powell had been partners on the trial team at Alabama together. Powell was the star and Rick more of a late bloomer. Hell, if it weren't for Powell coaching Rick before the final tryout, Rick knew he probably wouldn't have made the team at all. The man was a natural. And his best friend.

"So how's the caseload?" Powell asked, his expression one of genuine interest—another reason Rick loved Powell. Rick's parents couldn't hide their disappointment when they asked how he was doing, but Powell, who knew the deal—hell, he'd had a front-row seat for Rick's journey from the penthouse to the outhouse—was always supportive and encouraging.

"Thin," Rick said. "As it was last week and the week before that. Three workers' comp files. But, hey, I got a walk-through today.

If the judge approves, I'll get two thousand dollars in fees. Just enough to make overhead and buy groceries next month." Rick smiled. "So I got that going for me—"

"Which is nice," Powell finished, laughing at the line from *Caddyshack*, which was a staple in the usual banter between Rick and Powell.

Breakfast was wolfed down quickly, with the talk turning to women. With football season over, there was little else to talk about other than work. Walking outside, they said their good-byes.

"Let's get together at Phil's for a pitcher or two or three tomorrow night. Whattaya say?" Powell said, closing the door of his Honda and leaning his head out the window.

"Sounds good, but you never know. A home run may walk into my office and thicken the old caseload. Or, by some act of God, I could wind up with a date." Rick laughed. "I'll call you."

—

Ten minutes later Rick trudged up the dusty steps to his second-floor office. Located on a side street two blocks from the courthouse, the law office of Richard Drake, Esq. sat above Larry and Barry's Interior Design, a three-year-old company formed by two gay lovers from Missouri—Larry Horowitz and Barry Bostheimer. According to Powell, who seemed to know everyone and everything since joining the DA's office, Larry and Barry had done well for themselves since opening up shop. Whatever their financial condition, they had both been very supportive of Rick, even sending one of their friends—a lesbian dancer named Sharnice—to see Rick about a car accident. Rick was able to arrange a quick settlement with the other driver's insurance company, and since then Larry and Barry had acted as if Rick were the next coming of Clarence Darrow.

At the top of the stairs, Rick unlocked the door and flipped the lights on. The office had once been a two-bedroom loft, but Rick thought he'd made a nice conversion. The den that the front door opened to was now a reception area, where Rick's secretary, Frankie, sat. Behind Frankie's desk the carpet turned to tile, and there was a small kitchen with a coffee pot and a refrigerator. To the left of the kitchen was the prior master bedroom—now a conference room containing a long table with several chairs—and to the right was the smaller bedroom, which Rick used as his private office.

As Rick walked into his office, his eyes immediately locked on a picture on the wall. "ABA Regional Champions, the University of Alabama" was the heading stenciled under the photograph of Rick, Powell, and the Professor. *Should be another one saying "National Champions"* was the thought that went through Rick Drake's mind every time he looked at it. Along with *"You're a hothead, Drake. A liability in the courtroom."* Rick glared at the gray eyes of the Professor, which seemed to mock him from inside the frame.

Rick shook his head and tried to think about the day ahead, which, as usual, was not that busy. The workers' comp walk-through was at 11:00 a.m. in front of Judge Baird. Rick's client was Myra Wilson, who had fallen off a forklift at the Mercedes plant in Vance and broken her hip. She was set to arrive at 10:30 to review the settlement documents.

Rick retrieved the Wilson file from his desk and walked back into the reception area, where he paced and read, wanting to make sure that everything was right. Every so often he looked at Frankie's desk, expecting her to be there, but then reminded himself that she was off today. A forty-two-year-old mother of two whose husband, Butch, was a self-employed bricklayer, Frankie had worked out all right. She typed eighty-five words a minute, was usually in a cheerful mood, and worked steady hours without many complaints. Other than today, the only time she had taken off since being hired was the Friday before Labor Day when Butch had taken her and the kids to Panama City for a long weekend.

As he noticed a mistake in the Wilson papers, a paragraph inserted on page 2 closing future medical benefits—*The bastards always try that trick*—Rick was jarred by the sound he craved more than any other. The most wonderful sound in the world. The all-powerful phone. Ringing. In his office. And it wasn't even 9:00 a.m. *Be a client and not Powell*, he thought as he answered on the second ring, knowing that this could be the one. The one he knocked over the fence, turning Richard Drake into a household name.

"Richard Drake," Rick said in his most lawyerly voice.

"Dude, you'll never guess where I am." Powell. *Son of a bitch*, Rick thought, smiling in spite of himself as the elusive chase of the home run was put on hold until the next call. The life of the plaintiff's lawyer.

12

Tom watched his team from the jury box in the trial advocacy room—or, as his teams liked to call it, the "war room." He focused in particular on their eyes. Were they listening to the opposition's words, or were they trying to remember what they were going to say when they got up there? Tom taught the former, but from the look in their eyes he could tell they were doing the latter. *This team will be lucky to make it through regionals.*

At the bench sat Judge Art Hancock—venerable old Judge Cock as he was known by most of the Birmingham bar. Judge Hancock had been a judge since the midsixties. His rulings were always quick, precise, and usually right on point. He put up with no grandstanding by lawyers and each year routinely called at least one young lawyer down on the carpet for "acting a fool" in his courtroom. As a young lawyer, Tom had tried his very first case in front of Judge Hancock, and Tom felt that he had earned the judge's respect for knowing the basics and not going overboard with theatrics in front of the jury like so many inexperienced lawyers tended to do.

Now seventy-seven years old and showing it, Judge Hancock sat at the bench stroking one of his thick, bushy eyebrows. Tom and the judge had struck an agreement back in the early eighties where Judge Hancock agreed to come to Tuscaloosa and preside over a mock trial between Tom's A and B teams one day each year. It was great experience for the team, exposing them to a real judge whom they would see again in the future.

However, that wasn't the team's only treat today.

Sitting next to Tom in the jury box was without question the most dominant trial lawyer in the state of Alabama. Jameson Randall Tyler. "The Big Cat" as the Birmingham trial bar referred to him with both admiration and fear.

"They'll come around," Jameson whispered, nudging Tom's elbow and seeming to sense his mood. "There's a lot of growing that happens between years two and three."

Tom nodded, knowing Jameson was right. Rick Drake had proven that last year. A bull in a china shop his second year, Drake had blossomed into a real force as a third-year.

And then the bull came back for nationals . . .

"Had anything with Jerry lately?" Tom whispered back, trying not to think about Drake. Since talking with Ruth Ann, he had been racking his brain, thinking of attorneys he could refer her to, but he kept coming back to Rick Drake. Henshaw was a small town, and small-town juries liked hometown lawyers. The bottom line was that Drake was the only trial lawyer Tom knew with Henshaw ties that was worth a shit. Aside from the obvious problem that Drake was just eight months out of law school, Tom also didn't have a clue where he was living or what he was doing.

And there's that little incident where he tried to take your head off last year.

Jameson smiled. "Three last year." He paused. "All defense verdicts."

Tom also smiled, shaking his head. Jameson was a senior partner with Jones & Butler, the largest law firm in the state. His spe-
cialty was defending large personal injury cases, many of which
were filed by his former trial team partner, Jerry Snider. Jameson
and Jerry had won Tom's first national championship in 1979.
After graduation they had gone in opposite directions, Jerry forg-
ing a career as a plaintiff's attorney and Jameson as a defense lawyer. Both were considered at the top of their fields.

But as good as Jerry Snider had turned out to be—many
thought he was the best plaintiff's attorney in the state—he was
no match for Jameson if the facts were anywhere close to even.
Jameson regularly handed Jerry's ass to him, just like he did everyone else.

"Still dating that court reporter?" Tom asked.

Jameson's smile widened. "Actually, I'm dating two court
reporters," he whispered. "Rival services."

"Competitors?" Tom asked.

Jameson shrugged. "What can I say? They each try to outper-
form the other." He raised his eyebrows, and Tom laughed.

"You are such a bastard, Jamo," Tom said, slapping Jameson
on the back.

Jameson grinned. "Don't I know it."

A few minutes later the trial concluded and the teams shook
hands. Tom turned the floor over to Judge Hancock and Jameson,
who both offered constructive criticism and encouragement to
each of the participants, keeping all of their comments positive.
After the team was gone, Tom approached the bench, smiling at
the judge.

"Judge, as always we appreciate your patience. I'd love to hear
your thoughts on what you observed."

"Sure, Tom. Hey, you still keep a fifth of Jack Black in your
office?"

Tom smiled. He had forgotten about the Cock's love of sour mash whiskey. "I do indeed. Shall we reconvene upstairs?"

—

Five minutes later the three of them were in Tom's office, each drinking Jack Daniel's on ice out of plastic cups.

"Boys, I'm too old for this shit, you know it?" Judge Hancock said, laughing to himself and sitting on the edge of Tom's desk. "Godamighty, I love it, though. I think my heart would up and die if I had to go longer than two weeks without a trial." He took a sip of whiskey, coughed, and continued. "How you been, Tom?"

"Not bad, Judge," Tom lied, glancing down at the apology on his desk. The board meeting was tomorrow. "So what did you think of the team?"

"Oh, you know, Tom. You can tell they're well coached," the judge started. "They speak well, kept their questions on cross short and sweet, and used effective visual aids in opening and closing. But I wasn't wowed like I was last year. Now that team . . . shit fire and save the matches. That team got me excited."

"Drake and Conrad," Tom said, nodding and glancing at Jameson, who was standing by the window. "You know that team should've won the title. I . . . I mismanaged the Drake kid a little and—"

"He's the one that clocked you, ain't he, Tom?" Judge Hancock interrupted, laughing. "You know, I saw that on YouTube."

"Oh, Christ," Tom said, turning to look at the judge. "*You* get on YouTube?"

"Hell yes, I do," Hancock answered. "My grandson's junior high football highlights are put on there. Plus I like watching the old Alabama football games." He smiled. "Drake has a pretty good overhand right."

Tom felt his face getting hot but he knew he shouldn't be mad. He again looked at Jameson, remembering something he had wanted to ask him.

"Jamo, do you know what happened to Drake? Didn't he clerk for you guys one summer?"

Jameson's eyes narrowed. "Actually, he clerked both summers for us, and we made him an offer after the second. Even threw in a nice signing bonus when he accepted. But we terminated his contract after the incident with you, and I'm pretty sure he didn't get one from anywhere else." He laughed. "We let the little shit keep his bonus, though, because his contract didn't specify whether he had to return it. Ten thousand dollars. Not a bad start to a career as a solo practitioner, if that's where he ended up." Jameson paused, eyeing Tom. "Why the interest in Drake?"

Tom's stomach tightened and he looked down at the floor. A sense of guilt crept over him. He hadn't realized how devastating the altercation had been to Rick. *Jesus Christ, his whole career . . . I should've done something.*

Tom shook his head, looking back at Jameson. "Just curious. Drake's from Henshaw, and I have an old friend whose family was killed in a trucking accident in Henshaw. I'd like to refer her to someone with Henshaw ties."

Jameson smiled. "Can't say I know of any Henshaw attorneys, but that sounds like a case for Jerry. His firm takes them from Huntsville to Mobile now. No one could blame you for referring her to Jer."

"I know, and maybe I'll end up doing that," Tom said, looking down. "But I'd really like a Henshaw connection, and I think Jerry would be the first one to recommend that approach. He may live in Montgomery, but he's made his fortune in Greene County, where he was born and raised and where his momma still teaches Sunday school."

Jameson nodded. "I can't argue with that. In fact, I only know of one lawyer who's beaten Jerry in Greene County." Jameson smiled, and Tom smirked back at him.

"How do you fit that ego in the room, Jamo?"

"It gets harder and harder, Professor. But I can't help it." He sighed and drained the rest of his whiskey. "I just keep winning." He set the cup down on Tom's desk and extended his hand. "Good luck with finding her someone. I'll pray that whoever it is doesn't have to face me."

Tom laughed and shook Jameson's hand, holding it for a second. "Thanks for coming down, Jamo. It means a lot that you keep doing this."

"No problem. Actually, now that I'm representing the university, I had to be here anyway for meetings today and tomorrow."

"You must be joking," Tom said, smirking. "*You* are the attorney for this fine institution?"

Jameson held out his arms in mock protest. "What did Coach Bryant always say about coming here to coach? Momma called."

"Momma, my ass," Tom said, shaking his head. "So this is a billable trip?"

Jameson shrugged. "A man's got to make a living," he said, winking at Tom and shaking Judge Hancock's hand. "Judge, always a pleasure."

The Cock raised a toast with his plastic glass and Jameson walked out the door.

—

"So how are things *really* going?" Judge Hancock asked once Jameson had shut the door behind him.

Tom squinted at him. "What do you mean?"

"What the hell is this?" the judge asked, picking up the apology from the desk and shaking it.

Tom shrugged, wishing he'd put the damn thing in a drawer. "I don't know. Apparently, the YouTube video you saw has raised some eyebrows."

"This is bullshit," Hancock said, reading through the apology. "Total bullshit."

"I know. I wish that was all of it. I'm meeting tomorrow with the board. They want me to make *McMurtrie's Evidence* more user-friendly, and the dean said I can't kick anybody else out of class, even if they're not prepared."

"Jesus, Tom. You think the Drake deal is really pushing all that?"

"I don't know. Lambert's been on my ass ever since he was hired. I think he wants new blood, and he's trying to use the Drake incident as leverage to force me out." Tom sighed, rubbing his eyes. He was tired. Thinking about Ruth Ann's case and the board meeting had kept him up the night before.

"So you gonna sign this crap?" Judge Hancock asked, throwing the apology down on the desk. He fixed himself another drink and took a seat in the chair across from Tom.

"I don't know, Judge."

"You wanna know what the Cock would do?"

Tom smiled. "OK, Your Honor, what would you do?"

"If it were me, I'd take that apology to the board meeting tomorrow. I'd set it down real careful like on the table in front of them. Then, after I had their full and undivided attention, I'd unzip my pants and piss on the damn thing. When I was finished, I'd fold my dick back up and walk my ass outta there."

Tom laughed. "So you have to fold yours too?"

The judge took a long sip of whiskey. "The Cock is hung like Secretariat," he said, letting out a belch and stretching his legs. "But seriously, Tom, I wouldn't give them the satisfaction. The unappreciative, ungrateful sons of bitches. You've given your life to this school." He took another sip and grimaced. "And let me tell you something. It's not like you had to come back here to teach."

"What do you mean?"

Judge Hancock leaned forward, setting his cup on the edge of Tom's desk, looking very serious. "Tom, in fifty years I've seen every great trial lawyer in this state. Every damn one of them. Jameson Tyler is the second best I've ever seen." He paused, grinning. "You were the best."

"What?"

"I mean it, buck. You were the real deal."

Tom felt his face flush red. It had been a long time since he had thought of those days.

"You hear George McDuff died?" the judge asked.

"Heart attack, right?"

The judge nodded, and Tom felt a twinge of guilt. He had lost touch with his old boss over the years. George had never gotten over Tom's decision to teach law at Alabama. *You won't make any money; it's a dead end, Tom,* he had said, but Tom had gone nonetheless. He'd had to. The Man had called.

"You ever think about what would have happened if you hadn't gone back to Tuscaloosa?" A slight grin arose on the judge's face, as if he had been reading Tom's mind.

"More now than I used to."

"It's not too late, you know. You're not that old—what, sixty, sixty-five?"

Tom squinted at the judge. "I'm sixty-eight. What are you talking about, Judge?"

Judge Hancock placed both his hands on the desk for leverage and slowly rose to his feet.

"Tom, I've already said it once but I'll say it again. Son, you were the best goddamn trial lawyer I ever saw. It's not too late. Why not give it another go? You've done your part for the school. If they don't appreciate it, then fuck 'em." He paused, pointing his finger at the only picture that adorned Tom's wall other than the national championship plaques. It was of the Man, wearing the houndstooth hat and leaning against the goalpost. "Tom, Coach Bryant would not tolerate this bullshit. I knew the Man. If the Man heard how they were treating you, he would shove his boot so far up Lambert's ass that he'd be tasting the shoestrings. You know he would. I can just see him now." Judge Hancock put his hands on his hips and gave a mock scowl. "You turds. You goddamn turds. I'll give the ultimatums around here. Don't tell my boy to apologize. Build him a goddamn statue and stay the hell out of his way."

It was a pretty good impression, and Tom laughed.

The judge walked around the desk and put his arm on Tom's shoulder.

"Tom, I'm seventy-seven years old. I've gotten too old to give a shit about anything but the things that really matter." He paused. "I'm gonna tell you something, and I want you to listen. I understand why you came here to teach, but I also understand that it would've been a shame if Picasso had never painted. Or if Elvis Presley had never recorded a song." He paused. "Or if the Man had never coached. You have a gift for trying cases, and you're not too old. I think it would be great if the Professor made a comeback."

Tom scoffed. "A comeback. At sixty-eight years old? Are you out of your mind?"

"What does Augustus keep saying in *Lonesome Dove*? 'The older the violin, the sweeter the music.'" He patted Tom's shoulder and winked at him. "Think about it, Tom. It'd probably make some folks in this state piss in their pants." Judge Hancock laughed and walked to the door. Before leaving, he turned around. "I wouldn't refer out that Henshaw case too soon." Again, he winked. "Sounds like the perfect case for a guy I used to know."

13

Tom locked the door and took the stairs to the second floor. He was about to walk out the glass double doors that led to the faculty parking lot when he remembered that he had parked in the student lot adjacent to Coleman Coliseum. There was a basketball game tonight, and he had thought he might go to the game. He and Julie had gone to basketball games on a routine basis. Since her death, he had planned to go several times, but he had never followed through. *And I won't tonight*, Tom knew, feeling depressed as he walked slowly down the second-floor hallway that led to the next staircase. As he walked, it was hard not to gaze at the composites that hung on the walls. Class of 1969. 1972. 1977. He could still remember a lot of the faces. When he reached the first floor, there were more recent classes. 1997. 1999. 2004. 2009. In the 2009 composite, he searched out the face of Rick Drake, finding it in the third row. Rick was smiling, and Tom again felt a sense of guilt.

I can help him, Tom knew. Rick was from Henshaw, and Ruth Ann's case could jump-start his career. *The Cock has lost his mind. I'm way too old and out of practice to take on Ruth Ann's case.*

Shouldn't I just refer the case to Rick and try to work things out with the school? Do I really want to let Lambert run me off? Tom closed his eyes. *But what if the boy's temper gets the best of him again? This isn't a trial competition, this is real.*

Tom opened his eyes and shook his head, frustrated by his indecision. He walked away from the composites toward the door that led to the student lot. At the door a security guard sat with his legs propped up on a desk. When he saw Tom, he instantly shot to his feet.

"Hello, Professor. Do you need an umbrella or anything?"

Tom blinked, looking first at the guard—a first-year student named Jeffrey working his way through school by doing security at night—and then out the glass door, where he saw rain pelting the sidewalk and heard a clap of thunder.

"No, I'm good, Jeff," Tom said, reaching into his briefcase and pulling out a small umbrella. "Jesus, it's coming down."

"Yes, sir." They both looked out the door, and Tom caught sight of a lone figure carrying a pile of books down the sidewalk, the weight of the books causing the person to walk in zigzag fashion.

"That stack of books is bigger than her," Jeffrey said, beginning to walk toward the door. "She must've come out the doors to the student lounge. I should probably—"

"Don't worry about it," Tom said, catching his arm. "I'm headed that way. You stay here."

"Uh . . . OK . . ." Jeffrey said, stopping. "Thanks, Professor."

"No worries," Tom said, heading out into the rain, which was coming down sideways. Tom opened his umbrella, ran, and caught up to the figure.

"Need some help?" he asked.

The person looked up, and Tom recognized the face of Dawn Murphy.

"Professor!" she yelled, smiling at him. "I would run but I'm afraid I'll drop everything," she said, and, just as she said it, one of the books she was holding fell to the ground.

Tom picked up the book and set it back on her stack. Then he smiled at her and held the umbrella, which was barely big enough to cover just him, over her head.

"Here," he said, instinctively putting his arm around her. "Just hold on to your books and stay close."

She hesitated for a moment but then gave in, and Tom felt her body relax against his. Feeling self-conscious, Tom walked Dawn down the long cobblestoned sidewalk to the parking lot. When they reached a white Mustang hatchback, Dawn slid her purse off her shoulder and it fell to the ground.

"The keys should be on top," she said, shrugging and looking embarrassed.

Tom leaned down, unzipped the purse, and found the keys easily. He pressed the button and opened the passenger-side back door.

"My hero," Dawn said, throwing the books inside. When she turned around, Tom saw that the front of her T-shirt had gotten wet.

"Well . . . here you go," Tom said, holding out the keys and forcing himself to look at the ground.

"Professor, thank you so much," Dawn said, taking the keys from his hand. "I had five guys walk right by me and not even offer to help."

"Glad to help," Tom managed. Then he remembered the conversation with Dawn in his office after the first class. She had a young daughter and was in need of money. She lived with her mother. "So how is everything going?" he asked.

Dawn chuckled softly and shook her head. "Oh, fine. I have to go be a mom now. Tonight is parents' night at Julie's school and"— she looked down at her watch and sighed—"and I'm late and I'm gonna have to change."

Julie . . . Tom winced as he heard his wife's name out loud. He looked away, feeling the depression beginning to seep back in.

"You're getting wet," Dawn said, grabbing the handle of the umbrella and stepping toward him. Tom looked down at her, blinking rain out of his eyes. At some point while talking to her, he had covered her with the umbrella and forgotten about himself. Forgetting had felt good.

"Are you OK, Professor?" Dawn asked, her eyes and forehead crinkling up with concern.

Tom just gazed down at her. He knew he should nod or say something, lest Dawn might get uncomfortable, but he couldn't force out the words. He wasn't OK. He hadn't been OK for three years.

"Well, thanks again," Dawn said, leaning in and patting his shoulder.

She stepped out from under the umbrella and opened the door to her car. Feeling light-headed and foolish, Tom took a couple of steps back, waiting until the Mustang roared to life before he turned away. As he made his way toward his own vehicle, he heard Dawn's voice again and turned around.

"Bye!" she yelled, her window rolled down as she drove past.

Tom waved at her as she left, and he shook his head. *That girl is something else*, he thought, climbing inside his Explorer and letting down the umbrella. As he cranked the ignition and waited for the car to warm up, he leaned back in the seat and tried to relax.

What's going on with you? Tom wondered. Depression had given way to restlessness. He could feel something churning within him. Something reawakening. Like an old bike, whose chains had rusted and whose handlebars were covered with cobwebs, craving to be oiled up and ridden. Tom fumbled for his cell phone and scrolled down the contacts until he reached Ruth Ann. He highlighted her number and stared at the green Send key, hovering his right thumb over it. He owed Ruth Ann a call about her case, but he wasn't thinking about her case right now. Tom felt goose bumps on his arm, remembering the tingle he'd felt when Ruth Ann touched him. *Do it. Just call her.* He lowered his thumb and started to apply pressure.

No. Tom pressed End, feeling his heart pounding in his chest. "What's going on, Tom?" he said out loud. He laughed nervously and shook his head, trying to get a grip.

It's just the whiskey. It's just the booze and that foolishness the Cock was spouting and all this shit with the board. Just go home and get some rest.

Tom took a deep breath. "Go home," he whispered, forcing himself to put the car in gear and flinging the cell phone into the passenger seat.

"Just go home."

14

The next day Tom walked down the faculty hallway and stopped off in the restroom. As he took a leak in the urinal, he leaned his forearm against the concrete wall and his head against the back of his wrist. He had barely slept a wink the night before. He had left the parking lot and gone straight home, taking the time to let Musso out and refill his water bowl before turning out the lights and crawling under the covers. Once in bed he kept staring at the ceiling, unable to get the conversation with the Cock off his mind. He was still undecided about what to do with Ruth Ann's case or the board meeting he was about to attend. He also couldn't shake the weird feeling he'd had after talking with Dawn Murphy or his near booty call to Ruth Ann. He felt restless and unstable, as if the ground were moving beneath him.

Tom sighed, zipping up his pants. He started to flush the toilet but stopped when he noticed some bloody residue in the urinal. *What the . . . ?*

He hadn't been paying attention while he went, nor had he looked in the urinal before he had started. A couple of months ago he had noticed a few drops of blood after a long day of golf, but he hadn't thought anything of it. There hadn't been a repeat episode and there hadn't been much blood in the first place. He had thought it was probably stress or maybe a small infection that had gone away.

Shaking his head, he flushed the urinal. *Probably someone else.*

Tom walked to the sink and splashed water on his face. As he gazed into the mirror at his bloodshot eyes, he tried without success to suppress the frustration he felt at being called before the board. Tom had been to numerous board meetings in his forty-year career but never one where his actions were the subject of review. He knew acting defensive would not help his cause, but it was hard not to be irritated. *Where do these turds get off?* he thought, remembering the Cock's admonition to piss on the apology.

He exited the bathroom and walked down the corridor toward the large conference room at the end of the hall. When he reached the mahogany door, he paused, feeling a rush of adrenaline.

Bring it, he thought, gripping the handle and stepping through the doorway.

15

"He there yet?"

The cryptic text message splashed across Dean Richard Lambert's BlackBerry, with the familiar phone number written across the top. Lambert read the words and looked up as Tom McMurtrie entered the conference room.

"Y," Lambert typed, pressing Send and standing with the rest of the board members in the room.

"Hello, Professor. Thank you for coming today. Please . . . have a seat."

Tom McMurtrie's eyes fixed on the dean's, and Lambert felt his stomach tighten.

"I didn't realize I had a choice in the matter," Tom said, his voice pleasant but curt. "If you don't mind, I'd prefer to stand."

"Well, suit yourself. We're still lacking one other person, but . . ."

There was a loud knock at the door, and the dean's voice cut off. He smiled at Tom and looked around the room, taking a deep breath. "Come in."

—

When the door opened, Tom felt as if his stomach and testicles had both been kicked at the same time. He stared at the man standing before him, twisting his head in confusion.

"Professor," the man said, his voice lacking its usual joviality.

"Jamo?"

"Members of the board," Dean Lambert said, walking over and grasping Jameson's hand. "I trust you have all met the university's new attorney, Jameson Tyler."

Tom kept his eyes on Jameson, who continued to stare back at Tom despite shaking the dean's hand. Jameson put his hand out for Tom to shake, but Tom didn't move.

"What are you doing here?" Tom asked, his voice a low growl.

"Like I told you yesterday, I had to be up here anyway for a couple of *meetings*, and this is one of them," Jameson said, slapping Tom on the arm and walking down the table, squeezing shoulders, shaking hands, and kissing the lone female board member, Barbara Bostic, on the cheek before joining the dean at the head of the table.

"Well, it's good to see everyone," Jameson said. "Now please sit down."

Everyone did as they were told but Tom. He continued to stand bolt upright and glared at his friend.

"Please, Professor, sit down."

"As I told the dean, I'd prefer to stand."

Jameson didn't blink or show any outward emotion. He crossed his legs and gazed back at Tom. "OK, Professor. Let's get on with this."

"I'd like that very much," Tom said. *What in the hell is going on? Why didn't he mention this yesterday?*

"The board," Jameson began, looking around the room and then back at Tom, "per my recommendation, has decided to reprimand you for the incident involving trial team member Rick Drake. The board, along with thousands of other people, has watched the video of your altercation with Drake and finds that you acted inappropriately when you grabbed his arm and jerked him around."

Tom again felt like he'd been punched in the gut. He couldn't believe it.

"As a result of the incident with Drake and another, more personal matter, the board has decided to put a reprimand in your personnel file and has chosen to allow you to remain on the faculty only if you will agree to work under certain conditions."

Tom remained silent. He would hear it all before he commented.

"Condition number one," Jameson continued. "You will work under a zero tolerance policy. One more incident in any way similar to the Rick Drake altercation and you will be terminated immediately." Jameson paused, looking at Tom, who glared back.

"Condition number two. You will be supervised by another member of the faculty during your classes and during trial team practices and tournaments. Bill Stewart, the other Evidence professor, has volunteered for the job, and he will begin his surveillance effective tomorrow."

Tom almost laughed. He and Bill Stewart had a hate-hate relationship, which Jameson knew because Tom had told him. *So much, I've told him . . .*

"Condition three. You will sign the apology that Dean Lambert provided you on Monday and tender it to this board before we leave this meeting today." Jameson paused. "The board met last night to discuss this plan and it passed by majority vote. If you do not agree to work under these conditions, then it will have no choice but to terminate you."

"Last night?" Tom asked, his voice incredulous. The words felt like acid on his tongue. "*Before* or *after* you judged our mock trial?"

Jameson poured himself a glass of water and took a sip, not answering the question. The board members sat stoically in their seats. Tom ran his eyes down the table, and only one of them met his gaze. William Rufus Cole. The oldest member of the board looked at him with sad, angry eyes and slowly stood.

"There's something I want to say," Rufus said, his voice gruff.

Jameson smiled. "By all means, Rufus."

"I think the Professor is entitled to know that not everyone here agrees with this decision." Rufus Cole paused and cleared his throat. "The vote of the board was five to four. I was one of the four. It should be noted that the five board members who voted for this decision have all been added within the last two years and are not as familiar with the Professor's vast accomplishments as the rest of us are." He walked down the table and put his arm around Tom. "Let the record reflect, Dean Lambert, and let it be recorded in the minutes of this board meeting that William Rufus Cole from Choctaw County, Alabama, thinks that the board's action today is an *unadulterated, unmitigated, goddamn disgrace.* This man has given his whole life for this school. He played for Coach Bryant's 1961 national champions. None of you people remember that team, but *I do.* That team was the Bear's first national champion. The defense that Tom played on gave up twenty-five points. *For the whole year.* That team made not just the school but the whole state *proud.*" Rufus squeezed Tom's shoulder. "Then, when the Man asked him to come build a trial program and teach Evidence, what did he do? He came. And he won three national championships and wrote the *goddamn* book on evidence in this state."

"Please watch your language, Rufus," Jameson said, a thin smile covering his face.

Rufus pointed his finger at Jameson, and it trembled with anger. "You . . . you *fucking Judas.* You of all people should be standing by Tom on this, Jameson. You wouldn't be half the trial lawyer you are if it wasn't for the Professor."

"Rufus, my first and only loyalty in this matter is to my client, the University of Alabama. My client asked for a recommendation, and I have given it." Jameson turned his gaze to Tom. "So what'll it be, Professor? You've heard the conditions. Will you agree to abide by them?"

"Don't do it, Tom," Rufus said, his voice shaky and tired, having given out from the effort. He was now talking to and looking at only Tom. "I'm sorry."

"It's OK, Rufus," Tom said, patting his old friend on the arm. Then he turned to Tyler, forcing himself to remain calm.

"You mentioned something besides the altercation with Drake. A 'personal' matter. What does that involve?"

"It's bullshit, Tom," Rufus blurted. "Complete—"

"Rufus Cole," Dean Lambert said, standing and glaring at Rufus. "You have been warned twice. You can address this board appropriately or you can leave."

"Don't threaten me, you son of a—"

Rufus started to walk toward the dean, but Tom grabbed him by the arm and whispered in his ear, "Just sit down, Rufus. I appreciate the gesture, but it's not helping. OK?"

Rufus looked at him with pleading eyes, then nodded and took his seat. Tom turned back to Jameson, who was now standing.

"The personal matter involves a relationship you have with one of your students that the board believes is inappropriate. According to the dean, he saw you holding hands with one of your female interns on Monday and"—Tyler opened a file folder in front of him and slid an envelope down the table—"and we also have these."

Tom looked inside the envelope and couldn't believe his eyes. Dawn Murphy's smiling face was caught in close-up as Tom walked her down the sidewalk with his arm around her. The next one showed her wet T-shirt. In the last two, Dawn's body leaned into Tom's and her hand was on his shoulder, but their faces were blocked by the umbrella, making it appear like they were in some type of romantic embrace.

"You had me followed?" Tom looked up at the dean, whose eyes shifted to Jameson.

"Well . . . yes," the dean said. "After observing you holding hands with Ms. Murphy on Monday, the board was advised by our attorney to conduct surveillance on you. I think the photographs show the wisdom in Mr. Tyler's advice."

Tom glared at Jameson. "Since when is helping a student get to her car in the rain some type of offense?" Tom asked, trying to keep his voice steady as he put the photographs back in the envelope and slid them back to Jameson.

"It is my opinion and that of the board that the conduct captured in those photographs and described by the dean is inappropriate," Jameson continued, his voice grave. "Out of respect for you and the memory of your deceased wife, Julie, the board has decided, per my recommendation, that this allegation will not be included in your written reprimand, but you should know that it *was* a factor."

That was it.

For the third time in the last fifteen minutes, Tom felt like he'd been punched in the gut, but this one was too much for him to take.

He took two swift steps toward Jameson, grabbed him by the collar, slammed his back against the wall, and held him three feet off the ground.

"Professor, you're choking me."

Tom shook him and got within an inch of his eyes. "Don't you ever mention my wife's name in front of me again. Don't you ever refer to her as if you knew her. You address her as Mrs. McMurtrie, you backstabbing son of a bitch."

Tom heard the dean call security and felt an arm on his shoulder. It was Rufus.

"Let him down, Tom. It's OK. I want to do it too, but just let him down."

Slowly, Tom lowered his former student and confidant to the ground. "How could you do this to me? You were my friend, Jameson. I trusted you. Why . . . ?"

"Thanks for proving my case," Jameson whispered. Then, straightening his coat, he addressed the rest of the board. "I think you should now see the wisdom in your decision today and the reasoning behind my recommendation. What if he did that to a student? Or another teacher?"

"You baited him, you son of a bitch. You set him up." Rufus Cole lunged for Jameson, but Tom caught Rufus's arm. "That won't be necessary, Rufus."

"As university attorney, I hereby recommend that this board change its action from reprimand to suspension," Jameson said, his voice loud and authoritative. "The Professor is obviously not himself and needs some time to . . . get it together. Three months' suspension. Then, if he comes back and agrees to the conditions referenced today, he can continue on the faculty. All in favor?"

"There won't be need for a vote," Tom said, hearing the fatigue in his voice. The adrenaline rush was gone.

He walked slowly down the table and stopped when he reached the door. Turning, he forced himself to smile at Jameson. "Thirty years you've been my friend. I hope that selling me out was worth it to you."

"My client sought my advice and counsel, and I gave it. It would have been unethical to put loyalty to you over my client's interests."

"Unprofitable, more like it," Tom spat. "Dean Lambert has wanted rid of me since the moment he took over. He asked your opinion, and you gave the one that allowed you to bill hours and make money."

"I gave the one that was sound. You put your hands on two students. One in anger and the other in lust. There are grounds here for termination, but the board, in my opinion, is being lenient for all of the reasons that Rufus mentioned."

Tom shook his head, looking out over the board members. "I congratulate you on your ambush. I'll have you know that what the dean witnessed and what is seen in the photographs were both simply harmless displays of affection by a young student glad to get a job and appreciative of an umbrella. I hope this board won't take any action against her and will keep her name in confidence."

"No action against her is planned," Dean Lambert said. "The board sees you as the guilty party, Professor. As with Rick Drake, the student is an innocent, and her name will remain confidential."

Tom nodded, feeling the bitterness begin to invade his exhausted body. "This board has given me no alternative but to step down. I won't accept a suspension and I won't work under your bullshit conditions."

Jameson frowned disingenuously. "Professor, please know that no one here wants you to—"

"Shut up, Jameson," Tom interrupted. "I've had enough bullshit today. I'll have my things removed from the office this weekend."

"Professor," Dean Lambert said, his eyes and voice excited. "Perhaps as a show of gratitude and a way to bring closure to the situation, we could hold a banquet in your—"

"Not only no"—Tom cut him off—"but hell no. No banquets, no ceremonies, no bullshit." Tom paused, looking at all of them for a couple of seconds. "Just leave me the hell alone." He grabbed the doorknob.

"Professor, please . . ."

But Lambert's voice was lost in the sound of the mahogany door slamming shut.

16

Tom stood with his hands on his knees, staring down into the toilet bowl. He had walked straight to the bathroom after the meeting and vomited up his breakfast. Now, ten minutes of dry heaving later, he still felt nauseated, but he didn't have the energy to puke anymore. He flushed the commode and leaned his hands against the concrete. He couldn't believe it. Jameson Tyler had eaten in his home numerous times over the past thirty years, first as a student, then as a young lawyer, and finally as a trusted friend. When Julie had been dying, Jameson had come to the hospital a couple of times.

He was my friend.

The betrayal hurt Tom like nothing he'd ever felt in his life. He had always had a knack for reading people, and other than Rick Drake, he had never gotten it wrong. Tom had thought Jameson was from the old school. A tireless worker. Loyal to his friends. A winner through and through. Tom beat his fists softly against the concrete.

He's nothing but an opportunist, Tom thought. *He used his friendship with me for his own gain to climb the ladder at Jones & Butler, and when I couldn't help him anymore, he threw me out with the garbage.*

Tom heard the door to the bathroom swing open and he straightened up. Whoever was out there was using the urinal and whistling happily to himself. A faculty member oblivious to Tom's forced departure.

Tom unzipped his pants. He started to piss and gazed at the wall in front of him. *It's over,* he thought, still not believing it.

Forty years spanning five decades. Three national championships. Four editions of *McMurtrie's Evidence.* Three deans. Hundreds of faculty members. And thousands upon thousands of students.

Over.

Tom leaned his forearm against the wall. He was so damn tired. As he bent down to flush the toilet, he glanced into the bowl.

What the . . . ?

Tom's whole body tensed, and he blinked. Then he looked again, and he felt goose bumps break out on his arm. Instead of the familiar whitish-yellow residue of urine, all Tom could see was red. He took a step back and wiped his eyes, trying to refocus them. Then he looked into the bowl again.

Red. Everywhere. *Blood,* Tom thought, his heartbeat quickening as he remembered the trip to the restroom before the board meeting. He again looked away, this time for several seconds. He tried to think of something else. Maybe his eyes were playing tricks on him. He hadn't slept well all week, and he knew that tired eyes could fool you.

When he was satisfied he'd waited long enough, Tom took a deep breath and turned his head for a final look at the bowl.

"Holy shit," he whispered.

He left the toilet stall, went out into the bathroom, and tee-tered toward the sink.

"Everything all right, Professor?"

Tom looked at the man, a young faculty member named Will Burbaker, and nodded, forcing a smile.

"Just a little under the weather," Tom managed, running his hands, which were shaking, under the sink and then drying them with a paper towel.

"Sure?" Burbaker asked, looking at Tom's hands.

"I'm fine, Will," Tom said. "I'll talk to you later."

Tom walked to the door, his thoughts a jumbled mess. As he exited the restroom, he just wanted to go to his office and collect himself, but that wasn't going to happen.

A female reporter stuck a microphone in his face and grabbed his arm, looking back toward a cameraman. Several flashbulbs went off, and Tom was momentarily blinded. The fatigue from lack of sleep, the dehydration from vomiting, and the shock from pissing a bowl of blood, combined with the sharp light, made him dizzy. He started walking toward the stairs, with the reporter right on his heels.

"Professor . . . Professor, can you comment on the press release from the university announcing your retirement? You got a lot of scrutiny after the incident with former student Rick Drake last year in Washington, and we want to know whether that had anything to do with your departure. There's also rumors of an inappropriate relationship with a female student. Can you comment?"

Tom stopped at the head of the stairs, leaning against the wall and wanting to puke again. He had been retired all of fifteen min-utes and the press already knew. Jameson must have alerted them before the meeting. *The bastard thought of everything.*

"I don't have any comment," Tom said, glaring at the reporter.

Then, calmly and with as much dignity as he could muster, Thomas Jackson McMurtrie descended the stairs and left the building.

17

At 10:00 p.m. Tom sat on the couch in the den, clutching his cordless phone in a death grip. Musso had placed his head in Tom's lap and was snoring loudly, but Tom paid him no mind. Tom wasn't even paying attention to the television screen, where the nightly news was dominated by the story of his forced retirement. He had bigger things to worry about.

Tom had gone to see Dr. Bill Davis after leaving the law school. Bill had been Tom's urologist for the past ten years. Bill had taken blood and urine samples, and he'd also done a bladder X-ray. Though he hadn't elaborated on the possibilities, Bill had sounded worried.

Now Tom was worried. Bill had said he'd call tonight, but it was getting late. Tom knew he needed to think about what to do next. He had tenure with the law school, and the board's reasons for their punishment were horseshit. But did he even want to work for a board and a dean who would throw him out with the trash after forty years? And what about Ruth Ann's case?

The phone exploded to life in Tom's hand, and he cringed. He glared at the receiver, and the caller ID showed the name he'd been waiting for—and dreading—for the past five hours.

"Hello."

"Tom, Bill Davis."

"Hey, Bill." Tom closed his eyes and tried to steel himself. "So what's the verdict?"

Tom heard Bill take a deep breath on the other end of the line. "Tom, the X-ray showed a mass in your bladder. I think it's superficial. Probably only stage one or two, but we'll have to get it out to confirm."

"A mass?" Tom asked, slowly beginning to get it. "Bill . . . are you telling me I have cancer?"

For several seconds the line was silent. Then Bill sighed. "Yeah, Tom. Cancer of the bladder."

18

The office was a strange place on Saturday. Quiet, still—like an amusement park the morning after closing night, the rides still there but not moving. Even in Rick Drake's small one-horse office, things were different. The constant hum of Frankie's typing was gone. As was Frankie, whom Rick seldom asked to work on the weekend. And the phone, which didn't ring that much during the week, didn't ring at all on Saturday. It was a good time to get some work done—if you could stand being there on a day when the college kids started drinking before noon and everyone else, it seemed, was out enjoying the day.

Unfortunately, Rick wasn't getting any work done this morning. His phone was ringing off the hook with calls from reporters wanting his take on the Professor's forced retirement and whether Rick felt any vindication. Though Rick was stunned by the announcement, Rick's answer mirrored the Professor's. "No comment," he said. Over. And over. And over. Talking about the incident wasn't going to get him a better job or any new clients. It was just going to make him more of a joke than he already was.

Which would be tough to do, he thought, laying his head on his desk. Maybe after a little rest—the constant phone calls had kept him up most of the night—he'd be able to process what had happened. Right now he just didn't want to think about it. Closing his eyes, Rick took a deep breath and tried to relax.

Four loud knocks on the front door interrupted his quest for solace.

"Jesus Christ," he muttered under his breath. When he had arrived at the office, he hadn't noticed anyone waiting for him or tailing him, but maybe one of the stations had gotten wind of where he worked. *Why can't they just leave me alone?* he thought, hoping that it might be Powell as he walked toward the door.

Rick unlocked the door and cracked it a few inches, planning to slam it shut if he didn't recognize the person outside. When he saw who it was, his stomach tightened, and instinctively he let the door swing open the rest of the way.

"What . . . what do you want?" Rick asked.

"I need to talk with you about something," the Professor said, stepping through the doorway before Rick could invite him in.

—

Tom took off his overcoat and slumped onto a couch in what he guessed was the reception area of Rick's office. *This looks like a converted loft,* Tom thought, seeing a kitchen behind him and a couple of rooms to the right of it.

"I . . . have a conference room. We can go in there if you—"

"This is fine," Tom said, gesturing to a chair with rollers behind a desk. *His secretary's desk?* "Have a seat, Rick. This won't take long."

Rick sat in the chair and rolled it to where he was a few feet from Tom.

"Nice office," Tom said, forcing a smile and trying to sound genuine. "How long have you been here?"

"Five months," Rick said, and Tom heard a trace of irritation in the young man's voice. "You said you wanted to talk about something."

Tom looked away and leaned forward in the couch, placing his elbows on his knees. After Bill Davis's call, he had spent all night thinking about his options—or lack thereof. Sometime around dawn he knew what he had to do. When he saw his face plastered all over the morning newspaper, it just confirmed his decision. There were just a couple of loose ends to tie up.

Forming a steeple with his hands, Tom gazed into Rick's eyes. "I'm sure you've heard the news about my 'retirement.'"

Rick nodded but didn't say anything.

Tom looked down at the carpeted floor. "Rick, I need to go away for a little while. Maybe a long while. It's a zoo here, and I need to get away from it. Have you seen the newspaper this morning?"

Again Rick nodded.

"Well, it's going to be like that for a while, and . . ." Tom paused. "I'm too old to put up with it." Sighing, Tom looked up from the floor. "I'm sure you've been contacted."

"I've told them all 'No comment.'"

Tom nodded. For a moment neither of them spoke. Tom was so tired. *You have to do this*, he thought. *Suck it up.*

"Professor, why are you here?"

"I'm about to tell you. You're from Henshaw, right?"

"Right."

"Your family has a farm there, don't they?"

"Yes. What does that have to do with—?"

"Are you familiar with the intersection of Limestone Bottom Road and Highway 82?"

Rick wrinkled his eyebrows. "Professor, what—?"

"Just answer the question."

Rick slapped his hands against his legs. "There's a Texaco there. Been there forever. Used to be a bait and beer store."

"Do you know anyone that works there?"

Rick snorted. "The only person I know that's ever worked there is Rose Batson." Rick stood and took a step forward. "Now that's it. I'm going to ask you to leave unless you tell me what this is about."

"Do you have any staff, Rick? Associate, secretary, clerk, paralegal?" Tom knew Rick was about to blow a gasket, but this question was important.

"I have a secretary." Rick spoke through gritted teeth. "Now get the hell—"

"I'm going to refer you a case," Tom said, rising from the couch. "It's a wrongful death trucking case. A good friend of mine's whole family—daughter, son-in-law, and granddaughter—all died. The accident happened at that Texaco, Ms. Batson is the eyewitness, and the trucker was estimated to be going eighty miles per hour just before the accident by an Officer"—Tom took out the crumpled accident report from his pocket—"Ballard."

"Jimmy Ballard," Rick said, his voice barely audible. "Sheriff Jimmy Ballard."

"I wanted to refer her to someone from Henshaw who might know the people involved," Tom said, shrugging. "You passed the test." Tom paused and narrowed his gaze. "Do you want the case?"

—

Rick's heart pounded in his chest. He had read about the accident in the paper the day after it happened, and he had known there would be a lawsuit. He had even called Ms. Rose and Sheriff Ballard himself to inquire about it. Alas, despite his connections in Henshaw, the family that was killed was from Huntsville, and he had no way of getting his name in front of them. The rules of ethics prohibited a lawyer from directly soliciting a case from a potential client. He had chalked the case up as a pipe dream and figured one of the big dogs would get it. Now, here was the Professor. In his office and offering to refer the case to him. *Is this really happening?* Rick blinked his eyes several times as he gazed back at a man he had hated for over a year. During the intervening months since the incident at nationals, Rick had often daydreamed about chance confrontations with the Professor. At the grocery store. At the mall. At an Alabama football game. In his daydreams he always told the bastard off. Now he could barely speak.

"You . . . you have a lot of nerve," he managed. "Coming here after what you did to me."

"As I recollect it, you hit me in the face," Tom said. "I think I got the worse end of it."

"I had a job, you know. Not just any job either. *Jones & Butler.* A hundred K a year. Working for Jameson Tyler. They *fired me* after the incident at nationals before I had even worked a day. Said they couldn't have a hothead working for them."

"I know," Tom said.

"Of course you know," Rick said, feeling anger burn through his chest. "You and Tyler are all chummy. He probably called you right after he told me, and y'all probably had drinks to celebrate. Well, *fuck him.*" Rick took a step forward. "And fuck you too. I'd never take a referral from you. I don't care how great the case is."

Tom walked to the door, moving slowly and deliberately. When he reached the knob, he turned around. "I'm sorry, Rick. I didn't realize the incident had affected you so badly. That's in part why I'm here. I was hoping this case might in some way make up for how I've hurt your career."

Rick glared back, unable to form coherent thoughts. *"Just get out,"* he said.

Without waiting for any further response, Rick turned and walked to his private office, slamming the door behind him.

Listening, he heard a sigh and then the front door squeaked open and shut.

Jesus Christ, he thought, pacing the floor of his office, looking up at the regional championship photograph and cursing the gray eyes in the picture. *Where does he get off? Marching in here and giving me a pop quiz before he refers me a case. Well, fuck him. I don't need him. I don't need his help.*

Rick took a deep breath and glanced at his desk. Leaning up against it were his four thin file jackets. Three workers' comp cases and a car wreck. *Four measly files and you're turning down a multimillion-dollar death case in your hometown with Ms. Rose and Sheriff Ballard as witnesses? Are you out of your mind?*

Rick glanced around his office, knowing that he'd never get a job in this state working for a firm like Jones & Butler again. The incident would always keep him down. His only chance was to be a plaintiff's lawyer and have a million-dollar case walk in the door.

Rick felt panic from his head to his shoes as he realized what he had done. *My million-dollar case just walked out the door.*

Rick ran. Through the reception area. Out the door. And down the stairs. *Don't be gone. Please . . . don't be gone.* He barreled outside and almost fell on the sidewalk. Looking in all directions, he didn't see anyone.

"Having second thoughts?" a gravelly voice asked from behind him. Rick turned and saw the Professor leaning up against the brick outer wall of Larry and Barry's.

"I'm . . . sorry. I . . . you just caught me off guard," Rick stammered, leaning forward and grabbing his knees to catch his breath.

"Don't worry about it. Do you want the case?"

Rick looked up and slowly nodded. "I do, but . . . I've got one condition. You have to stay away. You can't be hanging around, second-guessing every decision I make. You can't—"

"Don't worry about that," Tom interrupted. "Like I said, I'm going away for a while. You won't be hearing from me again about this or anything else." Tom took several folded pieces of paper out of his front pocket and gave them to Rick. "This is the accident report and my notes on the case. It's all I have right now. There's a sticky note on top with the client's name and phone number." He paused. "Her name is Ruth Ann Wilcox, and . . . she means a great deal to me. My only condition is that you call her when you get upstairs. Don't wait until Monday. I want you to tell her that I had to go away and that you have a note from me." He stopped and pulled out an envelope from inside his jacket. "When you meet her for the first time, I want you to give her this envelope. I'll trust you not to open it before you see her." Tom handed Rick the envelope and grabbed his arm. "Promise me you'll give her the note."

Rick squinted up at him. "I promise."

Tom gave a quick nod and turned and began to walk down the sidewalk.

"Professor . . . why . . . ?" Rick stopped, unsure of what he wanted to ask. A million questions seemed to flood his brain.

When he reached the corner, the Professor turned and glared at Rick. "Second chances don't come around every day, son." He paused. "Don't fuck it up."

19

Dear Ruth Ann,

I'm sure you've seen or read the news by now. Because of the bad publicity surrounding me, I'm going away for a while. Rick Drake is a talented lawyer with Henshaw ties who will do a fine job for you. I recommend that you hire him to take your case.

Love,

Tom

Ruth Ann read the letter and then reread it. *Going away for a while?* She didn't understand.

"Did he say anything else when he gave this to you?" Ruth Ann asked, looking up from the conference room table at Rick Drake. *He is so young,* she thought.

"He said that you mean a great deal to him."

Ruth Ann nodded, blinking back tears. *I mean so much to him that he could just leave without saying good-bye.*

"Ms. Wilcox, I've taken the liberty of drafting this complaint," Rick Drake said, sliding several stapled sheets of paper across the desk. "We would file against Willistone Trucking Company for two counts of negligence. First, for their driver's negligence at the time of the accident. I've already spoken briefly with Sheriff Jimmy Ballard over the telephone, and he stands by the speed listed in the report: eighty miles per hour in a sixty-five-mile zone. That's a clear basis for count one." Rick paused and took a sip of water.

"What about the eyewitness's statement? Ms. . . ."

"Batson. Rose Batson. I've also spoken with Ms. Rose— everyone in Henshaw calls her Ms. Rose—and unfortunately she just repeated what's in her statement. The Honda turned in front of the rig." Rick shrugged. "However, she added that the rig was about a hundred yards from the intersection when the Honda began its turn, so hopefully we can retain an accident reconstructionist who can give the opinion that your son-in-law couldn't have seen the rig when he started to turn."

Ruth Ann cringed when Rick said "son-in-law" and felt an ache in her heart. Bob had been such a good man. Strong. Protective of his wife and child. Exactly the kind of man a mother would want her daughter to marry. *Not the kind of man that would pull in front of an eighteen-wheeler.*

"OK, that makes sense," Ruth Ann said. "You mentioned a second count?"

Rick nodded. "Count two is for the company's negligence in hiring, training, and supervising Newton."

Ruth Ann raised her eyebrows. "So you think the company was negligent?"

Rick nodded. "I looked at Newton's driving record this weekend. There's a database online with that information. His record shows two speeding tickets within six months prior to the accident."

"Two speeding tickets?"

Rick nodded. "Since Newton was speeding at the time of this accident, the prior tickets should've warned the company of a problem. I think we'll probably need more than that to get to a jury, but the tickets give us a good-faith basis for bringing the claim."

"How will we get more?"

"Well . . . based on the newspaper articles I read online, Harold Newton was hauling nine thousand gallons of Ultron gasoline at the time of the collision. Now, I doubt we have a claim against Ultron, but they might have information relevant to the case. Unfortunately, the Ultron plant in Tuscaloosa burned to the ground the night of the accident, so I'm worried that Ultron may not have any documents."

"Do you think there could be some connection between the fire and the accident?" Ruth Ann asked.

Rick shrugged. "The fire marshal determined that the fire was accidental, so it appears to just be a bad coincidence. However, even if Ultron doesn't have any documents, someone there had to load Newton's truck on the day of the accident, and I'm going to make an all-out effort to find and talk with those employees." Rick took a deep breath and sipped from a cup of coffee. "The articles also mentioned that the deceased truck driver, Harold Newton, had a widow."

Ruth Ann felt her stomach tighten. She remembered hearing about Newton's widow. Several times in the days following the accident she had thought of calling Ms. Newton, but she never had. *Too painful*, she thought, biting her lip.

"Why is that important?" Ruth Ann asked.

"It may not be," Rick said. "But if there was something going on with Willistone that was making Harold Newton have to speed, then his widow may know about it. She may blame Willistone for his death." He held out his palms. "Anyway, I think it's worth exploring."

Ruth Ann nodded. Then, pointing at the complaint, she looked at Rick. "When did you want to file this?"

"As soon as you're ready. We could file today if you wish."

Ruth Ann crossed her arms over her chest. *This is really happening,* she thought, gazing down at the draft complaint in front of her. She wished so badly that Tom was still here.

Ruth Ann closed her eyes. *Everything. These people took everything from me. They deserve to answer for it.* She saw Jeannie, Bob, and Nicole as she remembered them and she fought back tears. *This won't bring them back. Are you sure you want to put yourself through this? Wouldn't it be better to move on?*

"Ms. Wilcox, you don't have to decide today," Rick said. "I mean, if you'd like some more time to think about it . . ."

Ruth Ann stood, her body trembling. *I have to know why.* She turned her back on Rick and walked to the door of the conference room. Then she turned around and looked Rick Drake directly in the eye.

"File it."

PART THREE

PART THREE

20

Hazel Green, Alabama, is a one-stoplight town on the northern tip of the state. In 1939, two years before enlisting in the army and three years before joining the 101st Airborne, Sutton "Sut" McMurtrie bought a hundred-acre farm across the street from Hazel Green High School. A year later, on a cold and blustery day two weeks before Christmas, Sut's wife, Rene, gave birth to their one and only child, a son. Wanting the boy to have a strong name, Sut named him after his grandfather's hero, the general that Newt McMurtrie served under in the Civil War. Thomas Jackson. To the world, Thomas "Stonewall" Jackson.

Tom was two when his daddy left the farm for the war, and he didn't remember him going. But he did remember his return. Sut had been badly injured at the Battle of the Bulge when his battalion, led by General McAuliffe, refused to surrender at Bastogne. Sut came home in a wheelchair, wearing the Purple Heart given him by President Roosevelt. Despite his condition, when Sut had seen his son for the first time, he had picked six-year-old Tom up off the ground, sat him in his lap, and kissed him on the cheek and forehead. And for the first and only time in his life, Tom had seen his daddy cry.

The wheelchair had lasted a week. After breakfast one morning, Sut ran his rough fingers over Tom's head and slowly stood from the chair. Walking with a limp, he heaved the chair off the ground and stuck it in the garage. "Come on, boy, we got work to do," he had said. That summer, the summer of 1945, Sut and six-year-old Tom built the brick farmhouse that Tom gazed at now.

Tom breathed the fresh farm air and looked at the house he and his father built with their bare hands. He touched a brick, remembering how his daddy had laid each one individually. Feeling tears well in his eyes, Tom shook his head and looked away, toward Highway 231.

"Where the heck is he?" Tom asked out loud, looking down at Musso, who was chewing on an old shoe. They had arrived three days ago, but there wasn't much Tom could do without some help. The house was a mess, not having had a tenant in over five years, and the yard that surrounded the house and led into the fields of corn might have to be bushhogged, the grass was so damn high. Tom silently cursed himself, feeling guilty that he'd let the place go to pot.

Sighing, he watched as Musso stopped chewing, coughed, and then made a god-awful throat-clearing sound. When the dog stood up and raised his ears, Tom turned his head and saw a car pulling up the driveway.

"'Bout time," he said. As Musso barked and ran toward the vehicle—a Lexus SUV—Tom stood with his arms folded.

Once the car was parked, an enormous black man wearing a gray sweatshirt and jeans stepped out and immediately disarmed Musso, grabbing him behind the ears and stroking him. The dog stopped growling and started shaking his tail.

"Musso, you're even bigger and fatter than the last time I saw you," the man said, picking the sixty-pound animal up off his feet and letting him lick his face. Then, after planting his own kiss on the side of Musso's massive head, the man—all six foot four and two hundred forty pounds of him—set the dog down, walked toward Tom, and stopped a foot in front of him.

"Well, well, well," he said, extending his hand. "The Professor has gone to the farm."

Shaking his hand, Tom couldn't help but smile. In forty years of teaching, he'd had lots of students come and go, but—like all teachers—he had an all-time favorite. And he was looking at him now.

"Bocephus, you doing all right?"

"All right?" Bocephus smiled, feigning shock. "I'm living the dream, Professor. One day at a time. One case at a time. One million-dollar verdict at a time. We're talkin' wide . . . ass . . . open."

He laughed and caught Tom in a bear hug, holding him close. "It's not right what they've done, dog. Let me go after 'em. Don't you think it's time for Jameson 'Big Cat' Tyler to face Bocephus Haynes?" He let Tom go and laughed, pointing at Musso. "I'd treat him the same way that bulldog would."

As if on cue, Musso let out his patented throat-clearing sound.

"Yeaaaah," Bocephus said, turning to Tom and trying to make the same sound in his own throat. "That's what I'm talking about."

—

Bocephus Aurulius Haynes was born and raised in Pulaski, Tennessee, which is about forty-five minutes northwest of Hazel Green. His father had died young, and Bo had grown up working on a farm, just like Tom. Also like Tom, Bo had a taste and a talent for football. The local town leaders of Pulaski had wanted Bo to wear orange and play for the Vols, but Bo had never been much for doing what other folks wanted him to do. In 1978 he signed a scholarship with Alabama. A year later, against Arkansas in the

Sugar Bowl, Bo saw playing time on the Man's last national championship team. His junior year, Bo was a preseason All-American, but he blew his knee out in the first game of the season. Though he returned for his senior year and played on the Man's last team, he was never quite the same.

During Bo's rehab, the Man had asked Tom to talk to Bo about his future. Bo had no clue what he wanted to do, still reeling from the reality that his knee would prevent him from playing in the NFL. For a semester, Tom asked Bo to follow him through trial team practices and got him a job as an intern in the Tuscaloosa DA's office. Once he got a sniff of the law, Bo was hooked. Though his LSAT scores and grades weren't great, they were solid. And with recommendations from the Professor and the Man, Bocephus Haynes was admitted to law school in 1982.

The rest, as they say, is history. Bo graduated in the top ten percent of his law school class and was the bell cow on Tom's 1985 national championship trial team, making him the only student in Alabama history to have won national championships for both the Man and Tom. He had offers from every prestigious law firm in the state and even clerked a summer for Jones & Butler, working for a hotshot young partner named Jameson Tyler.

But the lure of the big firms had no impact on Bo. There was only one place Bo wanted to practice law, and he returned to Pulaski and hung up a shingle three months after graduation. Tom had never gotten the full story of why Bo wanted so badly to return home. When he asked him once, Bo had just shrugged and said, "Unfinished business."

Regardless of the reasons, twenty-four years later Bocephus Haynes was the most feared plaintiff's lawyer south of Nashville. But despite his amazing trial record—only one loss to go with countless victories—Bo had never forgotten where he'd come from. Or who had made his success possible.

Over the years Bo had called Tom several times a year and had stayed at Tom's house on football weekends. Tom had been to Bo's wedding, and Bo had been a pallbearer at Julie's funeral, the only former student Tom had asked. For years Bo had always told Tom the same thing: "If things ever get bad for you, if you ever need anything, I want you to do something for me. After you've prayed to God and talked to Jesus, you come see Bocephus."

Tom had laughed at the punch line, but now here he was. And Bo had done him one better.

Bocephus had come to see him.

—

It took the whole weekend to make the place livable. While Bo mowed the grass—he had to make two full turns around the massive yard to get it done—Tom cleaned out the house and contacted the utilities company to get the heat turned on. They also hiked out onto the farm a ways, and Bo cut down a tree for firewood. It had been years since Tom had walked the farm, and he was amazed at how grown up a lot of the brush had gotten. They had seen several deer and also heard the unmistakable squeal of a bobcat, which caused even Bocephus to raise his eyebrows.

On Sunday night Tom cooked steaks on the grill, and the two men drank beer and told war stories on the deck attached to the back of the house. For February the temperature was a pleasant sixty degrees, and for the first time in weeks, Tom laughed. After the meal was finished and the sun had long since gone down, Bo passed Tom a cigar and lit one of his own. With Musso snoring below his feet, Bo blew a cloud of smoke in the air and eyed Tom.

"So, how'd the surgery go?"

Tom looked down at the table, feeling some of his good vibes begin to dissipate. "As well as can be expected, I guess. Bill said he thought he got it all, and the biopsy matched his initial thoughts. The mass was stage two but superficial."

"Meaning?"

"It's treatable."

"Well, that's good, right?" Bo asked, seeming to sense Tom's drop in mood.

"Better than the alternative."

"Hell, yeah, it is," Bo said, smiling. "So, what are you gonna do now?"

Lighting his cigar with the tip of Bo's, Tom shrugged. "Don't know. Gotta get through the damn cancer treatments first. This"—he gestured to the cigar—"probably ain't helping."

Bo laughed. "One won't kill you. Now, how long will the treatments last?"

"The first one is next Friday. Bill referred me to Urology Associates in Huntsville, a Dr. Kevin Banks. I tried to schedule the appointments for Fridays so it wouldn't hurt your workweek too much."

"Professor, I would've taken you first thing every Monday morning if you had asked."

"I know you would have, Bo. Just trying to make it easier."

"Anyway, so the first treatment is next Friday. Then what?"

"Got four total per session, so three more after that. Wait two months. Then four more. Wait two months. Four more. Then they scope me and make sure none of it's come back. If the scope is clean, I'm good to go. After that they'll just rescope me every six months."

"And you said some folks live more than thirty years doing this?"

Tom nodded. "That's what Bill said."

"And the treatment puts you down for about thirty-six hours?"

Tom blew a cloud of smoke to the side and took a sip of beer. "What is this? A cross-examination?"

"Just trying to understand. Thirty-six hours, right?"

"Right."

Bo set his cigar in an ashtray and leaned forward on his elbows. "Then I have to ask you. What are you doing here, Professor? You need to be in Tuscaloosa, fighting to get your job back. For three out of the next six months, you're going to miss a day and a half per week due to the treatments. But the other five and a half days you'll be fine. The other three months you'll be fine. It's not like you've been sentenced to bed rest. You worked as hard as I did for the past two days, and you're a week removed from surgery and I'm twenty years younger." Bo paused, leaning back again. "So, what are you doing, Professor? It's not like you to quit."

Tom felt a flash of anger. "I'm not quitting, Bo. It's a zoo in Tuscaloosa right now. Reporters wanting interviews, newspaper articles, crazy allegations that are total bullshit. I didn't want to stick around and endure it in the face of cancer. I . . . I just needed a break from all of it."

"I get that, I do. But didn't you always teach us to hit first and hit hard? And if you couldn't hit first, strike back twice as hard as your opponent. Jameson and the board hit first, but we can strike back by suing them. You had tenure. You were forced out for bullshit reasons. It's straight-up breach of contract and maybe fraud."

Tom smiled, shaking his head. "Bo, I appreciate the pep talk. But that would just make things worse. The press would never let it go. Besides, I'm not even sure if I want to teach again. At this point in my life, I'm not sure what I want."

"So you're just gonna wait?"

Tom shrugged but didn't answer.

"For what?" Bo pressed.

"I don't know. If the treatments don't work . . ." Tom stopped, not wanting to say the obvious. "Bo, I'm sixty-eight years old. My wife is dead. I've lost my job and I'm too sick to start a new one. I guess maybe I came here to—"

"Whoa now, dog. You're startin' to sound like a country music song." Bo paused, taking a sip of beer. "But I feel you now. I get it."

"You do?"

"Oh, yeah."

"Then tell me. Because I haven't the faintest of clues."

"It's like that break between the third and fourth quarters in a football game. When the teams switch sides of the field and TV goes to commercial, and everyone on both sides of the field makes a four with their hands." Bo pulled his thumb back and held his hand over his head. "You know what I'm talking about?"

"I know the part of the game you're talking about. But what's your point?"

"That's where you are. This farm. This place. This is the sideline. You're about to start the fourth quarter, but you're not there yet." Bo paused. "They're still at commercial."

Tom laughed. "You're so full of shit, Bocephus."

"No, sir," Bo said, smiling back at him. "I'm speaking the truth. You've got one quarter to play, and you have to decide what to do."

Tom looked away, to the fields of corn past the freshly mown yard. "What if I'm at the end of the fourth quarter, Bo? What if I'm at the end and the other side's snapping the ball and taking a knee? There's time left on the clock, but there ain't a damn thing I can do. They're goin' run the clock out on me, and I can't win." Tom paused and looked into Bo's dark eyes. "What if that's where I'm at?"

Bo looked back at him, his eyes sharp, piercing Tom with their intensity. "Is that where you think you're at?"

Tom didn't answer. As the crickets chirped and the lightning bugs flashed around them, the question hung in the air like a bubble.

I don't know, Tom thought. *I just don't know.*

—

An hour later the food and beers were gone, and Bo had to go home.

"Jazz will have my ass if I'm not home by ten," Bo said, rubbing Musso behind the ears and opening the door to his SUV. "Oh yeah, I almost forgot." Bo reached into the car and pulled out two large manila envelopes. "The mail has started to come to my house like you asked, and you got these two packages."

Bo handed the packages to Tom, whose stomach tightened when he saw Rick Drake's return address on one of them.

"Thanks," Tom said.

"No problem. Your first treatment is next Friday at 9:00 a.m., right?"

"Right. You sure you don't—?"

"Don't ask me that again, Professor. You know I don't mind. If it wasn't for you, I'd probably be a PE teacher somewhere. You saved my life by introducing me to the law, and now it's time for Bocephus to pay his debts."

Bo winked at Tom, then started the ignition. A minute later the Lexus was pulling out of the driveway.

Tom brought the packages into the kitchen and made a pot of coffee. The other envelope didn't have a return address, so Tom opened Rick's first. Inside, the heading read "Ruth Ann Wilcox, as Personal Representative of the Estates of Bob Bradshaw, Jeannie Bradshaw, and Nicole Bradshaw v. Willistone Trucking Company, Inc." The date of filing was Monday, January 31, 2010. Rick had filed suit less than forty-eight hours after getting the referral. On the top of the first page there was a yellow sticky note with five words scribbled in blue ink—"I won't fuck it up."

Tom couldn't help but laugh. *Piss and vinegar*, he thought. *That boy is piss and vinegar and the rest balls.*

Tom opened the other package, still thinking about Drake. The boy was probably about to be hit with a firestorm of discovery by whoever was hired to defend Willistone. Tom cringed, remembering Rick's converted loft of an office and his lack of office staff. *He can't do it by himself. He has no partner, no associate, and no clerk, and he may have lied about having a secretary. How the hell is he going to handle everything?*

Sighing, Tom pulled a bound notebook from the second package. *What the hell is this?* he wondered. Flipping the notebook over to the front, Tom read the cover page out loud: "*McMurtrie's Evidence*, Fifth Edition (*Daubert* Excerpt)." Flipping through the pages that followed, Tom saw a nice summary of all the cases dealing with the *Daubert* expert witness standard since the publishing of his last supplement. *Well, I'll be damned* . . . The actual cases were also attached, with a notation on the front of each case that said "Still Good Law." Tom closed the notebook and ran his hand through the package to see if there was anything else. He pulled out a small piece of pink notebook paper. The message on the page was short and written in cursive handwriting:

> *Professor, I'm so sorry about your retirement. Please know that all the students are very upset about it, especially me. I was really looking forward to being your student assistant. Anyway, I finished your first assignment, and I wanted you to have the benefit of my work. Though you didn't ask, I went ahead and prepared an excerpt, summarizing the cases I found so that you would have it for your new edition. Please call me if you have any questions.*
> *Dawn*

Tom couldn't believe it. In his rush to get out of Tuscaloosa, he had forgotten all about Dawn Murphy. Reading the note again, he was relieved that it appeared that Dawn had no idea that she was implicated in his being forced to leave the school. *At least Jameson kept his promise about that.*

As Tom looked again at the notebook, he felt a lump in his stomach. The assignment had just been to find the cases, but Dawn had gone above and beyond. *This is exactly what I would have wanted*, he thought. She had anticipated correctly and finished in record time. *She's good*, Tom thought. *Very good.*

As Tom glanced from Dawn's work to Drake's complaint, an idea popped into his head. Dawn Murphy had wanted to be Tom's student assistant because she needed money to provide for her daughter.

Now she's out of a job . . .

Tom picked up Dawn's note. Below her name, she had left her home and cell phone numbers. *You told Rick that you would stay away. That you wouldn't interfere.*

He stood, walked into the den, and grabbed the phone. Looking at the note, he started to dial Dawn Murphy's cell number. He hesitated before pressing the last digit. *This is crazy*, he thought. *Just hang up the phone and stay out of it.* Tom started to lower the phone, and then his instincts took over. *Fuck it*, he thought, pressing the final digit and holding the phone to his ear.

21

Wilma Newton, bride of the late Harold Newton, now lived in Boone's Hill, Tennessee. According to Doris Bolton, Wilma's next-door neighbor in Northport, she had moved sometime around the first of November. Ms. Bolton had been nice when Rick dropped by. Invited him in for tea and talked about a host of different subjects. The weather. Her late husband, Earl. Alabama football. After he had been there almost thirty minutes, Rick had asked about Harold Newton. "Poor Wilma," she had said. "A widow at thirty-one. Damn shame." Ms. Bolton didn't have the address or number but said that Wilma and her girls had moved to Boone's Hill, Tennessee—"you know, over there by Fayetteville"—a few months back. Rick didn't know but nodded as if he did. Fifteen minutes later he was gone, having promised Ms. Bolton that he would come by for tea again sometime. "Roll Tide," Ms. Bolton had yelled from her front door as Rick opened his car. "Roll Tide," Rick had yelled back.

When Rick had returned to the office, he called information and learned that there were five Newtons in the Fayetteville,

Tennessee area. He started calling them and got a hit on the third when a girl who sounded about eight answered the phone, saying, "She's not here right now" when Rick asked for Wilma. Instead of leaving a message, he told the girl that he'd call back later and asked if her mother would be home that night. "She's working late at the Sands, so I don't know," the girl had said.

Rick then obtained the number and address for the Sands Restaurant online. He called the number and asked for Wilma. When whoever answered the phone said, "She's taking an order right now. Can she call you back?" Rick had politely declined, saying he'd call back later.

But he wasn't going to call back.

"Sure you want to just drop in on her?" Frankie asked, handing Rick his briefcase.

"I'm sure," Rick said, annoyed at being questioned. "She'll be more willing to talk if she knows I've come a long way. On the phone she could just tell me to go to hell and hang up on me."

Frankie was sucking on a green lollipop she'd gotten at the bank, and she made a loud smacking sound with the candy. "She could tell you to go to hell in person and slam the door in your face. Be a lot quicker to call. We called ahead with Carmichael, and you are meeting with him tomorrow night at five."

"That's different," Rick said, biting his lip. "We called ahead with Carmichael because we got to him through Ultron. If I just showed up at the Ultron plant in Montgomery and asked to talk with the loaders of Harold Newton's rig on the day of the accident, the plant manager would have me thrown off the premises."

"The restaurant manager could do the same thing tonight," Frankie said, sucking on the lollipop. "Could throw your skinny butt right out of there."

Rick started to snap something back but stopped himself. Sighing, he shook his head at her. "Thanks for the support."

"Just telling you like it is," Frankie said, biting off a piece of the lollipop and turning around. As her teeth began to grind the candy up, she added, "If you come back empty-handed, don't blame me."

Rick gritted his own teeth and, with Frankie's back turned to him, he made a choking gesture with his hands toward her. Then he opened the door and began thinking about how he would prove his secretary wrong.

He was so lost in his own thoughts, he almost ran over the young woman standing at the foot of the stairs.

"Are you Rick Drake?" the woman asked.

Leaning back from her, Rick sized the woman up. Black pant suit, brown hair cut off above her shoulder line, around five feet four inches tall with olive skin and brown eyes. Beautiful no doubt, but judging by the needy look in her eye, she wanted something from Rick. *Another reporter*, he thought.

"Look, if this is about the Professor, I'm not giving any interviews," Rick said, brushing past the woman and beginning to walk toward his car. He had continued to be pestered by various news outlets since the Professor's retirement, and his stance hadn't changed. He would not be made a fool of.

"I don't want to interview you," the woman said, catching up to him. "I want a *job*."

Rick had started to walk faster but then stopped in his tracks. "What?"

"Mr. Drake, I'm a second-year law student at Alabama and"—she sucked in her breath—"I was hoping to talk to you about a job."

Rick laughed and started walking again. "Tell Powell I said this was very funny, but I don't have time for pranks. I have a long trip ahead of me. How long have you been in the DA's office?"

Rick pressed the unlock button on his key chain and reached for the door, but the woman stepped in front of him.

"I don't know what you think this is," she began, "but I don't work for the DA's office and I don't know anyone named Powell. I want to work for *you*. I want to be *your* law clerk."

Rick started to make another smart-ass comment but stopped when he saw the look in her eyes. She was furious. *This can't be real.*

"You want to work for me?" Rick asked.

"Yes."

"Me?" Rick repeated.

"*Yes*, are you deaf?"

Rick chuckled. "Insulting me is probably not the best way to go about this."

The woman's face turned crimson. "I'm sorry, I—"

"I'm kidding," Rick said. "Look, I appreciate the offer, but the fact is that I just don't have the funds to take on a—"

"I'd work for free," she interrupted. "For the experience. If that's OK."

Rick's jaw dropped. "You're shitting me?"

For the first time the woman smiled. "No," she said, stepping closer to him. "I'm not. Here." She reached into the small briefcase she was holding and pulled out a sheet of crème-colored bonded paper. "This is my résumé. I'm in the top twenty percent of my class. I'm on law review. I clerked for Tomkins & Fisher last summer and got the defense perspective, but now I want some experience from the plaintiff's side. I'll work around my school schedule and I'll work weekends if need be. I . . ." She paused, gathering herself. "I want to be a trial lawyer . . . like you."

Like me? How did you even hear of me? Rick wondered, glancing down at the résumé. It was all there: 4.0 undergrad from Alabama, and a 3.8 at the law school. Top twenty percent, law review, etc.

"I . . . I don't know . . ." Rick said. He was stalling, trying to figure out what to do. *This is crazy.* He thought about the four-hour trip he was about to make. What would Wilma Newton be like? Receptive? Defensive? A grade A bitch?

Then he turned back to the woman, who, now that he had a chance to size her up, looked every bit the part of the eager law student. Naive. Sincere. Passionate.

"Look . . ." Rick began to tell her "thanks but no thanks," then stopped. *She might be able to help. If Ms. Newton won't talk to me, then maybe . . .*

He gazed into her brown eyes, which did not waver from his own. *Beautiful, smart, and she wants to work for me.* Rick almost laughed at the absurdity of it. Then, remembering the immortal words of Crash Davis—"Don't think; it can only hurt the ball club."—Rick made his decision.

"OK, I'll hire you but only on one condition."

"Name it," she said, her eyes narrowing.

"I'm leaving right now to go to Boone's Hill, Tennessee, to meet with a witness. It's four hours away, so we probably won't get back until past two in the morning. I'll brief you on the way, but you have to go with me. Now."

The woman didn't blink. Instead, she stepped around Rick and hopped into the front seat.

"Fine by me," she said, smiling up at him. "But I get to drive."

Rick gazed down at her, feeling completely out of sorts. He had not expected her to say yes. Forcing his legs to move, he walked around the front of the car and opened the passenger-side door. He had never sat in the passenger seat before, nor had he let anyone else, even Powell, drive his car. *This is surreal.*

He looked at his pretty new clerk and held out the car keys. When she took them, he held on to her hand.

"I guess before I let you drive my car I need to know your name."

The woman smiled. "It's Dawn." She squeezed his hand and then put the key in the ignition. "Dawn Murphy."

22

The Sands Restaurant had a Waffle House feel to it, Rick thought as he looked around the place and took in the scent of grilled hamburgers and coffee. There were several booths that lined the main window with a view of the parking lot, and Rick and Dawn had taken one of these. At a little after eight on a Thursday night in mid-February, the place was basically empty. A couple of rugged-looking gentlemen wearing jeans and heavy jackets sat drinking coffee at the counter, and there was a middle-aged couple at one of the tables. Rick and Dawn were the only other patrons, which suited Rick just fine. He knew Wilma Newton would be less likely to talk if there was a crowd.

"So you really think this is gonna work?" Dawn asked, raising her eyebrows and looking around. Rick had spent the drive briefing her on the case and the reason for the meeting with Ms. Newton. To his relief, Dawn had easily grasped the big picture, asking good questions, to some of which Rick hadn't had answers. But to his chagrin, Dawn had agreed with Frankie that he probably should've called ahead.

Only one way to find out, Rick thought, trying to look confident as a large, buxom woman walked around the counter toward them. *Is that her?* he wondered. As she got closer, his gut told him no.

"What can I get for y'all?"

She had short, curly red hair and teeth a dark shade of yellow.

"I think I'm gonna need a minute. Maybe some water to start off with," Dawn said in a friendly voice.

"And you?" the large woman asked Rick.

"Coke, please."

"All right. I'll be back with your drinks in a jiffy."

As she turned to go, Rick noticed a more attractive-looking waitress pouring tea into a glass at the table where the middle-aged couple sat. *Is that her?* This time Rick's gut was inconclusive.

A couple of minutes later the large red-headed waitress was back, drinks in hand. "Now what can I get y'all to eat?"

Rick had barely looked at the menu but knew what he wanted. Dawn nodded at him to go first.

"I think I'll have a cheeseburger and fries," Rick said, smiling at the waitress.

"You want that burger with everything?"

"Yes, ma'am."

"How about you, honey?"

"I think I'll have the same thing," Dawn said, closing her menu.

"Ma'am, I was wondering," Rick led in, feeling his heart rate speed up. "Is there a Wilma Newton working here tonight?"

"Who wants to know?" the woman replied, a suspicious look on her face.

"Just a couple of folks from Tuscaloosa, Alabama. In the neighborhood and wanted to speak with her. She used to live nearby."

None of what Rick said was a lie, but he still felt a little guilty. And anxious. *Maybe I should have called . . .*

The waitress maintained her suspicious look and didn't move from in front of their table. She then turned her head toward the table with the middle-aged couple.

"Hey, Wilma!" she yelled.

The attractive waitress Rick had noticed earlier looked up.

"Come over here. Got some folks from Tuscaloosa that want to see you."

As she walked over, Rick realized that she wasn't as young as he'd originally thought. Several lines ran down her forehead, no doubt the result of a hard life. Her hair was cropped off about midway down her neck, and like their waitress, she wore the Sands uniform.

"Hi, there," Wilma said in an unsure voice.

"Ms. Newton, my name is Rick Drake, and this is my coworker, Dawn Murphy. We're from Tuscaloosa." Rick smiled. "We were wondering if you might have a few minutes to talk with us."

Wilma Newton looked at them, her expression curious. The other waitress also continued standing in front of them, looking back and forth from Wilma to Rick and Dawn.

"Everything all right, Wilma?" she asked.

Ms. Newton continued to look at Rick and Dawn, sizing them up. "Yeah, no problem, Judy. Listen, why don't you let me take this table? These folks being from Tuscaloosa and all."

"Well, all right," the other waitress replied, hesitating before walking away.

Once she was out of earshot, Wilma's expression hardened and she glared at Rick. "I guess you folks want to talk about the wreck."

"Well, actually—" Rick began, but was quickly cut off.

"I already told the newspapers everything I know about it. I got nothing else to say. Now if you'll excuse me."

She walked off and disappeared behind the front counter and into the kitchen. Rick took a sip of Coke, wincing at Dawn.

"Still think not calling ahead was a good idea?" Dawn asked, a playful smile on her face.

Rick just shook his head. "I don't know," he said. "Maybe not. But let's give her some time. If she's our waitress, she'll have to bring the food out and then the check after that. We'll get a couple more cracks at her."

"Hope those go better than that," Dawn said, now laughing.

"Well, I didn't have much help from my new partner. Why don't you give it a try."

"Really?"

"Why not?"

A few minutes later Wilma Newton reappeared, carrying two plates.

"Cheeseburger and fries," she said, placing one of the plates in front of Dawn. "And the same thing," she continued, setting the other plate hard on Rick's place mat, making a rattling sound.

"Sorry," she said, throwing a dirty look at Rick that said, *Not really*. Before either of them could say anything, she was gone, walking back behind the counter and turning on the sink, where some dirty dishes had piled up.

"That went well," Rick said, but Dawn ignored him, got up from the booth, and walked over to the counter.

He saw her get the attention of Ms. Newton, who walked over and folded her arms. She started talking, and Rick could tell that Wilma Newton was listening. Once during their conversation, Ms. Newton pointed her finger at Rick. When she did, Dawn looked over and gave Rick a long look as if she was sizing him up. When she turned back to Ms. Newton, they both laughed, and Rick got a little self-conscious. *What the hell?* Five minutes later Dawn sat back down.

"She said she'll talk to us when she gets off. Around ten or so. If no one's in the place at nine forty-five and all her cleaning's done, she'll come over then."

She smiled proudly and looked at Rick, who was impressed.

"Well, how might I ask did you pull it off?"

Dawn grinned. "Promise you won't be mad?"

"Yes, promise. How'd you do it?"

"I told her to forgive you. That you couldn't help coming across like a jackass. It was just natural. I had begged you to call ahead so we wouldn't startle her like we obviously did. But that, you know, since we were already here, we'd really like to talk with her. We represent this poor lady whose whole family died in the wreck and are just trying to help her out."

"And that worked?"

"Yeah, partner, it did."

"What about when y'all looked over at me and laughed. What was that all about?"

"Oh, that. Well, after she agreed to talk with us, she looked at you and said, 'Kinda cute for a jackass, ain't he?'"

She laughed when she finished, and Rick smiled.

"Well, partner, I'm impressed," he said, saluting her with his glass.

"You should be."

—

Good as her word, at around 10:00 p.m. Wilma Newton walked over and sat down next to Dawn. She looked tired, her eyes a little red at the edges.

"Like I said earlier, I told the damn reporters everything I know, which wasn't much. But if y'all have some questions, go ahead and shoot."

She made almost all of her comments with her head cocked to the side, looking at Dawn. Rick nodded at Dawn to start things off.

"Thanks again, Ms. Newton. We know you must be tired. I guess we were first wondering how long Mr. Newton—Harold that is—had been working for Willistone prior to the accident."

"Well, Dewey—nobody's ever called him Harold as far as I know—started there in . . ." She paused, turning her eyes upward, thinking. "Probably around 2003. We bought the house in '04, so it had to be late '03. It was our first house . . ." She stopped, and Rick saw a tear running down her cheek. "I'm sorry. I haven't talked about this in a while. It's just . . . it's hard, you know? I got two girls at home. Daddy's girls both of them. They . . ." Now there was a steady stream of tears.

Dawn grabbed a napkin out of the dispenser on the table and handed it to Wilma, who dabbed her eyes.

"Would y'all like some coffee?" Wilma asked.

Rick could tell that maybe Ms. Newton wanted a minute to gather herself, so he accepted, as did Dawn.

A few minutes later she was back with three hot cups of coffee, a small layer of steam hanging over the top of each cup like fog lifting from the morning. The coffee smelled good and tasted better. There was something about a cup of coffee from a place like this, Rick thought. It was probably just Folgers or Maxwell House, but somehow it tasted better.

"Well, what other questions do y'all have?" Wilma asked, smiling, though Rick could still tell that she had been crying.

"What sort of schedule did your husband keep at Willistone?" Rick finally piped in, hoping he hadn't jumped the gun.

She looked at him a long time before answering. "Who did you say y'all represent?" she finally asked.

"Our client is Ruth Ann Wilcox. Ruth Ann's daughter, granddaughter, and son-in-law were killed in the wreck. She wants some answers about what happened, and I'm sure you do too."

"Dewey was a good driver. I just can't believe this was all his fault," she said in an accusing voice directed at Rick.

Rick did not immediately reply. *Handle this with care.*

"Ms. Newton, here is a copy of the accident report." Rick reached into his pocket and slid the report over. He gave Wilma several seconds to review it. In a quiet voice he continued: "The accident report shows your husband going eighty miles per hour at the time of the accident. The speed limit was sixty-five." Rick paused and placed both hands around his coffee cup. "We came here tonight to find out if you knew of any reason why Dewey would have been speeding on the morning of the accident. That's why I asked about his schedule with Willistone."

Wilma stared at the report. "Well, I just . . ." She stopped, appearing flustered. "Damnit," she whispered under her breath.

"Ms. Newton, please. We're trying to figure out—"

"It was pretty hectic," she said, meeting Rick's eye. "Dewey's schedule was hectic."

"How so?" Rick returned. *Keep her going.*

"I . . . I don't know. It was hectic." She stopped and looked down again. *She's stalling. Why?* Rick wondered.

"Was Dewey's driving schedule difficult for him to meet?" Rick asked.

Wilma didn't immediately answer, taking a sip of her coffee.

"You're gonna sue Willistone, aren't you? Regardless of what I say, you're gonna sue them." Wilma's voice was calm, even. Her eyes went from Rick to Dawn and then back to Rick.

"We've already sued them," Rick answered, maintaining eye contact with Wilma.

"Ms. Newton," Dawn said, putting her arm around her, "our client lost her whole family—just like you did, except imagine if the wreck had taken your girls too. She wants answers. She wants to know why this happened."

"It was an accident. Accidents happen," Wilma replied.

"His schedule, Ms. Newton. Was it hard for him to meet?" Rick again asked. *Come on, lady.*

Wilma Newton took a deep breath and looked up at the ceiling. She thought back to that terrible night in the hospital. Having to sign that form. Putting an end to her husband's misery.

"Yes," she finally answered, looking Rick right in the eye. "He had a hard time meeting his schedule. There was usually not much time to spare." *None, more like it.*

"Do you remember whether he was running late the day of the accident?" he asked. "Tell us about that morning."

"I don't remember a whole lot. He got up pretty early and left—that's about it." She stopped. *Why am I protecting those bastards? They were real nice at the funeral and all. "We're so sorry for your loss, Ms. Newton. Dewey was a fine trucker for us and a good man. We want to help you, and we'll be in touch."* But they hadn't been in touch. Wilma hadn't heard so much as a peep from the company since the funeral. *Willistone left me and my girls high and dry. No help. No nothing.*

She sighed and took a sip of coffee. *Fuck 'em*, she thought.

"Anything he said, anything at—"

"Look, what did you say your name was again?" Wilma interrupted.

"Rick."

"OK then, Rick. You want to know about Dewey's schedule? Well, it was *crazy*. Not just that day but every day. Dewey would drive twenty straight hours at times just to keep up. He knew that was more than the law allowed—he told me—but the company didn't care. Jack Willistone inspected the driver's logs himself every week, making sure that whatever was on the logs was compliant with DOT regulations, regardless of how many hours were actually driven. Dewey was so terrified of Jack, a lot of times he asked me to help him fill out his driver's logs so it looked like he was under ten hours.

"Dewey also got a couple of speeding tickets in the months before he died. He was pissed about 'em, but he said he didn't have a choice. If he didn't speed, no way he could make the load on time." Wilma sighed. "He wanted to quit. He even filled out his notice, but I"—she breathed deeply, her bottom lip trembling with anguish—"but I wouldn't let him turn it in. The money was so much better than he could've made anywhere else." She stopped and put her face in her hands.

"How could they get away with doctoring the driver's logs?" Rick asked. "Aren't they inspected by—?"

"DOT?" Wilma interrupted, her voice dripping with bitterness. "Jack Willistone has all the local and state DOT inspectors in his back pocket. He also has an in with the Alabama State Troopers' office. Dewey said Jack was Teflon." Wilma glared at Rick. "He's been getting away with this shit for years."

There was a pause, and Wilma saw Rick glance at his pretty partner. Then he returned his eyes to Wilma.

"Ms. Newton, would you be willing to tell a jury what you just told us?"

Wilma folded her arms. *Persistent bastard. Not sure I'd call him a jackass, though. Just doing his job.*

"I don't know," she said, looking down at her cup. "I'd really rather not get involved."

"I understand that, ma'am," Rick started, "but you may be the only person who can explain why Dewey would've been speeding the day my client's family died. The day Dewey died. If Jack Willistone has the DOT and State Troopers' office in his pocket, then no one there is going to be able to help. And I doubt any of his current employees are going to spill the beans." Rick paused. "But you could. You could pull the net over his whole operation. Forcing employees to falsify driver's logs is a federal crime. Not only could you give my client justice, but you could help put Jack Willistone where he belongs—in prison."

Wilma continued to gaze at the coffee cup, remembering Dewey's anguished face the day he tore up his notice. The resigned look in his eyes. *He knew it was just a matter of time.* Then she thought of the hours after she left the hospital, holding her girls as they cried their eyes out. *"Daddy can't be dead. He can't be. No. No. No."*

Wilma looked up from the coffee cup, first at Dawn and then at Rick Drake. Slowly, she nodded her head.

"OK," she said. "I'll do it."

23

Through the windshield of his El Camino, he watched them talk, knowing that he was too late. He'd already run the plates on the Saturn—he had friends everywhere, including the Alabama State Troopers' office—and confirmed what his instincts had already told him. The car belonged to Richard Drake. It seemed the plaintiff's lawyer and his hot-to-trot assistant were having a heart-to-heart with Ms. Newton. He cracked the window and blew cigarette smoke into the cool night air. He knew this complicated things, and he hated complications. He crushed the cigarette out on the dash and flipped the butt onto the floorboard. Then he dialed the number.

"Bone?" the familiar raspy voice answered.

"Yeah, boss." He paused, dreading what he was about to say. "We've got a problem."

—

Jack Willistone slammed the phone down on the hook.

"Damnit," he said out loud, bringing the side of his fist down on the complaint that lay on his desk. It had been served on him just eight hours earlier.

Jack had expected a lawsuit. He just hadn't expected it so soon. The accident was barely five months old, and the statute of limitations on trucking claims was two years. In his over forty years of hauling freight, Jack had been sued only twice, and both times the lawyers had waited until the bitter end to file the complaint. This lawyer, Richard Drake, had filed in four months.

One month prior to closing the merger with Fleet Atlantic.

An hour after he received the complaint, Jack got the call he was dreading. Out of an abundance of caution, Fleet Atlantic wanted to postpone the closing of the merger until after the disposition of the lawsuit.

"That might take years," Jack had said, but Fleet Atlantic's president wouldn't back down.

"A wrongful death lawsuit with three deaths and a speeding trucker is cause for concern on our end, Jack. I'm sure the case will resolve in your favor or settle, and then we can move forward with the deal."

The minute Jack hung up the phone, he had dispatched Bone to handle Wilma Newton, Dewey's widow. Since Buck Bulyard had died in the fire, Willard Carmichael and Dick Morris were bought and paid for, and the plant holding all of the documents was ash and rubble, the only possible weak link was Wilma.

But Drake got to her first . . .

Jack sighed. He would have Bone shadow Drake from here on out, but he would have to fix the Wilma Newton situation. *God knows what she might have told them if Dewey talked at home . . .*

Jack shook his head and grabbed the phone off the hook. *First things first*, he thought. Before he could figure out how to handle Wilma, there was a more pressing priority.

He dialed the number for his insurance agent.

"Hawkins," the voice on the other end of the line answered.

"Bobby, it's Jack. We got sued today in Henshaw."

"Damn, that was fast," Hawkins said. Jack had reported the accident to Hawkins the day after it happened, so Bobby was already up on all the facts.

"Tell me about it," Jack said. "Listen, Bobby, no fucking around with the lawyer on this one, OK?"

"What do you mean?" Hawkins asked, his voice incredulous.

"I mean I know you insurance companies cut costs by hiring lawyers on the cheap, and I won't tolerate that mess. I've paid BamaSure premiums for over three decades, and this is just my third lawsuit."

"I assure you, Jack, that we will retain a very capable attorney to handle this file."

"'Very capable'?" Jack asked, chuckling. "What the fuck does that mean? 'Very capable' is the way my dick performs after a six-pack of Budweiser, Bobby boy. I don't want 'very capable.' I want the goddamn best. I want a porn star. Am I clear?"

Several seconds of silence and then Bob's muffled voice. "Yeah, Jack. I think I get it."

"You think?" Jack asked. "Well, let me say it another way so there's no miscommunication. Unless you want me to take my six-figure account somewhere else, Bobby boy"—Jack paused—"I'd suggest you get me the fastest horse in the stable."

24

At five sharp the following evening, Rick and Dawn were escorted into a small conference room at the Ultron plant in Montgomery. Running on four hours' sleep, Rick knew he should be tired, but he was juiced on adrenaline. Every ten seconds Wilma Newton's words from the previous night popped into his head. Dewey Newton's schedule was "crazy." Dewey Newton's schedule forced him to speed. Dewey Newton, at Jack Willistone's direction, doctored his driver's logs to fraudulently show compliance with DOT regulations. *I have my star witness*, Rick knew, blinking and trying to focus on the task at hand.

The room had yellow cinder-block walls, and Rick had the feeling he was in a prison instead of a gasoline plant. Introductions were quickly made. Present were Hank Russell, a tall, heavy-set man with silver hair who was the president of Ultron's Montgomery plant; Willard Carmichael, a skinny man with a strawberry-blond mullet and mustache; and Julian Witt, a lawyer from Milhouse & Wright, one of the larger Montgomery firms. Witt wore a navy-blue suit with a red power tie, and after everyone had shaken hands he took the lead.

"Rick, we understand that you have filed a lawsuit against Willistone Trucking Company in Tuscaloosa County."

Rick smiled. "That's correct."

"That lawsuit arises out of a trucking accident that happened on September 2, 2009, involving a Willistone rig hauling Ultron gasoline and a driver named Harold Newton."

"Yes." Rick didn't like being cross-examined by another lawyer, but he could understand Witt's need to set the tone of the meeting and also grandstand a little in front of his client.

"Your secretary told Mr. Russell that you wanted to talk with any employee of this plant who may have worked at the Tuscaloosa plant on the day in question and loaded Newton's truck."

"That's right," Rick said. "And she was told that Mr. Carmichael had been one of the loaders that day."

"Correct. Well then—" A knock at the door interrupted Witt, and the lawyer looked irritated for half a second. Then, as if remembering something, his face broke into a grin. "Oh, I almost forgot. Come in!"

Rick squinted at Witt, then turned his head, not sure what to expect. When the door swung open, Rick's stomach tightened into a knot.

He couldn't believe his eyes.

"Julian, my boy!" boomed the unmistakable voice of Jameson Tyler.

For a moment Tyler stood at the door as if to let everyone in the room, especially Rick, get a good look at the Big Cat. Then he strode into the room, ignoring Rick and extending his meaty hand across the table, where Witt shook it eagerly.

"Jameson, I'm so sorry to have started without you."

"No worries, Jules."

Tyler grabbed the pot of coffee that lay in the middle of the table and made a show of pouring himself a cup. He still had not looked Rick's way, and Rick could feel the heat on his face. Rick glanced at Dawn, who raised her eyebrows as if to ask, *Who the hell is that?*

Jameson fucking Tyler, Rick thought, trying to stay cool.

As Tyler sat down at the head of the table—*Of course that's where he'd sit*—Julian Witt, whose obvious man crush on Tyler made Rick nauseous, turned his flushed face back to Rick.

"Sorry, Rick, but we thought it only fair to invite Willistone's lawyer to this little soiree."

Willistone's lawyer? Rick thought, feeling his stomach jump. This had to be a joke.

"*You* are Willistone's lawyer?"

Rick asked what he was thinking, unable to contain the contempt in his voice as he glared at the man who had withdrawn Jones & Butler's offer of employment to Rick nine months before.

Tyler's mouth curved into a thousand-megawatt smile. "I am indeed. And you represent Ms. Wilcox." Tyler chuckled, chewing on the tip of his pen. "I can't believe the Professor referred you this case. If I didn't believe he'd lost his mind before, I definitely do now."

Rick felt heat from the top of his forehead to the bottom of his feet as he glared a hole into Tyler, whose arrogant grin only widened. *How could he possibly know about the Professor?*

"Now, don't get mad, Rick. None of us here want another YouTube incident. Deep breaths now, boy. Deep breaths." Tyler's eyes moved to Dawn, and he cocked his head to the side. "Well, well, well . . ." he said, extending his hand. "Jameson Tyler."

"Dawn Murphy," Dawn said, giving Tyler's hand a quick shake, but Tyler didn't let go.

"You look familiar, Ms. Murphy. Have we met before?"

"I don't think so," Dawn said, her voice firm, wriggling her hand out of his grasp. "If we did, you must not have made much of an impression."

"I think you're wrong," Tyler said, pausing, still looking at Dawn. "We have. I just can't place it. What's your—?"

"Can we get on with this?" Rick interrupted, glancing at Hank Russell, Ultron's silver-haired president, who did not seem to be enjoying himself any more than Rick did, before glaring at Julian Witt.

"Go for it," Witt said, winking at Tyler, who had crossed his legs, his eyes containing that amused *I know something you don't* look Rick had remembered from his days clerking for the bastard.

"Mr. Carmichael, did you know Harold 'Dewey' Newton?" Rick began, trying to keep his voice calm.

Carmichael pulled on his strawberry-blond mustache and looked at the table. "I knew Dewey. Not well or nuthin', but I knew who he wuz."

Rick nodded, forcing himself to look only at Willard. "Do you remember loading his truck the morning of September 2, 2009?"

Again, Willard pulled on his mustache. "Can't say that I remember the date or nuthin'. It was around Labor Day, I 'spect. I just remember later that day hearing that Dewey done been in a bad wreck."

Rick leaned forward. "What do you remember about loading his truck that morning?"

Carmichael hesitated for a couple of seconds, looking around the table. *Great*, Rick thought, wondering how many times the poor SOB had already been through this with Julian Witt.

"Honestly, sir, I don't remember nuthin' much at all about loading the truck that morning. Everything seemed normal to me."

"Did Mr. Newton seem in a rush?"

"I think he's answered the question, Rick," Tyler interjected, but Rick didn't even look at the bastard.

"*Did Mr. Newton seem in a rush?*" Rick repeated, unable to control his irritation.

"Hey, boy," Tyler said, banging the table with his fist. "You deaf or something? He said he doesn't remember what happened that morning."

Again, Rick didn't look at Tyler. Instead, he glared at Julian Witt. "I came here because Mr. Russell said I could ask Mr. Carmichael some questions. If you want to cut the meeting off, *Julian*, just say the word. Otherwise, I'd like to keep going."

"W-well . . ." Witt stammered, glancing at Tyler and then back at Rick. "I think Jameson has a point. I mean, if Mr. Carmichael doesn't remember—"

"Willard, was Dewey in a rush?" Hank Russell's voice punctured the air like a knife.

"Mr. Russell—" Julian began, but Russell cut him off.

"I'm busy, Julian. I got a gasoline plant to run and I don't have time for this song and dance. Was he, Willard?"

"No, sir, boss. Not that I recall. But like I said, I just don't remember that much."

Hank turned to Rick. "Next question."

"Had you loaded Dewey's rig prior to that day?"

Willard shrugged his shoulders. "I 'spect."

"Do you ever remember him being in a hurry?"

Willard shrugged again but didn't say anything.

"Answer the question, Willard," Hank prodded.

"Not that I recall," Willard finally said, staring at the table.

"Did he ever say anything to you about the schedule he was on at Willistone?"

Willard wrinkled up his face like he didn't understand the question.

Rick tried again. "Did Dewey Newton ever complain to you about how much he was having to drive or whether he was having to speed to make loads on time?"

Willard shook his head. "Oh, no. Dewey never said nothing to me like that. Least not that I recall."

"I think that about covers anything relevant you could ask," Witt said. "I'm not going to let him answer anything else unless you set up a deposition."

"One more question," Rick said, tapping his pen on the notepad he'd brought with him and praying Witt wouldn't cut him off. A deposition was a discovery tool where a lawyer could ask questions of a witness under oath, and the answers were taken down by a court reporter and converted to a transcript. Rick might take Willard's deposition down the road, but depositions tended to be expensive, and he did not want to have to set up a deposition to ask one question. "I promise it's relevant."

Witt sighed but didn't say anything.

"Mr. Carmichael," Rick began. "Do you remember if anyone else helped you load Dewey's truck the morning of the accident?"

Willard again looked around the table, but none of the other men spoke. They all knew it was an appropriate question. *And all of them already know the answer.*

"Answer the question, Willard," Hank interrupted.

"It was Mule," Willard blurted. "I mean Dick. Dick Morris. We all called him Mule."

Rick turned to Witt. "Does Dick Morris work here at the Montgomery plant?"

"No," Witt said, his voice firm and matter-of-fact. "Nor does he work at any other Ultron plant. We have no information on Morris."

"I think he has family up near Faunsdale, but—"

"That's enough, Mr. Carmichael," Witt interrupted, glaring at Willard. "You are excused now."

Carmichael hesitated, then looked around Witt to Hank Russell, who waved him off. "You can get to work now, Willard. Thanks for coming in."

Willard Carmichael stood awkwardly and nodded to Rick. "Evenin.'"

Rick nodded back and also stood. Then he looked at Hank Russell. "Mr. Russell, thank you for setting this meeting up."

Russell rose from his seat and extended his hand. "My pleasure, son. Here's my card. Call me if you need anything else."

Rick took the card and put it in his pocket. Then he shook Russell's hand.

"Actually, Rick," Julian Witt interceded, "you should call me if you need anything else. Ultron is represented by counsel, and it wouldn't be appropriate for you to contact Mr. Russell directly."

Rick glanced at Russell long enough to see him roll his eyes, and Rick stifled a laugh.

"Sure thing, Julian," Rick said, motioning to Dawn that it was time to leave. He had reached the door when Witt's voice stopped him.

"By the way, Rick, that YouTube video is awesome." Julian chuckled, throwing a mock punch in the air, and Rick heard louder laughter to his side. *Tyler.*

Rick felt the adrenaline pour through his veins, but he didn't say anything. *That's what they want*, he knew. He waved at Hank Russell. "Thanks again."

25

Willard Carmichael smoked a pack of cigarettes during his shift. He also called home twice. He hadn't done either in—he couldn't remember when. Smoked or called home. Everything was fine at the house. Sally was about to go to bed. She had to be at the Cracker Barrel at six in the morning. Lindsay was out with a friend but due in by ten. *Everything is fine*, he thought.

Willard tried to stay calm, but it was a slow night on the yard, giving him time to think. And worry.

Willard was a world-class worrier. He worried about his thinning hair. He worried that Sally was cheating on him, since they worked separate shifts and hardly saw each other anymore. He worried Lindsay would get pregnant before she graduated. And he worried he'd get fired pretty much every day.

But he wasn't worried about any of those things tonight. Tonight he was thinking about Dewey Newton and the deal he made five months ago: *If you ever talk, I won't come back for the money. It'll be your life, Willard. Everything you hold dear . . .*

"But I didn't talk," Willard whispered to himself over and over throughout his shift. *I did exactly what he told me to do . . .*

At 1:00 a.m. Willard clocked out and walked to his car. When he climbed in the front seat, he lit up another cigarette and closed his eyes. The nicotine was helping but it wasn't enough. *I need to get drunk.*

He was thinking about what brand of six-pack he was going to buy at the filling station on the way home when he felt a blunt object press against the back of his head.

"Don't move, Willard," a male voice said. "Don't move and you might live to see tomorrow."

"What the—?"

Willard's face slammed against the steering wheel, and his head was jerked around. Now he saw the man, and he felt his bladder beginning to give way.

"Yeah, it's me, Willard. Remember our little agreement? I think you cashed in rather nicely."

"I didn't say a word, I promise," Willard said. "I told them I couldn't remember anything."

Now the gun was pressed into Willard's forehead, and he let go of his bladder.

"That's good, Willard. That's real good. I like it when people meet their end of the bargain. I was just thinking how awful it was going to be to take out your indiscretions on Sally and Lindsay. What is Lindsay now, sixteen? She's really pretty, Willard."

Willard was crying now, and his bowels had opened up too. "I . . . didn't . . . say . . . anything."

"Good, Willard. Good. Well, it's starting to stink in here. I'm going to go."

The man opened the car door but did not walk away. With minimal effort he forearmed the driver's-side window, and the glass pelted down on Willard Carmichael's crying face.

"One more thing, Willard. If I ever see you talking with Rick Drake or his little hottie assistant again, after I rape and kill your wife and daughter while you watch, I'm going to cut your dick off and choke you to death with it." The man winked at the petrified eyes that stared back at him. "Have a nice day."

26

Rick barely said a word from Montgomery to Tuscaloosa. *Of all the lawyers to defend this case*, he kept thinking, trying to tell himself that it was a good sign that Jameson Tyler had been retained by Willistone. *That means they know they're exposed. They wouldn't have retained a heavy hitter like Tyler if they weren't scared.* Though the thoughts were true, Rick couldn't block out the needling he'd endured from Tyler and Julian Witt. *It's always going to be like that*, he knew. *Every lawyer I encounter is going to bring up the YouTube video. If they don't bring it up, they'll know about it and they'll laugh behind my back.*

"You OK?" Dawn finally asked as the Tuscaloosa city limits sign came into view.

"Fine," Rick said, irritated at having his thoughts disturbed.

"Coulda fooled me," Dawn pressed, turning to face him. "You haven't said a word in over an hour. I was about to check for a pulse."

"I'm fine," Rick repeated. "It's just"—Rick shook his head—"I let those guys get to me, that's all."

"I think you handled them fine," Dawn said. "They were very unprofessional, and I think it pissed off Mr. Russell."

Rick shrugged. "Russell was cool." Reflexively, Rick reached into his pocket and pulled out the business card that Russell had given him. "Be sure to put this in the file," he said, handing it to her. "I probably shouldn't call him—Witt was right about that—but—"

"Rick," Dawn interrupted, her voice anxious. Glancing at her, Rick saw that she had turned the business card over. There were handwritten words on the back of the card.

"What does it say?" he asked.

"'Faith Bulyard,' and then a phone number."

Rick felt his stomach jump. "That name sounds familiar. Bulyard . . ." Rick thought back to the articles he'd read about the accident and the Ultron fire. "Damnit, why does—?"

"Buck Bulyard was the president of the Tuscaloosa plant," Dawn interrupted, her voice excited. "He died in the fire."

Rick raised his eyebrows at her in wonder. "How did—?"

"I read your investigative files this morning when I got to work. The articles also said that his wife, *Faith*, worked for Ultron."

Rick shook his head in bewilderment. "Why the hell would Russell put Faith Bulyard's phone number on the back of his business card? Do you think he gave me that by mistake?"

Dawn shook her head. "No way. This has to be a subtle way of him trying to help us."

"But why?" Rick asked. "Why would Hank Russell want to help us?"

"I don't know. But why else would he give you a card with Ms. Bulyard's name and number on it? The newspaper articles I read said that Faith Bulyard worked in . . . *record keeping*, I think. Oh my God, maybe she knows something."

Rick pondered the possibilities and knew Dawn had to be right. Hank Russell had seemed perturbed throughout the meeting with Willard Carmichael. Ms. Bulyard's name and number had to be his way of throwing a bone their way.

"Read the number out to me," Rick said, taking out his cell phone.

"You're going to call her now?" Dawn asked.

"No time like the present."

Dawn slowly read each digit of the phone number out loud, and Rick entered it in his phone. Then he waited. After six rings and no voice message, he ended the call.

"Just have to keep trying," Rick muttered, setting the phone in the console between the seats. "We need to get on finding Dick Morris too. Carmichael said Morris has family in Faunsdale, and my friend Powell has some connections there. I'll check with him if you'll do an Internet search."

"Will do. What about Ms. Bulyard?"

Rick started to answer but then his cell phone started vibrating. He picked it up, and the caller ID was the number he'd just called. "It's her," he said, his heart pounding.

"Hello," Rick answered, trying to sound calm.

"Yes. Did you just try to call me?" A female voice.

"Yes, ma'am. Is this Faith Bulyard?"

"It is. Who is this?"

Rick's eyes darted to Dawn, whose eyebrows were raised in anticipation. He nodded at her.

"Ms. Bulyard, my name is Rick Drake. I'm a lawyer in Tuscaloosa and I represent a woman whose entire family was killed back in September in a trucking accident with a Willistone Trucking Company driver who was hauling Ultron gasoline. I spoke with Hank Russell in Montgomery this afternoon, and he gave me your number as someone I should call." Rick shrugged his shoulders at Dawn, and she gave him a thumbs-up.

"Jesus Christ," Ms. Bulyard said. Then, barely audible, she muttered, "Why can't people just mind their own business." She sighed, and the irritation in her voice was palpable. "Look, I remember that accident but only because my husband . . ." There was a pause, and Rick heard coughing on the other end of the line.

"Ms. Bulyard?"

". . . my husband died the night of that accident. He died in a fire."

"I know, ma'am. And I'm so sorry." Rick stopped, not sure what to say next.

"What do you want, Mr. Drake?"

Rick sucked in a quick breath. "I want to meet with you, ma'am. Just for a few minutes if that would be OK. I know you worked in record keeping at Ultron, and I wanted to ask you a few questions." Rick crossed his fingers and held his breath while the other end of the line was silent for several seconds.

"I don't know . . ." Another sigh. "I . . ."

"Fifteen minutes, Ms. Bulyard. I doubt I'll need longer than that."

More silence. Then, finally, Faith Bulyard cleared her throat.

"OK, but we are out of town this week on the boys' spring break. Why don't you call me again next week, and we can meet at the house?"

It was all Rick could do not to scream out loud. "Thank you, ma'am."

When Ms. Bulyard said "Bye," Rick pressed End and looked at Dawn. "She'll meet us next week."

Dawn's squeal must have lasted a full five seconds and the sound was so genuinely happy that it warmed Rick's whole body. *It doesn't mean anything yet*, he told himself, trying to calm down. *Just because she's agreed to meet you doesn't mean she knows anything helpful.*

Still, it was a success after a day full of failures, and Rick wasn't ready to throw water on it yet.

He looked at Dawn. "Hey, are you hungry?"

"Starved," she said, leaning forward.

"Then let's go somewhere and get something. What do you say?"

When Dawn didn't immediately answer, Rick's spirits sank. *Nice work, Drake. Next time your instincts say do something, just do the opposite.*

"We don't have to—" Rick began, but Dawn cut him off.

"I'd love to, Rick, but I really need to get home. My daughter—"

"Your daughter?"

They looked at each other, and Rick came to the harsh realization that he really didn't know anything about Dawn. *She's a mom?*

"Yes," Dawn finally said. "My daughter. Julie. She's five, and my mother is watching her, but"—Dawn looked at her watch—"it's almost nine, and I'd like to be there to tuck her in before bed. I wasn't able to last night when we went to Boone's Hill, and she didn't sleep well." Dawn stopped, and Rick could see that she was frustrated. "I'm sorry, I really wish I could—"

"Don't apologize," Rick said, his mind working overtime to try to find a solution. Then, like an oasis in the desert, the yellow and red lights of Taco Bell emerged in the distance.

"I think I know how we can fix this," Rick said, smiling.

—

Fifteen minutes after going through the drive-through at Taco Bell, Rick pulled into Riverview Apartments, a small complex right outside of downtown Northport. They walked to the second story of the first unit, and Dawn pulled out a key from her purse.

"Here we are," she said, opening the door to Apartment 124.

As they walked in, Dawn whispered, "Let me go check on Julie. Be right back," and she disappeared down a short hallway.

Rick sat down on a couch and waited. The room carried a pleasant, fruity scent, and Rick breathed it in. *Smells like her*, he thought.

A few moments later Dawn returned, gave Rick a thumbs-up sign, and plopped down on the couch next to him. "Asleep," she said, letting out a sigh of relief. She was now wearing a pair of plaid flannel pajamas, and she smiled sheepishly at Rick. "I hope you don't mind, but I had to get out of those clothes."

"Not at all," Rick said, feeling a slight jump in his stomach. Just like in all outfits he'd seen her wear, Dawn looked good in pajamas. "I like your place," he said, forcing his eyes away from her.

"Thanks," Dawn said, getting up and beginning to put the food on a couple of plates. "We like it, but sometimes things can get pretty cramped. My mother . . ." She stopped for a second and looked up from the plate, her face red with embarrassment. "I live with my mother."

"Oh," Rick said, trying not to sound surprised but failing. He had assumed that Dawn's mother had just come over for the night to keep Julie.

"Lame, huh?" Dawn asked.

"No . . . not at all," Rick stammered. He fought to think of something to say that would ease the awkwardness of the moment. "I'm sure it's nice having help with Julie."

Dawn smiled. "It is nice. But still . . . a few years ago I would never have expected I'd be living with my mother with a five-year-old to care for."

"And I would never have expected I'd have my own law office. I thought I'd be at Jones & Butler bringing in eighty Gs, driving a sports car, and living in a bachelor pad in Homewood. Hamming it up with Julian Witt and standing in line to kiss Jameson Tyler's ass. Instead, I live in the same apartment I lived in while I was in law school, and I barely make enough to cover the bills. That's just"—he stopped, knowing he'd probably said too much—"that's life, I guess."

"So what's the deal with you and Tyler anyway? Did you clerk at Jones & Butler or something?"

"Both summers," Rick said. "After my first and second years, and got an offer after the second, which I accepted. And then . . ." Rick squinted at her. "Come on. I'm sure you've seen the YouTube video they were talking about."

"Sure, I've seen it," she said. "But there's gotta be more to it than that, right? I mean, the way . . ." She stopped, and Rick looked away, feeling heat on the back of his neck.

"I'm sorry," Dawn said, and Rick felt her touch his shoulder. "I can tell it's a sore subject, and it's none of my business." She shrugged. "Curiosity got the cat."

Rick again looked over at her, wanting to tell her but feeling a twinge of fear. He liked Dawn. In just two days of working together, he already felt a connection with her. She was smart, funny, and easy to be around. Everything you could want in a law clerk.

"You really want to know?" Rick asked.

Dawn looked at him, her eyes kind. She nodded. "But only if you want to tell."

Rick looked down at the floor. He had never told this story to anyone, not even his parents. He saw the hallway in his mind and felt the heat behind his eyes and on the back of his neck. He had been so angry. If the Professor had just let him get out of there . . .

Rick sighed, feeling that terrible mixture of disappointment, failure, and anger again. Then he started talking.

27

"I was on the trial team at Alabama. The Professor's team. I never dreamed I'd make it, much less be one of the advocates. My second year of law school, I was a bull in a china shop. My best friend, Powell, was much smoother, and when the Professor teamed me and Powell together, that sort of relaxed me. Let me be myself. I don't know, it just worked. I started coming into my own. We cruised through all our practice matches, and regionals was a breeze. We killed Stetson in the finals in New Orleans. Then in the spring we competed for the national championship in Washington, DC. We won our first four matches easily and faced Georgetown in the semis.

"To this day I can't say what really happened. I know the judge was awful. From the get-go he seemed to overrule all of our objections and sustain all of Georgetown's. And I couldn't stand that team—they had two girls, and one was very annoying. Red hair, freckles, a little hefty, and a nasal voice that made you cringe, but the judge adored her.

"At one point he sustained one of her hearsay objections. I argued that the statement I was trying to get in—essentially a confession by the defendant to the crime—was an admission by party-opponent, which is one of the recognized exceptions to hearsay. He said it was hearsay and sustained the damn objection. He was so obviously wrong, and it was going to cost us the trial. We were the prosecution that round, and we had to have the defendant's confession as part of our case-in-chief.

"I just lost it. I told the judge that I was astonished. Then I accused him of favoring the other team and asked that he recuse himself from the trial. The judge stared at me for a long time. I looked at Powell, and his face told me all I needed to know. I had blown it.

"Anyway, the judge threatened to hold me in contempt if I had another outburst. I quickly apologized and went on. The rest of the trial was uneventful. I actually thought my closing was the best I had ever done. But in the end all five judges voted for Georgetown, each reminding me that a good lawyer had to keep his cool. Judges make honest mistakes all the time, and my outburst would have cost me a real trial. They just couldn't send us on.

"I was inconsolable. Powell tried to talk to me, but I couldn't handle it. I'd let him down. Let everybody down. I just wanted out of there. The Professor yelled something to me as I opened the door, but I didn't stop. When I got out in the hallway, I felt someone grab my arm, and it was, well, sort of instinctive. I was . . . so . . . mad. I'm not even sure my eyes were open when I swung the punch. I hit him, but he didn't even look fazed. His face turned red, and all he said was . . . I'll never forget it . . . He said, 'You're a hothead, Drake. A liability in the courtroom.'"

—

"There's no sound in the video." Dawn said, breaking the silence that had engulfed the apartment when Rick had stopped talking. "You said something back, didn't you?"

"I told him to go fuck himself," Rick said, looking sheepish. "The next day Jameson Tyler called and terminated my contract with Jones & Butler. Said that the firm was embarrassed by the incident and that they didn't have room for a hothead who couldn't control his emotions. I tried to get another job somewhere else, but no one would touch me. Hanging up a shingle was the last resort, in case you were wondering."

Dawn ate a chip and looked at her plate, trying to take it all in.

"Have you talked to the Professor since?"

"Just once," Rick said, shaking his head. "When he referred me Ruth Ann's case."

"It's a good case, isn't it?"

Rick shrugged. "It's not a guaranteed win if that's what you're asking."

"But he could've referred it to anyone, right?"

Rick nodded. "Sure. What's your point? Oh, let me guess. You took Evidence from the Professor and worship the ground he walks on like everyone else."

Dawn's face turned pale. "I . . . uh . . . I did have Evidence with him, and . . ."

Something's wrong, Rick thought. Dawn looked visibly upset, like she might cry.

". . . I did like him," Dawn continued. "I thought he was a good teacher."

She's just worried you're going to be mad at her for liking him, Rick realized, feeling guilty.

"No worries," Rick quickly recovered. "He was a good teacher." For a moment he paused. When he spoke again, his words were soft, just above a whisper.

"Can I ask you a question?" *Don't do this*, Rick tried to tell himself, but it was no use.

"Sure."

"Why do you do it? Working for me, I mean. You're smart, beautiful. Grades are fantastic. You could be working for someone who could afford to pay you. Why this job? Why me?"

Dawn looked up, and her face was even paler than before.

You moron, Rick thought. *Can't you just enjoy a good thing?*

"Like I said when we first met. I wanted to see the life of a plaintiff's lawyer to get a broad view before making any long-range career choices. I think this is good for me. And I'm enjoying it. I've already done more for you this week than I did all last summer clerking for Tomkins & Fisher."

"That's a good group," Rick said.

"I like working for you better," Dawn said. The color had returned to her face, and her eyes radiated with warmth.

"I like it too," Rick said, holding his fist out, which she nudged with her own.

—

Dawn watched from the window as Rick's Saturn pulled out of the complex.

"I have to tell him," she whispered, looking down at the check she held in her hand. It came in the mail today and was for the agreed amount, written from what must be a personal checking account. At the top left corner was a Tuscaloosa address, above which in bold letters was his name. "Thomas J. McMurtrie." Dawn closed her eyes and leaned her head against the cold glass. "I have to."

28

When Jameson Tyler walked in the door of his two-story townhouse in Homewood, he was too wired to go to sleep. The whole drive home he kept thinking of the young lady that had accompanied Rick Drake to the Ultron plant. Dawn Murphy . . . He knew he had seen the girl before, and her name had tickled a memory. *But it can't be*, he kept telling himself. Still, he couldn't shake the feeling, and a few minutes later he pulled up the folder entitled "Professor Investigation" on his computer. Then he clicked on the photographs and waited for confirmation.

Well, I'll be damned, he thought, smiling, as the first photograph popped up on the flat screen. *It can be.*

Jameson had never met "Dawn" before, but he definitely knew who she was. As he looked at her perfectly shaped breasts poking through the wet T-shirt, he couldn't help but laugh out loud. How in the hell did she end up working for Rick Drake? Jameson shook his head, but his gut immediately told him the answer. *Same way Drake ended up with the Wilcox case.* The Professor.

"You can't take back your sins, Tom," Jameson laughed as he continued to admire Dawn Murphy's rain-soaked body. *Referring Drake a case he can't handle and getting your paramour a new job isn't going to help them.* Jameson clicked off the computer and began to whistle as he walked down the hall to fix himself a drink.

It's just going to make my life easier.

29

As the sun set over Henshaw County, Rick stood in the middle of the intersection of Limestone Bottom Road and Highway 82, drinking a twenty-ounce Sun Drop and waiting for the verdict. Next to him a white-bearded man with a black Stetson hat, also holding a Sun Drop, pointed east.

"With the Honda right here when it started its turn and the rig a hundred yards out"—the man had placed an orange cone a hundred yards down the shoulder of the road—"the bottom line is . . ."

Rick held his breath. He was paying two thousand dollars for this opinion.

". . . it's just impossible to tell whether the driver of the Honda should've seen the rig before starting his turn."

Shit, Rick thought, glancing over to the edge of the highway, where Dawn's expression registered the same thought. *Shit . . .*

At seventy-five years old, Ted Holt had been reconstructing accidents for fifteen years, which was a retirement gig after he had spent most of his life working for the Swift Trucking Company in Fort Worth, Texas. Rick had gotten to know Ted during Rick's time clerking at Jones & Butler, as Holt was Jameson Tyler's go-to expert in wheels cases. Rick remembered Jameson saying that Ted was "the best in the business" and that the affable Texan could make a jury eat out of his hand.

When Holt had stepped out of his rental car to begin his inspection, looking ever the Texan with his jeans, plaid flannel shirt, and black Stetson, Rick had smiled, knowing he'd gotten the jump on Tyler.

Now, though, none of that mattered.

"Honestly, Rick, I just can't say," Ted said, talking in his slow drawl. "At ninety-five yards, which is still in the dip, Bradshaw probably should've seen the rig. At a hundred and five yards, Bradshaw probably can't see shit. But at a hundred"—Holt rubbed his chin—"it's just too close to call. We're talking a couple of yards and split seconds. I"—he scratched his head and walked out of the road as a car began to come toward them—"I wouldn't feel comfortable taking the stand."

Great. I'm sure you'll feel comfortable depositing my two thousand dollars, Rick thought, taking a long sip of Sun Drop and trying to calm down.

But as the sugar from the soft drink flooded his system, Rick knew he was being shortsighted. If Ted couldn't give him a strong opinion, then he'd rather know that now than find out at trial after Tyler had torn him and Rick to shreds.

"I appreciate you shooting straight with me, Ted," Rick managed.

Ted nodded, and Rick could tell he felt bad.

"If it makes you feel any better, I doubt Jameson will find anyone either."

That did make Rick feel better. Sort of.

"Anyway," Ted said, slapping Rick on the back. "Sorry I couldn't help."

—

Rick and Dawn stood in front of Rick's Saturn as the last vestiges of sunlight began to dissipate, neither speaking. Like a punch-drunk boxer, Rick tried to steady himself from the blow of Holt's unhelpful opinion. He knew he couldn't afford another opinion. He'd have to try the case without an expert and hope to hell that Holt's prediction that Tyler would not be able to get one was correct. Turning his head, Rick looked beyond Ms. Rose's store to the south, where miles and miles of farmland stretched across Henshaw County and into Marengo County. The Drake farm was only three miles away.

Rick had hoped that after a successful meeting with Ted Holt, he and Dawn could stop by the farm and tell his parents about his new case. It had been a long time since he'd had something good to share with them. They had both been so disappointed when Jones & Butler terminated his contract, especially Rick's father. "Seven years of putting you through college and law school and you blow everything we worked for in a matter of seconds," Billy Drake had said, storming out of the house after Rick broke the news. Since then Rick had barely talked with his father, and while his mother was more approachable, the sadness in her voice and eyes was difficult to take.

"How can y'all drink that?" Dawn finally asked, nodding at the plastic bottle in Rick's hand.

"Sun Drop?" Rick said, unable to suppress his smile. "Are you kidding? How can you not?"

Dawn smirked. "There's so much sugar . . ." She had barely taken three sips of hers, but like a good sport she'd tried to tough it out.

"So . . . what now?" she asked.

Rick looked into her brown eyes, thinking of the other night at her apartment. Things had been a little uncomfortable since then, neither of them quite knowing how to act around each other.

"Well," Rick began, forcing his eyes away from her, "it looks like our case on liability will rest in the capable hands of Sheriff Jimmy Ballard. We'll have to pump the speed angle and not emphasize whether Bradshaw should have seen the rig. I just hope Ted is right about Tyler. If Tyler finds an accident reconstructionist and we don't have one to cancel him out, that could hurt."

Rick sighed as they both climbed into the Saturn. He pulled the car toward the exit onto Highway 82, and he hesitated, knowing that he could turn right and be at the farm in five minutes. His mother probably had a good dinner waiting, with plenty for him and Dawn.

Shaking his head, Rick turned the wheel left. As they headed toward Tuscaloosa, he felt Dawn's hand touch his forearm.

"Hey," she said, smiling. "I know that didn't go like you hoped, but don't forget about Wilma. Even without an accident reconstructionist or Rose Batson, and even if Dick Morris and Faith Bulyard turn out to be dead ends, we've still got Wilma."

Rick couldn't help but smile back at her. She was right. If Dewey Newton's widow told the jury that her husband was forced to speed to meet his schedule and that she helped him fraudulently record his driver's logs, then combined with Sheriff Ballard's testimony that Dewey was speeding, nothing else would matter. Wilma would be a lot more powerful than any hired-gun accident reconstructionist.

Rick nodded, feeling a deep sense of resolve. Softly, almost to himself, he repeated Dawn's words.

"We've still got Wilma."

30

Wilma Newton left the Sands fifteen minutes after closing time, tired and wishing she could go home. But now she had to crank it up for job number two. She grabbed a pint of Jack Daniel's out of her glove box and took a swig. "Goddamn," she said out loud, feeling the burn of the whiskey as it made its way down her throat.

It was about a twenty-minute drive from the Sands to the Sundowners Club, and Wilma had found that she did better when she started out with a buzz. Ironically, staying semidrunk allowed her to focus better on the job at hand—pleasing the men that came in. Flirting with them, persuading them to pay for a private dance, and literally talking and dancing the money out of their pockets. When the buzz wore off and she was back to the real world—picking up her kids from Ms. Yost's house or refilling a pitcher of iced tea at the Sands—she hated what she had become. Unfortunately, it was the only way she could support her kids by herself.

She had come back to Boone's Hill because it was the only home she had ever known. Her mom and dad were dead, but Ms.

Yost—her mom's best friend—was still around, and Wilma had been able to rent a small house down the road from her.

Lately, the rent was getting hard to pay. Also, Laurie Ann would start middle school in the fall. She was pretty and wanted to be a cheerleader. Those outfits cost money—more than Wilma had. She wanted Laurie Ann and Jackie, her youngest, to have the things she never had. Since there was nobody around but her, she knew she had to do something.

So a month earlier she had gone looking for a second job. She worked 2:00 p.m. to 10:00 p.m. at the Sands Monday through Saturday, so she had her mornings and late nights free. Her first thought had been a morning waitressing gig, but then she had met Darla Ford. Darla had come into the Sands for a cup of coffee right before closing one night. Said she was a "dancer" and needed a little energy boost before she started work. They struck up a conversation—Darla was a regular chatterbox—and Wilma asked her what a waitress might make at the club. Darla laughed and said, "Not much." The money was in the "skin." The dancers—the good ones—made twice what the waitresses made. Then she told Wilma that she had made fifty thousand dollars the year before.

Wilma had not hesitated. Fifty thousand dollars! She had gone to the Sundowners Club that night, and after enduring a job interview that included taking off all her clothes, leaning over to touch her toes, and getting slapped on the ass by the owner, Larry Tucker, she was hired.

The first weekend had been awful, and she thought she might be fired. She was uptight, nervous, and, according to Darla, a "buzzkill." Darla, whose stage name was Nikita, finally made her do three quick shots of whiskey, and things got better. During the last two hours of the first weekend, she had three men ask for lap dances. After that she picked a stage name and Smokey was born.

She was now over a month into her job, and she was doing pretty well. On course to make $30K if she kept it up.

As she parked in the lot, which was framed in the neon blue light of the Sundowners Club sign, she took another shot of Jack and closed her eyes, allowing the hot liquid to settle into her stomach before turning off the car. *Showtime.*

—

He watched her walk into the club before he stepped out of the car. He lit a cigarette and leaned against the El Camino, taking in his surroundings. The Sundowners Club was like so many other joints he'd been in. Concrete-slab building, parking lot with only a couple of light poles, long neon sign marking the front door, and broken beer bottles strewn everywhere. *Good place to get a tire blown out*, he thought, stomping out his cigarette. He reached in the car and took a little Afta and dabbed it on his stubbly face. He wore a golf shirt, khaki pants, and a pair of dusty boots. Six feet three inches tall, he knew he wasn't handsome, but he had never had much problem with the ladies, or anything else for that matter. Of course, he didn't give a shit, which he knew was the secret to his success. With women, with work—hell, with everything. Jim Bone Wheeler, a.k.a. the Bone, just didn't give a shit.

As he walked toward the front door, he laughed out loud thinking of the thousands of dollars in cash in his wallet and his assignment from the boss.

31

This is my lucky night, Wilma thought. Lap dances were twenty dollars a pop and this man, James, had already paid for five of them. They were sitting at a table in the corner of the club, and she was drinking a Jack and Coke, which he had bought for her. Def Leppard's "Pour Some Sugar on Me" was blaring from the speakers, and Darla Ford, a.k.a. Nikita, was sliding down the pole on the main stage while Tammie Gentry, a.k.a. Sweet & Nasty, was pouring a sack of flour all over Nikita and herself. It was one of the highlight dances that always drew a big crowd. Most nights Wilma liked to be walking around during this dance, trying to seize on the momentum by landing a few lap dances right after the show was over. But tonight she had already hit the jackpot.

As Nikita and Sweet & Nasty's show was coming to a close, James leaned over and whispered in her ear, "Listen, is there a VIP room where I can get a private dance without all these folks around?"

For a moment Wilma panicked. Lap dances were performed on a long bench near the back of the building. There was a small divider every few feet, separating the bench into little stalls. She was not aware of a more private area.

"I'll be right back, honey."

Without waiting for an answer, Wilma approached the main stage. Darla was walking down the steps, covered in a towel.

"Smokey is smokin' tonight," Darla said, hugging Wilma. "How was the show?"

"Great, as always," Wilma replied. "Listen, this guy back there"—Wilma positioned herself so Darla could see—"is asking about a VIP room. Do we have one of those?"

"You're shitting me," Darla answered, walking to the bar while Wilma tagged close behind. "Seven and Seven, Saint Peter," she bellowed, and the bartender—a bearded man named Peter—slid the already-made drink over to Darla. "Aren't you a sweetie," she said, winking at him and downing half her drink in one swallow. Then she turned and looked at Wilma.

"Listen, honey, if he'll pay a hundred dollars, then go through that door past the benches. There is a stairwell that will take you upstairs to a hallway with two rooms. You can use either one. The first has an old beat-up leather chair, and the other one has a couch."

"What do you do up there? I mean, I guess you're supposed to . . ." She stopped because she didn't have a clue what she was supposed to do.

"Anything and everything. There are no cameras up there. No rules like there are on the floor. If you like him and he's nice, show him a good time. If not, then don't."

"How long should I stay up there?"

"As long as he's paying and you're comfortable."

Wilma had another question, but she wasn't sure how to ask it. She looked back at James and then Darla.

"Have you ever . . . ? I mean . . . up there have you ever let the guy . . . ?"

"Yes, honey. I have." She put her hands on Wilma's shoulders. "But only because I've *wanted* to. I've gotten hot just like the guy. The guy's hard, he's throwing money at you, it's, you know . . . you're still a woman. But I don't do it because he's paying for it—I do it because I want to. There's a difference." Darla drained the rest of her drink and put her glass on the bar.

"One more thing," Darla said. "Me and Tammie are the only girls in this joint to ever get a VIP dance. It's a status symbol around here. Larry will notice it and you may get a raise. But—and, honey, this is a big but—you don't need to take a guy up those stairs if you think he might try to force you to do something you don't want to do. That's a big buck over there. Just be careful and have fun." She slapped Wilma on the ass and walked away.

Wilma looked at Peter and was about to order another drink when she felt two firm hands on her shoulders.

"Well, what'll it be? How about that private dance?" James asked. Wilma tried to return to Smokey mode, turning her back to him and leaning over the bar.

"Saint Peter, James here wants to buy me another drink. Right, James?" She looked back at him with what Dewey always called "the bedroom eyes."

"Yes, ma'am. How about making it two?" he said to the bartender, and then to Wilma he whispered again, "How about that private dance?"

"You got a hundred dollars?" she asked, trying to sound as sexy as possible.

"I got a thousand dollars. And I want to spend every dime of it on you."

Wilma was stunned beyond words. After a few seconds she leaned over the bar and motioned Peter over and whispered something in his ear.

"Will do," Peter said, looking over his shoulder at James and back at her.

"Right this way," Wilma said, taking his hand and walking toward the door. Without allowing herself to think, Wilma led him up the stairs and into the first room she saw. There was the leather chair—brown with several patches—positioned right in the center of the room. There was a coffee table to the left of the chair and an old jam box on the floor against the wall on the right. Wilma put her drink on the coffee table and turned quickly to James.

"Sit down and I'll be right back." She walked down the stairs in time to see Peter placing the fifth of Jack Daniel's on the floor behind the railing.

She picked up the bottle and looked at the stairs. *What in God's name am I doing?* She put the bottle down and folded her arms. It wasn't too late. She could go into the dressing room, put on her clothes, and be at Ms. Yost's house in thirty-five minutes. There were other ways to make a living. Then she saw the faces of her girls. Laurie Ann couldn't be a cheerleader if she couldn't afford the uniform. And that wouldn't be the last thing. Wilma wanted more for her girls. College. Opportunities. A real chance. Everything she never had.

She picked up the bottle and unscrewed the top. She cocked it back and took a long swig. "There's a difference," she whispered out loud, repeating what Darla had said, trying to believe it, as she ascended the stairs. She took another swig of whiskey outside the door and brushed her hair back with her hand.

Then, steeling herself as best she could, she opened the door.

But when Wilma saw who was now sitting in the leather chair, she almost dropped the bottle of whiskey.

—

"Hello, Wilma."

"Hi." It was all she could get out. *Jack Willistone?* Behind her the door closed, and Wilma wheeled to see James.

"Relax, Smokey the Bear," James said, his voice much harder than it had been down on the floor. "Just hear the man out."

Wilma turned back to the chair but her feet were glued to the ground.

"Wilma, please . . ." Willistone said, gesturing to the table in front of the chair. "Sit. I'd like to talk to you about some things. Explain, so to speak, why I'm here."

Though still in shock, Wilma forced her feet to move, and she did what he said.

"It's about Dewey, Wilma. We don't think we've really done enough for you since Dewey's death. How have you been getting along?"

Wilma tried to gather herself.

"I'm making it if that's what you mean. I . . ." She wanted to ask him about James, what the connection was, but she wasn't ready yet.

"I imagine times have been tough, though, what with Dewey not around."

She just nodded her response. *Where is this going?*

"Well, that's why I'm here." He scooted forward in the leather chair so that their knees almost touched. "I want to help you."

"Why?" Her thoughts had become words.

"Two reasons. One, because you're the widow of someone who was a very valuable employee, and I don't think we've treated you the way we should've."

That sounded all well and good to Wilma—the shock had worn off now—but it rang hollow. *Why the strange rendezvous if that was it?*

"So what's the second reason?" Her voice was tough, and she hoped it conveyed a simple message. *Let's cut the bullshit.*

"Our company has been sued by the estate of the family that was killed in the wreck with Dewey. They say Dewey caused the family's death because of his bad driving." He stopped to take a sip of his drink.

Wilma, who had been leaning forward with her elbows on her knees, now sat back and folded her arms. *I should've known*, she thought.

"They also say that we—the company, I mean—were negligent in hiring, training, and supervising Dewey." He stopped again, and she knew he was gauging her reaction.

"OK . . ."

"We wanted to ask you a few questions about the lawsuit."

She looked over her shoulder at James, who continued to stand by the door. "We?"

"Well, me mainly. Bone here was just the instrument I used to set this up."

"Bone?" She again looked over her shoulder, and this time James winked at her.

"Nickname," he said.

"We actually call him JimBone. 'Bone' for short. Don't ask me where that name came from." Willistone was laughing now, and Wilma was furious.

"He has been paying me for lap dances all night, and he requested a VIP dance in this room," she said through clenched teeth. "Was all that part of the plan?"

"Actually, yes," Willistone said, sporting a humorless smile. "I figured if Bone could get you in this room, you would have already made the decision to whore yourself out." He paused, and Wilma felt her skin turn cold. "What I am about to offer is a much easier way to make a lot more money."

"I'm out of here," Wilma said, standing from the table. "You people are crazy." But before she could do anything but stand up, JimBone caught her by the arm.

"I don't think so, little lady. Why don't you hear what the man has to say? I think you're gonna be pleased."

"Let me go or I swear I'll scream," Wilma said.

"Scream all you want," Jack said. "I told Larry this meeting might be rough."

Again, Wilma was stunned. "Larry . . . knows about this?"

Jack laughed. "Larry and I go way back. Who do you think was one of his initial investors? No telling how many pickle tickles I've gotten in this room. But go on, scream. Let loose with a humdinger if it'll make you feel better."

Tears formed in the corner of Wilma's eyes as she sat back down on the coffee table. *Damn, damn.*

"Wilma." Willistone's voice was quieter. "We know you've been through a lot, and I'm sorry we've had to use these tactics." He paused. "Have they contacted you?"

She was still crying. All she could think about was that Jack was right. She had agreed to prostitute herself the minute she entered this room.

"Have they contacted you?" Jack repeated, his voice louder. She felt a hand on her shoulder. It was James . . . JimBone . . . *whoever.*

"Come on now. Answer the man's questions. Nobody's going to hurt you."

"Have they contacted you?" Willistone asked for the third time.

"They?" Her voice was weak.

"The family. Lawyers for the family. Anybody that would be against us in this lawsuit."

She knew it was pointless to lie. *They probably already know and are testing me.*

"Yes," she said, looking at Willistone.

"Who?"

"The lawyer. Rick I think is his name. He and this girl—I think his assistant—came to see me at the Sands a couple of weeks ago. They asked about Dewey. About the accident."

"What did you say?"

"He was most interested in the schedule y'all had Dewey on. I . . . I was mad at y'all. I—"

"You what?"

"I told him that the schedules were crazy. OK? Everyone knew they were crazy. And"—Wilma sucked in a breath—"and I told them about how I helped Dewey fix his driver's logs sometimes. So they looked good."

There was a pause as Willistone got up from the chair and snatched the bottle of whiskey off the coffee table. He took a long pull on the bottle, nodded his head, and then took another, smaller, sip.

"We're gonna have to fix this, Wilma. That won't do." He shook his head. "That won't do at all."

"Plan B?" JimBone asked, eyeing Willistone.

Willistone peered over Wilma's shoulder to JimBone and slowly nodded.

"Yeah, I think so. A variation anyway." Willistone looked back at Wilma.

After a couple of seconds he sat down beside her at the coffee table and draped his arm over her shoulder. She was scared. More scared than she'd ever been in her whole life.

"I think we can fix this, but it would have been easier if you hadn't talked." He smiled and gently stroked her hair.

"Let me ask you something, honey," Willistone continued. "You came up here because you thought you were going to at least get a thousand dollars, right?"

She nodded.

"You were prepared to take your clothes off and dance nekkid for Bone over there, right?"

Another nod.

"Judging by what I know happens in this room, you were prepared to go even further. Right?" When she made no response, he nudged her elbow. "For that thousand you would have done more than just dance, right, Wilma?"

She was crying again, and Willistone finally stopped talking. He got up and moved back to the leather chair, crossing his legs as he sat.

"Well, I'm not going to ask you to do any of those things."

When he didn't elaborate, Wilma wiped her eyes and tried to focus.

"What do you want?" she asked.

"Simple. All I want you to do is to suddenly lose your memory when you get to trial. And I'm prepared to pay you a hundred thousand in cash for that amnesia. Fifty thousand now and the rest after the trial."

"You want me to . . . lose my memory?" she asked, confused by the request.

"Yeah. Blow off Drake for any deposition. Keep telling him you're too busy to talk. If he corners you, just be vague. Don't agree to any more specifics. Just tell him you'll testify to what you've already told him. Then, when called to testify, just forget the crucial stuff. The only thing you have to deny outright is helping Dewey rig the logs. Understand?"

Wilma nodded.

"Good. So, do we have a deal?"

Wilma shivered. *This is wrong*, she knew. Beyond a shadow of a doubt, she knew. Just as she had always known that Dewey's driving schedule was wrong. *But where else am I ever gonna make this kind of money?*

She took the whiskey bottle from Jack's hand and cocked it back, feeling it burn the back of her throat.

She spilled some of the liquor down her chin, and Jack wiped it off with the back of his hand.

"Well?" he said.

Before she answered, she took another long sip and placed the bottle on the floor.

"Two hundred thousand," she said. "Half now and half after trial. If I do what you say, I get the money regardless of how the trial goes. I shouldn't be punished if y'all lose anyway."

"Well, you little bitch," Willistone said, laughing. "Are we negotiating?"

"Yes. I think I should get more for lying under oath. You bastards did run Dewey to death and you know it."

Willistone crossed his arms, his eyes not leaving Wilma's.

"Did we bring that much?" he asked, still looking at Wilma.

"Yeah, boss," she heard JimBone say in the background.

"OK, Wilma. But before I agree to that, I've got a few extra conditions too." His voice was cold. Mean. "We seem to have a disagreement about whether you're lying or not when you say you don't remember. I think saying you don't remember is more truth than fiction, but you obviously don't feel that way. So . . ." He leaned in closer, and Wilma already regretted asking for more money. *I am so stupid.* "If I'm paying for a lie," Willistone continued, "I want the real McCoy. Instead of not remembering at trial, you've got to testify that the schedules were fine as far as you knew. That if anything, Dewey had a light load and needed more runs. Got it?"

"What about before trial?" she asked. She was trembling but couldn't stop.

"Just stay away from the family's lawyer. When he contacts you, tell him you'll testify but that you don't have time to talk with him. Put him off. If he does get to you, be vague and blow him off as fast as you can. Try to let him think that you are his star witness without giving him any more information. Then at trial you become our star. He calls you to the stand and you bury his ass. *Comprende?*"

She almost said she couldn't do it. In fact, she wanted to say that. She wanted to just go back to the first deal he proposed. Not remembering would have been a lot easier. *But I can't go back*, she knew, thinking of when she had been thirteen on a weekend trip with her family, climbing to the third platform at Point Mallard Water Park in Decatur, Alabama. The third platform was the highest. When she got up there, she wanted to walk back down the ladder, but she couldn't do it. She had to jump. She felt the same way now. She nodded her agreement to Willistone.

"All right, Wilma. Second condition. If you tell anybody about our arrangement or if you fail to carry out your end of the deal, then you're dead, you hear me?"

He got close enough to where she could smell the whiskey on his breath. She again nodded.

"And your little girls. We won't hesitate, Wilma. And that lady . . ." He snapped his fingers and closed his eyes. "What's that old hag's name, Bone?"

"Ms. Yost."

"Ms. Yost too. We won't hesitate, Wilma. Do you understand?"

Ms. Yost? The girls? They knew all about her. And they would do it. She knew they would. She tried to maintain a poker face as she nodded, but she knew she was grimacing.

"And one more thing."

He was closer now, and she could feel the whiskers of his face on hers.

"If you want two hundred thousand, you're gonna have to give me some of this," he whispered, moving his hand up under her G-string.

For a split second she almost tried to run. To scream. To do anything. Then she looked into Jack Willistone's cold, hard eyes.

It's no use, she thought. *They'll find me. Wherever I go . . . they'll find me.*

"Done," she whispered back.

PART FOUR

PART FOUR

32

Faith Bulyard lived at the end of a cul-de-sac off Rice Mine Road in Northport. The two-story home had a circle driveway and what looked to be a big backyard, though a privacy fence made it hard to see. Rick pulled up to the curb in front of the house and cut the ignition. It was 5:30 p.m., and though it was dark outside, the street lamps provided a nice view of the house. Rick could see several lights on inside the Bulyard home.

"Looks like somebody's there," Dawn said.

Rick nodded, feeling butterflies in his stomach. He needed this meeting to go well. Up to this point the day had been a total failure. Earlier that morning Rick had taken the deposition of Jack Willistone, the president of Willistone. Other than learning that Dewey Newton was headed to an Ultron station in Montgomery on the day of the accident, there had been no useful information disclosed. Ruth Ann's deposition had also been taken, and though she was a sympathetic witness, there weren't any points that Rick could score with her. Tomorrow Tyler would depose Rose Batson, which Rick knew wouldn't be good for the home team. Rick had tried several times to talk with Ms. Rose again in the last month, but she'd blown him off each time, saying she'd already said her piece.

At least she answers her phone, Rick thought. Faith Bulyard was clearly screening his calls. There was no telling how many times he had tried. Morning. Afternoon. Night. Both on the cell number he'd gotten from Hank Russell and on the home number that Dawn had found.

Rick had wanted to drop in on Ms. Bulyard sooner, but there just hadn't been time. The last four weeks had been a blur. The morning after the meeting with Ted Holt, Rick had received a box of discovery from Tyler, which contained interrogatories, a request for production and one for admissions, all of which had to be answered within thirty days. While trying to answer all of Tyler's discovery, Rick and Dawn also had to keep the four other files in his office going.

Finally, there was Wilma Newton. One of Tyler's interrogatories had asked for the names of all witnesses who had knowledge of facts that would support the claims in the lawsuit. Rick had hoped to surprise Tyler with Wilma at trial, but the interrogatory left no wiggle room. Rick had no choice but to list her as a witness.

He'll take her deposition, Rick knew.

"Hey, you OK?" Dawn asked, nudging Rick on the arm.

Rick took a deep breath. "Yeah, just a little nervous. I doubt this is going to go well."

"We won't know until we know," Dawn said, opening her door a crack and then looking back at him. "Dropping in on Wilma turned out to be the right thing to do. Maybe this will too."

Maybe, Rick thought, opening his own door and walking the cobblestone path toward the house. *But I doubt it.*

—

A woman of about fifty answered the doorbell, looking suspiciously at Dawn and Rick.

"Can I help you?"

"Ms. Bulyard?" Rick asked, trying to sound as pleasant as possible.

"Yes."

Rick sucked in a quick breath. "My name is Rick Drake and this is my law clerk, Dawn Murphy."

Ms. Bulyard narrowed her eyebrows. "OK . . . oh . . ." Her eyes flickered as she looked from Rick to Dawn and then back to Rick. "You're that lawyer who's been calling."

"Yes, ma'am. I was hoping you could give me those fifteen minutes now."

Ms. Bulyard—who was a tall, athletic woman—looked behind her and then at her watch. "I really wish you had called. I was about to go to the gym, and I need to get back to fix dinner for the boys."

"I did call, ma'am. I've called several times and left at least a dozen messages. Please, it will only take fifteen minutes."

Ms. Bulyard turned her back on them, and for a minute Rick thought she was going to slam the door in their faces. Then she turned her head and motioned for them to follow. "Come on. Let's go into the kitchen. I'll make some coffee."

Five minutes later the three of them were seated at a round table in the breakfast nook of Faith Bulyard's kitchen. The aroma of fresh-brewed coffee filled the room, and Rick breathed it in, beginning to feel better about the meeting. He heard footsteps and yelling upstairs, sprinkled in with laughter.

"Sorry for the noise," Ms. Bulyard said. "The boys just got home from football practice and . . ." She sighed, smiling. "What can I say? They're teenage boys."

Rick smiled back at her. "No worries. I was a teenage boy not that long ago, and my mom still tells me I'm too loud in the house."

Ms. Bulyard laughed and took a sip from her coffee cup. "So how can I help?"

Instead of explaining all of the background again, Rick chose to get right to the heart of it. "We met with Hank Russell over a month ago at the Ultron plant in Montgomery. Ultron's lawyers were there, so I couldn't really talk with him. He gave me his business card, and after we left the meeting we noticed that your name and cell number had been handwritten on the back. We thought he might be trying to help us and that you must know something about the accident that killed our client's family or perhaps something else that might be relevant . . . like maybe the schedule that Willistone's drivers were on."

Ms. Bulyard held her coffee cup with both hands, gazing down at the dark liquid. After several seconds she sighed and looked back up. "What you have to understand is that Hank was sort of a mentor for my husband, Buck, who . . . died in the fire."

"We're sorry for your loss," Rick offered.

"Thank you," Ms. Bulyard said, drinking a sip of coffee. "Anyway, Hank was a few years older and had been with Ultron longer. When problems would arise, Buck liked to run them by Hank and get his take before he called the corporate brass." She paused. "Buck talked with Hank about the Willistone . . . problem."

"The Willistone . . . *problem*?" Rick repeated.

Ms. Bulyard nodded. "They were too good to be true. Once Buck signed the contract with Jack, deliveries picked up by twenty percent. Everything ran faster. We delivered gas faster and more efficiently than we ever had, which meant our clients were able to sell more gas and we made more money. The partnership with Willistone made Buck the most valuable plant president in the southeast. At that time the only Ultron plant in Alabama was in Tuscaloosa. The Montgomery plant was under construction, but it wasn't a reality yet. Hank Russell was actually working at the Chattanooga, Tennessee plant at the time."

Rick narrowed his eyebrows. "So working with Willistone was good for your husband and good for Ultron. How is that a problem?"

Ms. Bulyard took another sip of coffee. "Like I said, they were *too good*. Buck said he thought they were breaking DOT regulations. He had looked at some of the bills of lading and the times didn't match up."

"What do you mean?" Rick asked.

"When a Willistone driver picked up a load at the plant, he got a bill of lading. The bill had the pickup time stamped on it, and it also had the expected delivery time. So, let's say we had to deliver gas to a Chevron station in Huntsville. It's about three hours from Tuscaloosa to Huntsville, give or take fifteen minutes. Willistone would pick up the load and our loader would stamp the time on the bill as 1:00 p.m. and the delivery time might be 3:00 p.m." She shrugged. "Well, that only gives the driver two hours to get there."

"So . . . were they late a lot?"

Ms. Bulyard shook her head. "That's just it. *They were never late.* Like I said, our clients loved Willistone because they were always on time."

"Then how did . . . ?" Rick stopped, feeling his stomach constrict into a knot.

Ms. Bulyard smiled sadly. "How do you think?"

"They had to speed," Dawn piped up, her eyes wide as she looked at Rick.

Ms. Bulyard nodded. "Buck knew it and I'm pretty sure he told Hank about it. Buck thought we'd eventually get bitten by it and"— she gestured with her hands to Rick and Dawn—"I guess we did."

Rick blinked his eyes, trying to process everything Faith Bulyard had just said. "So, according to Buck, it sounds like these bills of lading would have been very damaging evidence."

"They would have been," Ms. Bulyard said, shaking her head. "But now they're gone."

The fire, Rick thought, also shaking his head. "Did you see any of the bills of lading that Buck was talking about? The ones where the numbers didn't match up?"

Faith Bulyard shrugged. "I'm sure I did. That's probably why Hank led you to me. My job was records custodian, so I always signed the bill when the loader brought it to record keeping." She sighed. "I just never paid attention to the times. My signature reflected that we had received the bill and the delivery had gone out of the plant. It was purely a record-keeping function, and I never looked at the times. I . . . I didn't have a clue what was going on until Buck told me." She cut off, and her eyes welled with tears again.

"Would any of the gas stations have kept copies of the bills of lading?" Rick asked, feeling desperation kicking in.

"No. The driver would get a copy and we would keep the original. That's it." She shrugged. "You might see if Willistone has any of them, but I doubt they do."

Rick had already asked Willistone in his request for production for bills of lading, and they did not have any. Also, since Newton's rig had exploded in the accident, there was no hope of getting Dewey's copy of the bill.

"Ms. Bulyard, do you have any personal knowledge beyond what your husband told you regarding the pickup and delivery times being too tight?"

She shook her head. "Just what Buck told me."

Rick felt his spirits sink. If Faith Bulyard had any personal knowledge beyond what Buck had told her, then he could destroy Willistone and probably add Ultron as a defendant. *A conspiracy to make faster deliveries by forcing Willistone's drivers to speed to make the load on time.* Combined with Wilma's testimony and the evidence of Dewey Newton going eighty in a sixty-five, Ultron and Willistone would be begging for a multimillion-dollar settlement. *But with the documents gone and nothing beyond hearsay evidence . . .*

Rick sucked in a breath, knowing that Buck's statements to Faith would not be considered hearsay if he sued Ultron. *Admission by party opponent*, Rick remembered, thinking back to the Professor's Evidence class. *Buck was the president of the company. His comments to Faith would be an admission by party opponent, which by definition isn't hearsay.* Then Rick felt his stomach tighten. *But they'd also be protected by the husband-wife privilege. If I sued Ultron based solely on Faith's memory of what Buck told her, Faith could claim the privilege and kill the case.*

"Is there anything else?" Faith asked, looking from Rick to Dawn. "I really need to get to the gym if I'm going to be back in time to make dinner."

"Ms. Bulyard, if we sued Ultron for negligence, would you be willing to take the stand and tell a jury what your husband told you about the bills of lading?" Rick asked, feeling his heart racing in his chest.

Faith raised her eyebrows. "You want me to sell out my own husband so you can win a trial?"

"No. I want you to expose a conspiracy between two big companies that ended up killing my client's family," Rick said, his voice firm. "No way Hank Russell risks his job to help us. With the documents gone, you're my client's only hope of a jury hearing the truth. Please, Ms. Bulyard . . ."

"No," Faith said, shaking her head. "I . . . I can't. I'm sorry."

Rick started to protest, but Dawn's voice, hyper and high, cut him off.

"Ms. Bulyard, do you think Willistone or Ultron had something to do with the fire that destroyed the documents and killed your husband?"

Damnit, Rick thought, sensing an opportunity being lost as Faith's face turned pink. "Don't worry about that, Ms. Bulyard," he said, shooting Dawn a hard look. "What we really need is—"

"I don't give a damn about what you need," Faith said, standing up from the table, her hands trembling with anger. She pointed a shaky finger at Dawn. "The fire marshal *ruled out* arson." Then she turned to Rick and pointed at the door. "Your fifteen minutes are up."

33

"I'm sorry," Dawn said, hanging her head once they were back in the car.

"Don't worry about it," Rick said, trying not to be mad. Even if Dawn hadn't interrupted, his gut told him that Faith Bulyard wouldn't have budged on testifying.

"I shouldn't have blurted it out like an amateur. That was really uncool, and it messed up what you were doing."

Rick shrugged. "I think we probably got all we could get from her. Besides, she didn't really answer your question."

"True," Dawn said, nodding her head and coming out of her funk. "She didn't answer the question. And after everything she said about her husband and Willistone, the fire seems even more fishy than before. Those bills of lading would've killed Willistone."

"Ultron too," Rick added. "If Buck Bulyard knew about the DOT violations and acquiesced to them because his company was making more money, then we could have also sued Ultron. But with Bulyard dead and the documents destroyed in the fire . . ." He sighed. The meeting had been one big tease. The information they learned was fantastic. *But we can't prove any of it in court.*

"I guess, unless we were to sue Ultron, everything Buck Bulyard told Ms. Bulyard would be hearsay," Dawn said, reading Rick's mind.

"Yep," Rick said. "With Ultron as a defendant, it comes in as an admission by party opponent. Without Ultron in, it's rank hearsay."

"But we can't force her to testify because of the husband-wife privilege," Dawn added.

"Bingo. Glad I wasn't the only one paying attention in Evidence."

"So we can't get anything she told us into evidence?" Dawn asked, her agitation matching Rick's.

"Nope."

"What about Wilma? Think she might have seen a bill of lading or two?"

"I guess it's possible," Rick said, shrugging. "Our better bet would be Dick Morris."

Again, Dawn hung her head. "I'm sorry, Rick. I know I should've found Morris by now, but we've been so busy the last month and—"

"It's not your fault," Rick cut her off as he pulled the Saturn into the parking lot outside his office. "I've been trying to find him myself with no luck, and my buddy Powell, who goes to Faunsdale every year for the Crawfish Festival, hasn't had any luck either."

"Isn't the Crawfish Festival going on this weekend?"

Rick chuckled and opened his car door. "Yeah, and Powell's going again. He said he'd ask around, so maybe he'll get lucky."

As they walked toward the building, Dawn caught Rick by the arm. "I really am sorry for ruining the conversation with Ms. Bulyard. I just got too excited."

"Don't worry about it," Rick said, opening the door that led to the stairs. "I think she was done talking anyway."

Rick waited for Dawn to walk through and then followed her up the steps.

When they stepped into the reception area, Rick saw a piece of paper taped to the computer screen on Frankie's desk. *Must have got some mail this afternoon,* he thought, knowing that Frankie liked to tape deadlines from the court or deposition notices on the computer screen so she'd remember to calendar them. Rick started to walk down the hall to his private office but stopped when he heard Dawn's voice.

"Rick, you better come here."

He did as he was told, and Dawn pointed to the computer screen.

"Read it," she said, her eyes looking anxious.

Rick strode to Frankie's desk and ripped the page off the screen. When he saw the case caption, his stomach turned a flip. Then he read the words.

I'll be damned.

It was an Order from the Circuit Court of Henshaw County. Rick glanced up at Dawn, knowing his eyes looked a lot wilder than hers. Then he lowered his gaze to the paper, his hands shaking as he reread the order.

"This case is set for trial on June 7, 2010."

34

Faith Bulyard didn't go to the gym. Instead, she cracked open a bottle of wine and poured herself a glass. Then another. And then another. By the fourth glass, her hands stopped shaking. Then she cracked open another bottle and walked down the hall to her bedroom. The boys would be fine. In the months since Buck's death, they had leaned on each other. Once one of them walked downstairs and saw the empty bottle on the kitchen table, they'd know to leave her alone. Faith shut the door to her bedroom, locked it, and took a long sip from the glass. The first month after Buck's death she had drunk herself to sleep every night. The next month she had cut back to twice a week. By the end of November, she found she was able to go long stretches of time without drinking. Only when someone brought Buck up or when a particular memory struck her did she turn to the bottle.

Tonight was one of those nights. Talking with Rick Drake and Dawn Murphy had brought it all back. The sadness. The emptiness. And most of all the guilt.

It's my fault, she thought. *If I had only been more under-standing . . .*

Buck hadn't been himself the night of the fire. He had got-ten home from work and immediately poured himself a Jack and Coke, which was unusual because Buck wasn't a big drinker, espe-cially during the week. Faith knew something was wrong and asked Buck about it, but Buck just waved her off. While she and the boys ate dinner, he paced in the den, watching the news. When Faith heard glass shatter, she ran into the den, and Buck wasn't even making an effort to clean it up. On the television screen a reporter was talking as a field burned behind her.

"Everyone died," Buck had said. "Everyone."

Faith watched as the reporter recapped that there had been an accident in Henshaw with a Willistone Trucking Company eighteen-wheeler hauling Ultron gasoline and a Honda Accord. Faith had put her arm around Buck, trying to console him. She knew immediately that this was what Buck had always worried about when doing business with Jack Willistone.

"Have you talked to Hank yet?" she had asked.

When Buck turned to her, the fear in his eyes had been palpa-ble. "Hank can't help. Not this time." It looked like he had wanted to say more, but instead he walked past her and grabbed his keys. At the door to the garage he stopped and without turning around said, "I'm sorry, Faith. For everything."

Five hours later Faith got the call from the fire department.

If we had just been able to talk. If we could talk . . .

She drank a gulp of wine, set the glass on her bedside table, and rocked back and forth on the bed. In the last two or three years of their marriage, Faith knew something had been wrong. Buck had rarely touched her, but Faith had been too selfish to notice. She was so busy with the kids' different activities, work, and all of her social clubs that she barely had time for sex herself. Being the manager of the plant, Buck worked late a lot, but sometimes he smelled funny when he got home. Smoky, like he'd gone to a bar. *Had he been having an affair?* She knew it was possible, maybe even probable. Their lives had become all about their boys, neither of them making time for the other.

Buck had talked with her many times in the last few months of his life about his worries over Willistone, but she had never given him the advice she should have: *Cut the cord. It doesn't matter how great things are now. Eventually, dealing with Jack is going to burn you.*

And it had. *Literally,* she thought, laughing bitterly as the tears fell. She didn't have any evidence that the fire was intentionally set, but it had never seemed right to her.

Faith took another sip of wine and was pondering pouring another glass when the phone came alive on the bedside table. She closed her eyes, deciding not to answer it. *Maybe it was for one of the boys.* She cringed when she heard Junior's high-pitch yell.

"Mom, it's for you!"

Great, she thought, sitting up again and grabbing the handle of the phone. *Please let this be quick.*

"Hello."

"Well, hello, Faith." The voice was male, loud, and eerily familiar. "This is Jack Willistone."

35

Rick sat on the dusty couch and sipped bad coffee from a paper cup. As was customary whenever he was nervous, he was fighting a queasy stomach and had already taken about four trips to the bathroom this morning. Now, though, in the living area of Ms. Rose's apartment at the back of the Texaco, there was nowhere to go. He'd have to suck it up and hold it in. He leaned forward and, looking down, noticed that his pants were showing leg between the cuff and his socks. *Nice*, Rick thought. Sitting next to him, Jameson Tyler was the picture of cool. Charcoal suit, red power tie, crossed legs, not a single hair out of place. They were waiting for Ms. Rose to take her leave from the front desk, which should be any minute.

Taking a deep breath, Rick reviewed his notes and prayed that Dawn or Powell would find Dick "Mule" Morris soon. Rick had called Wilma last night, and she had no memory of seeing any bills of lading. So, unless they found Mule Morris and Mule remembered the bills or Dewey Newton's crazy schedule, all the information gained from Faith Bulyard would be useless.

Dawn was back at the office now, making phone calls and searching every corner of the Internet, while Powell had gone to the Crawfish Festival this morning. *We'll get him*, Rick told himself, thinking of the trial date looming less than two months away. *We have to.*

The sound of foot patter jerked Rick's eyes open, and his stomach tightened. Seconds later the door to the room opened, and Rose Batson stepped through, looking pissed off and ready to kick ass.

"All right, let's get this over with. I got thirty minutes."

—

"Ms. Batson, let me show you what I'm going to mark as Defendant's Exhibit A," Tyler said, his voice gentle and deferential, two qualities that Rick could not conceive Jameson Tyler possessing. *Give the man an Oscar*, Rick thought, trying not to cringe as Tyler placed Ms. Rose's statement in front of her.

Outside of Rick, Tyler, and Ms. Rose, the only other person in the apartment was a striking blond court reporter named Vicki. Vicki had set her stenograph machine on a coffee table in the living area.

"OK." Ms. Rose took the statement and glanced down at it. She was sitting in a worn La-Z-Boy, which Rick figured was the chair she watched TV in every night.

"Ms. Batson, what is Exhibit A?"

"It's the statement I wrote after the accident." Ms. Rose sounded firm but guarded, and she looked at Tyler as if he might be a dangerous animal. *Which, of course, he is*, Rick thought.

"And would you please read it into the record, ma'am."

Ms. Rose took a pair of bifocals out of her shirt pocket and held the piece of paper in front of her. Then she read: "Walked outside to get a breath of fresh air. Saw eighteen-wheeler coming west on 82. Saw a Honda coming east. Honda put blinker on to turn on Limestone Bottom. Honda turned in front of the rig, and trucker put on the brakes. When crash occurred, I was knocked out for a few minutes." Ms. Rose took off her glasses and looked up from the paper.

Tyler smiled. "And does what you just read fairly and accurately depict your memory of the accident?" Tyler said, his voice remaining in that deferential tone that Rick had never heard before.

"I don't remember much about the accident," Ms. Rose started. "I wrote this right after it happened and I didn't have no reason to lie."

Tyler crossed his legs and paused. "Ms. Batson, you wrote Exhibit A shortly after the accident occurred, correct?"

"Yes, that's what I just said."

"And that's your signature at the bottom of the page, correct?"

"Yes."

"Ms. Batson, your statement indicates—and I quote—'that the Honda turned in front of the rig, and trucker put on the brakes,' correct?"

"Right," Ms. Rose said, shooting Rick a glance. "That's what I saw."

"And I believe you've told me over the phone that the rig was just a hundred yards away from the Honda when the driver of the Honda started turning. Is that correct?"

Rick tensed, recognizing a setup question when he heard one. A sense of dread came over him.

Rose nodded. "Yes. There and abouts."

"I have nothing further," Jameson said, turning and smiling at Rick as Rick's dread intensified.

—

He has an expert, Rick thought, walking through the gravel to his car with his head down, anxiety pulsing through his veins. *Why else would he ask her to confirm the distance? He talked to her before just like I did, and he's found someone that will say that Bradshaw should've seen the rig.* Rick felt a wave of nausea. If Tyler had an accident reconstructionist and he didn't, then . . . *He hasn't disclosed an expert yet. I could be reading too much into it.*

Rick tried to shake off his anxiety but it was impossible. He had known this deposition would be bad for his case, but he felt uneasy, as if he was missing something important.

He had almost reached his car when Tyler's voice stopped him.

"See the order setting trial, Rick?" Tyler asked, pointing his keyless entry device at the crimson Porsche parked next to Rick's Saturn. The court reporter, Vicki, was walking next to him.

"June 7," Rick said.

Tyler put his file in the Porsche, bent over, and started the car, while Vicki walked around the vehicle and opened the passenger-side door. Rick had not realized they had ridden together.

"That's pretty close," Tyler continued, leaving his car door open and approaching Rick. "You know, even with Ms. Batson's testimony, which almost assures that we'll win at trial, my client would still appreciate a settlement demand. No use trying a case if the parties can agree on something."

Despite the bastard's arrogant delivery, Rick felt goose bumps break out on his arm at the mention of settlement. "I'll talk with Ms. Wilcox and get back to you," Rick said.

"You do that," Tyler said. "You might also want to talk with the Professor. I would hope that he'd want you to cut your losses and get something for his friend."

Rick snorted, feeling his blood pressure rise. "I think I can manage that decision on my own."

"I bet you can," Tyler said, laughing. Then he sighed. "You know, for the life of me I can't understand why the Professor referred this case to you. I mean, I guess he didn't want to refer Jerry a dog, but still. One of Jerry's minions could have probably settled this case pretty quick. So why you?" He paused. "You want to hear my theory?"

"Do I have a choice?" Rick asked.

"I think he wanted to get back at the student that did him in. I think he must not think much of Ms. Wilcox either. Maybe she's an old flame that ended bad, or one of Julie's friends that he didn't care for. Anyway, I think he referred you this case because he knew you couldn't handle it. The incident with you was part of the reason for his retirement, so he wanted to stick it to you by giving you a case that you would most certainly lose." Tyler paused. "What a *bastard*," he said, chuckling. "But that's not even the worst of it. Hiring his whore to work for you. Now that just takes the cake."

Rick felt a wave of heat roll down his body. "What did you just say?"

Tyler's smile spread wide across his face. "His whore." Tyler reached into his jacket pocket and pulled out a manila folder. "Here, see for yourself."

Rick took the folder. When he saw the first photograph, his heart constricted. *What th— ?*

"My favorite is the wet T-shirt shot," Tyler continued, pointing as Rick flipped through the photographs. "No one can accuse Tom of having bad taste in his old age. Ms. Murphy is a fine piece if I ever saw one. Well . . ." Tyler ripped the folder from Rick, who was too stunned to say anything.

"Let me know if your client wants to put this case out of its misery," Tyler said, slapping Rick on the back and grabbing the open door of the Porsche. "We've just retained an accident reconstructionist, and it would be nice to avoid that expense." Tyler smiled, showing all of his teeth. "Have you hired an expert yet, Rick?"

"Y-y-you're wrong," Rick stammered, ignoring the question. "About Dawn."

Tyler shook his head. "Am I? Are you paying Ms. Murphy?"

When Rick didn't answer, Tyler laughed long and hard. "Dawn Murphy is in the top twenty percent of her class, son. Lives with her mother and has a five-year-old kid." He paused. "That ain't the type of girl who works pro bono."

As Rick struggled to say something, anything, Tyler sat down in the Porsche. He put the car in gear and whipped it around, slinging gravel to the side. Then he pulled in front of Rick and rolled down the window.

"Wake up and smell the coffee, Rick. The Professor is playing you like a fiddle."

36

Rick sped back to Tuscaloosa in a stunned fog. All he could see in his mind were the photographs that Tyler had showed him. Dawn hugging the Professor. Dawn, wearing a wet T-shirt, leaning into the Professor. The outline of Dawn's nipples through the wet T-shirt. And the needy look on the Professor's face. Just below the fog of his confused thoughts, he knew he should be concerned about the case. As Rick had dreaded, Tyler had retained an accident reconstructionist. Rick, on the other hand, had been shot down by Ted Holt and couldn't afford a second opinion.

But the anxiety over Tyler's expert was drowned out by his anger at seeing the photographs. *If it's true . . .* He squeezed the steering wheel until his knuckles turned white. *Tyler's just trying to get under my skin. It can't be true. It can't be . . .*

But Rick knew that some of Tyler's comments had the ring of truth to them. Why did Dawn work for him? She did have a young child and did live with her mother. How could she afford to work for free? Rick had always questioned Dawn's motivation. *So, if she's lying, then who would want to pay her to work for me?*

Rick could think of only one person and again squeezed the wheel, seeing the photographs play through his mind like a PowerPoint presentation. *Only one way to find out*, he knew as he reached downtown and turned onto Greensboro Avenue.

He parked the Saturn in front of the office and jumped out of the car, his heartbeat racing. *Just be cool*, he told himself as he took the steps two at a time, his anger increasing with each step. *Just . . . be . . . cool . . .*

Rick opened the door and didn't bother to shut it. "Dawn!" he yelled, forgetting everything but the photographs. *The Professor is playing you like a fiddle*, Tyler had said, and Rick's entire body tensed as he remembered the look on the SOB's face. "Dawn!"

"Well, hello to you too," Frankie said, and Rick wheeled to face his secretary. He hadn't even noticed her when he had barreled in. "Where's—?"

"In the conference room."

Rick started for the door as Frankie added, "She has a visitor."

Rick jerked the door open and glared into the room. "Are you . . . ?" He stopped when he saw who was there.

"Hey, brother," Powell said, eating from a massive bag of vinegar and salt potato chips and drinking a canned Miller High Life beer. "Want a cold one?" Powell twisted a can out of the six-pack sitting on the table and tossed it to Rick. Rick caught it and looked at Dawn, whose face was glowing red. She too was drinking from a Miller High Life can. It was hard to look at her without thinking of the wet T-shirt photograph.

"What's going on?" Rick asked. "You two know each other?"

"We just met," Dawn said, sounding giddy. "I thought I was good at finding people, but your friend here . . ." Dawn looked toward Powell, who popped a chip in his mouth and winked at Rick.

"Will someone please tell me what's going on?" Rick asked, still not getting it as he held the lukewarm beer in his hand.

"I found him, brother," Powell said, standing up and licking his fingers. "I found Mule."

37

Faunsdale is a sleepy town about forty-five minutes west of Tuscaloosa. In most respects it's like every other small town in the state. It has one school, where all the kids go, one stoplight, and a couple of restaurants. But for one weekend every April, Faunsdale becomes the center of Alabama. The Alabama Crawfish Festival was started in 1992 by John "Ca-John" Broussard, who got his nickname from his roots in southern Louisiana. The center, or hub, of the festival is the Faunsdale Bar & Grill, also called Ca-John's, which Ca-John bought in 1995. There is a cooking area in the street outside the restaurant, where thousands of pounds of crawfish are prepared. On the Friday of the festival, crawfish is served starting at 11:00 a.m. and continues to be served until the last song is sung on Saturday night. Faunsdale is known for good crawfish, good beer, and good music, and Alabamians and even folks from other states flock there every April.

Powell loved the Crawfish Festival, having attended the last three years by himself. This year he'd gotten there early and started asking questions. After three hours, two beers, and a half pound of crawfish, he'd run into a man named Doolittle Morris, whom everyone seemed to call Doo. Doo's job at the festival was to run the mechanical bull, which had been set up right outside of Ca-John's. After admittedly asking several questions about the operation of the mechanical bull, which Powell was fascinated by, he finally got around to asking Doo if he knew a Dick Morris. Doo had laughed long and hard.

"Only all my life," Doo had said. "Mule's my cousin."

So now here they were. Rick and Dawn. Seated in the back of Ca-John's, gazing across the table at Dick "Mule" Morris.

Rick immediately understood the reason for the nickname. The man must have been six feet five inches tall and well over three hundred pounds.

"Listen, I can make this quick." Mule said. He spoke with a slight lisp and his eyes were droopy. "The day Dewey died, he didn't even get to our place until nine forty-five, 'cause his rig wasn't ready." Mule chuckled. "Ol' Dewey was just a-cussing. We got the trailer hooked on pretty quick but it didn't matter. It was still almost ten before he hit the road, and he had to be in Montgomery by eleven." Lowering his voice, Mule placed his gigantic elbows on the table and added, "I still remember the last thing he said to me."

Rick's adrenaline had hit overload, but he forced the question out with as much calm as he could muster. "What did he say, Mule?"

"He said, 'Guess I'll either make it or I'll get a ticket. Same shit, different day.'"

Rick wanted to kiss Mule Morris on the forehead.

"Mule, had you loaded Dewey Newton's truck prior to the day of the accident?"

"Oh, yeah. I probably saw Dewey in there once, maybe twice a week."

"Did he ever complain about his schedule before the accident?"

Mule nodded. "Dewey was always bitching about that, and it wasn't just him. All those Willistone drivers did."

Rick glanced at Dawn for a second, and her eyes were as wide as saucers. *Holy shit*, he thought.

"I tell you what you need," Mule continued, leaning back and rubbing his chin. "Every time a driver left the yard with a load, we did a bill of lading. The bill would have the time they were supposed to deliver the load already on it, and we'd stamp the pickup time on the front. The bill for Dewey's run the day of the accident was stamped 9:57 or something like that and the delivery time, like I said, was 11:00. That ain't enough time to get to Montgomery by the speed limit." He paused. "I stamped a bunch of bills, and there was a lot of that going on. I told our plant manager about it, and he said not to worry." Mule shrugged, shaking his head. "So I didn't."

"We've tried to get the bills," Dawn chimed in. "But the Ultron plant burned to the ground the night of the accident."

Mule opened his mouth, then nodded, as if he had just remembered something. "The fire . . ." He shook his head and took a deep breath. For a second Rick thought he was going to say something else, but instead he just smiled. "Is there anything more I can help you with?"

Rick looked at Mule, knowing there was just one other thing. *The most important thing.* "Mr. Morris, will you testify to everything you just told us at trial?"

Mule's smile widened, and he slammed both hands on the table. "Damn right I will. I liked Dewey Newton. He's dead because of the schedule he was on, same as the people in that Honda." Mule stood up and grabbed a coaster from the table across from them. He turned the coaster around and wrote two phone numbers on the back. "Here's how to reach me. Just let me know when and where, and I'll be there." He slapped Rick on the back. "You got a card?"

Rick fumbled in his back pocket for his wallet and pulled out a business card. Mule snatched it from him and leaned down. "I may send y'all a little surprise in the mail. A little extra butter on the bread, if you know what I mean."

Rick didn't have a clue what he meant, but he smiled back. "Sounds . . . good," Rick stammered.

"All right, then. Best get back to the festival. Been aiming to ride Doo's bull all night." He stuck out his hand, and Rick shook it. "Damn nice to meet you Rick. Ms. Dawn."

Rick watched Mule walk all the way out of the bar. Then he turned to Dawn, whose eyes were just as wild as his own.

"Holy shit!" they both screamed at the same time.

Rick grasped Dawn in a bear hug and squeezed her tight, and she squealed in pain and delight. All thoughts of the conversation with Jameson Tyler were gone. Dick "Mule" Morris was on the team and batting cleanup. *This case just went from good to a grand slam home run*, Rick thought.

They were both so excited that neither of them noticed the stubbly-faced man who followed Mule out the door.

38

Mule Morris drove a 1987 Ford F-150 pickup truck and lived in a clapboard house three miles from the Faunsdale Bar & Grill. After drinking three more beers and eating another pound of crawfish, Mule said good-bye to his cousin and headed home. It felt good telling someone about Dewey Newton. He had felt guilty for six months for not saying something right after it happened and even guiltier for accepting the $5K to stay silent. He didn't owe nobody nothing, and he was tired of having a guilty conscience.

Mule saw his little piece of heaven up on the right and pressed the brake to begin slowing down.

Nothing happened.

What the . . . ? Mule slammed his foot this time on the brake, and still nothing. "Oh, shit." Up ahead, past his house, Highway 25 made a sharp right turn. He slammed his foot three more times on the brake and still nothing. The yellow sign marking the ninety-degree turn gave a maximum speed to safely make the turn at twenty-five. Mule looked at the speedometer. He was going fifty-five.

"Fuck!"

Mule Morris turned the wheel hard right and braced himself.

The truck crashed into the metal railing that guarded the far side of the highway, and for a second Mule thought the railing would hold. But the truck was going too fast. It broke through the railing and hurtled down the steep embankment. Mule squeezed the wheel till his knuckles were chalk white. *If I can make it all the way to the bottom, maybe it flattens . . .*

The truck flipped on its side, and Mule's shoulder exploded in pain.

Somebody tripped my brakes, he thought, picturing the man who made him the bribe. Then out of the corner of his eye he saw the clump of trees through the windshield.

I'm going to die.

39

Rick, Dawn, and Powell laughed all the way back to Tuscaloosa. While Rick and Dawn had been meeting with Mule, Powell had won the annual Crawfish Eating contest, and for his victory he had been given the Crawfish Cup, a huge bowl of a trophy that had a picture of a crawfish emblazoned on the side of it. Since the contest, Powell had delighted in filling the cup with beer and drinking from it, which he was doing now in the backseat of the Saturn.

"All right, Delta Dawn, your turn," Powell said, handing her the full cup.

"Powell, I've had enough. And would you please stop calling me that."

Of course her protests just led Rick and Powell to serenade her with "Delta Dawn" for the tenth time since she'd said she hated the song because her ex-husband used to sing it to her all the time.

"All right! Enough!" Dawn took the cup from Powell and turned it up. Spilling a little bit down her chin, Dawn finished and handed the cup back to Powell. "There, happy?" she asked, smiling.

Powell made a mock-serious face. "Ms. Dawn, it gives my heart great joy to see you drink from my trophy."

Dawn shook her head and started to say something, but Powell began singing again, and Rick couldn't stop himself from joining in. As Powell's voice rose higher than Rick's, Dawn covered her ears, and Rick's entire body tingled with happiness.

Good times, he thought.

40

Mule opened his eyes. The truck was on its back, but he was still alive. He couldn't move his right arm, but everything else felt OK. He kicked at the windshield, and after three efforts, the glass shattered.

I'm going to make it, he thought.

Pulling his body forward with his left arm, he was almost out of the truck when he saw the boots on the dirt. Mule squinted upward.

"You," he said, not believing his eyes.

"Me," the man said. "Hard to stop when your brakes give out, huh, Mule?"

"Fuck you, you mother— "

Mule saw the boot coming but there was nothing he could do. His nose exploded in blood and pain. Mule tried to move forward, but now the man was stepping on his hand.

"Before you die, Mule, I want you to know that I spared your daughter and ex-wife. They were both so damn ugly I wouldn't have fucked either with your dick. I am going to have to kill

Doolittle, though. And his wife . . ." The man whistled. "Now that is one nice piece of ass."

Mule struggled but he couldn't move.

Doo . . .

Then he saw the boot coming again and he closed his eyes.

—

JimBone Wheeler took a few steps back and lit a cigarette, admiring his handiwork. *Too easy*, he thought. Tailing Drake and the girl had turned another profit. Last night it was Faith Bulyard, whom the boss said he'd handle himself. Tonight Mule Morris was the spoils. *And he's all mine*, JimBone thought, knowing that, given what JimBone had seen and heard in the bar, there was only one way to handle this problem.

This is just too much fun, he thought. He wasn't really going to kill Mule's cousin and he didn't even know whether Doolittle Morris had a wife or not. "Just fucking with you, Mule," he said, laughing out loud.

After enjoying as much of the cigarette as he wanted, he went over to the patch of gasoline he'd seen on the ground and let the cigarette drop from his fingers. He watched the small flame ignite and slither like a snake toward the truck. Then he walked away.

About halfway up the embankment he heard the explosion, but he didn't turn around. JimBone just smiled, remembering something the boss had once told him.

Sometimes the only way you can put out a fire is by starting one.

41

Rick and Dawn dropped Powell off at his apartment. "You sure you're OK to walk up those stairs?" Rick asked, laughing.

"Drinking and walking is not against the law, sir." Powell pointed at Rick. "As a district attorney, I know these things."

Powell took Dawn's hand and planted a kiss on it. "Ms. Dawn, I have a new appreciation for Tanya Tucker after meeting you." He opened the door and stumbled forward, singing the words to "Delta Dawn" as he walked, holding his trophy up high.

"He kills my soul," Dawn said, smiling as she watched Powell walk away.

As they drove to the office, Rick caught himself glancing at Dawn every few seconds. At Powell's urging, Dawn had done a few more "cannonballs" from the Crawfish Cup, but she didn't appear drunk. Just relaxed. *And beautiful*, Rick thought.

"Do you mind if I come in and get some coffee?" Dawn asked when Rick parked in front of the office. "I doubt I should be driving."

"Not at all," Rick said. *Not at all.*

When they got upstairs, Rick made a pot of coffee, and they stood in the reception area. *Stop staring at her*, Rick told himself.

"What?" Dawn asked, punching him on the shoulder.

Rick shook his head. "Nothing. Just . . . I can't believe this is happening. With Mule saying what he said, we can add Ultron as a defendant. We can tell the jury that Ruth Ann's family died because of a conspiracy between two huge companies to make more money by encouraging speeding and DOT violations. Newton was speeding at the time of the accident and complained about his schedule at the time of pickup. You heard what he told Mule. 'Guess I'll either make it or I'll get a ticket.'"

"'Same shit, different day,'" Dawn added.

Rick slapped his hands together. "Mule told the plant manager—"

"Buck Bulyard," Dawn interrupted.

"About what was happening and—"

"Bulyard told Mule not to worry about it."

"Right," Rick said, again slapping his hands together. "So we have evidence that a higher-up at Ultron knew about the situation and let it go."

"Time to sue the bastards," Dawn said, laughing and causing Rick to laugh.

"Sue the bastards," Rick repeated, making a mock toast with his drinkless hand. "Think Willistone and Ultron will want to settle?" Dawn asked.

Rick wrinkled up his face. "Are you kidding? They'll be begging for a settlement. I can just see Tyler now—"

"That arrogant SOB," Dawn cut in. "So how did it go with Ms. Batson? We were so busy with Mule, I never got a chance to ask you about that. Was Tyler his normal asshole self?"

Rick felt his stomach tighten as the conversation with Tyler came back to him. Tyler's hiring of an accident reconstructionist. The allegations against Dawn. The photographs . . .

"It was a good day," Rick said. "Let's not ruin it." He took a step closer and glanced down at her breasts, their outline barely visible underneath her conservative black blouse. He saw the wet T-shirt in his mind, the hard nipples poking against the damp fabric.

"OK," Dawn said, creasing her eyebrows slightly. "I . . . I had fun after the festival. Powell really is a trip."

Rick took another step toward Dawn. "He is."

Again, neither of them spoke, and Rick took another step closer, violating her personal space. He wasn't sure what he was doing—he knew he should confront her about the things Tyler had said—but the heat he felt below his waist was unbearable. The confusion and anger from the conversation with Tyler, the elation over the meeting with Mule, and his pent-up, long-repressed desire for Dawn had combined with the alcohol to make him loopy.

Dawn averted her eyes and looked down. "So, what do you want to do now?" she asked, her voice soft. She looked up at him, and Rick finally let himself go.

He pressed his lips to hers and plunged his tongue into her mouth with an energy that was desperate and uncontrollable. When his mind returned to the photographs, he squeezed his eyes shut and kissed her harder, moving his hand up under her shirt. He expected her to protest but she didn't. Instead, she pressed into him, and her hands began fumbling at Rick's belt buckle.

Rick caressed her breasts, but his mind could not stop seeing the wet T-shirt. Dawn had leaned into the Professor and hugged him, just as she was leaning into Rick now. He could almost hear Tyler's laughter. *Wake up and smell the coffee, Rick. The Professor is playing you like a fiddle.*

Rick started to kiss Dawn again but then pulled away from her. He turned his back and wrapped his hands around his neck. "I'm sorry," he said.

"I . . . Don't be," Dawn said, sounding confused. "It's OK. I . . . I want to." She walked over to him and gently put her hand on his arm. "I want to," she whispered.

She raised on her tiptoes to kiss his neck. "Rick—"

Before she could say anything else, Rick wheeled around. *Don't do this*, he thought, but the words were already coming out of his mouth. "Is the Professor paying you to work for me?"

"What?" Dawn took a step back.

"It's a simple question. Is the Professor paying you to work for me? Jameson Tyler thinks he is and said so today. I blew Tyler off because you told me you were working for the experience, and I didn't think you'd lie to me. But now I'm asking. Is he paying you?"

Dawn's lip began to tremble and she looked down at the floor. "Rick—"

"Answer the question," Rick interrupted, feeling anger boiling inside him as the truth shone on Dawn's face.

"Yes," Dawn croaked, closing her eyes. "I'm sorry. I meant to tell you but—"

"Bullshit," Rick said as the confirmation burned through him like buckshot. "You lied to me and didn't mean to tell me shit." Rick turned away, feeling heat behind his own eyes. How could he have been so stupid to think that a young, pretty, smart law student would voluntarily work for him for free? *You are an idiot.*

"Rick, please listen," Dawn said, her words distorted with emotion. "The Professor *has* been paying me to work for you. I . . . I know I should have told you earlier, but the Professor told me not to say anything to you about it. He said that you wouldn't understand that he was trying to help you."

Rick's jaw stiffened. He didn't want to hear this crap. "Let me ask you, Dawn, when the Professor was giving you these instructions, was it in his bedroom, or did y'all just find a place at school to do it?"

"*What?*" Dawn stopped trembling and glared at Rick, which only seemed to fuel his anger. He took a step toward her.

"Tyler showed me photographs of you leaning into the Professor and hugging on the Professor and wearing a wet T-shirt. So, my question is, when you struck this deal with the Professor, did you do it before you had sex? Afterwards? *During*? Are you meeting him on the weekends and giving him a little consideration for his payment? Tyler called you the Professor's *whore*. Is that—?"

Rick couldn't finish the question, because Dawn's slap caught him right across the face. Before he could say anything else, she slapped him again, this time harder, and stuck her finger in his chest. "Don't you *ever* call me that again. The Professor is paying me to work for you because he felt guilty that he was forced to leave after hiring me to be his student assistant. I accepted because I'm a single mother and his offer was better than what I could get working as a law clerk for any other firm in town. Yes, I took the deal, and yes, I should've told you about it, but the rest of what you said is an outright lie."

Rick knew he needed to calm down, but he couldn't contain his emotion. "I saw the photographs. I *saw* you leaning into him and hugging him."

"I don't know what you're talking about," Dawn said. "What photographs? I remember the Professor walking me to my car in the rain one night when I didn't have an umbrella. I hugged him at the car to thank him. That's it!"

"Why should I believe you?" Rick asked, feeling the bitterness in his words. "You've lied to me from the beginning. About everything. Tell me why I should believe a word you say."

Dawn put her hands on her hips and glared at him, not saying anything. Her lip had started to tremble again. "Rick . . ." She cut herself off and bit her lip. "You know what? I don't care if you believe me or not." Then, blinking back tears, she calmly walked to the counter, where the coffee had finished brewing. She poured herself a cup and grabbed her purse from the floor. When she reached the door, she paused but did not turn around. "I quit," she said.

"Don't let the door hit you on the way out," Rick said, walking toward the door and catching the knob before it closed shut. "And tell the Professor that I don't need his help or his hand-me-downs. I'm sure you'll be seeing him soon. *Tell him!*"

Rick watched her as she slowly descended the steps, his blood boiling with anger and bitterness. Part of him wanted to stop her, but he was just too angry. He started to slam the door, but Dawn's voice stopped him.

"You know what, Rick?" Her voice cracked with emotion, and when she turned around, tears streamed down her face. "The Professor was right about one thing. You *are* a hothead. And a liability. Maybe not in the courtroom, but you're a liability to your*self*. If you would just have calmed down and let me explain . . ." She chuckled bitterly and wiped her eyes. "But it doesn't matter now. All that matters is you're still hung up on what happened between you and the Professor."

42

Jameson Tyler woke up at 5:00 a.m. and, before getting ready for work, checked the computer in his office. He clicked on the website for the *Tuscaloosa News*, waiting impatiently the two seconds it took for the site to open. When he saw the front page headline, he laughed out loud. "Student Believed to Be in Inappropriate Relationship with Professor Revealed."

When he had leaked the details the day before, he had known the *News* would be all over it. But the front page? *Even better than I could have hoped.* The photograph was perfect too. Nothing overly salacious. Just Ms. Murphy's picture from the law school directory.

Jameson laughed. The case might not be perfect but it was starting to come together. Rose Batson's testimony had allowed him to retain an accident reconstructionist, which Drake didn't have. Plus, according to Jack Willistone, Wilma Newton was "handled," and there was no need to depose her. Though Jameson was uncomfortable letting a client "handle" anything, his adjuster, Bobby Hawkins, had instructed him to leave Willistone alone— saying that Willistone's "cowboy shit" always had a way of working out. So Jameson would follow his marching orders, which was a lot easier to do with Batson deposed and an expert on board.

And now there should be considerable tension in the Wilcox camp, Jameson thought, laughing all the way down the hall.

"Everyone's right about you, Jamo," he said out loud as he climbed into the shower. "You are such a bastard."

43

Rick drove for hours. Up and down McFarland. Back and forth down University and over to Paul Bryant Drive. He cranked the radio loud and he just drove. All he wanted was for the conversation with Dawn to have not happened. Why had he gotten so mad? *Are you gonna let your temper blow things with Dawn like it ruined nationals?*

At 7:30 a.m. he stopped at McDonald's for two sausage biscuits and a couple of coffees. He figured Powell would probably be hungover from the night before and craving some grease.

As he walked back to his car, he almost spilled one of the coffees when he glanced at the newsstand and saw the front page headline of the *Tuscaloosa News*. Rick quickly put the food in his car and fiddled in his pocket for change. He walked back to the stand, bought a paper, and skimmed the contents of the article as fast as he could.

As he read, anger and adrenaline again broke through his fatigue. The *News* wouldn't run this story unless they had it on good authority. He shook his head and trudged back to the Saturn, trying to calm down. *It says "believed to be,"* he thought. *Not "is" or "was." They qualified it.* He sighed. She could still be telling the truth. Rick looked at the photograph on the front page and for a second pictured Dawn's horror when she saw it. He closed his eyes and beat his head softly on the steering wheel. *This is so fucked-up.*

Rick drove over to Powell's apartment in a confused haze. He knew he needed to get some rest. But he couldn't sleep. Not with all the crazy thoughts swirling around in his head.

Seeing Powell's place brought on a deep sadness, and he felt numb as he walked up the steps. Everything had been so right when he and Dawn had dropped Powell off last night. Now everything was so incredibly wrong.

When he reached the door, he extended his hand to knock, but the door swung open. Powell, wide-eyed and alert, stared at Rick.

"Dude, where you been?" Powell's voice was frantic, and he ushered Rick inside. "I was about to drive over to your place."

"Just, uh, out and about," Rick said. "I brought you some—"

"I been trying to call you since three this morning," Powell interrupted. His face was red, and he looked more agitated than Rick had ever seen him.

"I left my cell phone at the office. Powell, what's—?"

"That's when Doolittle Morris called me," Powell continued as if Rick hadn't said anything.

Rick felt his whole body tense. Doo? Mule's cousin. "OK, what—?"

"Dude," Powell interrupted again, running his hand through his sandy hair and sighing. "Mule is dead."

PART FIVE

PART FIVE

44

Tom cast his line out over the creek and slowly reeled the hook back in, grateful for the change of season. Tom had always been a hot-weather person, and the first week of June had brought temperatures into the nineties. For some reason the heat seemed to relax his aching bones. It also seemed to make "the torture"—Tom's phrase for his chemo treatments—more bearable. As the sound of a bobcat's squeal cut through the air, Tom recast his line, smiling at the memory of the fear in Bocephus Haynes's eyes when Bo had heard that same sound several months before. The squeal also stirred Musso, who was lying at Tom's side, from his sleep, and the bulldog cocked his head from side to side and cleared his throat.

"Easy, boy," Tom said.

"Easy, my ass," came a voice from behind Tom, which he recognized right off.

Tom laughed. "Bocephus, I was just thinking about you."

"You sure those things are harmless?" Bo asked.

"As a mouse," Tom said, shaking his head and inspecting his line. "Bobcats are only dangerous if they're rabid, and besides, he's not as close as you think."

Tom recast his line, and this time the hook landed a good thirty feet away.

"Nice form. Caught anything?" Bo asked.

"Nope. May try to catch a buzz here in a few minutes. There's beer in the cooler in the back of the truck."

The creek was at the edge of the farm, a good two miles from the house. Though Tom had walked this trek many times, he had decided to drive today because of the soreness from that morning's torture. Bo must have followed the wheel tracks to find him.

"So what gives me the honor?" Tom asked as Bo handed him a beer and they both popped the tops. "Can't you get enough of me?" Bo had taken Tom to his treatment earlier that morning and as always had stayed until Tom had rid the poison from his bladder.

"Thought you might like to see this," Bo said, reaching into his pants pocket and pulling out a folded piece of paper. "I printed it off the *Tuscaloosa News* website. I get on there from time to time to read about the football team, and this article jumped out at me. It ran in today's paper." Bo paused. "Front page."

Tom set the fishing rod on the ground and unfolded the piece of paper. His fingers tensed when he saw the headline. "Still No Word." Underneath was a photograph of him.

"Jesus, when will they let it go?" Tom said, sighing and taking a sip of beer.

"Just read it," Bo said.

Tom lowered his eyes and read as fast as he could. He stopped when he got to the part about Dawn. "Finally, the Professor has not responded to the allegations that he was forced into retirement due to the board's belief that he was having an inappropriate relationship with a student, which the *News* reported in April was allegedly with his student assistant, Dawn Murphy."

Tom looked up from the article, and Bo was squinting at him.

"I don't remember you mentioning anything about a girl, Professor."

"Do you have the article from April?"

Bo nodded, reaching into his pocket and pulling out another piece of paper. Tom snatched it from his hand and cringed when he saw the photograph. It was the picture of Dawn that was in the law school face book. He had looked at this same photograph when he called on Dawn for the first time.

She did nothing wrong, Tom thought as he read. *Tyler said the board would take no action against her. So why release her name? Why now?*

Tom folded both articles and looked up at Bo, who continued to gaze at Tom with his piercing black eyes.

"Well?" Bo pressed.

"Dawn was my student assistant. I had just hired her. When I gave her the job, she got emotional, and the dean saw me holding her hand. Then a couple days later I helped her to her car in the rain. She hugged me, and somebody was watching. They took photographs and showed them at the board meeting."

"That's it?" Bo asked.

Tom nodded, feeling anger pulse through him.

"That's *bullshit*, dog."

"When I told them I was leaving, they said they weren't going to take any action against Dawn."

"*They* being Jameson Tyler."

Tom nodded.

Bo snorted, beginning to pace beside the creek bed. "I told you, Professor. Tyler's a *motherfucker*, and there's only one way to deal with a motherfucker. And you know that way. *You know it.*"

As Bo paced, Tom glanced up at the pine trees that surrounded the creek on both sides. When his daddy had needed time to think, he'd always come here. Tom would be sent out by his momma "to find Sut," and Tom would invariably find him here, fishing by the creek bed, the only sounds the chirp of the crickets and the occasional song of a bluebird. Now, as the sun began to set and light shone through the pines, Tom recast his line and searched for his own answers. He had not heard from Dawn yet, and she was the only person who knew the number at the farm. He had given it to her when he hired her to work for Rick.

Why hasn't she called? Tom unfolded the article again and looked at the date. The article had run on April 10, 2010. That was almost two months ago. Tom had sent her checks for April and May, but he hadn't been checking his mail. *Did she send them back?*

Tom slowly reeled his line back in to shore as Bo finally stopped pacing. "Thanks for letting me know about this," Tom said.

"So what are you gonna do?" Bo asked, the challenge evident in his voice.

Tom sighed, not looking at Bo. Instead, he gazed at the dying sunlight as it flickered across the creek. It would be dark in less than an hour.

"What can I do, Bo?" Tom asked, hating himself as he heard the words come out of his mouth.

From the corner of his eye, Tom saw Bo cross his arms, but his former student didn't say anything. Several seconds passed with the only sounds being Musso's snoring and the chirps of several crickets.

"You're serious?" Bo finally said, sounding disgusted.

Tom looked at him. "Yes, I'm serious. What can I do? I'm a sixty-eight-year-old cancer patient. At the treatment this morning, they scoped me again and found some more of the shit. Not a full mass, just fragments of one. The doctor here thinks Bill probably just didn't get all of it the first time around, which he said happens sometimes. Course, it could mean the cancer has already come back. Either way I've got more surgery in my future."

Bo's arms remained crossed. "So what? You've got to have more surgery. You just gonna quit?"

Tom felt heat on the back of his neck. "Listen, Bo—"

"No, you listen, Professor. I'm not blind. I've seen all that mail piling up on your kitchen table. I bring it every time I come, and there's a steady flow. You haven't opened a letter in months. If that's not quitting, I don't know what is."

Tom threw down his fishing pole and stood from the log, his legs shaking from the effort. "I don't need a lecture from you."

Bo also stood, walking in front of Tom. "I think that's *exactly* what you need, dog. What the hell are you doing out here? Are you just gon' stay out here the rest of your life?" Bo grabbed Tom's shoulder, making him stop. "You know what I think?" Bo asked.

"No, Bo." Tom turned around, brushing Bo's hand off his shoulder. "What do you think?"

"I think you're scared, Professor."

Tom glared back at him. "You think *I'm* scared. *Me?*"

"As a prissy schoolgirl," Bo said.

Tom felt a flash of anger and he wheeled toward Bo, his hands tightening into fists. "Now, you listen here, Bocephus. I appreciate all that you've done, but I'm about to—"

"You're about to what?"

Tom blinked, hesitating.

"Go on, say it. You know what you want to say. You're about to whup my black ass. Right? That's what you want to say. When I challenged you, you came back at me. Now, you're pushing seventy years old and eighteen hours removed from chemotherapy. I'm a six-foot-four-inch, two-forty-pound black man who did fifty pull-ups this morning and stopped 'cause I wanted to, not 'cause I couldn't do any more. But when I threatened you, your first reaction was to fight. That's what you do when challenged, Professor. You fight. That's who you are."

Tom turned away.

"So what's the holdup?" Bo asked, continuing his rant. "The cancer? So it came back. So what? The doctor will take it out, you'll go through some more chemo washes, and it'll be gone for good. You're old? So what? I've seen you work as hard as a man twenty years younger. You're still strong as a bull, dog."

"I don't know what to do, goddamnit!" Tom yelled, unable to take it anymore. "And yes, you're right, Bo. I'll admit it. I'm scared, OK. Happy? The old professor is scared. I'm sixty-eight years old, my wife is dead, I don't have a job, my family has moved away, my old dog is about to die, and I don't have a *fucking* clue what to do."

"What do you want?" Bo asked, his voice quieter.

"Part of me wants to go back. Fight . . ." Tom sighed. "The other part"—Tom glanced at his sleeping dog—"just wants to go where Musso's going soon . . . see Julie again." He stopped, feeling his chest swelling with emotion. "Bo, part of me was glad today. When the doctor said the cancer was back, part of me was happy. I . . ." Tom stopped, unable to continue. He stared at the ground but looked up when Bo's shoes came into his line of sight. "Look, Bo—"

"No, *you look*," Bo interrupted, digging his finger into Tom's chest, his eyes spitting fire. "You're telling me you just want to die? That dying is an option here? Well, forgive me, Professor, but *fuck you*. My daddy died when I was five years old. He was hung by a rope by twenty white men wearing sheets and hoods. You ask me why I practice in Pulaski. Well, I'll tell you why: 'cause every day I want to show the bastards who hung my father that Bocephus Haynes hasn't forgotten. I'll never stop fighting, Professor. *Never*. Fighting's in my blood. It's what I was born to do. You can't fake who you are. When I said you were scared, you didn't hesitate. You rose to fight. By quitting you're going against who you are." Bo stopped, breathing heavy.

"I'm not quitting," Tom said. He glared at Bo, tiring of the lecture.

Bo glared back, but after several seconds his face broke into a smile and he glanced down at the ground. "We are who we are, Tom. And me and you, we're like that bulldog over there."

Tom wrinkled his face in confusion as he looked at Musso, snoring away.

"Yeah," Bo continued, smiling at Musso. "You look at Musso, what do you see? A docile, sweet dog that licks your face and likes to lay around all day. That's how he is 'cause that's how people for years have conditioned him to act. His ass has been domesticated. You hear me?"

"I hear you, but what are you trying to—?"

"I'm getting to that. Now, the English bulldog wasn't meant to be a damn lapdog. The English bulldog descended from the bull mastiff, a fighting dog. A war dog. Back in the day the bulldogs were used by the police to catch wild bulls that had gotten loose. *Wild bulls.* They'd grab the bull by its nose, close their eyes, and hold on until the officer could corral the bull. That's what Musso is. At his core that's what he is. And let me tell you, it's a shame you'll never see it. Musso is about gone and hasn't ever been challenged. But you can bet your ass, Professor, that even now, even as old as Methuselah in dog years, if Musso was ever threatened he would not walk away and lay in the grass and die." Bo paused. "Mark my words, as Jesus Christ is my witness and Bocephus Haynes is my name, *that dog would fight.*"

For a long time Tom gazed at Bocephus as a gentle breeze filtered through the pine trees. Finally, he couldn't help but smile.

"Where'd you learn so much about bulldogs?"

"Jazz loves the History Channel," Bo said, smirking. "Shit's on all the time."

Tom laughed and his groin flared in pain. He squinted at Bo. "So you're telling me I'm a bulldog?"

Bo smiled but his eyes remained intense and he took a step closer. "What I'm trying to say is you've been challenged by the law school and Jameson Tyler, and you're going against who you are by not coming back at them. It doesn't matter that you're sick or old. You are who you are. Just like I am." He paused. "Just like Musso is."

Bo reached forward and grabbed Tom around the back, squeezing him tight. "That's my closing argument, dog."

Bo started to walk away but then stopped, keeping his back to Tom. "Professor, I'm sorry about the last sentence of today's article. I just thought you might need a push in the right direction."

Tom wrinkled his brow and pulled out the article. He had stopped reading it after the part about Dawn. He skimmed down to the last sentence. Tom felt his blood pressure go through the roof as he read the words aloud.

"Believed to be sick and possibly near death, the Professor has retired to his family farm in Hazel Green, Alabama."

"They didn't get the 'sick and near death' part from me, but I think it's a nice touch," Bo said, beginning to walk away.

"Goddamnit," Tom said. "They'll descend like vultures on this place. What the hell were you thinking, Bo?" Tom was exasperated. "Bo!"

As Bo reached the edge of the clearing, he turned and smiled. "You can't hide out here forever, dog."

45

As the sun began to rise over the cornfield, Rick gazed at the brick farmhouse. *Stop procrastinating*, he told himself. *Just do what you came to do.* He took a sip of coffee from a Styrofoam Hardee's cup, but still he didn't move from the car. He glanced down at the passenger seat, where he'd put the article that ran in yesterday's paper. Powell had brought the article by last night with an address. "Go see him, Rick," Powell had urged. "Go get it from the horse's mouth. He is the Professor, for God's sake. He will help you."

Rick wasn't so sure. The Professor hadn't been very helpful in the last year. He'd cost Rick a job with the best law firm in the state. He'd referred him a case that was going down the tubes. And despite Rick's request not to interfere with the case, the Professor had hired him a law clerk who was now long gone. His "whore," Rick thought, remembering Jameson Tyler's words.

Rick took another sip of coffee knowing that none of that mattered anymore. He was three days from trial, and he was at the end of his rope. The Faunsdale Police Department had determined that Mule Morris's pickup had flipped down the embankment of

Highway 25 and exploded upon impact with a tree. The preliminary conclusion was that Mule's brakes had gone out, causing him to lose control of the vehicle.

But Doolittle Morris wasn't buying it. "Mule was a certified-by-God mechanic, and that truck might have been old but it ran like a top. No way the brakes would just go out." Doo, who was distraught over his cousin's death, had no doubts over who was to blame when Rick and Powell caught up with him the day after the accident. Doo had shook his fist at them both and had to be restrained by several friends, his eyes burning with rage. "I wish I'd have never seen either of you turds. My cousin is dead because of you."

And deep down Rick knew that Doo was right. *Mule died three hours after he spoke with me and Dawn*, he thought. *He kept his truck in mint condition and had no known enemies.* There was only one logical conclusion in Rick's mind. Jack Willistone had hired someone to follow him and that person had taken out Mule. *Murder*, Rick thought, trying not to be paranoid but knowing he was right. Just thinking about it left his body covered in gooseflesh, and Rick now drove with one eye permanently fixed on the rearview mirror.

Finally, there was the Wilma Newton dilemma. Tyler still hadn't deposed her, and Rick knew that Jameson Tyler wouldn't just overlook a witness with damaging evidence against his client. *Tyler is the best*, Rick thought. *If he doesn't take her deposition, there's got to be a reason.* Rick felt a gnawing in the pit of his stomach. He'd sent Wilma an affidavit weeks ago, setting out exactly what she'd told him and Dawn at the Sands, but Wilma had yet to send it back. She had also gotten spotty about answering phone calls. Rick had called three times last week with no answer. *I need that affidavit signed before I put her on the stand*, Rick thought.

He sighed, his head hurting from all the questions he had and doubts he felt. Glaring at the farmhouse, he wished there was somewhere, anywhere, else he could go. But he knew there wasn't. Other than Powell, Rick had no friends in the legal community who could help him. And Powell had told him to come here.

Rick grabbed the door handle, trying to summon the courage to move. With his other hand he felt in his pocket for the photograph he now kept with him at all times. A picture that Ruth Ann had given him during their first interview. He didn't even have to look at it, the images were so burned into his mind. Bob Bradshaw's beaming, proud face. Jeannie Bradshaw's smile, her mouth slightly open as if someone had just made her laugh. And finally, Nicole Bradshaw holding a teddy bear under her arm, looking shy, vulnerable, and so young.

This ain't about you, Rick told himself. *It's about them.*

Taking a deep breath and then a last sip of coffee, Rick opened the door.

46

Tom woke to the sound of knocking. He turned to look at the alarm clock and yelled as the soreness from yesterday's torture sent a flare of pain through his groin. 6:00 a.m. "Who the hell . . . ?" He rolled off the bed and looked down at the floor, where Musso remained snoring away. "Christ, boy, at least make an effort." Tom put on a pair of sweatpants as the knocking continued. "I'm coming," he yelled, and again felt a pull in his groin. Finally, Musso let out a weak bark and crawled off the bed.

"That all you got?" Tom snapped, shaking his head. "Fighting dog my ass," he muttered as he walked down the hall to the den. "If this is Bo, so help me I *am* gonna whip his ass," Tom said, limping through the den and beginning to wake up.

Tom stopped when he saw Rick Drake's face behind the glass window.

"Can I come in?" Rick asked through the glass.

Tom squinted back at him, wanting to make sure he understood right.

"Can I come in?" Rick repeated. "Please, Professor . . . I . . . I know it's early but I need to talk with you."

Tom finally forced his legs to move forward. He unlocked the dead bolt and opened the door. He stood in the doorway but didn't move back to allow access in.

"What's this about, kid?"

Drake let out a breath. He looked like death warmed over, his eyes bloodred.

"I need your help."

—

They sat in the den, as the kitchen table was still completely cluttered with unopened mail. Tom sat in his rocker and Rick on the couch. Tom had made a pot of coffee, and Rick leaned forward, holding his cup with both hands. The boy looked tired and scared.

"So how did you find me?" Tom asked, crossing his legs and drinking some coffee.

"Powell," Rick said, placing his cup on the coffee table in front of him and then pulling a folded newspaper from his pocket. "He gave me this article." Rick handed it over and Tom opened it, knowing full well what it was.

"The article mentions that you retired to a farm in Hazel Green," Rick said, picking up his cup and gazing into it. "I think Powell managed to get your forwarding address from a friend at the post office in Tuscaloosa. He wouldn't tell me the rest."

"Well, you found me," Tom said. "What's on your mind?"

Rick drank some more coffee and finally raised his tired eyes. "I need to talk with you about the case you referred me, but . . . first . . ." Rick sighed, looking back down at the cup.

"First what?" Tom asked. He stopped rocking and watched the boy, noticing sweat beads on Rick's forehead. After a half cup of coffee, Tom was finally awake and was beginning to realize how difficult being here must be for Rick. *Whatever he came here to do, it's killing him to do it.*

"First . . . I wanted to say I'm sorry about punching you in Washington. I shouldn't have done that. I lost my temper. I . . . I lost control of my emotions and it cost us the national title. I'm sorry."

Rick stopped and met Tom's eye, but Tom didn't say anything. *Did I just hear him right?*

"Second," Rick continued, "I'm sorry about how the law school forced you out. That's a lot my fault too and—"

"Hold it," Tom interrupted, putting his hand up for Rick to stop. "Son, I appreciate the apology, but you didn't cost me my job. That was going to happen regardless of what happened in DC."

Rick wrinkled his face in confusion, and Tom cursed under his breath. "The incident was just the pretext, all right? If it hadn't been our fight, it would've been something else. Dean Lambert wanted new blood, and Tyler gave him the ammunition to get rid of me."

"Tyler?" Rick asked. "Jameson Tyler?"

Tom nodded. "He became attorney for the university right before I was forced out. He orchestrated the whole thing." Tom shook his head and stood, his agitation growing. "You said you needed to ask me some things about Ruth Ann's case."

Rick looked up from his cup. "I do, but . . . there's one other thing." The look of anguish on Rick's face told Tom all he needed to know.

"Dawn?" Tom asked.

Rick nodded. "I have to know the deal. The newspaper—"

"The deal is simple," Tom interrupted. "My last week I hired Dawn to be my student assistant. When I hired her, she was so relieved to get the job that she started crying, and the dean walked in my office while I was patting her hand." Tom shrugged. "Later in the week, in the pouring-down rain, I walked Dawn to her car under an umbrella so she wouldn't get wet. She gave me a hug as a way of saying thanks." Tom sighed. "Somehow Tyler captured the whole thing in some photographs that paint a skewed picture. Dawn is . . ." Tom chuckled. "Well, hell, you've seen her. She's attractive. Her T-shirt is wet in the photographs. I guess it probably looked bad but nothing happened."

"You promise that was it?" Rick asked.

"I promise."

"You paid her to work for me?"

Tom crossed his arms. "I did. I felt bad she'd lost her job when I was let go. And . . . I thought you could use some help."

"I told you not to interfere," Rick said.

"I know," Tom said. "But you needed help." He paused. "She helped you, didn't she?"

Now it was Rick who stood, not answering the question.

"Didn't she?" Tom pressed.

"Doesn't matter," Rick finally said, stepping behind the couch and gazing out the glass sliding doors to the deck. Sunlight poured through the panes, casting Rick's entire body in an orange glow. "She confessed her arrangement with you, and I said some things that made her quit. My temper . . ." Rick's voice drifted off, and Tom could see the regret in the boy's eyes. *Did something else happen with Dawn?* he thought about asking him, but then held his tongue.

"Like I said, it doesn't matter," Rick repeated, sighing and turning to face Tom. "The only thing that matters now is that the biggest case of my life is three days away and I don't have a clue what to do."

Tom was jolted by the desperation in Rick's voice and body language. *He is scared to death*, Tom thought, walking over to the rocker and plopping down in it. He gestured at the couch, and Rick took a seat.

"OK," Tom said, crossing his legs and narrowing his gaze. "Tell me about it."

—

For the next hour, Rick told the Professor everything.

"I'm just not sure what to do," Rick said, wrapping things up. "But one thing I know, Ruth Ann won't settle for any amount of money. She wants Willistone called on the carpet for everything they've done." Rick sighed. "The problem is that with Mule dead the only way to expose Willistone is to put Wilma Newton on the stand. I mean, come on. The trucker's wife sticking it to the trucking company. But—"

"You're worried because you don't have any sworn testimony from her," Tom interrupted, rubbing his chin.

"Right. And Willistone's lawyer hasn't deposed her either, and we disclosed her as a witness months ago. It doesn't make sense that they wouldn't depose her unless—"

"They've talked to her and aren't worried. Course, that might not be it. Willistone is probably being defended under a policy of insurance, and insurance companies are known to cut costs. They may have instructed the lawyer not to depose her."

Rick nodded, throwing his palms up in the air. "So, that's the dilemma. Any suggestions?"

Tom refilled both their coffee cups. Rick's coffee buzz had hit overload, but he accepted the cup without argument. He had been up now for almost twenty-four hours, and he needed all the fuel he could get.

"That is a dilemma, Rick, but the safe play would certainly be to not call her. You can still win without her, and if she were to turn . . ."

"It could kill the case."

Tom shrugged in agreement.

"But without her I could lose. With Rose Batson sticking to her statement and Tyler's expert saying Bradshaw should've seen the rig before making his turn, their contrib case is pretty strong. You know as well as I do that in Alabama, if a jury finds a plaintiff just one percent contributorily negligent, then they are supposed to award a defense verdict. Also, the case loses its heat. I mean, *the truth* is that Willistone was breaking the law by requiring its truckers to speed and falsify their driver's logs. Newton was speeding on September 2, 2009 because he had to speed to make the load. He'd gotten two tickets in the months leading up to the accident. Mule Morris would've nailed Willistone and Ultron to the cross."

"Rick, we both know the truth is worthless if you can't prove it. Morris is dead and because of the fire you have no documents that are helpful. Ms. Bulyard didn't give you anything, so—"

"All I've got is Wilma," Rick blurted, his frustration mounting. "I know, I know. So you wouldn't call her?" Rick asked, meeting Tom's eye.

Tom squinted back at him with a noncommittal look. "I didn't say that. I just said that was the safe play. Nobody could fault you for it."

Rick sighed, feeling the first twinge of anger. *So maybe, maybe not, huh? Thanks for nothing, old man.*

"Rick, trying a lawsuit is ninety-five percent preparation and five percent gut. Once you've prepared yourself to the fullest, once you know your case backwards, forwards, and every whichaway you can know it, then you gotta let go and trust your gut. You can't script everything out. Sure, you develop a plan, and you follow the plan. But there are times in a trial when all the preparation in the world doesn't matter. In those situations you just have to trust your gut to make the best decision available."

"Trust my gut?" Rick asked, unable to hide the sarcasm from his voice. "Well, my gut's telling me I need help. That's why I came here."

"I've given you the best advice I can," Tom said.

Rick looked up at the gray eyes of his mentor, seeing the truth in them. Advice was fine and Rick appreciated it. But he needed more. Bob, Jeannie, and Nicole Bradshaw deserved more. So did Ruth Ann.

"Professor . . . thank you for the advice, but . . ." He sighed.

"But what?" Tom asked.

"I know it's pretty late in the day to be asking, but . . ." Rick paused, taking a deep breath. He couldn't believe what he was about to do. "Will you try this case with me?"

47

"No," Tom said, hating himself the minute the words were out of his mouth. He stood and turned his back on Rick, gazing into the kitchen, where the table of unopened mail seemed to glare back accusatorily at him. *I can't,* Tom thought. *I'm too old, too sick, and I don't have time to get prepared.*

"Why?" Rick asked, and Tom could hear the disappointment in the boy's voice. "Didn't you hear me? I really need—"

"No, you don't," Tom interrupted, turning around to face Rick. "I wouldn't have referred this case to you if you weren't ready. You've lived and breathed this case for half a year. You have a difficult decision to make, and I can't tell you the way to go. *You* have to choose. Even if I were to say yes, it doesn't change the Wilma Newton dilemma. *You* have to trust your gut and make that call. I would just be a distraction. If the *Tuscaloosa News* or the television stations got wind of it, they could turn the trial into a circus. You don't want that and neither do I."

"You're really saying no?" Rick said, still not believing it.

"You don't need me," Tom said. "I . . ." He started to mention the cancer but stopped.

"If I didn't need you, I wouldn't have come here," Rick said, brushing past Tom toward the kitchen. "I wouldn't have banged on your door at six in the morning. That's a cop-out, Professor, and you know it."

Rick stopped when he reached the door to the kitchen. "What are you doing here, Professor?" He slowly turned, and his eyes burned with anger. "Seriously? You get run off by the law school and you split town? The school puts their spin on everything and you don't say anything? What's that all about?"

Tom again fought the urge to say something about his health.

"You once told our trial team that if we ever needed anything once we got out in practice, you would be there." Rick's voice cracked. "You're a *liar*, Professor."

"You've asked too much, son. You want me to try a case with you three days before the trial starts. Have you lost your mind?"

"You're a liar, old man," Rick repeated, ignoring Tom's response. "And I've seen those photographs you're talking about. The wet T-shirt ones. And you're right. They do look bad."

Tom froze. To his knowledge the photographs hadn't been put in the newspaper. "How . . . ?"

Rick laughed bitterly. "Oh, I haven't told you the best part. The defense lawyer for Willistone showed me those photographs. I guess he noticed Dawn working for me and recognized her. He got a real charge out of showing them to me, calling Dawn your *whore*, and telling me that the only reason you referred the case to me was to see me fail. I mean, why else refer a multiple-fatality wrongful-death case to a kid nine months out of law school?"

"Who?" Tom asked, already knowing the answer.

"Don't act like you don't know," Rick said. "I've sent you a copy of every pleading in the case."

"Say it," Tom said, his voice stifled by anger.

Rick smirked, opening the door, and Tom lunged forward, grabbing his arm. "Say it, you son of a bitch."

"Isn't this how we got in all this trouble to begin with?" Rick asked, looking down at his arm. "Aren't I supposed to punch you now? Where are the YouTube cameras when you need them?"

Tom let go of Rick's arm and glared at the boy. "Say it," he repeated.

"Tyler," Rick said, stepping back out of the open door. "The defense lawyer is Jameson Tyler."

48

Rick squealed his tires as he sped out of the driveway, but Tom wasn't watching. He had already knocked all of the mail off the kitchen table and now was on his knees, going through the letters and packages from Rick that he had ignored for months. It didn't take him too long to find what he was looking for. Willistone's answer to the complaint was almost twenty pages long, denying all claims and asserting a number of affirmative defenses, including contributory negligence. Tom quickly turned to the last page and put his finger on the signature line. His stomach instantly turned to acid.

"Jameson R. Tyler, Attorney for the Defendant."

"Son of a bitch," Tom cursed, throwing the answer across the room. He leaned against the table, feeling dizzy. He wasn't supposed to do much the day after a treatment, and he felt sick to his stomach. The room began to spin.

"Fuck!" he screamed, shaking his head and beginning to pace the kitchen floor. *That son of a bitch*, Tom thought, remembering

Jameson's words after the mock trial: "Good luck with finding her someone. I'll pray that whoever it is doesn't have to face me."

Tom's entire body shook with anger. *I told him everything. Described the whole fucking case and mentioned I was thinking of referring it to Drake. He probably laughed his ass off when this case came in.* Tom bit his lip so hard that it bled. *He showed Rick the photographs and called Dawn my whore.* Tom punched the cabinet above the microwave so hard that his fist went through the wood with a loud crash, sending splinters everywhere.

In the den, Musso growled and rose to his feet, ears up, watching his master.

Tom licked his knuckles and glared at his dog. "You got something to say?"

Musso growled louder, and Tom turned away, stumbling over the mail, toward the door, which Rick had left open when he left. Tom knew he should sit down, but there was no way he could rest. He needed to move. To think. To do something. He looked back for Musso, but the dog was already on his heels.

"Come on, boy," he ordered, shutting the door behind them and walking toward the cornfield. "Let's go for a walk."

49

Tom sat on a rock, looking down at the shallow stream at the edge of the farm. He was exhausted, and he didn't know if he could make it back to the house. *What was I thinking? Walking all this way the day after a treatment. I'm too damn sick to go on a two-mile hike.* Below him, Musso's breath came in gasps. It was way too hot for him to be walking this far. After going down to the stream for a drink of water, Musso had collapsed at Tom's feet.

Closing his eyes, Tom let his mind wander. Rick needed him. Rick, whom Tom had referred Ruth Ann's case to, had come to him. Had fallen on his sword and asked for help. *That was big for him,* Tom knew. Huge.

And Tom had said no.

Standing on wobbly legs, Tom gazed up at the sun. When he'd heard it was Jameson, he'd had an adrenaline rush like he hadn't had since playing football. He had wanted to track Rick down and tell him he'd changed his mind.

But now the adrenaline was gone. Reality had set in. Regardless of what Bocephus had said, he was too old and sick to whip Jameson.

The cry of a bobcat rang out to the left, but Tom didn't even turn his head. *What use am I anymore?* Below him, Musso let out a low guttural growl, but Tom didn't pay him any mind. *I did Rick a favor. The last thing he needs is a chemo-filled wash up to babysit during his first trial. Even if I helped a little on the front end, I couldn't stand up to a full-blown trial. Hell, I haven't tried a case in forty years, and Jameson . . . is the best.*

The bobcat's cry rang out again. *Regardless of what the Cock said*, Tom reflected, *Jameson is in his prime. He's the best lawyer in the state. Rick at least gives Ruth Ann a fighting chance. He was just panicking this morning. That's the only reason he asked me to try the case with him. When I didn't give him an easy answer, he panicked. Come Monday he'll be fine. He's trying the case in his backyard, and he'll be fine.*

Musso whined, and Tom looked down at him. In thirteen years the only time he'd ever heard Musso whine was when the dog wanted to go out. "Musso, what's . . . ?"

This time the cry of the bobcat was more of a squeal, and Tom turned around, searching out the sound. It was much closer than before. Behind him, Musso's whine grew louder, but the dog had yet to move.

Instinctively, Tom reached down for his shotgun, but it wasn't there. In his anger after learning about Jameson, he had forgotten to bring his gun or his cell phone. Tom felt his body tense.

"Where are you?" he yelled, hoping his voice might scare the animal off.

The high-pitched squeal he got in response sent a chill down his spine. Tom turned slowly in a circle, squinting, trying to focus . . .

There. Twenty yards away, crouching in some brush by the edge of the creek, he saw it. It had a black-speckled yellow coat, and its yellow eyes were looking straight at Tom. It had been years since Tom had actually seen a bobcat on the property. Usually, they stayed a fair distance away and all you heard was an occasional cry. As he had told Bocephus over and over, bobcats were harmless. *Unless they are . . .*

Tom saw the foam flying from the animal's mouth and heard another blood-curdling squeal as it bared its teeth.

. . . rabid. He's rabid and . . .

. . . I'm shit out of luck. Tom was two miles from the house without a gun or a phone. He took a step backwards and instantly knew it was the wrong move. The bobcat lunged forward, heading straight for him. Tom only had a few seconds before it would be on top of him. Moving his body to the side, he put his left foot in front of his right and held his hands out, seeing the animal's yellow eyes closing in on him.

I'm not strong enough, Tom thought. *If he gets ahold of me . . .* Taking another step back, Tom saw the yellow eyes of the bobcat veer to the left, and then Tom was stumbling, having stepped on an uneven rock. Putting his hands up to protect himself, Tom waited for the moment that he'd see nothing but yellow as the bobcat pounced. *It's over,* he thought.

But as Tom's head cracked against something sharp, he didn't see yellow.

All he saw was white.

50

"ALL RISE!" the bailiff bellowed. "THE HENSHAW COUNTY CIRCUIT COURT IS NOW IN SESSION, THE HONORABLE BUFORD CUTLER PRESIDING."

Heart pounding in his chest, Rick stood as Judge Buford J. Cutler strode through the doors of his chambers and up to the bench. Rick had once heard his father describe the judge as hard on crime and not real personable—a lot of folks said the J stood for "Jackass."

"All right," Cutler said, banging his gavel a couple of times. "*Wilcox v. Willistone Trucking Company*. Are the parties here?"

"Rick Drake for the plaintiff," Rick said, trying to sound confident. Beside him stood Ruth Ann dressed elegantly in an ankle-length black skirt and a white sweater top.

"Jameson Tyler for Willistone Trucking Company," Tyler said, looking his typical best with a blue pinstripe suit, white shirt, and baby-blue tie. Next to him sat another lawyer from Jones & Butler—a young guy. Jack Willistone, also wearing a dark suit, rounded out the defense table.

"Pretrial motions?" the judge asked, peering over the bench.

"Your Honor, we have filed a motion in limine regarding the exclusion of any mention of the fire that destroyed the Ultron plant on September 2, 2009," Tyler responded. "The fire was ruled an accident by the Tuscaloosa fire marshal, and any mention of it would be irrelevant and highly prejudicial to the defendant."

"We have no objection," Rick said, knowing Tyler was right and not wanting to fight a battle he couldn't win.

"OK, that's easy. Granted. Are we ready to bring in the jury pool?"

"Yes, Your Honor," Tyler said.

"Yes, sir," Rick added. *Here we go.*

51

Faith Bulyard sat at Gate A22 on the Delta wing of Birmingham International Airport. The plane wouldn't board for another fifteen minutes, but she had ordered the boys to go to the bathroom. They had a long trip ahead of them. Faith gazed down at the three tickets she held in her right hand and blinked back tears. Now that she was here, she was having a hard time controlling herself. She'd already taken two Xanax this morning, but might have to take a Valium if the Xanax didn't do any better. *This is wrong,* she thought. *Wrong, wrong, wrong.*

Faith's hands began to shake and she reached into her purse for the Valium. When she did, she heard the familiar beep showing she had a new text message. She opened the phone and saw that the message had come from a number she didn't recognize. There was a photo attachment, and Faith clicked on it without thinking.

When she saw the picture, she dropped the phone. A person sitting next to her reached down to pick it up.

"No!" Faith yelled, causing the person—an elderly black gentleman—to jerk his hand back and look at her with wild, scared eyes. Faith grabbed the phone and pressed her face close to the screen. It was grainy but what it depicted was unmistakable. Buck was on his knees and there was a man behind him. Underneath the photograph the message was simple. *"Hope you're on that plane. Wouldn't want this to get in the wrong hands . . ."*

Faith closed out of the message and covered her face with her hands.

"Flight 1432 to New York now boarding," came a female voice over the loudspeaker.

"Let's go, Mom!" Danny yelled, bounding up to her with Junior right behind. The boys grabbed their bags and got in line, but Faith couldn't seem to make her feet work. *As bad as that picture is, it's just the tip of the iceberg. The video . . .*

Faith cringed as she remembered the clipped telephone conversation she'd had with Jack Willistone after Rick Drake and Dawn Murphy had left her house. "You're going to get a video delivered to your door in about an hour. I'll give you another hour to watch . . . and digest it. Then I'll call you."

Faith had watched the video and seen the last vestiges of the life she'd perceived she had with Buck crumble in front of her. When the next call came, the message was even more to the point. "Unless you want your boys to know their daddy was a rope sucker, I suggest you never, ever talk with the lawyers you just met with again." The phone clicked dead when Jack finished, and Faith had lived in fear ever since. Last week the plane tickets came in an envelope, with a handwritten note. "Unless you want the video to become public, I'd make plans to spend next week in New York."

Now here she was, doing exactly as she was told. *This is wrong*, she thought again. *A bully never stops. Next he'll want money. Or sex . . .* Faith remembered the way Jack had looked at her with a predatory gaze at a fund-raiser a few years back. *He won't stop with money . . .*

"Mom, let's go!" Junior waved to her from the front of the line. Next to them a clerk waited to take the tickets Faith still held in her hand.

Faith forced her legs to move forward. It didn't matter. All she had now were her boys, and all they had of their father was their memories of him. *I won't ruin that for them. I don't care what I have to do.*

52

At 1:00 p.m. Judge Cutler pounded his gavel and motioned for his bailiff to usher the jury in. For the past three hours, Rick and Tyler had whittled a jury pool of thirty-six down to twelve. They had started with voir dire, where first Rick, then Tyler got to ask the jury questions about their prior experiences with truckers, car accidents, lawsuits, and whether any of them knew any of the lawyers or witnesses in the case. Then each side was allowed to strike from the pool twelve people for any reason except race. The result of the process was walking into the courtroom now. Seven men. Five women. Rick had wanted more women than men, because he thought they'd be more sympathetic. Unfortunately, the pool was male-heavy, and Tyler was able to strike most of the women.

Fortunately, however, Tyler couldn't strike all the jurors who knew either Rick or the Drake family. Sam Roy Johnson was a black man who owned an auto parts store on the west side of town and had played football with Rick's father. Judy Heacock was a retired schoolteacher who had taught both his parents. Now they were both on the jury.

My jury, Rick thought, nodding at Sam Roy as he sat down in the front row. Rick was beginning to understand why the Professor had recommended him. *I may not have the experience or the talent to hang with Tyler*, he reasoned, *but I do have the home field advantage. No one likes playing the Packers at Lambeau, and that's what this is gonna be like for the Big Cat.* Instinctively, Rick glanced over at the defense table, and the smug look on Tyler's face seemed to say that this was the *perfect* jury—exactly the twelve people Tyler wanted. *Whatever*, Rick thought, knowing that Tyler was just following one of the Professor's mantras. *Never let them see you sweat.*

Rick glanced out in the galley and caught the eye of Powell, who was taking off work this week to help Rick with the trial. Powell nodded and gave the thumbs-up sign.

Rick nodded back, feeling his stomach twist into a knot. He had practiced two versions of his opening statement—one with Wilma in it and one with her out—and he still wasn't sure which one he was going to use. Last night Wilma had texted Rick saying she couldn't miss more than one day of work and asking which day she was going to testify. The request was reasonable—most witnesses didn't want to sit at the courthouse more than a day—but it still made Rick queasy. *What if she doesn't show?*

After trying to call her several times and getting no answer, Rick texted back, telling her to be at the courthouse Tuesday morning and to bring the signed affidavit with her.

Now the time was at hand, and he had to make his call. *Trust your gut*, Rick thought, remembering the Professor's advice and knowing he must follow it.

"Are you OK?" Ruth Ann asked.

Rick looked at her, but before he could answer, Judge Cutler banged on the bench with his gavel.

"Counsel, are we ready for opening statements?" the judge asked.

"Yes, Your Honor," Tyler said, rising and buttoning his coat.

Rick felt goose bumps break out on his arm. *What's it gonna be, Drake?*

"And is the plaintiff ready?" Judge Cutler cut his eyes to Rick, who couldn't seem to make his feet work. *You have to choose.*

"Mr. Drake?" Judge Cutler said, leaning over the bench. "Are you ready to give your opening statement?"

"Yes, Your Honor," Rick finally said.

"OK," Judge Cutler said, gesturing to the jury. "Please proceed."

Rick slowly stood and buttoned his coat. "May it please the court," he began. "Your Honor . . . Counsel . . ." Rick gestured at both the judge and Tyler before facing the jury box.

"Members of the jury . . ."

—

". . . and finally . . ." Rick paused; he had saved the best for last. "You're going to learn that Dewey Newton's driving schedule was crazy. You're going to learn that he was put on a schedule that forced him to speed. These people"—Rick pointed at the defense table with malice and glared at Tyler, then back at the jury—"gave Dewey Newton no choice but to lay the hammer down. On September 2, 2009, Dewey Newton wasn't going eighty in a sixty-five because he wanted to. He wasn't going fifteen miles over the speed limit just because he was negligent. No, ladies and gentlemen, it goes much deeper than that. You're going to learn that Dewey Newton *had to speed.*" Rick paused, making eye contact with Sam Roy Johnson. Then Judy Heacock. "After you have seen all the evidence and heard all the testimony, I am confident that you will find that this case is *not* just about an accident. This case is about *greed.* Willistone Trucking Company forced their driver to break the law in order to make a delivery, and their negligent and wanton behavior killed three innocent people." Rick again paused, letting it sink in. Then he nodded his head. "Thank you."

He walked back to his table and sat down. He had sweat through his shirt, but he knew no one could tell, because he had his jacket on. *That was OK*, Rick thought, knowing it was better than OK. He had managed to plant the seed of the conspiracy without technically committing Wilma to the stand. He couldn't prove any of what he'd said without Wilma, so he knew he would have to call her. But by not mentioning her by name, the damage wouldn't be as bad if she flaked on him. Somehow, on the fly and in the heat of the moment, he had found middle ground.

Rick turned his head, and Powell's beaming grin let him know all he needed to know. He had nailed it.

Maybe I am cut out for this shit after all.

53

Jimmy "Specks" Ballard had been the sheriff of Henshaw County for eighteen years. The physical feature that you could not escape when you looked at Sheriff Ballard was the freckles that covered almost every square inch of his face. He had been called Specks for the first time by Coach Silas Mooney, in the seventh grade, because his face looked like it was covered with specks of dirt and the nickname had stuck. Around Henshaw, most folks addressed him as either Specks or Sheriff Specks. All except Rose Batson, who thought it was a mean name and rode Coach Mooney to the day he died about it every time he came in her store.

As the sheriff strode into the courtroom Tuesday morning to be sworn in, Rick tried to contain his excitement. Judge Cutler had adjourned yesterday after Tyler's opening, which had predictably focused on Rose Batson's statement and his accident reconstructionist's expert testimony. Now it was time for Rick to put on his case, and he had always known his first witness would be the sheriff. "Hit First and Hit Hard" had been the Professor's mantra, and

Rick was leading off with the strongest part of the case. Newton's speed.

After Sheriff Ballard had taken the oath, he sat in the witness chair, leaning back and nodding at the jury. He looked relaxed, his khaki uniform unbuttoned at the top to reveal a thick clump of red chest hair. As Rick approached the bench, the sheriff nodded at him.

"Sheriff Ballard, would you please introduce yourself to the jury," Rick said, gesturing with his arm to the jury box, where several of the jurors were smiling.

"Specks Ballard," the sheriff said, smiling back at them and then looking at Rick.

"Sheriff, would you prefer that I call you Specks?" Rick asked, taking a piece of advice his father had given him last night.

The sheriff beamed with pride. "Well, your momma and daddy have for fifty years; I don't see why you can't."

Laughter from the jury box, and Rick smiled, taking the time to look Jameson Tyler right in the eye. *Welcome to Henshaw, baby.*

Rick slowly walked to the end of the jury box, a good twenty feet away from Specks. He wanted the sheriff to be center stage. *During direct examination, the witness is the star,* the Professor had always said. *You want it to seem like the witness is just having a conversation with the jury. Your only role is to facilitate that conversation.*

Rick paused, glancing at the jury and then back at Specks. Rick knew this would be the high-water mark of the trial for him. The hardest lick Rick could deliver was Newton's speed, and it was up to the sheriff to drive it home.

"Specks," Rick began, taking a deep breath. "Did you investigate an accident on September 2, 2009?"

—

An hour later Rick sat down knowing it couldn't have gone much better. Specks was fantastic, leaving no question that Dewey Newton was going eighty in a sixty-five at the time of the accident. Specks was most effective when Rick had him get off the stand and diagram the wreck on a chalkboard, showing the jury how he calculated Newton's speed based on the number of skid marks found at the scene. The last thing on the board when Rick sat down was a big eighty, and Tyler had to move it out of the way and erase it before he could begin his cross.

"Sheriff," Tyler began, "when you investigated this accident, did you learn whether anyone saw it happen?"

"Yes, sir. Ms. Rose did."

"And by 'Ms. Rose' you mean Rose Batson, correct?"

"Yes, sir."

"And isn't it true that Ms. Batson was the only eyewitness to the accident?"

"Yes, sir."

"And when you arrived on the scene, you asked Ms. Batson to write a statement, correct?"

"I did. I always ask the eyewitnesses to write down what they saw."

"And why do you do that, Sheriff?" Tyler looked at the jury, watching them as Specks answered.

"Well, it helps us figure out what happened. An eyewitness usually got no reason to lie. They just write down what they saw."

"And that's what Rose Batson did immediately after the accident, correct?"

"Yes, sir."

Tyler walked along the edge of the jury box, nodding his head. "You've read Ms. Batson's statement, correct?"

"I have," Specks answered, shooting a worried glance Rick's way.

"Well, isn't it true, Sheriff, that Rose Batson indicated that Bob Bradshaw pulled out in front of Dewey Newton's rig?"

Rick was out of his chair. "Objection, Your Honor. Hearsay."

Cutler cut his eyes to Tyler, who held out his palms. "I'm not offering it for the truth, Your Honor. At least not through this witness. I'm just offering it to show the sheriff's state of mind in conducting his investigation."

Tyler was the picture of confidence as he waited for the judge.

"Overruled," Judge Cutler said. "Answer the question, Specks."

"Well, that's what her statement says," Specks said.

"You aren't suggesting that Rose Batson was untruthful in her statement, are you, Sheriff?"

"Oh, no. Ms. Rose would never lie. When she says something, you can bet it's the gospel."

"The gospel," Tyler said, smiling at Specks and then the jury.

"Yes, sir," Specks said.

"I have no further questions," Tyler said, winking at Rick as he took his seat.

Judge Cutler turned to Rick, who was stunned by the brevity of Tyler's examination. *What was that? Six questions?*

"Redirect, Counsel?"

Rick started to say something but stopped himself. There was no way he could counter Tyler's cross. It was short, effective, and went straight to the theme of Tyler's case. It was the perfect lead-in to Batson's testimony, where the jury would get to see Ms. Rose's statement. *Which Specks called "the gospel,"* Rick thought.

"Counselor?" Judge Cutler repeated, scowling at Rick with impatience.

"No, Your Honor," Rick said, trying to sound confident. *No big deal*, he thought. *You still got Newton's speed on the table. Tyler scored the only points he could score. He's not the best trial lawyer in the state for nothing.*

"Very well, call your next witness," Cutler ordered.

Rick glanced down at the table. He'd placed his cell phone between his notebook and file, and the red light wasn't blinking.

He had asked Powell to roam the courthouse and text him if he saw any sign of Wilma. He'd also sent Wilma another text this morning, asking her to contact him as soon as she arrived at the courthouse. *She's still not here*, Rick thought, staring at the cell phone and feeling his stomach twitch. What was most disconcerting was that Wilma had not made any contact with Rick since her text Sunday night—no returned phone calls, no texts, no nothing. *This stinks*, he thought.

"Counselor?" Judge Cutler pressed, and Rick glanced up, realizing he'd let almost ten seconds lapse without a word. He glanced at the jury, and Judy Heacock had a worried look on her face. *Pull it together, Drake*, Rick told himself. *Wilma's not here and we can't call Rose right now—not after what Specks said. We need a little gap before they hear "the gospel."*

Rick looked to his right, and Ruth Ann met his eye. "You ready?" Rick whispered.

Ruth Ann nodded, looking anxious but determined.

"Your Honor," Rick said, standing. "The plaintiff calls Ms. Ruth Ann Wilcox."

54

Thirty miles away and half-cocked on Jack Daniel's, Doolittle Morris pulled his pickup to a stop in the gravel driveway off Highway 25. Doo took a sip of the pint of Jack Black he'd been holding between his legs and wiped his mouth, gazing at the clapboard house. The grass, which Mule had always kept like a golf green, had grown high, covering the front porch, where Doo and Mule used to sit and pick guitars on Monday nights. Neither of them could play for shit, but they liked getting together and blowing off steam, drinking a little whiskey, and playing the chords they knew. Doo sighed, stumbling out of the truck and slamming the door. "Goddamnit, Mule," Doo said out loud, kicking at an empty paint bucket that lay in the front yard.

For over a month Doo had been putting off this chore. After the visitation, the funeral, and the investigation, Doo just didn't have it in him to clean out Mule's house. But the house couldn't just sit out here forever. It was Doo's now—Mule had left everything he owned, which wasn't much, to Doo—and Doo knew the longer the house sat, the harder it would be to sell. All of Mule's stuff had to be cleaned out, the yard had to be mowed, and judging by the different shades of paint and the empty paint bucket, he'd have to finish the paint job his cousin had started before his death.

"Goddamnit," Doo repeated, his eyes stinging with tears as he climbed the steps of the porch and saw Mule's guitar leaning against one of the rocking chairs. *Maybe I can get it all done in a day or two*, Doo thought, taking the key out of his pocket and opening the door. The stench of rotten food and a stale house hit him like a ton of bricks.

Maybe not.

55

Ruth Ann came off just as Rick had expected. Poised. Polite. Graceful. And emotional at the right times, as when she teared up describing how old Nicole was at the time of her death. Rick's direct lasted until noon, and Cutler ordered a recess for lunch.

At 1:00 p.m. the jury was back in the box, and Cutler addressed Tyler.

"Are you ready for cross-examination, Counselor?"

Rick's stomach tightened as he glanced at Tyler and then back at Ruth Ann. He knew he had prepared Ruth Ann well and that there were hardly any points Tyler could score with her. Regardless, he was terrified. As he'd heard Powell and the Professor say many times, there was nothing in a trial as scary as turning over your client or witness to the other side for questioning.

"Your Honor," Tyler said, standing and buttoning his coat. "We do not wish any more suffering on Ms. Wilcox for this terrible accident. We have no questions."

Tyler bowed slightly, and Ruth Ann, the relief evident on her face, said, "Thank you."

Rick couldn't believe it. *No questions.* He glanced at the jury and saw several of them nod, including Judy Heacock. *Bastard scored points and didn't ask a single question.*

"OK, then," Cutler said, also looking a bit surprised as his eyes shifted to Rick. "Call your next witness."

Rick again glanced at his cell phone, which still showed nothing from Wilma or Powell. This time, though, it didn't matter. He couldn't finish his case-in-chief with Ms. Rose, because he didn't want to end on a downer. He had toyed with not calling Batson at all, but he knew Tyler would have a field day with that. "They didn't want you to hear from the eyewitness," Tyler would hammer in his closing. *Better to bury her in the middle and end with a flourish with Wilma,* Rick thought, praying that he'd hear from Wilma soon.

"Your Honor," Rick said, standing and sucking in a quick breath. *This isn't going to be fun,* he knew. "The plaintiff calls Ms. Rose Batson."

—

Rick had resolved to handle Ms. Rose like ripping off a BAND-AID. He didn't pull any punches, having her describe everything she remembered. When he finished, he had basically brought out all of the points he knew Tyler would make, albeit not emphasizing them as he knew his adversary would. *He can't say I'm hiding anything,* Rick thought, walking back to his table. Sitting down, he checked his cell phone, and there were still no new texts or missed calls. He looked at his watch. 3:00 p.m. Tyler would finish around 3.30, which would leave time for one more witness. *And I only have one more witness,* Rick thought, beginning to feel sweat beads on his forehead. *If Wilma doesn't show in thirty minutes, I'm toast.*

56

Wilma Newton sat in the passenger-side seat of the El Camino. She wore a long black dress, appropriate for a funeral. "Handpicked by the boss," JimBone had said this morning as he watched her get dressed. Wilma sighed, wishing she could wake up from this nightmare but knowing it was only starting. She had spent most of the last forty-eight hours in a Rufilin-filled haze. JimBone had started drugging her from the moment he picked her up, which had been Sunday morning, and every time she drifted back into lucidity, he force-fed another pill down her throat.

Last night she had been awake long enough to realize that they were staying at a Quality Inn in Tuscaloosa. The room was a business suite with a Jacuzzi right in the middle of it. *Nice room*, Wilma had thought, but then she'd been forced to take another pill, and the haze had set back in. Occasionally, she opened her eyes and saw him on top of her, but she couldn't feel anything. It was as if she were watching a horror movie and she was the main character.

As they pulled onto the courthouse square, a sense of dread overcame Wilma. *This is it.* She thought of Rick Drake and that pretty girl he brought with him to the Sands. Of the lady whose family died. Of Dewey. Poor, sweet Dewey. *This is all so wrong.* She closed her eyes and tried to shake it off. *I can't go back.* She took a tube of lipstick out of her purse and applied a fresh batch.

"All right, you know what to do," JimBone said as he pulled into a parking space a block from the courthouse. "And you know what the consequences are if you don't."

His look was cold. Businesslike.

"I know."

As if she could forget. Since cutting the deal, JimBone had visited the Sundowners Club once a week to remind Wilma of those consequences, and just two weeks earlier Jack Willistone himself had made an appearance.

She opened the door and stepped onto the sidewalk, clearing her mind of everything but her girls. "Nothing for me. Everything for them," she whispered to herself as she walked toward the marble stone building with the words "Henshaw County Courthouse" imprinted on the front.

57

Fifteen minutes later there was still no sign of Wilma, and Rick knew Tyler was near the end.

"Ms. Batson, you are the only eyewitness to this accident, correct?" Jameson asked, his voice rising to reach all corners of the courtroom.

Ms. Rose shrugged. "Far as I know. Weren't nobody else at the store."

"And based on your statement, the Honda turned *in front of the rig*, correct?"

"Yes."

"And the rig was *just a hundred yards away* when the Honda started turning?"

"Yes."

Tyler nodded and looked at the jury, as if telling them without words, *I told you so.* "No further questions."

Judge Cutler immediately turned to Rick. "Redirect, Mr. Drake?"

"No, Your Honor," Rick said, wishing there was something else he could ask Ms. Rose but knowing there wasn't. He was out of time.

"Very well," Cutler said, turning to smile at the jury. "Mr. Drake, please call your next witness."

Rick's stomach tightened into a knot as he thought of any possible way to delay the trial. A bathroom break was as good as he could do. Rising from his chair, he started to ask for one, but before he could speak he felt a hard tap on his shoulder. He wheeled around and saw Powell, grinning, his face red as a beet. *She's here, dude. She's here.*

"Your Honor," Rick said, turning back to the bench and forcing his voice to be firm. "The plaintiff calls Ms. Wilma Newton."

58

The judge's bailiff opened the double doors and ushered Wilma through them. From the back of the courtroom, Wilma could see the judge. The jury. Rick Drake, looking dashing in a black charcoal suit. And to her left, sitting at the defendant's table, Jack Willistone. She walked slowly, trying to be elegant. *Nothing for me. Everything for them. Nothing for me. Everything for them.* She repeated it over and over in her head as she passed Rick and sat in the witness chair.

"Raise your right hand please, ma'am," Judge Cutler said in a booming voice.

Wilma did as she was told.

"Do you swear to tell the truth, the whole truth, and nothing but the truth, so help you God?"

Wilma saw the doors open and another man enter the court-room. Her stomach tightened. The man had sandy blond hair and a six-foot-four-inch frame and wore his customary golf shirt and khakis. JimBone Wheeler was in the house.

"I do."

—

"Ms. Newton, would you please introduce yourself to the jury," Rick said, walking along the jury railing and looking into a few of the jurors' eyes before looking back at Wilma. Wilma's late entrance had given him no time to talk with her or ask her about the affidavit. *Can't worry about that now*, Rick thought, trying to stay focused and calm. His heart was beating so fast he could barely keep his voice steady.

"My name is Wilma Newton."

"Where are you from, Ms. Newton?"

"I was born in Boone's Hill, Tennessee. Moved to Tuscaloosa when I was eighteen years old to be with my husband."

"Who was your husband, Ms. Newton?"

"Dewey."

"And what was his full name?"

"Harold Newton."

"The same Harold Newton that was killed in the accident that we're here about today?"

"Yes, sir."

She's doing great, Rick thought, his heart still pounding in his chest. *She looks good. Sounds genuine. Let's ease into it.*

"At the time of his death, was Mr. Newton employed by Willistone Trucking Company?"

"He was."

"How long had he been employed by Willistone?"

"Not sure exactly. Seven, eight years."

"And what was Dewey's position with the company?" *Take it slow.*

"A driver. Trucker, I guess. Not sure if he had a job title or anything. He just drove the truck."

"And did you have personal knowledge of how often he worked?" *Let's lay a little foundation.*

"I was his wife. Sure. When he wasn't home, he was on the road. Plus he would talk about his work schedule."

"He was on the road a lot, wasn't he?" Rick asked.

"Objection, Your Honor. Counsel is leading the witness," Tyler said, standing.

"Sustained," Judge Cutler responded. "Don't lead, Counselor."

Rick walked a little toward Wilma, pausing. The objection had given him a dramatic opening. All the jurors were focused on him.

"Ms. Newton, would you please describe for the jury what Dewey's schedule was like at Willistone." Rick walked back to his spot at the end of the railing, catching a few jurors' eyes. Most of them, though, were watching Wilma. *Perfect.* He turned and waited for her response.

God, please forgive me, Wilma thought, looking at JimBone and Jack Willistone out in the galley. *Nothing for me. Everything for them.*

"It was fine," Wilma said in a calm, clear voice.

There was a gasp from one of the jurors, and Rick was sure he had misheard.

"Ms. Newton, could you repeat your answer? I didn't hear you."

"It was fine. Dewey always told me he liked the schedule he was on. Normal hours. Decent pay."

She smiled and Rick froze. *Oh, holy shit.*

"But . . . didn't you . . . ? I . . . I met with you." Rick struggled to put his words together. "You said . . . you told Ms. Murphy, my associate, and me that it was crazy . . . that Dewey told you it was crazy. That Dewey told you that Willistone was forcing him to drive more than the law allowed. Right?"

"Objection, Your Honor. Counsel is leading the witness. His question also calls for hearsay." Tyler looked at Rick when he finished his objection, and the bastard's smugness was palpable. *He expected this,* Rick thought.

"Sustained on leading. Don't lead your witness, Counselor." Judge Cutler leaned over the podium and made eye contact with Rick. He looked concerned, no doubt realizing that the witness was testifying contrary to Rick's opening statement.

"Ms. Newton, did we meet back in February of last year to discuss this case?" *Let's try this again.*

"Yes." Wilma had not flinched. She was poker faced and, actually, pleasant.

"Did we discuss Dewey's schedules at Willistone?"

"Yes, we did."

"And how did you describe them then?"

"I'm sure the same way. I mean, that was a long time ago." She looked right at Rick, then the jury, many of whom were sitting on the edge of their seat.

Damn, damn, damn.

"Ms. Newton, did you not tell me that Dewey's schedules were crazy? That was your word, wasn't it? 'Crazy'? Did you not say that?"

"Objection, Your Honor. Mr. Drake just asked Ms. Newton four questions. Could he break it down a little?"

Tyler's arrogant and patronizing voice made Rick's stomach churn, but Rick forced himself not to look at the bastard. *Just try to stay calm.*

"I'll rephrase, Your Honor," Rick said, walking toward Wilma.

"Go ahead," Cutler said.

"Ms. Newton, did you ever in my presence describe Dewey's schedules at Willistone Trucking Company as 'crazy'?"

She leaned toward Rick, glaring back.

"Absolutely not," she said. "I would never have said that."

"Did you ever in my presence say that Dewey told you that he was being forced to drive twenty hours at a time?"

"Never. I remember you asking me questions like that and wanting me to say those things, but I never did. Dewey loved that company," she said, looking at the jury. "And they treated him good."

I can't believe this is happening, Rick thought. He knew he needed to regroup, but he was unable to stop the next question from coming out of his mouth.

"You told me that Dewey got a couple of speeding tickets because Willistone's schedule forced him to speed, didn't you?"

"No, Mr. Drake. I never said that."

"You also said that Jack Willistone inspected the driver's logs himself every week, making sure that whatever was on the logs was compliant with DOT regulations, regardless of how many hours were actually driven."

"No, I *never* told you or anyone else that."

"Ms. Newton, you told me that Dewey was so scared of Jack Willistone that a lot of times *you* helped him fill out his driver's logs so it looked like he was under ten hours."

Wilma shook her head. "I don't know what you're talking about. My husband never said those things, and I never helped him fill out his driver's logs."

Rick felt heat sting his forehead. *This is a fucking ambush.* "Ms. Newton, I met with you. You told me everything I just asked you about."

Tyler rose but then shook his head and sat back down without raising an objection.

"Mr. Drake, I remember our meeting and I remember you wanting me to say those things." Wilma looked right at the jury. "But I never, *ever* said those things. Dewey's schedules were reasonable at Willistone. He . . ." Wilma's voice cracked and her lip trembled. "Dewey loved that company."

When Rick was in the seventh grade, a fifth-grader smarted off to him, and Rick grabbed the little SOB by the collar. When he did, the fifth-grader kicked him in the balls as hard as he could, and Rick lay in the school parking lot in pain for fifteen minutes.

This felt worse.

He felt the jury's eyes on him. The judge. Tyler. He had trusted his gut and . . . *I was wrong.* He looked over at Ruth Ann, who was glaring at Wilma. *I failed her. She came to me and . . . I failed.* Rick's hand went into his front pocket and he felt for the photograph of Bob, Jeannie, and Nicole Bradshaw. As Rick envisioned the photograph, his legs began to shake. *I failed them too.*

Rick knew he needed to regroup but he didn't know how. He had fallen into a trap. Rick glanced at Tyler, and the Big Cat's amused expression told him all he needed to know. *He knew all along,* Rick thought again.

The courtroom was silent as a morgue. Rick turned to the galley and saw Powell hold his face in his hands, and Rick wished he could do the same. *I should've taken her deposition or gotten her to sign the affidavit. I should not have put her on the stand without getting her sworn.*

Rick turned around, feeling the sweat on his forehead, as the silence was broken by the sound of the double doors in the back of the courtroom squeaking open and footsteps clacking on the hardwood floor. Rick was frozen in place. He couldn't think of a single thing to say or do.

"Mr. Drake," Judge Cutler said, and Rick managed to look up at him. "Would you like a short recess?"

"I . . ." *You can't take a recess now,* Rick thought. *Not like this. Not with Wilma's testimony emblazoned in the jury's mind.* But what else could he do? There weren't any questions left to ask her. "I—"

"Your Honor, may I approach?"

The hard, gravelly voice cut through the air like a knife. It did not belong to Tyler or his associate. And though it sounded familiar, Rick was so numb with shock he didn't turn around.

"Who are you?" Judge Cutler asked, sounding annoyed. Then Rick saw Cutler's eyebrows raise, and the judge cocked his head to the side. "Well, I'll be . . ." The judge didn't complete the thought, and his face changed from irritation to awe.

Finally, Rick forced his head to turn toward the voice. When he saw who was there, his knees gave a little. *What the hell . . . ?* Then he caught Jameson Tyler's face and saw initial recognition replaced by a look he had never seen before on the arrogant bastard.

Fear.

"Your Honor, my name is Thomas Jackson McMurtrie."

59

"I'm sorry I'm late," Tom said, setting his briefcase down on the counsel table next to Ruth Ann. He caught her eye and leaned toward her. "I am so sorry," he whispered. "I know it's a lot to ask, but I need you to trust me. OK?" Ruth Ann's face was white with shock but she nodded. Tom took her hand. "I'm going to make this right, I promise."

"Late?" Judge Cutler asked, sounding confused.

Tom squeezed Ruth Ann's hand and then turned to face the bench. "Yes, sir. I intended to be here yesterday, but I got into a little scrape on my farm."

"You're Professor . . . McMurtrie, right?" Cutler asked, holding up a book that he kept on the bench. It was *McMurtrie's Evidence*. Second Edition.

"Yes, Your Honor."

"I thought you were . . . I mean, the papers said you were almost . . ." Cutler blushed red, and he caught himself before he said the word, but Tom knew where he was going.

"Dead?" Tom offered, smiling and thinking of something John Wayne had said in the movie *Big Jake*. "Not hardly, Judge." Then, turning and taking a long stride toward Jameson Tyler, who was now standing in front of the bench, Tom repeated himself. "Not hardly."

Tom stood straight, looking down on his former student. His former friend. Tyler cut his eyes to Judge Cutler.

"Your Honor, I don't know what the Professor is doing here, but I object to this interruption."

Tom took a step closer to Tyler, their toes almost touching now.

"Your Honor, I'd like to enter my appearance as additional counsel of record for the plaintiff, Ruth Ann Wilcox." As he spoke, Tom never took his eyes off Tyler.

Tyler rolled his eyes, then brushed past Tom's shoulder and stepped in front of him. "Judge, it is way too late in the game to be trading horses."

"It's not a trade, Judge. I'll be joining Mr. Drake. There's nothing in the rules of civil procedure that would prevent a party from retaining additional counsel during a trial."

Judge Cutler leaned back in his chair and rubbed his chin. He looked past the lawyers to Ruth Ann and banged his gavel.

"Ms. Wilcox, would you please approach the bench."

Ruth Ann walked toward them, her eyes on Tom and then on the judge.

"Ms. Wilcox, the Professor here—er, Mr. McMurtrie, I mean—has asked to join Mr. Drake as your lawyer in this case. I presume you're OK with that?"

Ruth Ann looked at Tom, and for a split second Tom thought she might say no. Then her mouth curved into the smallest of smiles and she nodded at Cutler. "Yes, Your Honor, I'd like that."

"Your Honor, I object," Tyler said, his frustration obvious. "This is ridiculous . . . I mean—"

"Overruled," Cutler interrupted. "I've made my decision." He banged his gavel. "Ladies and gentlemen of the jury," he said, turning to face them, "Thomas McMurtrie will now be joining Rick Drake as counsel for the plaintiff." He turned to the lawyers. "Please proceed, gentlemen."

—

Tom and Rick followed Ruth Ann back to the counsel table.

"What are you *doing*?" Rick asked.

Tom could tell the boy was overwhelmed by shock.

"Taking you up on your offer," Tom said.

"It's a little late for that, isn't it?"

Tom smiled. "Better late than never. I take it Ms. Newton has changed her story."

"One hundred eighty degrees," Rick said, raising his eyebrows. "You've read—"

"I've read everything," Tom said.

Rick gazed wide-eyed at Tom as they reached the table. "How?"

Tom started to respond but felt a rough hand on his arm. Ripping his arm away, he turned to see Tyler.

"You've got a lot of nerve showing up here, Professor." Tyler chuckled, glancing at Rick, then back to Tom. "Well, isn't this something? Rick Drake and the Professor together again. The papers will have a field day. Now, y'all play nice and don't fight. We wouldn't want any more things turning up on YouTube."

Tyler smiled and started to walk away, but before he could, Tom caught his arm, pulled him close, and didn't let him go. Keeping his face a mask of perfect calm, Tom whispered in Jameson's ear, "Taking you to the woodshed is going to be so much fun, Jamo." Tom winked, then let go of Jameson's arm just as he tried to jerk it away, causing the Big Cat to stumble.

His face crimson, Tyler straightened his suit and stepped backwards toward the defense table, his eyes never leaving Tom's.

"Counselor, do you have any further questions for this witness?" Judge Cutler asked, looking at Rick and gesturing toward Wilma Newton, who remained seated at the witness stand.

"I . . ." Rick started, then looked to Tom.

"Yes, we do, Your Honor," Tom said. "May we approach?" Tom was already walking, Rick behind him. "Trust me," Tom whispered under his breath to Rick.

"What now?" the judge asked, clearly irritated.

"Your Honor," Tom started as they arrived at the bench again, "we'd like to treat Ms. Newton as an adverse witness and cross-examine her. Also, I'd like to take over for Rick. Rick may have to be a rebuttal witness against Ms. Newton, so it wouldn't be appropriate for him to ask her any more questions."

"A rebuttal witness?" Tyler asked, sounding exasperated. "Judge, a lawyer cannot be a witness in his own case. And they haven't laid the proper predicate for Ms. Newton to be treated adverse."

"I'm not sure about Mr. Drake testifying, but Ms. Newton seems clearly adverse to the plaintiff's position," Judge Cutler answered, looking down and rubbing his eyes.

"Well—" Tyler started to say something but the judge interrupted.

"Look, I'm going to allow the cross-examination. But it's 4:20. Why don't we call it a day? The jury is tired. I'm tired . . ."

"Judge, I don't think I'll be long," Tom said. "Just give me till five."

Cutler took a long look at Tom. "You got a lotta nerve, McMurtrie." He sighed. "You played for Coach Bryant, didn't you?"

"Nineteen-sixty-one team. Defensive end," Tom said.

Cutler shook his head and gave a tired smile. "Hell of a team. All right, you've got till five o'clock."

As they walked back to the counsel table, Rick whispered, "Professor, do you know what you're doing?"

I sure as hell hope so, Tom thought, feeling his nerves kick in as he realized he was about to try a case in front of a jury for the first time in forty years. He looked at Rick and forced a smile.

"Let's see if this old dog has a few tricks left."

60

"All right, Mr. McMurtrie. Your witness," Judge Cutler said.

Tom walked slowly toward Wilma Newton. The last three days had been a whirlwind, leading up to this moment. He had reviewed all the pleadings. All the discovery. All the depositions. Every piece of paper Rick had sent him. He'd also digested Rick's concerns about Wilma Newton and done a little investigation. Tom had hoped to get to court before Wilma took the stand, but making sure everything was ready had taken longer than he had expected. *But I made it*, he thought, adrenaline coursing through his veins. *Hopefully, I'm not too late.*

Tom had not cross-examined a witness in front of a live jury in forty years, and he could feel the rapid drumbeat of his heart. *Calm, slow, Andy*, he told himself. It was a phrase he used to think to himself when he tried cases. Something he taught to his trial team. *Calm, slow, Andy.* Calm and slow were self-explanatory. Be calm. Talk slow. Andy was the trick. Andy was for Andy Griffith. If you talked and acted like Andy, you'd be calm and slow. It was a visual that everyone could understand. *Calm, slow, Andy.*

Tom's eyes moved from Ms. Newton to the jury, trying to make eye contact with as many of them as possible. Then he positioned himself at a forty-five-degree angle between the witness chair and the jury box and looked at Wilma, who returned his glare.

"Ms. Newton, my name is Tom McMurtrie. Rick Drake and I represent Ruth Ann Wilcox." Tom grandly gestured with his arm at Rick and Ruth Ann. "You understand that we called you as a witness today, right?"

"Yes, sir."

"Now"—he rubbed his chin and looked at the jury—"why do you reckon we would do that?" His eyes remained locked on the jury. He had just broken two of his own cardinal rules. *Number one, never ask an open-ended question. Exception: unless the answer can't hurt you. Number two, never ask a question you don't know the answer to. Exception: unless it doesn't matter what the answer is, the question speaks for itself.*

"I don't know. I . . ." Wilma stopped.

"Maybe—oh, I don't know—because we thought you might say something good for our case."

"I don't know."

"You don't know." Tom was incredulous. "You must think we're stupid, Ms. Newton."

"Objection, Your Honor," Tyler stood. "Counsel is being argumentative and badgering the witness."

"Your Honor, I'm allowed a thorough and sifting cross-examination. I'm also allowed to question this witness's credibility."

"Overruled," Judge Cutler said.

Tom returned his gaze to Wilma. "Ms. Newton, if we had known you were gonna come in here and testify that the defendant was good to Dewey, treated Dewey well, and had Dewey on a reasonable schedule, why . . . we'd have to be out of our minds to put you on the stand, right?"

"Well . . ."

"Answer the question, Ms. Newton," Tom insisted.

"I don't know. Like I said earlier, Mr. Drake wanted me to say that Dewey's schedule was crazy, and I told him I wouldn't do it."

She was beginning to look a little flustered. Her face was turning red. *Good*, Tom thought. *Not getting under your skin, am I?*

Tom walked down the jury rail. He could tell all eyes were on him. *Cross-examination is about the lawyer. You're the star. You want the jury to be watching you. Paying attention to you.* He had preached it to his kids. Now he was doing it.

"You told him you wouldn't do it."

"Yes."

"And you were clear about it."

"Crystal," she said, glaring at Tom.

Tom walked all the way over to the counsel table and got within a few feet of Rick.

"So, let me get this straight. You told Mr. Drake . . ." Tom placed his hands on the counsel table and leaned to within a few inches of Rick's face. "I . . . will . . . not . . . testify . . . that . . . Dewey's . . . schedule . . . was crazy, right?"

"Well, I don't know if I was that—"

"Clear? You just said you were *crystal* clear, didn't you?"

Tom took a few steps away from the table toward Wilma. He was twenty feet away.

"Yes."

"You told him you would not testify that Dewey's driving schedule was crazy, right?"

Tom edged closer. Fifteen feet.

"Yes."

"You told him you would not testify that Dewey's schedule forced him to speed, right?"

Still closer. Ten feet.

"Right."

"You told him you would not say anything bad about Willistone, right?"

Five feet.

"Yes. That's right." Wilma had a scared look on her face.

"And you were *crystal* clear, right?"

Two feet.

"Yes."

"Yet, despite how crystal clear you say you were, Mr. Drake put you on the stand today."

The Professor had stopped walking and resumed the forty-five-degree angle between him, Newton, and the jury.

"Yes."

"Ma'am, is it not fair to say that if you were as crystal clear as you say you were with Rick Drake, then he'd have to be the dumbest person on the face of the earth to have put you on the stand." Tom's eyes turned to the jury. It didn't matter what the answer was.

"I don't know why Mr. Drake called me to the stand. I'm not a lawyer."

Tom saw the opening he was waiting for.

"What do you do for a living, Ms. Newton?" Tom saw that her face had turned red.

"I'm a waitress. At the Sands Restaurant in Boone's Hill."

"That's where your first meeting with Rick occurred, right?"

"Yes, sir."

"Now it wasn't just you and Rick in this meeting, was it?" Tom rubbed his chin.

"No, there was a woman with him."

Tom looked at the jury. "And her name was Dawn Murphy, correct?"

"I know her first name was Dawn. I can't remember her last."

Tom walked to the counsel table, reached inside his briefcase, and pulled out the face book he used when he taught his Evidence class.

"Professor, what are you doing?" Rick whispered, leaning his head over so that the jury couldn't see him. "Dawn—"

"I know what I'm doing," Tom whispered back. Then he returned to the witness stand.

"Forgive me, Ms. Newton, but I used to be a law professor, and Dawn Murphy was in my class. I want to show you a picture of her in the law-school directory so that I know we're on the same page." Tom pointed to Dawn's picture with the words "Dawn Murphy, twenty-six years old, Elba, Alabama" underneath it. "Is that the woman you saw with Rick Drake at the Sands Restaurant?"

"Yes, it is."

"Your Honor, we'd like Ms. Murphy's photograph admitted as Exhibit 1."

Once the photograph was admitted, Tom held it up and showed it to the jury.

"Ms. Newton, you talked with both Mr. Drake and Ms. Murphy here"—Tom gestured with his finger at the photograph—"about Dewey's schedules, correct?"

"Yes."

"And your testimony today is that you were *crystal* clear with both of them that Dewey's schedules were normal?" Tom asked, resuming his position in front of Wilma.

"Yes."

"Ms. Newton, if Dawn Murphy takes this witness stand and testifies that you told her and Rick Drake that Dewey's schedule at Willistone was 'hectic,' 'crazy,' and 'hard for him to meet,' would she be a liar?"

Wilma shrugged. "I didn't say those things. So . . . yes, she would be lying."

"This girl right here," Tom again held the photograph up for the jury to see. "If she tells this jury that you said Dewey was forced to speed to meet his schedule, would she be lying?"

"Yes."

"And if she says that you told her and Mr. Drake that you changed Dewey's driver's logs to make sure he met the ten-hour rule, would she be a liar?"

Wilma leaned forward in the stand. "Yes, sir."

Tom walked to the end of the jury railing, watching the faces of the people inside the box. He could tell they were all locked in.

"Ms. Newton, this meeting between you, Rick Drake, and Dawn Murphy happened back in February, correct?"

Wilma shrugged, and Tom saw the fatigue in her eyes.

"I think so. That was a long time ago."

Another opening.

"Ms. Newton, let's go back just a couple of weeks. Isn't it true that in the last two weeks you have spoken with Rick Drake on the phone a couple of times?"

"Yes."

"And during these phone conversations, Rick told you he was going to call you as a witness in this case, didn't he?"

"He might have. I don't remember."

"That was two weeks ago, ma'am. You sure you can't remember him telling you he was going to call you as a witness today?"

"I think I already knew by then he was going to call me."

Thank you, Wilma, Tom thought, walking to the counsel table. "Subpoena," he whispered to Rick, who handed him a folder. Rick also handed Tom his cell phone with a text message pulled up on the screen. When Tom saw it, he smiled. "Nice."

"That's right, Ms. Newton," Tom said, returning to the witness chair and slipping Rick's phone into his pocket. "By that time Mr. Drake had issued this subpoena, hadn't he?" Tom handed the subpoena over to Wilma.

"Yes."

"He had gone through the time, money, and trouble of having a Tennessee subpoena issued, requiring that you be here today."

"I guess."

"Your agreement to show up wasn't good enough. He thought you were such a good witness that he was going to ensure your attendance today, right?"

"I don't know what he thought."

"Your Honor, we'd like to admit the Tennessee subpoena requiring Wilma Newton's attendance here today as an exhibit."

"Any objection?" Judge Cutler asked, looking at Tyler.

"No, Your Honor." Tyler's voice sounded tired.

"Counselor, it's almost five. Are you about to wrap up?"

"Just a few more questions," Tom said. "Ms. Newton, let's go back to Sunday night. You sent Mr. Drake a text message then, didn't you?"

"I don't remember."

Tom took the phone out of his pocket and held it over his head, looking at the jury and then back to Wilma. Then he handed the phone to Wilma. "Does this refresh your memory?"

Wilma looked at the phone but didn't say anything.

"Ms. Newton, why don't you read what you wrote to Mr. Drake two nights ago to the jury."

"'I can't miss more than one day of work. What day do you want me to testify?'" Wilma read, speaking in a flat voice.

Tom, watching the jury, saw an elderly woman on the front row and a black man on the back row glaring at Wilma. *She's losing credibility*, Tom thought.

"That was your text message to Mr. Drake two nights ago," Tom asked, turning back to Wilma.

"Yes." She tried to sound nonchalant but her voice had a crack in it.

Blood in the water, Tom thought. *Time for the good stuff.*

"Ms. Newton, do you know Jack Willistone?"

Wilma's eyes widened slightly. "Of course. My husband worked for his company."

"That's right," Tom said, pointing to the defense table where Jack Willistone sat. During forty years of living in Tuscaloosa, Tom had met Jack Willistone several times, usually at fund-raisers for politicians whom both men supported. Jack had always struck Tom as disingenuous. A smart, analytical man playing the role of the loud-talking, good-old-boy redneck. To his credit, Jack did not appear rattled by being called out.

"Mr. Willistone is the owner of Willistone Trucking Company, correct?" Tom asked.

Wilma nodded. "Yes."

Tom smiled at the jury. "But that's not the only way you know him, is it?"

"I . . . I don't understand."

"Ms. Newton, when you're not waiting tables at the Sands, you have another job, don't you?"

"Yes," she answered, her voice clipped.

"Where?"

Wilma sighed, looking down. "The Sundowners Club. Right outside of Pulaski."

"I see," Tom said, now pacing down the jury rail so the jury could see Wilma better. "Is that a restaurant too?"

"No."

She was going to make him pull it out of her, and Tom could've kissed her for it.

"A bar?"

Now her look was angry. "There is a bar in the club, yes."

When he reached the end of the rail, he said softly, "What kind of club is it, Ms. Newton?"

"A dance club," she said.

Tom leaned forward a little and raised his eyebrows. *I'm gonna keep going,* he tried to convey with his eyes.

"An exotic dance club . . ." she continued, pausing before adding, "I'm a dancer there."

"And as a 'dancer'"—Tom made the quotation symbol with the index and middle fingers of both hands—"you take your clothes off and 'dance' for *customers* of the club, correct?"

"Your Honor, I object," Tyler said. "This questioning is clearly meant to harass and embarrass this witness."

"On the contrary, Judge," Tom said, looking at the jury, "this questioning goes straight to the heart of this witness's bias."

"Overruled," Cutler said. "Let's get to the bias part, Professor."

Tom paused, continuing to look at the jury. They were awake and alert. Listening.

"Ms. Newton, Jack Willistone is one of your customers, isn't he?"

Wilma froze, her face turning white. "I don't . . . I . . . wouldn't say that."

"You wouldn't?" Tom pressed.

"No."

"OK," Tom said, rubbing his chin for effect. "Well, let's go at it a little differently. Ms. Newton, who drove you to court today?"

Wilma's eyes widened. "Wha-what?"

"Objection, Your Honor." Tyler was off his feet, his face red. "What possible relevance could Ms. Newton's ride to trial have on this case?"

Tom never took his eyes off Wilma Newton as he responded. "Again, Your Honor, this questioning goes straight to this witness's bias."

Out of the corner of his eye, Tom caught movement in the galley, and he knew instinctively what was happening. A quick glance confirmed his instincts.

"Overruled," Judge Cutler said. "Get to it quick, Mr. McMurtrie. Everyone here is pretty tired."

"Ms. Newton, the man standing up and trying to get out of here—the one standing right behind Jack Willistone . . ." Tom paused. "Did he drive you to court today?" Tom pointed to a man about six foot four with stubble on his face wearing a golf shirt and khakis.

Wilma nodded, looking scared to death.

"You have to answer out loud, Ms. Newton," Tom said. Glancing, he noticed that the stubbly faced man had returned to his seat.

"Yes."

"Does that man work for Jack Willistone?" Tom asked, looking at the jury first, then at the stubbly faced man, and then fixing his eyes on Jack Willistone.

"I . . . I don't know."

"Didn't you spend several hours in the VIP room at the Sundowners Club two weeks ago with Jack Willistone and the man sitting behind him in the courtroom?"

Wilma Newton's face had turned chalky white. "I . . . I don't remember."

"You don't remember?" Tom almost laughed, loving the evasive response. "Do you know Peter Burns, Ms. Newton?"

"Yes." Her voice was barely audible.

"He's the bartender at the Sundowners, right?"

Wilma nodded.

"Would it surprise you to know that Peter remembers you going up to the VIP room two weeks ago for several hours with Mr. Willistone and the man who drove you to court today?"

Wilma looked down at her clasped palms.

"Has your memory returned yet, Ms. Newton?" Taking a step closer, Tom glanced at the jury. Every juror's eyes were open and alert. "You spent three hours in the VIP room two weeks ago with Jack Willistone and the man who drove you to court today, didn't you?"

Wilma finally looked up. "Yes, sir, I did."

Tom caught several of the female jurors moving their hands to their lips in surprise, and one male juror crossed his arms, his expression one of disgust.

"I'm a dancer, OK?" Wilma croaked. "I... I knew Mr. Willistone from when Dewey worked there. I was just doing my job."

"For three hours," Tom reiterated. "Two weeks before trial."

"Yes," Wilma said.

"That must have been quite a financial windfall. Though I don't know from experience... I hear those VIP dances are pretty pricey." Tom paused. "How much did Jack Willistone pay you?"

Wilma shrugged, again looking down. "I don't remember."

"Another memory loss. Well, Ms. Newton, I'm sure he paid you something for a three-hour dance, didn't he?"

"Yes, he paid me."

"He was a customer of yours that night, wasn't he?"

"Yes."

Tom nodded. "Isn't it also true, Ms. Newton, that the man sitting behind Mr. Willistone in the courtroom today has come at least once a week to the Sundowners Club for a VIP dance for the last three months?"

"Yes."

"And each time he's paid you."

"Yes, of course. He's a regular."

Tom looked at the jury. "And then this same man, this 'regular' as you call him—the man sitting behind Jack Willistone in the courtroom—drove you the four and a half hours to court today, correct?"

Wilma nodded. "Yes."

Tom held his eyes on the jury for several seconds. Then he looked at Judge Cutler.

"No further questions, Your Honor."

—

Rick watched the whole thing in awe. Wilma had been a trap set by Jack Willistone. *But the Professor blocked it. He suspected something, did the investigation, and turned it on them.* Rick shook his head as the Professor took the seat next to him. *But how? How could he do that in three days?*

"Mr. Tyler, are you going to have any questions of this witness tomorrow?" Judge Cutler asked.

Rick glanced across the courtroom, where Tyler was looking out the window.

"Mr. Tyler!" the judge bellowed.

Tyler turned his eyes to the judge and slowly stood. He looked at Wilma Newton for a second, then shook his head.

"I have no questions, Your Honor."

"Fair enough. The witness is excused. Members of the jury, it has been a long day and you've been very patient. We will start back up tomorrow morning at nine."

Cutler banged his gavel, and the sound of rustling filled the courtroom as people began to head for the doors. Rick turned to the Professor.

"How did you do that?"

Tom shrugged. "It was nothing really. After I processed everything you told me and reviewed the file, it smelled funny to me. I did some investigation."

Rick's eyes widened. "In *three* days?"

Tom smiled. "I had a little help."

Rick squinted and started to say something else, but the Professor held his hands up. "I'll tell you everything, OK? But let's get moving. Tomorrow is another day. We just bloodied their nose a little bit but the fight's not over. Tomorrow the jury's going to learn what Wilma Newton really told y'all. I set the jury up for it," Tom said, smiling. "I even showed them a picture."

Rick felt his stomach tighten. *Dawn.* "Professor, I don't think that's—"

"We have no choice, Rick. You heard His Honor. He's not going to let you testify, and we need someone to tell the jury what Wilma Newton really said. Dawn's our only option."

Rick nodded. "Professor, I have no idea where she is. What if we can't find—?"

"Don't worry about that," Tom said, turning from the table. "I have someone working on it, and . . . we will."

61

Jameson Tyler remained seated at the counsel table. Legs crossed, fist on his chin. Thinking.

"Mr. Tyler, you ready to go?" his associate, Clark McPheeters, asked. McPheeters had packed both their briefcases. "Mr. Tyler?"

"Yeah, Clark. Yeah. Tell you what," Tyler said, grabbing the keys out of his pocket, "why don't you go get the car and swing it around? Pick me up out front. I want to talk to Mr. Willistone for a second."

McPheeters smiled and took the keys.

Probably never driven a Porsche before, Tyler thought, but the usual egotistical pleasure he would have gotten from such a scene was gone. *Fuck me*, he thought, finally getting up from his seat.

When Tyler saw Jack Willistone outside the courtroom, his adrenaline shot up, and he didn't hesitate. He grabbed the big man by the collar and pushed him into the wall.

"I didn't need that today, Jack. We . . . we did not need that," Tyler said, seething.

Jack just smiled. "I don't want to hurt you, Barrister. So I'm going to ask nicely. Take your goddamn hands off me."

Tyler loosened his grip, and Jack pushed him hard, causing him to stumble several steps backwards.

"What's your game?" Tyler asked, quickly regaining his balance.

Jack smiled again. "Winning."

Tyler took a few steps closer to Jack, close enough where he could smell tobacco on the big man's breath and clothes.

"Mine too," Tyler said. "Mine too. But not like this."

"I don't know what you're talking about."

"Wilma Newton. You know damn well what I'm talking about. Bob Hawkins told me to stay away from you and let you handle Ms. Newton. But your John Wayne cowboy shit just about fucked us today. Now the jury thinks you might have paid Wilma Newton to testify. We don't need that kind of help."

Jack took a step closer. They were almost nose to nose.

"All that jury heard was that I paid for a long VIP dance." Jack laughed. "So I like looking at titties. So what? My company runs trucks through Pulaski, I was in the area, and I wanted to see some skin. Are you telling me you *really* can't handle that?"

"What about the *driver*? The guy who drove Wilma to the courtroom and who watched the VIP dance with you?"

"An old friend who lives near Pulaski. He likes titties too. I'm not sure why he drove Wilma to court—I was as surprised as anyone else to see him at court—but I bet it's got something to do with that diamond-shaped body part underneath her zipper. You ever driven four and a half hours for a piece of snatch, Tyler?" Jack paused, stepping closer. "Yeah, I bet you have. So that's the deal. That old man didn't prove nothing today."

Tyler stepped away, shaking his head.

"By the way," Jack continued, "what happened out there today, Tyler? I thought you were supposed to be the best lawyer in the state. A fucking Jedi. Darth fucking Vader. What in the *fuck* happened?" Jack asked, spittle flying as he spoke.

Tyler said nothing.

"I tell you what happened," Jack continued. "That old SOB whupped your ass." Jack paused and crossed his arms mockingly. "'I have no questions, Your Honor,'" he mimicked. "You choked, Tyler. First time this whole case you had to work a little bit, and you choked all over yourself."

Tyler had had enough. He walked toward Jack, stopping when he was a foot from him.

"You may be good at handling things, Jack, but *you*, not me, fucked up today. I didn't ask any questions because I couldn't fix your fuckup." Tyler turned to walk away, but then stopped and looked back. "And I am Darth Vader, you belligerent fuck."

As he walked away, Jack spoke once more, determined to get the last word.

"Then who was that old SOB? Yoda?"

"Yeah," Tyler muttered, not turning back. *Fucking Yoda.*

62

JimBone answered the phone on the first ring. It had been thirty minutes since he left the courthouse, and he was anxious as hell. The whole plan had been fucked, and he knew Jack was pissing bullets.

"Yeah, boss."

"Good job, Bone. Come by my house next Wednesday night around six thirty and I'll give you the rest of what I owe you."

JimBone couldn't believe his ears. *He doesn't even sound mad.* "Uh . . . OK. Your house six thirty next Wednesday. Sounds good. What about the bitch?" JimBone asked, winking at Wilma Newton, who sat in the passenger seat of the El Camino.

"Tell her to rent a car to drive home in and explain the deal to her. Explain what happens if she ever tells anybody. She doesn't get the other half of the money for at least a month. We have to wait for things to die down a little."

"Will do, boss."

"And Bone . . ." There was a pause on the other end of the line, and JimBone heard the exhalation of what he knew was cigar smoke. "We have to fix some of what the old SOB messed up. Remember the photograph of the girl he showed the jury?"

JimBone smiled. "I do indeed."

—

Wilma gazed out the window as JimBone completed his phone call with Jack Willistone.

"Sounds good, boss," JimBone said. "I'll handle it." He hung up the phone and looked at Wilma. "Well, well. Looks like you earned your keep, Smokey the Bear."

Wilma didn't immediately answer, continuing to look out the window. *It's over*, she thought. *It's really over. A hundred thousand more dollars. Was it worth it?*

"Hey, bitch," JimBone said. "I'm talking to you."

No. No. Never.

"Can we go home now? I'd really prefer just going home, but I'm sure what I prefer doesn't matter," Wilma said, continuing to stare out the window.

"No, it doesn't, Wilma," JimBone said, laughing. "You're not as dumb as you look."

"So what are we going to do?" she asked.

"You're going to rent a car and drive your sweet ass home, but"—he looked at his watch—"since the rental car places in T-town are probably all closed by now, I'm just going to drive you back to the hotel."

"What are you going to do?" Wilma asked.

JimBone reached into his jacket pocket and pulled out a pack of cigarettes. He lit one and took a long drag. Blowing smoke up into the ceiling of the car, JimBone chuckled.

"Don't you worry about that," he said, reaching into the backseat and retrieving a brown paper bag. "Here, I think you'll like this," he said, taking the bottle out of the bag and handing it to her.

It was a fifth of Gentleman Jack.

"That's a little higher quality than what we normally drink," JimBone continued. "Go ahead, take a swig. Hell, take several swigs." He reached across her, opened the dash, and dropped a pill box into her lap. "Just make sure you wash one of these down," he said, laughing.

"Not tonight, please." Wilma felt like crying. "I did what you asked me to do."

"Relax, Smokey the Bear. The Bone has work to do tonight. I just don't want you in the way." He winked at her and laughed louder. "Now take one of those pills before I force them down your throat."

She did as she was told, swallowing the pill and taking several nips from the bottle, concentrating on the feel of the liquid burning as it went down. Then she passed the bottle to JimBone.

"When am I gonna get my money?" she asked, watching him take a long swig.

"Owwww! Goddamn, that's good!" JimBone bellowed.

She had never seen him so excited, and it scared her. He gave her the bottle and tuned the radio to a country station.

"It's going to be about a month, but don't you worry. You'll get it. That old bastard fucked some things up, but the Bone's gonna make everything right tonight." He puffed on his cigarette.

She took another swig of the whiskey and started feeling the first inkling of a buzz. *God forgive me*, she thought as JimBone turned up the radio. It was George Strait's "Amarillo by Morning." One of Dewey's favorites. Dewey had loved old country.

She took another sip and the numbness began to really set in as the whiskey and the roofie began to work its magic. *What have I done?* Her mind tortured her with visions of the people she'd betrayed. She could see Rick Drake's unbelieving face. *You lied to me, you bitch*, he must've been thinking. Sweet Dawn Murphy, whom Wilma had called a liar. Did "making everything right" mean that JimBone was going to hurt her too? *Is there no end to my treachery?* Ruth Ann Wilcox, the poor woman who had lost her whole family. She had come to Henshaw looking for answers. For justice. *And I tried to steal it from her.*

Finally, there was Dewey. *The bastards ran him to death, and I helped them cover it up.* She took another sip—this time a longer one—and felt JimBone's hand riding up under her blouse and up her thigh. *I am Judas*, she thought, spreading her legs to allow better access. Numb all over.

God forgive me.

63

As the sun dipped below the horizon in Faunsdale, Doolittle Morris finally made it to Mule's bedroom. Slowly but surely Doo had gone through the whole house, stacking on the porch the furniture that was worth keeping—an old grandfather clock and a recliner—and leaving the rest where it lay for whoever bought the house when Doo sold it. Now all that remained was the bedroom. Stumbling through the door, Doo couldn't help but laugh when he saw the old silver boom box lying on top of the dresser on the far wall. "Goddamn," Doo said out loud, walking over to the boom box and seeing a cassette tape in the slot. The white cassette had yellowed over time, but Doo could still read the faded letters of the title. *John Anderson's Greatest Hits.*

Doo laughed again and took a sip of beer. After finishing the pint of Jack Daniel's, Doo had fortuitously found a six-pack of High Life in Mule's fridge, which he had killed half of already. He was drunk and ready to go, but he wasn't leaving until he finished the job. *Only going to do this once*, he kept telling himself. *One and done.*

Doo pushed the Play button on the boom box and waited to see if the damn thing still worked. When the sounds of John Anderson's "Swingin'" blared through the speakers, Doo let out a rebel yell and began to sing along.

The bedroom was basically barren. Other than the dresser, the only things in the room were a bed and a small table next to it.

Doo continued to sing as he sat on the bed and went through the top drawer of the bedside table. Nothing there, so Doo lowered his hand and opened the bottom drawer. His voice caught in his throat when he saw the worn leather Bible.

Doo set his beer on the table, reached into the drawer, pulled out the Bible, and ran his fingers over the leather. Softly, he opened the cover. When he did, several documents and photographs fell out. When he saw the first document, he let out a long sigh of relief. It was the deed to the house.

"Thank God," Doo said out loud. He had been worried he was going to have to go down to the courthouse to find the deed. The photographs were baby pictures of Mule's two girls taken while they were still in the hospital. Though Mule hadn't seen them much since his wife ran off, Doo knew that Mule loved his daughters very much. Feeling his eyes beginning to burn again, Doo started to close the Bible but stopped when he noticed a single piece of white paper jutting out in the middle. Doo put his finger on the paper and opened the Bible to the page where it had been placed. A passage of Scripture had been highlighted. Proverbs 5:22-23. "The evil deeds of a wicked man ensnare him; the cords of his sin hold him fast. He will die for lack of discipline, led astray by his own great folly."

Doo shook his head and unfolded the piece of paper.

"What the hell?" Doo said, not understanding. Blinking his eyes and trying to clear his head of the booze, he reviewed the document again. And then again.

When he finally got it, he felt the hair on his arms stand up.

"*I . . . will . . . be . . . damned.*"

64

"She's not here," Rick said, continuing to knock on Dawn's apartment door in vain.

Tom could hear the panic in Rick's voice, and he was beginning to feel it himself. It was getting late and they had been trying for hours to find Dawn without success. She had yet to answer her cell or home phone, and Rick and Tom had each called at least a dozen times. Now, as a last resort they had come to her apartment, and it also appeared to be a dead end. Peeking through the outside window, Tom saw that no lights were on, and neither Tom nor Rick had seen Dawn's car in the parking lot.

"I just don't get it," Rick said. "Where could she be? She's not here. She wasn't at the law school, and she's not answering her phone. I thought we'd at least find her mom here, but she's gone too. Everyone's freakin' disappeared." Rick banged his fist against the apartment door. "You said you had someone working on it. Have you heard anything?"

"Nothing," Tom said, checking his cell phone for texts. "Look, I don't get it either, but she has to turn up. I called the registrar of the law school on the way back into town, and she checked the records for me. Dawn is enrolled for summer school and went to class yesterday. She's here . . . somewhere."

Rick nodded and started to say something but was interrupted by the sound he'd been waiting two hours to hear. His cell phone was ringing. Feeling his heart clench, Rick ripped the phone out of his pocket and pressed the answer button. *Please be her.*

"Hello, Dawn?"

For several seconds Rick heard nothing on the other end of the line.

"Who is it?" Tom asked, stepping closer to Rick.

Rick shrugged his shoulders.

"Hello," Rick repeated. "Who is—?"

"They're going to kill her." The voice came out in a strained whisper, and Rick felt goose bumps break out on his arm.

"Kill who?" he asked, his voice also a whisper. More silence. "Kill *who*?" Rick repeated. *Who is this?* "Kill wh— ?"

The line went dead.

"Who was is it?" Tom asked.

"I don't know. A woman, I think. All she said was, 'They're going to kill her.' She obviously knew my cell phone."

"They're going to kill her?" Tom said, rubbing his chin.

"Yeah."

They looked at each other, both getting it at the same time.

"Oh, Christ," Rick said, his face going white. "Dawn . . ."

65

Dawn Murphy turned off the computer and gazed at the blank screen. It was almost midnight but she had finished the brief. Mr. Tomkins would be able to review and revise it tomorrow, which had been her goal. Sighing, she forced herself off the swivel chair and began turning off the lights in the office. After her debacle with Rick, she had called Daryl Tomkins at Tomkins & Fisher, and he had been thrilled to hire her back. She knew she was lucky to have a job but she didn't feel lucky. She felt depressed. Sad. Tired. And most of all, confused.

She knew this was the week of Ruth Ann's trial. There hadn't been any press coverage yet, but she remembered the date. She had wanted to call Rick and wish him luck. In fact, she had picked up the phone several times and started to dial the number, but she just couldn't go through with it. Not after all the things they had said to each other.

She opened the back door to the office and stepped out into the night. The parking lot was barren except for her white Mustang, and the only sounds she heard were the passing of cars on Greensboro a few blocks up. She shut the door behind her, putting the key in the dead bolt and twisting it.

"Kinda late for a pretty girl like you to be out."

Dawn turned to the sound of the voice, her stomach tightening into a knot. The lot was sparsely lit, and for a moment she didn't see him. Then, standing by her Mustang, she saw a tall man dressed in khaki pants and a golf shirt. As he stepped toward her, she noticed that his hair was sandy blond and he had a patch of stubble on his face.

"Can I help you?" Dawn asked, her voice shaky. She reached into her pocket for her cell phone but then remembered that the battery was dead. *Damn, damn, damn.* The man was in front of her now. He had continued to approach as if his appearance were completely natural. He smiled at her and extended his hand.

"Yes, Ms. Murphy," he said, squeezing her hand until she shrieked in pain. "You can help me a great deal."

66

Tom pulled the Explorer into the parking lot in front of Rick's office at just past midnight.

"Damnit," Rick said, his voice hoarse from fatigue.

After leaving Dawn's apartment, they had driven up and down McFarland and Skyland Boulevards, checking restaurant parking lots, the mall, and every other place they could think of. Nothing. Then they had moved to the strip on University Drive, walking in all the bars and restaurants there. Still nothing. Now they were downtown and dead out of options.

"Maybe she's out of town," Tom broke in. "That's better than . . ." Tom didn't finish, but he didn't have to.

Rick shook his head. "Why would she go out of town in the middle of summer school?"

Tom sighed. "I don't know." He closed his eyes. *Think, damnit. Think.* He looked at Rick. "Do you know if she's taken another job?"

Rick shrugged, looking down at the floorboard. "Like I said, I haven't talked to her since she quit. I have no idea. But"—he snapped his fingers and jerked his head up—"she clerked at Tomkins & Fisher last summer. Maybe—"

But his words were drowned out by the sound of screeching tires as Tom floored it out of Rick's parking lot. Tomkins & Fisher was on Second Street. Three blocks away.

Please be there, Tom thought, looking at the clock on the dash. 12:13 a.m. It was so late. The trial would crank back up in less than nine hours, but Tom wasn't worried about the trial or the case.

Please be all right.

67

JimBone Wheeler couldn't believe his luck. After dropping Wilma off at the hotel, he had picked up Dawn's tail just before dark while she was leaving her apartment. He had followed her here but had been forced to wait, because there were video surveillance cameras inside both the front and back doors of the law office. Now, nearly five hours later, the parking lot was empty, Dawn Murphy was alone, and there was no sign of the Drake kid or anyone else. *Better to be lucky than good*, JimBone thought, wrapping his hand around Dawn's mouth with a chloroform-drenched paper towel as she tried to twist away from him.

The knife was in his jeans pocket. He could stab her, take her purse, and leave, and it would be a job well done. But where was the fun in that? Besides, why would someone just kill a pretty thing like Dawn Murphy? She was beautiful. Young. Sexy. Dawn stopped writhing as the chloroform did its magic. JimBone looked down at her face, unable to contain his smile as he thought of the fun he was about to have.

Beautiful, young, sexy women didn't just get killed for money. They got raped. Sodomized. Brutalized. Then, only after having been properly defiled, were they killed, rumpled up in a garbage bag, and thrown in the river.

She'd be just another hot-to-trot coed killed by a crazed pervert. JimBone followed the news. A killing like this happened in college towns all the time. Or at least enough not to raise too many eyebrows.

JimBone had parked on the curb on the street adjacent to the parking lot. There were no streetlights. No way anyone could see him unless they were looking for him. *Just too easy*, he thought as he carried Dawn's body up to the El Camino. He opened the door and was about to push her into the car when pain engulfed every part of his body.

Someone or something was squeezing his testicles. *Son of a . . .*

JimBone grabbed for his crotch, but then his face was pressed into the windshield. Howling in pain as his balls were squeezed together, JimBone felt hot breath on the back of his neck.

"Hurts, doesn't it?" a deep male voice said as the pressure intensified.

JimBone tried to elbow the man, but it was no use. The man was too strong. JimBone reached into his pocket for the knife, and the pressure on his balls suddenly eased. Turning on a dime, JimBone lunged with the knife, missing badly and sprawling on the pavement. When he got up, a pistol was pressed into his forehead.

"Hasn't anyone ever told you not to bring a knife to a gunfight?"

"Jesus Christ," JimBone said, looking at the man, who was as tall as him and black as the ace of spades.

"No, dog. Bocephus Haynes. You're as far from Jesus as you're ever gon' be."

JimBone gulped, then turned his head as tires screeched behind Bocephus. Bocephus also turned, taking a couple of steps back. When he did, JimBone's survival instincts kicked in.

And he ran.

"I don't think so, motherfucker," Bocephus screamed after him, and JimBone heard the sound of the gun firing up in the air.

JimBone Wheeler never looked back.

—

"She's OK!" Bo yelled, calling over his shoulder and pointing back at Dawn, who was crumpled against the side of an old El Camino.

Tom and Rick reached Dawn at the same time, and Rick knelt down and placed the side of his head on her chest.

"She's breathing," he said, looking up at Tom.

Tom stepped back and looked in the direction where Bo had been running.

"Wait here, Rick."

Tom ran back to the Explorer and put it in gear. After a couple of minutes of driving, he caught up with Bo, who was running at a dead sprint and approaching the bridge that connected downtown Tuscaloosa to downtown Northport.

Underneath was the Black Warrior River.

"Jesus," Tom muttered.

He saw another man stepping over the railing of the bridge. Bo was fifteen yards away. Ten. Five.

Bo lunged for the railing.

"Bo!" Tom yelled out the window of the car. But Bo was too late.

The man on the bridge jumped.

68

"I can't believe you kept following him," Tom said, looking across the booth at Bo, who was as pissed as Tom had ever seen him.

"I can't believe I let him get away," Bo said, tapping his knuckles on the table in disgust.

They were at the Waffle House on McFarland. Both of them had a cup of coffee in front of them. Rick was out in the Explorer with Dawn, who had just come to a few minutes before, while Powell Conrad paced back and forth across the tile floor, talking furiously into his cell phone.

"I don't care if they're off tonight, Sheriff, we need more people searching the banks of the river," Powell yelled into the phone, causing Tom to chuckle with pride. His former students were showing off tonight.

Tom squinted across the booth at Bo. "So when did you find her?"

"'Bout five minutes before y'all got there. I checked every law office downtown for a white Mustang hatchback and finally saw it just after midnight." Bo paused, taking a sip of coffee. "You still need the bartender, Burns?"

Tom shook his head. "No, we don't need Burns to testify anymore, because Wilma Newton admitted to everything he was going to say. Send him home."

"So the cross went well?" Bo asked, his face breaking into a grin.

Tom shrugged. "It probably could've gone better."

"Aw, don't play that poor-mouth routine with me, dog. You nailed it, didn't you?"

"It went pretty good," Tom said, smiling. "I couldn't have done it without your help, Bo. The stuff you dug up from the Sundowners Club was golden. I can't thank you—"

"No need for that now. You coming back is thanks enough for me. Now, when are we going after the school?"

Tom smiled. "First things first, Bo. We got a trial to win."

"Well, it looks like you'll have your star witness tomorrow," Bo said, nodding toward the front door.

Tom turned to see Rick leading Dawn by the arm toward them.

Dawn blinked as her eyes adjusted to the lights. She held tight to Rick but looked at Bo. "Thank you so much, Mr. . . ."

"Haynes," Bo said. "Bocephus Haynes."

"Yeah, thanks again, Mr. Haynes," Rick said, extending his hand, which Bo shook.

"No problem," Bo said, standing from the booth. "Now I understand that Ms. Murphy here is going to play a major role in a trial that starts in about"—Bo looked at his watch—"seven hours, so I'm going to leave y'all to it. Professor, let me know if you need anything else." Bo started to walk away, and Tom called after him.

"Bo?"

Bo turned at the door, a tired smile on his face.

"You gonna stick around?"

"I'm always around, dog."

Bo winked and bowed slightly. Then he turned and walked out the door.

For a moment there was silence as all three of them watched through the glass windows as Bo strode to his car. Even Powell, continuing to blare instructions through his cell phone, stopped pacing and watched Bo walk away.

"Thank God for him," Rick said, turning to face Tom. "You sure picked the right guy to help."

Tom just nodded. Any debts that Bocephus Haynes had ever owed him had been paid in full. *And then some.*

"Is somebody gonna tell me what's going on?"

Dawn's groggy voice startled them, and Tom and Rick both turned to her. Dawn wrinkled her eyebrows, looking back at each of them and then down at the table. Rick's eyes also went to his coffee cup.

This is awkward, Tom thought. It was the first time the three of them had ever been together.

"Yes, Ms. Murphy," Tom finally said. "But first there's something I need to say." Tom paused, searching for the right words. "I owe you both an apology. Ms. Murphy, you got caught in the school's plans to force me out, and they used you as a pawn. Our interactions were entirely innocent, but because of the way things looked, the board was able to spin it into something it wasn't. I'm sorry for the embarrassment the allegations have caused you. I'm also sorry for instructing you not to tell Rick that I was paying you to be his law clerk. I should've known the truth would eventually come out. I was trying to help Ruth Ann and Rick without sticking my own neck out there. For that I'm sorry." Tom stopped and turned his eyes to Rick. "And Rick, I—"

"Save it," Rick interrupted, his voice harsh. Tom's stomach tightened, and for a second he feared that he had made a mistake in rehashing the situation.

"You came back today," Rick continued. "If you hadn't walked in the courtroom when you did, the case would have been toast." Rick paused and looked Tom in the eye. "You put your neck out there today, Professor. Whatever issues there were between us are water under the bridge." Rick hesitated and then turned his head to look at Dawn, who met his gaze. For a moment neither of them spoke, and Tom could feel the energy of the feelings between them.

"I'm sorry about the things I said," Rick started. "I—"

"You're forgiven," Dawn broke in, "if you forgive me for not telling you about my arrangement with the Professor."

Rick smiled. "Done."

Again they just looked at each other, and Tom looked away, wanting to give them their moment.

"But y'all still didn't answer my question," Dawn finally said, turning to face Tom. "What is going on? Why did someone try to kill me tonight?"

Before Tom could answer, Powell Conrad plopped down in the booth, slamming his cell phone on the table. "Well, folks, after a whole lot of encouragement, the Sheriff's Office and the city police department have every available deputy searching the river right now. If the bastard ain't dead, we'll get him. And if there's a link to Willistone, we'll find it."

"Nice work, son." Tom said, hearing the fatigue in his voice. *We have got to get some rest*, he realized.

"Will somebody pleas—" Dawn started, but her exasperated voice was drowned out by Tom.

"Wilma Newton changed her story today," Tom said, slowly rising from his seat. "We called her to the stand, and she said her husband's schedules were fine and that he was never forced to speed. She said he never doctored his logs to meet the ten-hour rule."

"But she told us those things," Dawn said. "I was there."

"I know," Tom said, smiling down at her. "And tomorrow the jury is going to know. You are our first witness in the morning. Look, people, tomorrow is going to be a long day." Tom slapped his hands together and looked at each of them before zoning in on Rick. "We have to counter Wilma with Dawn, and then we have to be ready for Jameson. You can bet his folks will be singing the same song Wilma did today, except with more force behind it. Plus he's got an expert and we don't." Tom paused. "We've got to fix that."

"How?" Rick asked, also standing.

Tom smiled. "I don't know . . . but I've got an idea. For now, though, we need to get some rest. And given what's happened already, I think we should stick together. Let's all go to my house. It's probably dusty, but it'll do for the night."

"Good idea," Powell chimed in. "I could probably arrange for an officer to watch—"

"No," Rick said, cutting Powell off and turning to Tom. "Whoever the man that tried to kill Dawn is, he probably knows where we all live here. If he survived the fall, then he'll come back for more. An officer won't stop him."

"Well, son, do you have another suggestion?" Tom asked.

Rick nodded. "Yes, sir, I do."

69

JimBone made the call from a pay phone in Northport at six the next morning. His clothes were still wet, and his testicles were so sore he could barely walk. *Fucking nigger bastard*, he thought, already planning his revenge. He had heard of the great Bocephus Haynes, Pulaski's only black trial lawyer. And he was certain that Mr. Haynes would hear from him again. But first he had to break the news.

The phone picked up on the first ring.

"Well?" Jack Willistone said, forgoing a greeting. Even at the break of day, Jack sounded alert and irritated.

"No dice, boss. I about had her in the car, but Drake and the old geezer showed up before I could get away with her."

"Jesus Christ superstar," Jack muttered. "Did they see you?"

"I . . . I'm not sure. There just wasn't enough time to set it up," JimBone said.

Silence filled the line. JimBone knew to keep his mouth shut and not to apologize.

"OK, Bone. Just be at my house next Wednesday."

JimBone smiled, relieved that payday was still going forward. "Will do, boss."

—

Jack Willistone slammed the phone down and began to pace the floor of the kitchen. It wasn't like JimBone to fail. No one could account for the old SOB's surprise yesterday; even Jack had been caught off guard by that. But nabbing the girl should have been easy as pie. *Must've been out of his control*, Jack thought. Then he shook his head. It didn't matter. Failure was failure. *Bone will be taking a pay cut. He just doesn't know it yet.* Jack sighed and gazed through the bay window to McFarland Avenue below, where he could still see the remains of the Ultron plant. He knew there wasn't anything else he could do.

Buck Bulyard was dead. Dick "Mule" Morris was dead. Willard Carmichael and Wilma Newton were bought and paid for. The Ultron plant and the documents it held were ashes and dust, and Faith Bulyard had been "handled." *So what if Murphy testifies? Taking her out was just added insurance. Newton's testimony is out there, even if it is tainted, and there's nothing sweet little Dawn Murphy can do to take it away.*

Jack smiled and lit a cigar. *Murphy is irrelevant. With what we've done, Tyler should be good enough to either win outright or keep the verdict below the policy limits.*

Jack blew a smoke cloud in the air and chuckled softly.

Either way I win and the merger goes through . . .

70

As the sun began to rise over the cotton field, Rick walked out onto the porch. Billy Drake leaned against the railing, holding a twelve-gauge shotgun. Three packs of birdshot were lying in a box on the ground beneath him. Behind his father, Rick noticed that a hunting rifle and a .38-caliber pistol were leaning against both rocking chairs.

"Got enough ammunition?" Rick asked, handing Billy a mug of coffee and taking a sip from his own.

"I think we'd manage pretty good. He'd have to bring a pretty big posse to get past this porch."

Rick nodded and drank some more coffee.

"I'm glad you patched it up with your teacher," Billy said. "I always liked him. He played for the Man."

Rick knew that his father had been offered a scholarship to play football for Bear Bryant but had turned it down. Billy Drake hadn't gone to college. Instead, he'd taken over the family farm at the age of eighteen, when his own father died of a heart attack.

"I like the girl too," Billy said, chuckling. "And I can damn sure tell that you do."

Rick turned his eyes from the rising sun and gazed at his father. "Is it that obvious?"

Billy just smiled. Rick smiled back. For several minutes neither of them spoke as the sun made its gradual ascent over land that had been in Rick's family for almost a century.

"Dad, I don't know how to thank you," Rick said, his voice thick with emotion. "I . . . really didn't know where else to turn."

"No need for thanks," Billy said, fixing Rick with eyes that would pierce glass. "You did right coming here, Rick. You're my son and this is our land." Billy turned his gaze out over the railing. "God have mercy on the poor son of a bitch who declares war on us."

71

At 8:55 the next morning, Powell Conrad was waiting in the lobby, pacing the floor and listening on his cell phone as Trish Ball droned on about the investigation of the Black Warrior River.

"They been calling every fifteen minutes like you asked, but there's nothing so far. Those boys been up all night and are wanting to know if they can quit or if you still want to drag the river."

Powell sighed. *Bastard probably got away.* Peeking through the small window on one of the double doors, he saw Dawn Murphy sitting at the witness stand and the Professor rising to his feet.

"Just tell them to stop, Trish."

"OK, what about—?"

"I got to go, Trish. We're starting back up here."

He hung up the phone and began to head into the courtroom.

"Hey, boy."

Powell turned at the sound of the voice. Doolittle Morris glared back at him, wearing navy-blue overalls over a khaki work shirt and chewing on a toothpick.

"You need to tell your secretary that it's OK to give out your cell phone for emergencies," Doo said. "You may have just cost me ten dollars' worth of gas."

"Doo?" Powell squinted at the man. "What are you doing—?"

"Got something for you," Doo said, taking a folded piece of paper out of the pocket of his overalls. "Went over to Mule's yesterday to clean his house out. Found this in the boy's Bible." Doo unfolded the piece of paper and handed it to Powell. "Mule musta thought it was important else he wouldn't a put it there."

Powell glanced down at the page. When he saw the title, the date, and the names, his heart almost stopped. "I'll be damned."

"That's what I said," Doo chimed in. "Worth the gas, then?"

Powell looked up at him, still not believing what he was holding. "Doo"—Powell turned to look back through the double doors—"this might be worth a whole goddamn gas company."

72

"You were working for Ms. Wilcox's attorney, Rick Drake, at the time of this conversation with Wilma Newton, correct?"

Jameson Tyler wasn't even completely out of his seat before hurling his first question on cross, and Dawn cringed.

"Yes," she said, trying to sound composed. *Just relax*, she told herself.

She knew the Professor's direct had gone well, with Dawn hitting all the high points of the conversation with Wilma—Dewey's schedule forced him to speed, Jack Willistone checked the driver's logs himself, and Wilma helped Dewey doctor the logs to make it look like he was within the ten-hour rule. *That was easy*, Dawn thought.

Now came the hard part. Jameson Tyler was tall, handsome, and his eyes shone with intensity as he walked toward her like a tiger stalking his prey. It was hard not be intimidated, but Dawn knew she had to be strong.

"So you were paid to be there that night, right, Ms. Murphy?"

"Right."

"But you were being paid by Ms. Wilcox's other attorney, Tom McMurtrie, correct?"

Dawn felt heat on her neck. *How could he possibly know that?* "Yes."

"Whom you were also having an affair with, correct?"

"Objection, Your Honor," Tom said, bolting to his feet. "The question has no relevance and is meant to harass the witness."

"The question," Tyler began, looking at the jury before meeting the judge's eye, "goes straight to this witness's bias, Your Honor. The defense is entitled to the same *thorough and sifting* cross-examination as the plaintiff."

"Overruled," Cutler said. "Answer the question, Ms. Murphy."

"No." Dawn said. "That is a lie."

"Oh, really?" Tyler said, smiling. "Ms. Murphy, you read the *Tuscaloosa News*, don't you?"

"Sometimes."

"Remember seeing your picture on the cover of it with the headline 'Student Believed to Be in Inappropriate Relationship with Professor Revealed'?"

"Yes, I remember seeing that picture, but those allegations are not true."

"Isn't it true, ma'am, that you're just here trying to help your boyfriend out?"

"What?"

"Oh, come on, Ms. Murphy. You honestly expect this jury to believe that you're here out of the goodness of your own heart?"

"Objection, Your Honor," Tom said. "Counsel is arguing with the witness."

"Overruled," Cutler said, a hint of impatience in his tune. "Get on with it, Mr. Tyler."

"Which is it, Ms. Murphy? Are you here for money or love?"

There it is, Dawn thought, remembering the Professor's instructions: *answer the leading questions firmly with denials. But if he ever gives you an open-ended question, let . . . him . . . have . . . it.*

Dawn glared at Jameson Tyler. "Let me tell you why I'm here, Mr. Tyler. I'm here to tell the truth about what I saw and heard when Rick Drake and I interviewed Wilma Newton. I haven't been paid a dime to be here and I've *never* had a relationship with Professor McMurtrie other than as the Professor's student assistant and as Rick Drake's law clerk. I—"

"Ms. Murphy, I'm going to stop you right there," Tyler interrupted, his voice for the first time losing its arrogant, sarcastic tinge. "Now—"

"Oh, no, you're not," Dawn said, standing up from the witness chair. "You asked me why I'm here, and I'm going to finish my answer. *You*, Mr. Tyler, have made false allegations about me and the Professor for three months. The truth is you have no proof whatsoever that I had an affair with the Professor, because there is none. But you're trying to mislead this jury by continuing your lies."

"Your Honor, may I approach?" Tyler asked, walking past Dawn to the bench.

He was smiling but his face had gone pale.

The Professor was right. He's got no comeback, Dawn thought.

"We'd ask that you strike Ms. Murphy's answer for being unresponsive," Tyler said, his voice hurried and frustrated. "Her comments about me are clearly irrelevant."

The Professor cleared his throat, smiling. "Your Honor, I objected when counsel started down this road on the basis of relevance and you overruled my objection." He paused, and his smile vanished. "Respectfully, Judge, Mr. Tyler asked for the tongue lashing he just received. The witness's testimony should stand."

Cutler hunched his shoulders and looked down at the bench, then back at Tom. "You're saying he opened the door to it."

Tom nodded. "That's exactly what I'm saying."

Cutler turned to Tyler. His gaze was unsympathetic. "I agree with the Professor . . . er . . . Mr. McMurtrie. The witness's testimony will not be stricken. Move on to something else, Counselor."

Jameson Tyler blinked but he didn't say anything. He looked at Dawn and then back to his own counsel table, where his associate looked like he'd tasted something bad.

"I . . ." Tyler stammered and grabbed the index finger of his right hand. He looked at the jury and smiled.

He's got nothing, Dawn thought.

". . . have no further questions."

—

Rick was stunned. *That's it? He got nothing. Plus Dawn made him look like a bully.*

"Redirect, Mr. McMurtrie?" Cutler asked, looking at the Professor, who had just made it back to the table.

"No, Your Honor."

"OK, then, the witness is excused."

Dawn stood and walked past the counsel tables. She kept her eyes straight ahead, not looking at Rick or Tom, and Rick felt a pang in his heart. *She doesn't want the jury to see her smiling at us*, Rick knew. Still, he couldn't help but feel sad. *Am I gonna see her again?*

"Ladies and gentlemen of the jury," Cutler said once Dawn had exited the double doors in the back of the courtroom, "we are going to take a one-hour lunch recess. Please return to the jury room at one o'clock."

Rick was out of his seat the minute Cutler's gavel hit the bench. *Please still be here*, he thought, bursting through the doors and looking in both directions for Dawn. When he saw her standing next to Powell, relief flooded his body.

"Hey—" Rick started to say, but Powell cut him off.

"Dude, you're not going to believe this," Powell said, thrusting a sheet of paper in front of Rick.

Rick looked at Dawn, but she was pointing at the page.

"You have to read it," she said, her eyes wide with excitement.

Rick looked down. The top of the page had the blue and red logo of Ultron Gasoline. Underneath the logo the title of the document read "Bill of Lading." It was dated September 2, 2009. There were six columns underneath the title. "Cargo: nine thousand gallons. Loaders: Carmichael, Morris. Driver: Newton. Location: Montgomery. Time of delivery: 11:00 a.m. Time of pickup: 9:57 a.m."

All of the information on the document was typed except the time of pickup, which was stamped. The stamp was red, so the document had to be original.

"Where did you get this?" Rick asked, looking up at Powell.

"Doolittle Morris came by the courthouse this morning and gave it to me. Said he found it in Mule's Bible, where Mule kept important documents."

"Holy shit," Rick said, looking at Dawn. "Mule never mentioned he had the actual bill of lading, did he?"

She shook her head. "He never said he had any documents, but . . . didn't he say he might send you something in the mail?" She smiled. "A little extra butter—"

"On the bread," Rick finished, slapping his hands together. "You're right!"

"What's wrong?"

Rick turned at the sound of the voice, and the Professor was standing behind him.

"I think we just found the smoking gun," Rick said, handing the document to Tom.

The Professor reviewed it quickly and his eyes widened. "Holy . . . shit," Tom said, whistling.

Rick laughed. "I know."

"It's no good to us if we can't put a witness on the stand to authenticate it," Tom said, his voice sober. He looked up and turned the document around so Rick could see it. "We'll need to find the records custodian and . . . we'll need to find her fast."

Tom pointed to the bottom of the page, where, in a smaller font than the rest of the document, was the following sentence: "I certify that I received this bill on the date above." Underneath the sentence was a signature line, below which was the typed title "Records Custodian." Above the line was a signature written in blue, original ink. The handwriting wasn't great, but Rick could make it out. Even if he couldn't have read it, he knew who it was. Who it had to be.

She told us, Rick remembered. *She signed every one of them.*

73

Faith Bulyard sat on a stone bench in Central Park, eating a Mickey Mouse ice cream bar and watching the boys throw the football. It was a beautiful but hot summer day in New York, and Faith could feel sweat pooling in her belly button underneath her tank top. Every so often, out of habit she'd reach into her front pocket for her cell phone, but it wasn't there. She had turned the damn thing off and left it at the hotel. *Good riddance*, she thought, watching her boys. The only people in the world she cared about were right here with her, and the only person who would be wanting to reach her this week was Jack Willistone.

Faith bit into the chocolate Mickey Mouse ear and closed her eyes, relishing the sweet, comfortable taste. It was Wednesday afternoon. They had two more days in New York and then it was back to reality.

"Hey, Mom," Junior said, pointing at a couple who were walking toward them.

Junior was snickering and Faith looked at the couple, noticing that they were both men and were holding hands. Their T-shirts read "Celebrate Pride Weekend."

"Look, Danny. Queers."

The words hit Faith like a punch to the gut.

Both boys continued to giggle as the two men walked past the bench. Faith tried not to watch but she couldn't help herself. Her husband had been like these men and she hadn't known it. They'd been married for twenty-five years.

"Can you believe those rope suckers?" Junior said, walking over to Faith, his brother right behind him.

Again, Faith's stomach tightened as if she'd been punched. *Rope sucker . . .* She'd only heard that term used once before in her life: *"Unless you want your boys to know their daddy was a rope sucker, I suggest you never, ever talk with the lawyers you just met with again."*

"They really flaunt it here," Junior continued. "Like being a rope sucker is just as natural as—"

"Don't you *ever* call them that again," Faith said, surprising herself with the anger she felt. She was shaking. "You can call them gay or homosexual, but do not make fun of them—do you understand, young man?"

"Mom, what's the—?"

"Don't you 'mom' me. You promise me you'll *never* make fun of another homosexual person, male or female, again."

When Junior didn't say anything, Faith pointed her finger at him. "Promise me now."

"OK, jeez, I promise. What's got into you?"

"I'm your mother," Faith said, still shaking. Her ice cream was dripping down her closed fist but she didn't care. She was going to make this point if she had to beat it into them with a sledgehammer. "When you act like an ignorant brat, I'm going to tell you. Homosexuals are people too, and the Bulyards don't make fun of people, do *both* of you understand?" She peeked around Junior to Danny, who was staring back wide-eyed.

"Yes, ma'am," both said at the same time.

"Good," she said, feeling light-headed.

She plopped back down on the bench, opened her fist, and gazed at the remains of her melted ice cream, which had dripped onto her shorts.

"Mom, are you OK?" Danny asked.

Faith looked up into the boy's innocent eyes. Behind him, Junior's face blushed crimson with shame. Faith hadn't yelled at either boy at all since their father's death. Lip trembling, Faith tried to speak but the words wouldn't come. All she could think about was the text that Jack Willistone had sent her at the airport.

It's never gonna stop, she thought. *I can turn my phone off and pretend it will be over soon, but it won't be. Jack Willistone will never turn loose of an advantage. Buck knew that. That's why Buck . . .*

Faith wiped her eyes but the tears came anyway. She had long suspected that Buck might have taken his own life. That Jack had threatened Buck with the same evidence he'd shown Faith, and Buck had decided to walk into an inferno rather than have to deal with the repercussions. She had listened to Buck's 911 call a million times, and it just didn't sound right to her. Buck was smart. He wouldn't just barrel into a fire to save a building. He didn't love Ultron that much.

But he loved his boys . . . She could still remember the photographs Buck kept of Junior and Danny in his car, which she now kept in her own. *The boys worshipped him and he them. He took his own life so they wouldn't have to be ashamed of him.*

"Mom, why are you crying?" Danny asked, sitting beside her.

Junior continued to stand but moved closer and put his hand on her shoulder.

If Buck died to protect their memory of him, don't I owe it to him and them to keep his secret? she thought. She pictured Jack Willistone's arrogant face. *That's what he's counting on.*

"Mom, I'll never make fun of another gay person as long as I live," Junior said. His eyes were blue like his father's, but his voice carried more command.

He is so strong, Faith thought. *He's basically raised his brother for me these last seven months, while I—*

"Danny never will either, right, Danny?"

"Right," Danny said.

Faith looked at both her boys. Her strong boys, whom she was trying to protect. And then she thought of Jack Willistone, holding Buck's sexuality over her head for the rest of her life. *He thinks he can control me. He thinks he has me checkmated.*

"What's wrong, Momma?" Danny asked.

Faith looked at him. Danny had her own brown eyes, and he was a good-natured, happy-go-lucky boy. He was also very concerned about always looking cool. He hadn't called her Momma in five years.

Hearing the words seemed to break Faith out of her spell. She stood up from the bench and felt the sun burn into her back. For seven months she had been numb, feeling nothing. Now she felt everything. She was hungover, sunburned, and sticky from ice cream and sweat. She felt uncomfortable to the point of misery and yet . . .

. . . she felt better.

"Momma . . ."

Danny stood next to her, and the words soaked into her body like hot chicken noodle soup. God, it felt good to hear those words.

"Nothing's wrong, sweetie," Faith finally said, turning to Danny and placing her hand on his cheek. "Momma's just fine. Let's go back to the hotel."

—

Thirty minutes later they were back in the hotel room, and the boys turned on the TV. Faith lay on the bed and stared at the ceiling, thinking. Stretching her arms over her head, she smelled her own body odor and almost gagged. Then she glared hard at her cell phone. For a second she reached for it, but then just as quickly she stopped and got off the bed. Seconds later she was shutting the bathroom door and turning on the tub. She had a lot of decisions to make and a lot of thinking to do.

But first she needed a bath.

74

Rick entered the courtroom at exactly the same time as Judge Cutler. It was 1:00 p.m. on the dot, and he had unsuccessfully tried to reach Faith Bulyard for the last hour. Even worse, Dawn and Powell had driven to her house in Northport and found no one home, nor any sign of her.

"Any luck?" the Professor asked as Rick took his place beside him.

"Nothing," Rick said, feeling unsteady on his feet. Things were happening too fast.

"Counsel, call your next witness," Judge Cutler directed from the bench.

Rick looked to the Professor, whose entire demeanor registered perfect calm.

"What are we gonna do?" Rick asked. "We're out of witnesses and we can't find Faith. Like you said, the bill of lading is worthless if we can't put Faith on the stand to authenticate it. Your cross of Wilma and Dawn's testimony this morning saved us from getting killed, but we need something substantive. We can't win this case with just Newton's speed, because Ms. Rose's statement that Bradshaw pulled in front of the rig cancels it out. It's a wash, and that's all the Wilma fiasco was. A wash." Rick rubbed his forehead. "Professor, we have to get that bill in front of the jury."

"I know," Tom said. "Look, I have a plan. Just trust me, OK?"

Rick sucked in a breath as the Professor stood.

"Your Honor, at this time we'd like to offer a certified copy of Harold 'Dewey' Newton's driving record from the Alabama Department of Public Safety," Tom said, standing and delivering a copy of the exhibit to the judge and then another to Tyler. The driving record showed Dewey Newton's two speeding tickets in the six months prior to the accident.

Rick exhaled, grateful that the Professor was here. In the wake of Wilma's testimony, the chase for Dawn last night, and trying to find Faith Bulyard, Rick had forgotten all about Dewey's driving record.

"Any objection?" Cutler asked, darting his eyes to Tyler.

"No, Your Honor."

"Very well, the document is admitted. Counsel, call your next witness."

Rick's stomach tightened into a knot. *We don't have a next witness.*

"Your Honor, the plaintiff rests," Tom said, and Rick could hardly believe his ears. *How can we rest? We've finally got a document that helps us. We just need a recess so we can find Faith and get her down here.*

"Professor . . ." Rick whispered, but Tom ignored him.

"Are there any motions the defendant would like to bring at this time?" Cutler asked, looking to the defense table, where Tyler was already standing and walking toward the bench. At the close of the plaintiff's case-in-chief, it was customary for the defendant to make a motion for judgment as matter of law.

"Yes, Your Honor," Tyler said, and Tom also started to approach. Rick followed and grabbed the Professor's forearm. "Professor . . ."

Tom turned and put his arm around Rick, whispering slowly into his ear, "You're just going to have to trust me, son."

75

Wilma Newton awoke to the sound of knocking.

"Housekeeping!" a female voice said.

Wilma tried to get up but couldn't. "Come back later," she managed.

She rolled over and felt a wave of nausea. She was on the floor of the hotel room, her arms cradled over the telephone. *What the hell . . . ?* She let go of the phone and tried to stand but she was too weak. The room began to spin, and she grabbed the side of the hot tub. She again tried to stand, but the nausea was too much and she puked in the tub.

"Damn. Damn," she said out loud.

She looked around, trying to get her bearings. JimBone was gone. *Good.* She looked at her knees, which were red and partially skinned. Then she glanced back at the phone, which still lay on the floor below the bedside dresser. She closed her eyes and saw a fleeting vision of herself rolling off the bed and crawling on the carpet toward the bedside table, reaching for the phone. She had known JimBone would try to kill Dawn and had wanted to warn

Rick. *Did I get him?* she wondered. She couldn't remember and wasn't even entirely sure she had made the call. Everything was a blur. *Please let her be all right*, Wilma prayed.

After several dry heaves she tried to stand. When she did, another rush of nausea came over her. This time she made it into the bathroom. After puking for several more minutes, she ran some water at the sink and looked in the mirror. *Whiskey and roofies apparently don't mix well*, she thought, looking into her swollen eyes and feeling disgusted and ashamed. She barely recognized herself. *Who the hell am I?*

She walked out of the bathroom. The bed was unmade, but she could still see the note. It was lying on a pillow like a mint left by housekeeping.

You talk. You die.

Despite how weak she felt, she managed to laugh. *Man of few words that JimBone.* Crinkling up the note, she stood and saw her figure in the mirror facing the bed. She felt her lip starting to quiver and tried to hold it in.

She had been raped. Beaten. Broken.

And bought. She let go and the tears came. It was over.

Finally.

76

"So let me get this straight, Mr. Willistone," Tom began, taking his customary stance at a forty-five-degree angle between the witness stand and jury box.

Tyler's motion for judgment as a matter of law had been denied, and Jack Willistone, Tyler's first witness, had just testified on direct examination that Dewey Newton was supervised appropriately and that Dewey's driving schedules were within DOT guidelines.

"On September 2, 2009, Willistone Trucking Company knew that Dewey Newton had received two speeding tickets in the past six months while trying to make deliveries on time."

"Yes," Jack responded without hesitation.

"Armed with that knowledge, Willistone Trucking Company put Mr. Newton on the road that day."

"Yes. Two tickets in seven years is an acceptable driving record."

Jack remained calm and matter-of-fact.

Tom walked across the courtroom and stood behind Ruth Ann's chair. "And while on the road that day, Dewey Newton had an accident that killed Ruth Ann Wilcox's entire family." Tom let his eyes move to the jury, then back to Jack.

"Yes, there was an accident. Mr. Newton also lost his life."

Jack was appropriately somber. Tom nodded, then walked slowly back to within a few feet of the jury railing. *Time to throw the curve.*

"It takes about an hour and a half to get from Tuscaloosa to Montgomery on Highway 82, doesn't it, Mr. Willistone?"

Jack wrinkled his brow. "I . . ."

"You're familiar with that route, aren't you?"

Tom was taking a chance here but not a big one. He could prove this fact with another witness. But it would be more effective later if Jack would give it to him.

"Well . . . yeah," Jack said, his brow still furled. "That is a standard run for our crew."

"Takes an hour and a half, doesn't it?"

Jack shrugged. "'Bout that. Give or take five minutes either way."

"You couldn't do it in an hour, could you?" Tom asked.

Jack glared at Tom, the two men locking eyes. For the first time in the examination, Jack Willistone looked put out. *I know something you don't know*, Tom tried to say with his eyes.

"Are you asking me if it's possible?" Jack asked, recovering and forcing himself to chuckle.

"That's exactly what I'm asking," Tom said, glancing at the jury. "For example, let's say a driver decided to go eighty miles an hour the entire way. He could make it then, couldn't he?"

Jack shrugged. "I don't know."

Tom looked at the jury for effect, and he could tell they were all listening. "If Dewey Newton had to make it to Montgomery in one hour from the Ultron plant in Tuscaloosa, he'd have to go over the speed limit of sixty-five miles per hour, wouldn't he, Mr. Willistone?"

Jack folded his arms across his body. "That's not what happened here, but, hypothetically, the answer to your question is yes."

"Dewey was going eighty at the time of the accident, wasn't he?" Tom pressed.

"According to the officer," Jack said, nodding.

"According to the *sheriff*, Mr. Willistone. You're not telling this fine jury in Henshaw County that Sheriff Ballard was wrong in determining Dewey Newton's speed, are you?"

"No," Jack said. "That's not what I'm saying."

"And if the schedule you put a driver on forces him to speed, then you've violated DOT regulations, haven't you?"

"Well . . . yes, but Dewey's schedule was fine."

Tom glared at Jack, pausing for effect. "Yet on September 2, 2009"—Tom lowered his voice—"at the time of the accident that killed Bob Bradshaw, Jeannie Bradshaw, and two-year-old Nicole Bradshaw . . ."

Tom's voice was now just above a whisper, his eyes locked on the jury.

". . . Dewey Newton *was* speeding, correct?"

"Yes."

Tom kept his eyes on the jury, making eye contact with several of them. "I have no further questions, Your Honor."

—

Jack's body tingled with adrenaline as he walked back to the defense table. It had been a long time since Jack had faced off against a man who had shown no fear in his presence. This man—this Tom McMurtrie—was different. Jack could see it in the son of a bitch's flat eyes. He had come after Jack. Challenged him. Still, what bothered Jack wasn't his own performance during McMurtrie's examination but the questions themselves. *The only reason the bastard asks those questions is if he's got something else. He's setting us up.*

As Judge Cutler banged his gavel to announce a break, Jack, as gracefully as possible, stood from the table and walked out the double doors of the courtroom into the lobby. He dialed the first number before the doors closed behind him.

It was time to circle the wagons.

77

Tyler's accident reconstructionist, Eugene Marsh, was the next witness for the defense. Marsh's testimony was short, sweet, and effective.

Based on Rose Batson's testimony that the rig was a hundred yards from the intersection of Limestone Bottom Road and Highway 82 at the time the Honda began its turn, Bob Bradshaw should've seen the rig and not pulled out in front of it. Even with Newton's speed, Bradshaw caused the accident by pulling into the intersection.

Rick could barely watch. When Ted Holt told him that it was impossible to say whether Bradshaw could've seen the rig, Rick had doubted that Tyler could find an expert. *Never doubt Jameson Tyler*, Rick thought, ashamed that he hadn't at least tried to get someone else once Tyler disclosed Marsh. *I didn't have the money*, Rick pointed out to himself. He could've disclosed Holt, but what would that have accomplished? *Tyler's hired gun says it's our fault, and our guy's not sure. Win for Tyler.*

Rick sighed and glanced down at his phone. He had turned the volume to silent, but the screen showed no missed calls or texts. Faith Bulyard still hadn't responded, and it was getting late in the day. *She has to have heard my messages by now,* he reasoned. Neither Powell nor Dawn had texted either, so they must not be having any luck. *We have to find her,* Rick thought, squeezing his hands together. *We have to.*

As Tyler smiled and said, "No further questions," Rick turned around, hoping he might see a smiling Powell or Dawn walking through the double doors. Instead, all he saw was a mass of people. The galley was now completely full, and there were a few people standing near the back. *What's going on?* Rick wondered. Though this was his first jury trial, he knew that most trials were not attended by an audience. Several of the faces looked familiar. Law students that he'd seen roaming the halls, one of whom nodded at him. There was also Professor Burbaker, who taught property law, and Albert Sweden, the Cumberland School of Law trial team coach. Rick even thought he saw the judge from Birmingham who had come down in the fall to judge one of their practice trials.

This is crazy, Rick thought, turning around as the Professor strode toward Eugene Marsh.

—

This is crazy, Tom thought, genuinely shocked by the crowd that had filled the Henshaw County Courtroom. But it wasn't just the number of people—it was who they were. Judge Art Hancock sat in the third row from the front. The Cock was looking sporty, with a golf shirt and khaki pants. He also wore a smile, winking at Tom and shooting him a thumbs-up. Next to him sat Rufus Cole, who wore a suit a size too small and had his arms crossed. Rufus nodded at Tom and mouthed, "Kick his ass," pointing at Tyler. Tom forced himself not to smile.

There were numbers of others he recognized. Former students. Professors both current and former, including Will Burbaker, who had last seen Tom doubled over the sink in the men's room. Dean Lambert was there, but he averted his eyes when Tom glared at him. There was also a line of reporters, including the young lady who had interviewed Tom the day he was forced out.

The best, though, standing at the very back of the courtroom and leaning his six-foot-four-inch frame against the double doors, was Bocephus Haynes. Bo eyed Tom, and then his mouth broke into a humorless smile. It was the smile of a predator whose prey was near. "I'm always around," Bo had said, and he had meant it. Tom nodded at his friend, and Bo gestured to the witness stand. Then he formed a zero with the index finger and thumb of his right hand. This morning Tom had called Bo with one final assignment. And as usual Bo had delivered.

Let's do this, Tom thought, turning toward Eugene Marsh and feeling the energy in the room.

They're here to see me, he told himself. *Some want me to fail. Some want me to succeed. And some are just curious. But they're here to see if this old dog has anything left*. Tom felt a twinge of pain in his abdomen. *I'm overdoing it*, he thought. In the bathroom during the last break, he had seen a trickle of blood. He knew he should call Bill Davis, but now wasn't the time. *Now it's time to kick ass*. Tom took a deep breath. *Calm . . . slow . . . Andy . . .*

"Mr. Marsh," Tom said, his voice booming to the back of the courtroom. "Your opinion came with a price today, didn't it?"

—

Tom spent fifteen minutes covering every aspect of Marsh's payment arrangement with Jameson Tyler and the Jones & Butler firm. Marsh was making three hundred dollars an hour and had already collected twenty thousand dollars prior to the trial starting. He stood to make ten thousand dollars for his testimony today.

"So you're giving a thirty-thousand-dollar opinion—correct, Mr. Marsh?" Tom made eye contact with Sam Roy Johnson, who made a whistling gesture with his mouth. It was an obscene amount of money for an expert.

"That's how much I charge, yes."

"Now Mr. Tyler contacted you through the National Trucking Association. Is that correct?"

"Yes."

"You are one of the association's recommended experts, right?"

"I . . . guess."

"And that's because all you do is testify for trucking companies, correct?" Tom asked, looking out at Bo, who nodded.

"Well . . . I . . ."

"You've given testimony in how many cases, Mr. Marsh?"

Marsh shrugged. "Maybe thirty."

"And in every single one of those cases, you either found that the trucker was not negligent or that the other driver was contributorily negligent, correct?"

"I don't remember," Marsh said.

Tom glared at the bastard. "You've *never* testified against a trucking company, have you, Mr. Marsh?"

Tom motioned for Bo to walk down the aisle. Bo did as he was told and handed Tom a list of cases and a deposition transcript.

"Forty-two total cases," Bo whispered. "All for trucking companies. This deposition was taken three months ago. Page forty-seven, line fifteen, he testifies he's never given an opinion against a trucking company. *Stick this up his ass.*"

Tom turned to Marsh, who still hadn't answered the question, his eyes alternating between Tom and Bo.

"Mr. Marsh, are you going to answer the question?" Tom asked, striding toward him with the deposition in hand. "Surely, you haven't forgotten your testimony in the *Hockburger v. Swift Trucking* case from only three months ago?"

"I . . . don't understand."

"Isn't it true, Mr. Marsh," Tom boomed, slamming the deposition transcript onto the stand in front of Marsh so that he could read the highlighted language, "that you have never testified against a trucking company?"

Marsh gazed down at the transcript and then back at Tom. "Yes, that's correct."

Tom walked back to Bo. "How many for Tyler?"

"Three."

Tom turned back around. "And three of those times you have testified for Jameson Tyler and the Jones & Butler law firm?"

Marsh looked unsure of himself and scared. "I think that's right."

"And they paid you each time, correct?"

"Yes."

"How much did they pay you in those other cases?"

Marsh shrugged and looked down at his hands. "About the same."

Tom looked at the jury. "So you've made about a hundred twenty thousand dollars on the Jones & Butler nickel. Is that correct?"

"Something like that."

Tom let the answer hang in the air for several seconds. A hundred twenty thousand dollars was probably more money than half the jury collectively made in a year. Tom had made his biggest and best point. *Now time for the setup.*

"Mr. Marsh, you'd agree that visiting and understanding the accident scene is very important to coming to your opinion, correct?"

Marsh smiled, relieved to have the subject changed. "Yeah, probably the most important."

"And you've testified to going out to the scene three times to look at it, correct?"

"Yes."

"In your whole life"—Tom spread his arms wide—"you've only been to the intersection of Limestone Bottom Road and Highway 82 three times, correct?"

Marsh wrinkled up his face in confusion. "Well, yes, I—"

"No further questions."

78

"Your Honor, the defense rests," Tyler said as Eugene Marsh stood from the witness stand and left the courtroom.

Tom was not surprised. *Jamo is keeping it simple*, he thought. *Marsh gives him contrib, and Jack Willistone testified that the schedules were appropriate. Unless we can locate Faith Bulyard, all we've got on negligent supervision and training is two speeding tickets.*

"Very well," Judge Cutler said. "Members of the jury, it is almost five o'clock, so we are going to recess for the day. We will start back at nine in the morning."

Cutler nodded at his bailiff, who escorted the jury out of the courtroom.

As they filed out, Tom wondered where they stood right then. *Are we winning? Losing? Is it a dead heat?* It was impossible to tell from the looks on their faces. They all just looked tired.

When the jury had all exited the courtroom, Judge Cutler lowered his gaze to the counsel tables. "Counsel, please approach."

Once Jameson, Tom, and Rick were in front of him, Cutler looked over their shoulders to the crowd that remained in the courtroom despite the jury's adjournment. "Gentlemen, it appears that this case has garnered some public attention. I'll advise each of you not to discuss the facts of this case with the press until after the trial. Is that understood?"

"Yes, Your Honor," all three attorneys said at basically the same time.

"Mr. McMurtrie, will the plaintiff be calling any rebuttal witnesses in the morning?"

Tom paused, glancing at Rick. The answer to this question was yes, but he didn't want to give Tyler any information he didn't have to.

"We may, Your Honor," Tom said. "We will be deciding that question tonight."

Judge Cutler frowned but didn't say anything. Tom knew that Cutler might press a younger attorney like Rick for a clearer answer, but the judge didn't seem to know how to handle Tom. *That's an advantage I hope to exploit tomorrow*, Tom thought.

"OK, is there anything more to take up tonight?" Cutler asked, yawning into his fist.

"No, Your Honor," Tyler said.

"No, Your Honor," Tom repeated.

"All right, then, we're adjourned till tomorrow at nine."

—

Tom quickly made his way through the crowd, shaking hands with the people he knew and telling the reporters that he'd have no comment on anything until after the trial. When he finally made it to his car, he saw a familiar figure leaning against the hood.

"So you decided to take the Cock's advice," Judge Hancock said, smiling and extending his hand, which Tom shook.

"Just helping out an old friend and a former student."

"Right," the judge said, chuckling. "None of this is for you."

Tom finally smiled. "Maybe a little."

Judge Hancock slapped Tom on the back. "Well, I'm glad to see it." The judge took a couple steps away, then turned back. "And I'm not the only one, buck. You see this?" The judge had been holding a folded newspaper under his left armpit, and he handed it to Tom.

"State Legend 'The Professor' Trying Trucking Case in Henshaw County." Above the title was a photograph of Tom and Coach Bryant that had been taken a couple years before the Man's death during a reception at the law school to honor Tom's first national championship.

"Five months after his forced retirement and subsequent disappearance," the article began, "Professor Thomas Jackson McMurtrie, defensive end on Coach Paul 'Bear' Bryant's 1961 national champions, founder of the trial program at the University of Alabama Law School, coach of three national championship trial teams, and author of *McMurtrie's Evidence*, has emerged in Henshaw County, trying a trucking case with former student Rick Drake."

Tom skimmed the rest of the article, which described the nature of the case, Tom's dramatic appearance Tuesday during the cross-examination of Wilma Newton, and Tom's strange partnership with Rick Drake, "a student partly responsible for the Professor's forced retirement."

Tom raised his eyes from the paper and met the Cock's eyes.

"This has got some folks pretty stirred up," the judge said. "You saw the crowd today?"

Tom nodded. "They weren't all friends."

"Most were." Hancock paused and looked down at the ground. "I've been a judge in Jefferson County for forty-five years, Tom. I've *never* traveled to another county just to watch a trial. Never until today." He smiled again. "And you know what?"

"What?"

"I'll be here tomorrow too."

"Well, I doubt anyone else will," Tom said.

"You're wrong, buck. Like I said, what you're doing here, coming back after all you been through, has got folks stirred up. That article was positive. Reverent even. You're the Professor, goddamnit, and I think the news and the general public have started to realize it." The judge walked away but then turned back and squinted into the setting sun. "And so have your friends." He paused. "You know, sometimes a man can be so consistently good that people take him for granted. I remember another man kinda like that. Coached football and wore a houndstooth hat." The Cock nodded. "People will come tomorrow, Tom. Rest assured . . . *people will come.*"

—

"What was that all about?" Rick asked, reaching Tom just as Judge Hancock began walking away. Rick had stayed behind to iron out the jury instructions with Tyler's associate.

"Just an old friend wishing us luck," Tom said, trying to refocus, a little overwhelmed by the Cock's words of support. "You get the jury instructions worked out?"

Jury instructions comprised the law that Judge Cutler would read to the jury after closing arguments, just before the jury was given the case to decide. Alabama had published a pattern set of jury instructions for negligence cases, and Tom had been involved, along with a panel of four other lawyers and judges, in drafting them.

"Yeah, nothing unusual. Just sticking with the patterns. You should recognize them pretty well." Rick smiled, but he looked exhausted and stressed.

"You OK?" Tom asked.

"We still haven't found Faith Bulyard. I've left her at least a dozen messages on her cell phone." Rick sighed. "Powell and Dawn spoke with several of her neighbors, and one of them thinks she may have taken her kids on a trip. Wherever she is, she may not have cell phone service. I—"

"If we don't get the bill of lading in, it's not the end of the world. It . . ." But Tom stopped. He didn't want to sugarcoat things. "It would sure help, though. It would make Jack Willistone look like a liar and kill all of his credibility. It would also make Dawn's version of what Wilma Newton said at the Sands ring true."

"I know," Rick said. "I know . . ."

He hung his head, and Tom patted his shoulder.

"Just stay after it. She probably just has the phone turned off or is spending the afternoon at a place where her signal is weak."

Rick nodded. "I hope that's it."

For a moment neither man spoke. They were both dog tired, but there was a lot of work to be done tonight.

"You think tomorrow will be it?" Rick asked.

Tom shrugged. "Hard to say for sure, but probably. If Faith shows up, we'll be calling two rebuttal witnesses. Then post-trial motions and closings. Still, I think there's a good chance we'll finish."

Rick raised his eyebrows in confusion. "*Two* rebuttal witnesses?"

Tom smiled. "That's right," he said. "I made a stop on the way to trial this morning, and we have a little surprise in store for Jameson tomorrow."

79

An hour after the trial had adjourned, Jack Willistone pulled into the drive-through of a Burger King half a mile from the Ultron plant in Montgomery. After ordering, he paid in cash and came to a stop at the curb by the back exit of the restaurant. He flashed his lights, and five seconds later a man he didn't recognize opened the front passenger-side door and sat down next to him. Another man opened the back passenger-side door and stuck a small handgun in the stranger's side. Jack looked in the rearview mirror at the man in the back, and JimBone Wheeler, wearing a crimson Alabama hat over his now-bald head, nodded. Then Jack eased the car out of the parking lot.

"Willard Carmichael, I presume," Jack said, not looking at the stranger.

"Y-y-yes, sir."

"Willard, has anyone contacted you about testifying in a trial this week?" Jack asked.

"N-n-no, sir. Like I told him"—Willard cocked his head toward the backseat—"no one's called me or talked to me since that boy came up a few months ago and asked questions. Your man back there nearly killed me after that, and I haven't heard nothing from nobody since."

Jack continued to drive, turning left onto a dark street with several trailers lined up adjacent to each other.

"Why we going down my street?" Willard asked, his voice and legs shaking.

Jack laughed, and Bone joined him. "I've seen the pictures of your wife, Willard. What's her name?"

"Sally," Bone said.

"That's right, Sally," Jack said. "Like the song." Then he sang the chorus to Eric Clapton's "Lay Down Sally," his voice booming in the car.

Bone laughed, raised the gun, and stuck it in the back of Willard's head.

Jack pulled into a gravel driveway and cut his lights. The beige trailer had a couple of lights on, and a VW bug was parked out front.

"Please, mister, I swear no one's called me," Willard said, his teeth chattering.

"Nice trailer," Jack said. "You think Sally's in there making dinner for you and Lindsay?"

"Please . . ." Willard repeated.

"Did you keep any documents from the Ultron plant in Northport before it burned to the ground?"

"What?"

Jack slapped Willard with the back of his hand. "I'm *real* busy, Willard. I'm not going to repeat myself all night. Did you keep any documents from the plant?"

"No," Willard said, rubbing his nose. "I swear to God, no."

"What about Mule? Did he keep anything?"

"I . . . I don't know. I—"

"I think I'm gonna take Lindsay," Jack said, turning to look at Bone. "Haven't had a virgin since high school. You take Sally, all right?"

"Fine by me," Bone said. "Want to kill him now or make him watch?"

"Please, I swear I don't know nothing. You'll have to ask Mule if he took anything. I—"

"Mule is dead," Jack said. "Had a tragic car accident." Jack turned and glared at Willard. "At trial today the lawyer for the family asked some questions that sounded like he knew the time when Dewey picked up the load. Since all the documents are gone and Mule is dead, the only person he could have gotten that information from is you. Now, before I have you strapped to a chair and force you to watch me take your only daughter's virginity, I want you to tell me how in the hell that lawyer could know anything about the pickup time or delivery time of that load."

Willard Carmichael began to cry.

"Willard, crying ain't gon' stop me from busting Lindsay's cherry."

"I've told you everything I know," Willard said, sounding resigned. "I don't know how anyone could know anything about that load. I didn't keep no documents, and I haven't talked to no one."

Jack made eye contact with Bone, who shrugged.

"Kill me," Willard said, his voice almost monotone. "Please, shoot me before you go in there. I—"

"I don't think that's going to be necessary, Willard. You've convinced me. But . . . if I find out you're lying, I think you know what the consequences will be, don't you?"

"Yes, sir," Willard said.

Jack eased the car forward, and Willard let out a relieved sob.

Three minutes later they were back at the Burger King.

Jack parked in the back and looked into the rearview mirror. "Keep him out of sight until I tell you otherwise."

Bone nodded, and Jack turned to face his terrified passenger. "Willard, our mutual friend in the back is going to be keeping you company until the trial is over. If you do exactly what he says, everything will be fine. If you don't, then business in the Montgomery County Coroner's Office is going to be up by three. Understand?"

"Yes, sir," Willard whined, his hands shaking as they reached for the door handle. "Can I go now?"

Jack nodded, and Willard climbed out of the car, with Bone close behind. Before the door closed shut, Jack had his cell phone out.

There was just one more thing to take care of.

80

Faith was surprised when she heard her cell phone ringing. *When did I turn it back on?* she wondered, sitting up from the bed and wiping the sleep from her eyes. She gazed at the bedside table, confused it wasn't where she had left it.

"Boys, where's my—?"

"Here," Danny said, bringing it to her. He and Junior were busy playing the in-room Wii, which was one of the amenities this hotel had to offer. "I turned it on to see if it had any games, but they all sucked."

Faith's heart caught in her chest. *He's been in my phone,* she thought. *Could he have seen the texts from Jack?* Suddenly alert, she looked at Danny but saw no signs of agitation or anxiety. *All he did was check the games.*

"Aren't you going to answer it?" he asked as the phone rang for the third time. "You need to check your messages too. You have, like, ten."

Faith barely processed Danny's last comment as she pressed the answer button.

"Hello."

"Hello, Faith." Jack Willistone's familiar voice chilled Faith's entire body.

"What do you want?" Faith asked.

"I want to confirm that you're in New York, where you should be. In thirty seconds I'm going to call the hotel where I told you to stay. If you don't answer, then all the videos of Buck the gay porn star get released."

The phone clicked dead in her hand, and Faith shook with anger. *Who does he think he is?*

Thirty seconds later the in-room phone began to ring, and Faith picked up. "Satisfied?"

"Very," Jack said, chuckling. "Has anyone contacted you regarding the trial in Henshaw County?"

Something Danny had just said tickled at Faith's brain, but she couldn't remember it.

"No. I haven't heard anything."

"You promise?"

"Yes. Why? Why the hell are you so worried about me anyway? I told you all I did was stamp documents and store them. I don't remember anything, and all the documents burned in the fire."

"Just covering all my bases, Faith dear. No one has contacted you, correct?"

Faith heard a loud beeping sound and she looked at the cell phone on her bed. The light had come on, and Faith glanced down at it. The voice message symbol had "10" next to it, and she also had three text messages and twenty missed calls. *What the hell?*

"I haven't spoken to anyone," Faith said, still gazing at the phone.

"Good," Jack said, and Faith heard what sounded like relief in Jack's voice. *What's going on?* "If someone does call, you call me immediately, you understand? Your sons' memory of their father depends on it."

"I know what's at stake."

"You better."

When the phone clicked dead, Faith grabbed the cell phone and held her finger over the voice mail notice.

"Mom, we're hungry," Junior said. "It's almost eight o'clock. Can't we go somewhere?"

Faith gazed back at the phone. *Jack wouldn't have called if he wasn't worried*, she thought. Ten messages and twenty missed calls. *He knows someone is trying to reach me.*

"Come on, Mom, get dressed," Junior pressed.

"If you listen to all those messages, we might as well order room service," Danny said.

Sighing, Faith turned the phone off and set it back on the dresser. *What good would it do to hear them? Whatever it is*, she thought, *I'm not going to do anything.*

She grabbed a sundress from the closet and walked to the bathroom but stopped at the door to look back at her boys. "Why don't we go to Little Italy tonight?"

81

Wilma got home about 8:00 p.m. All she wanted to do was kiss her girls on the forehead and go to bed, but when she pulled in the driveway she was met by a surprise. Ms. Yost's car was not there. The house was dark—not a single light was on. *What's going on?*

She parked in the driveway and quickly walked to the front door, fumbling in her purse for the keys. She finally got the door opened and turned the light on. There on the coffee table was a note. She ran to it, a sense of dread coming over her. When she picked it up, she held it for a split second before reading. *Please, God. Don't let anything have happened to my babies.* She could see JimBone's face. *Please.*

She began to read.

Dear Wilma,

I have tried for some time now to find justification for your actions. But I can no longer stand by and watch you do this to your children. I knew you were a stripper. People talk, you know.

I didn't approve, but I wasn't going to cast stones. A couple of weeks ago a lady from church said she'd heard you were a prostitute. I didn't want to believe. Then I heard that message on your answering machine. I left it for you to hear.

With a heavy heart I have reported you to DHR. Your kids are now in the custody of the county. Jackie doesn't know. She thinks she's on a field trip. But Laurie Ann is devastated. I'm sorry, but I had to tell her. I hope that you will change your ways.

I know it doesn't seem so, but I'm your friend, Wilma. I'm doing this for your children. I hope that one day you can be with them again.

With love,

Carla Yost

Wilma was numb. *No. It was all for them. Everything. All of it. For them. Not me. Them.* She walked back to her bedroom and saw the blinking light on the answering machine. *No.*

She pushed it. "You have one saved message," the monotone message voice said. "Received 10:30 p.m. Monday."

"Monday? What was I doing . . . ?" Wilma closed her eyes, thinking of all the roofies he had forced her to take. The long blackouts. *No.*

The message began with static. Then his voice.

"Ah, God, Wilma this is so good. You. You are so good."

It was JimBone. She could hear panting in the background. Then a low moan. She recognized the sounds as her own. But she couldn't remember.

"My God, woman. Now you better beg for it. Come on now, bitch. Beg."

She could hear a thud and knew it was the back of his hand hitting her head.

"Fuck me," her own voice whined from the machine, slurring the words.

"Damn. Damn! Wilma. You are one good whore. Come on now, bitch. You're being paid top dollar for this dick. Let me see your best. Don't pass out on me."

She heard laughing and more panting. Then his voice again.

"Since you won't remember any of this, sweet Wilma, I'm leaving you a little reminder of the greatest couple of nights of your life. Courtesy of the Bone."

Click.

—

She must've lain on the bed for two hours without moving. Crumpled up in the fetal position. Slowly whispering, "No. No. No. Nothing for me. Everything for them. Nothing for me. Everything for them." At some point she lost control and started sobbing. Crying so hard she thought her heart would stop. Finally, she got up and walked over to her dresser. She pulled the pistol out of the top drawer and slowly loaded it.

What comes around goes around.

She knew it was true. Your actions eventually catch up to you. She took off all her clothes and turned on the overhead light in the bedroom. Then she looked in the mirror and pointed the pistol at her head.

You deserve this. You fucking earned it, you whore.

Then she closed her eyes.

And pulled the trigger.

82

When Rick hung up the phone, his face told the story.

"Still nothing?" Tom asked.

"Nothing," Rick said, his face ashen and his eyes bloodred. "What are we going to do? Without Faith the plan doesn't work."

Tom rubbed his chin and glanced inside the courtroom, seeing the bailiff walking out of Cutler's chambers. They had run out of time.

"Whether it works or not, we have to follow it," Tom said, opening the door. "We can't wait."

"ALL RISE!"

The courtroom was again filled to capacity. As he walked down the aisle, Tom kept his eyes straight ahead, forcing himself not to look. His stomach was starting to hurt on a regular basis but he ignored the pain.

As Judge Cutler strode into the courtroom, Tom calmly placed a copy of the bill of lading on Tyler's table.

"We plan to introduce the original today as part of our rebuttal," Tom said. "We were given it yesterday afternoon by Dick Morris's cousin."

Tyler glanced at the document, but if he was surprised by it he didn't show it. *Never let them see you sweat*, Tom thought, admiring his former friend's cool.

"It's too late to be surprising us with documents, Professor," he said. "You'll never get it into evidence."

"Really? Well, I have a lot of surprises in store for you today, Jamo," Tom said, smiling. "And I've got a little bit of experience with evidence."

Tom turned away just as the judge was seating himself behind the bench.

"Mr. McMurtrie and Mr. Drake," the judge said, looking at them. "Are you going to be calling any rebuttal witnesses?"

Tom felt a rush of adrenaline as the judge met his eye. "Yes, Your Honor. Yes, we are."

"Very well, call your next witness."

Tom looked at the jury, who all appeared alert and ready to go. Then he glanced at Tyler, who was going over the bill of lading with his associate. *Time for the next surprise, Jamo*, Tom thought, his heartbeat racing. He nodded at Rick for the go-ahead, and his young partner rose to his feet and spoke in a voice that carried to the back of the courtroom.

"Your Honor, the plaintiff recalls Ms. Rose Batson."

83

As Rose Batson walked down the aisle, Jameson Tyler put a sticky note on the bill of lading and handed it to his associate.

"As subtle as you can, hand this to Mr. Willistone," Jameson said, trying to keep his voice steady.

If they get that document in, the case is over, he thought. *Pickup at 9:57 and due in Montgomery by 11:00. If that bill is legit, then Newton had to speed to make it on time. And we lose. We lose big.*

Tyler turned to watch Rose Batson take her seat at the witness stand. *Why the hell is he calling her again?* he wondered, feeling uneasy. This was not how he had envisioned the morning going. He had thought he'd be moving for judgment as a matter of law right now and getting the negligent training and supervision claim thrown out. Now it appeared that the Professor and Drake might have found the smoking gun on negligent training and supervision and . . . *Rose Batson is about to testify? Again?*

Tyler smiled at the jury as if he didn't have a care in the world, but he had begun to sweat underneath his starched dress shirt.

What in the hell is going on?

—

Jack Willistone forced himself not to laugh. *"What the fuck is this?"* had been scribbled in blue ink on the yellow sticky note, underneath which was the bill of lading for Dewey Newton's fateful trip. Jack had never actually seen the bill but knew what it was. Yes, it was bad, and under normal circumstances the document would destroy them. *But these aren't normal circumstances*, Jack thought. *These are the circumstances I have created.*

The bill of lading was stamped and signed, as all bills of lading at the Tuscaloosa Ultron plant were, by its records custodian, Faith Bulyard. *Who happens to be in New York City right now and ain't coming back.*

Jack smiled and scribbled his reply to the sticky note.

"Piss in the wind."

84

"Ms. Batson, how long have you worked at the filling station at the intersection of Limestone Bottom Road and Highway 82?" Rick asked, gesturing to the jury so that Ms. Rose would direct her answer to them.

Last night, after disclosing his "stop" at Ms. Rose's store and his idea to recall her to the stand, the Professor had insisted that Rick conduct the examination. "She'll be more comfortable with you asking the questions, Rick. She trusts and likes you. We need to work this one as a team. You handle the witness . . . and I'll take care of Tyler." Rick wasn't sure he agreed with the plan, but he was humbled that the Professor believed he was up to the challenge. *Just relax*, Rick told himself. *You can do this.*

"Forty years," Rose answered.

She wore her normal outfit for work. A Texaco shirt, short sleeved, with her name stitched over her heart, and a pair of jeans.

"And in those forty years, how many times have you driven east on 82 and turned left onto Limestone Bottom to get to your store?"

Rose smiled. "Well, ever' day, I 'spect. For thirty years I lived about a mile west of the store, so that was my normal way a goin'. The last ten years I been livin' at the store, but every day I go downtown for a piece of pie and a Co'-Cola down at Eunice's. Come back 82 and turn left on Limestone Bottom."

Rick pulled out a marker board from the corner of the courtroom, set it in front of the jury, and took the top off of a black marker. "So, I'm no mathematician, but if we give you two weeks' vacation every year, you would have made this turn three hundred fifty times a year for forty years." Rick wrote "350 x 40" on the board. "Is that right?"

Rose shrugged. "I didn't take that much vacation."

Rick nodded. "So it would really be more than three hundred fifty days a year?"

"More like three hundred sixty."

Rick erased "350" and replaced it with "360."

"OK, three hundred sixty times forty is"—Rick worked the problem for the jury—"carry the two . . . fourteen thousand four hundred times. So . . ." He turned back to Batson and pointed at the board. "So, you've made the left turn from 82 onto Limestone Bottom about fourteen thousand four hundred times."

"Your Honor, this is all very fascinating," Tyler said, rising to his feet, "but we object. The number of times Rose Batson made this left turn is completely irrelevant." Cutler motioned for counsel to approach the bench, and Tom joined Rick and Tyler in front of the judge.

When they were out of earshot of the jury, the judge peered down at Rick. "Mr. Drake?"

Rick had hoped to be further into the examination before Jameson's objection, but Tyler was no dummy. He had to know where Rick was going by now, and he wasn't going to wait another second.

"Judge, I'm just laying some foundation," Rick said. "I can link it up if you give me a few more questions."

"A foundation for what?" Tyler asked. "Rose Batson is a store clerk at a Texaco. She is not an expert. She can't give opinions on the accident."

"She has made the same turn that Bob Bradshaw made on the day of the accident over fourteen thousand times," Rick said. "She has spent forty years at that Texaco. She knows that area better than any person on the face of the earth, and her opinion as a lay-person would be beneficial to the jury."

Cutler scratched the side of his face and pulled a book in front of him, which Rick instantly recognized. He glanced at the Professor, who nodded.

"Section thirty-five, part five," Tom said, and Cutler looked down at him.

"Uh . . . thank you. This is your book, right, Mr. McMurtrie?"

"Yes, sir," Tom said. "Second edition."

"Are there other editions?" the judge asked.

"Yes, sir. There is a third and a fourth. The lay opinion section, though, hasn't changed. Ms. Batson's testimony should come in under the cases cited in it."

"Your Honor, as I'm sure Tom says in his book, the general rule is that lay opinions do not come in." Tyler's usual calm and cool manner had been rattled, and his voice had risen to a higher pitch.

"That's true, Judge," Tom continued. "But I think you'll find this case to be similar to *Matthews Brothers v. Lopez*, where the Alabama Supreme Court affirmed a trial court's allowance of a lay witness to give his opinion on how long skidmarks had been on the pavement of a highway. Ms. Batson, like the lay witness in *Matthews Brothers*, has so much experience with the scene of the accident that her opinions will aid the jury in understanding what happened."

Cutler continued to peer at the hornbook, running his finger along the page and whispering to himself. Finally, he looked up from the page. "OK, Mr. Drake, I'm going to allow you to continue, but I'm not yet sure whether I'm going to allow Ms. Batson's opinions to come in. That will depend on what you're asking her about. Mr. Tyler, you are welcome to object when the opinions are asked for." He turned to Rick. "Please proceed."

Rick walked back to the board and pointed at the number he'd written on it. "Ms. Batson, you've made the left turn from Highway 82 onto Limestone Bottom over fourteen thousand times."

"Yes."

"And is that the same turn you saw Bob Bradshaw making the day of September 2, 2009?"

"Yes, it is."

"In the over fourteen thousand times you've made this turn, have you ever started to turn and then seen that a car was coming in the other direction?"

"Objection, Your Honor." Tyler was out of his seat again. "Ms. Batson's experience with this turn is irrelevant."

Rick smiled, not looking at Tyler. "Your Honor, Ms. Batson's experience with this turn establishes the foundation for the opinions I want to ask her about."

"Overruled. Let's get on with it, Mr. Drake."

"Ms. Batson, you may answer the question."

"Several times, yes. I can't give you a number or nothing, but that has happened before. There is a little dip in the road about a hundred yards from the light and when a car is in that dip, it can be hard to see. A couple of times I haven't seen the car and barely missed having a wreck."

Rick shot Tom a look, and his face said it all. *Now.* Rick turned to the witness, noticing that Tyler had already stood behind him, ready to object.

"Ms. Batson, you have testified in this case that the rig was a hundred yards away from Bob Bradshaw's Honda when the Honda began its turn. Is that correct?"

"Yes, sir."

"So was the rig in the dip you were talking about?"

"Yes, sir."

"Ms. Batson, based on the over fourteen thousand times you've made the same left turn that Bob Bradshaw was attempting, in your opinion could Bradshaw have seen the rig before he started his turn?"

"Objection, Your Honor," Tyler said. "May we—?"

"Overruled," Cutler said, cutting him off. "You can answer the question, Ms. Batson."

"It's just impossible to tell," Rose said, looking right at the jury. "I don't see how anybody could say one way or another. We're talking about split seconds. It's happened to me several times, and I've never been hit, because the other car wasn't hauling ass. With how fast that rig was moving—"

"Objection, Your Honor." Tyler was out of his seat, his face as red as his tie. "Ms. Batson's answer has gone beyond the scope of the question. I'd ask that any comments regarding the rig's speed be stricken."

"Sustained," Cutler said. "The jury will disregard Ms. Batson's description of the rig's speed."

Rick nodded, knowing it didn't matter. *Like they can forget.*

"Thank you, Ms. Batson. I have no further questions."

—

It was all Rick could do not to give a fist pump as he walked back to the counsel table. *I can't believe it worked.* But he knew he shouldn't be surprised. The minute Judge Cutler started flipping through his copy of *McMurtrie's Evidence*, Tyler didn't have a prayer. *It was like arguing with Moses over the Ten Commandments.*

As Rick took his seat, Tom nudged him with his elbow. "Great job," Tom said. "That's one down."

And one to go, Rick thought, glancing at his cell phone. There was still no word from Faith. Given the brevity of Tyler's cross-examinations, Rick figured they had fifteen minutes before they would have to call their next witness.

Our last witness.

Rick reached into his front pocket and touched the photograph of the Bradshaw family. Then he looked at Ruth Ann. Dark circles had formed under her eyes but she gazed stoically at the witness stand. *It's almost over,* Rick wanted to tell her, feeling an ache in his heart for this woman who had lost so much.

All she wants is the jury to know the truth.

And there was still a chance they might know. A small chance but . . . *a chance.*

Rick squeezed his phone and began to pray. *Fifteen minutes.*

—

"Ms. Batson, you're not an accident reconstructionist, are you?" Tyler asked, his voice dripping with sarcasm.

"I don't even know what that is. I run a gas station. Damn good one too."

"You've never had any instruction on how to analyze an automobile accident for fault, have you?"

"I reckon not."

"You've never investigated an automobile accident?"

"No."

"You have no idea whether Bob Bradshaw should have seen Dewey Newton's rig on September 2, 2009?"

"Like I said, it's impossible to tell. We talkin' split seconds."

"You saw Bob Bradshaw's Honda turn directly in front of the rig, didn't you?"

"Yes, I did."

"And that's what you wrote right after the accident happened, correct?"

"Yes."

"Nothing further, Your Honor," Tyler said, shaking his head at the jury as if he couldn't believe Rick and Tom had wasted the jury's time with such an unqualified witness.

"Redirect?" Cutler asked, shooting a glance at Rick.

"No, Your Honor."

"Very well. Ms. Batson is excused. Call your next witness."

—

Tom turned to Rick, who shook his head. *Damnit,* Tom thought. *Come on, old man, think. If Faith's not gonna show, how else can we get this document in?*

"Mr. McMurtrie, will the plaintiff be having any further rebuttal?"

"Let me see that bill again," Tom whispered, and Rick slid it in front of him. Tom scanned the contents, looking for something, anything, that might help.

"Mr. McMurtrie?" Cutler pressed.

Tom's eyes moved over the page at warp speed. *Come on, there's gotta be another way. There has to . . .*

Tom's heart caught in his chest when he saw it. *Well, I'll be . . .* He cocked his head and blinked several times, making sure he was seeing what he thought he was seeing. *How the hell did I miss that?*

"Mr. Mc— "

"Your Honor, may we approach?" Tom asked, standing and holding the document.

"What are you doing?" Rick asked.

"Just watch," Tom said, approaching the bench as Cutler motioned him forward.

"What is it, Counselor?" Cutler asked, clearly irritated at being ignored.

"Your Honor, yesterday we were presented with this document." Tom handed the bill to the judge. "It is the bill of lading for Dewey Newton's gasoline delivery the day of the accident. Apparently, one of the loaders, Dick Morris, who is now deceased, had kept it at his home, and his cousin found it. We have given a copy to defense counsel and plan to introduce the document as part of our rebuttal."

Cutler scanned the document quickly, looking unimpressed. "OK, so let's get on with it. I got a jury waiting, Professor."

"I understand that, Judge, but we just obtained the document and need more time to get a witness in court to authenticate it. Could we have a short recess? Maybe till after lunch?"

"Your Honor, I object," Tyler said. "They've had plenty of time to get a witness here to testify. Besides, all we've seen of the document is a copy. If all they have is a copy—"

"Looks like blue ink on the signature and initials," Cutler interrupted, handing the bill Tom had given him to Tyler.

"Even so," Tyler said, reading as he talked, "we would object to a recess."

Cutler sighed, looking back at Tom. "I have a feeling this trial would have run a lot smoother if you hadn't shown up, McMurtrie. I'm gonna allow the recess."

Yes, Tom thought, feeling an adrenaline surge. *There's still a chance.*

"It's eleven now, so you have two hours. We'll start back at one o'clock."

"Thank you, Your Honor," Tom said, and started to walk away.

"McMurtrie."

Cutler's voice stopped him, and Tom turned around. The judge motioned him forward.

"Tell me something," Cutler said, leaning over the bench and talking in a low voice. "Is that Lee Roy Jordan in the back row?"

Tom creased his eyebrows in surprise and slowly turned his head, finally letting himself look at the crowd. Up until now he had blocked everything out. He saw a lot of the same faces as yesterday. Former students, Will Burbaker, Rufus, the dean, the Cock. But when his eyes reached the back row, his stomach almost dropped. Lee Roy was wearing a blue blazer, white shirt, and a crimson tie. He was now a successful businessman in Dallas, and it had been years since Tom had seen old number 54, whom most viewed as the greatest middle linebacker in Alabama football history.

Next to him was Billy Neighbors, who had anchored the offensive *and* defensive line on the '61 team and was now a stockbroker in Huntsville. From Tom's view, he counted eight more. All wore blue blazers, white shirts, and crimson ties just like they used to for ball games.

It was a show of solidarity. From men who knew what loyalty was all about. The 1961 national champions. Tom caught Neighbors's eye, and he nodded. Tom nodded back.

Win. It was unspoken but it showed in Neighbors's eyes. As it did in Jordan's and the rest's. Like Tom, they had learned at the foot of the Man.

"Yes, sir," Tom said, turning back to the judge. "That's Lee Roy."

"Jesus aged Christ," Cutler muttered. "You've turned my courtroom into the damned Bryant Museum."

He banged his gavel and turned toward the jury box. "Members of the jury, we will be taking a recess for lunch. Please return to the jury room by one o'clock."

—

Rick grabbed Tom by the arm on the way back to the counsel table. "What if Faith doesn't show by one o'clock? I still haven't heard—"

"Faith's not our only option," Tom said, placing the bill on the table and pointing at the middle of it. "The truck was loaded by two people."

"I know that, Professor, but Mule is dead and Willard Carmichael was a dead end. He didn't remember any—"

"He'd remember his initials, wouldn't he?" Tom asked, placing his hand on the page where Willard Carmichael had scribbled "WBC" in blue ink next to his name.

Rick squinted at the page and his eyes widened. "I . . . can't believe I didn't see that before. Is that enough to get it in?"

Tom shrugged. "If Faith doesn't show, it's all we've got. Willard states that this is his handwriting and that he normally initials all bills and gives them to record keeping."

"Won't he also have to say that it was made and kept in the normal course of business by Ultron?" Rick asked.

Despite the stress he felt, Tom smiled with pride. "Glad you paid attention in class. Yes, those are the buzzwords, and we'll have to think of a creative way of proving them without confusing Willard. But first we have to get him here." Tom looked at his watch. "We've got an hour and fifty-five minutes."

"I'll get him here," Rick said, taking out his cell phone and running for the double doors.

85

"What do you mean, 'piss in the wind'?" Tyler asked, slamming the bill of lading into Jack Willistone's chest. "This document fucks us. I mean it fucks us up the ass with a sledgehammer."

Tyler was on the edge of losing control, having lost every battle of the morning. Tom got Batson's lay testimony in. Then he got his recess. If he were to authenticate the bill, then the whole complexion of the case changed. The bill would be the smoking gun that Willistone was negligently supervising Newton and forced him to speed to make the delivery. In other words . . . *We're fucked.*

"Old Yoda's really putting you through it, ain't he?" Jack said. "Well, let me ask you, how does he get this document into evidence?" Jack stuffed the bill back into Jameson's chest.

"Best way would be to call the records custodian who signed the bottom. Faith . . . Bulyard it looks like," Tyler said, squinting at the page. "He might also try bringing in one of the loaders, but Morris is dead."

"So his only options are Faith Bulyard and Willard Carmichael?" Jack asked, his chuckle turning into a full-bore laugh.

"Right. Is that funny to you? If either one of them shows up, then—"

"Relax, Darth," Jack said. "Yoda's all out of options."

86

Rick hung up the phone and walked in a daze through the doors and toward the counsel table, not even noticing as a reporter snapped a photograph of him.

When he reached the counsel table, the Professor quickly rose from his notes. "What is it? Did you fi— ?"

"He's gone, Professor. According to Hank Russell, Willard Carmichael didn't report for his shift last night. He's not answering his cell phone or his landline, and his wife doesn't have a clue where he is. He's . . . disappeared."

Rick sat down, feeling numb. Another dead end. He turned his head to search for the man he knew had to be responsible. Jack Willistone was seated at the defense table, looking right at him, and . . .

You son of a bitch, Rick tried to convey with his eyes.

. . . smiling.

87

"Counsel, please approach," Judge Cutler said as he walked into the courtroom at 1:00 p.m. sharp.

The judge appeared wired and anxious, clearly growing weary of the publicity the trial had generated. *He's in no mood to hear our excuses*, Tom knew, cringing as a jolt of pain went through his groin and abdomen. The pain was getting hard to ignore. He would ask for another recess, but even if Cutler allowed it, what would that buy them? They had no idea where Faith had gone, and Willard was missing. *And I doubt I can make another day of trial*, Tom thought, grabbing his side as another jolt of pain hit him.

"Are we ready to proceed, Mr. McMurtrie?" Cutler asked.

"Your Honor, during the break we learned that Willard Carmichael didn't report to work last night and is believed to be missing. Mr. Carmichael was one of the witnesses we planned to call to authenticate the bill of lading. The other witness, Faith Bulyard, is out of town and we've been unable to locate her. Given these circumstances, we'd ask for the trial to be recessed until at least tomorrow morning."

Cutler started shaking his head before Tom finished. "I'm not going to do that, McMurtrie. This jury's been patient and so have I, but we can't postpone this case indefinitely while you search for a witness. You should've gotten your witnesses in line prior to trial."

"With all due respect, Your Honor, we just received this document yesterday and have done all we could do to find the two witnesses. If you would just—"

"I gave you two hours. I'm not going to do any more than that," Cutler snapped. "Now do you have any further witnesses, McMurtrie?"

—

As the question hung in the air and silence engulfed the courtroom, Jameson Tyler could almost taste victory. If the bill of lading didn't come in, Tyler knew he had the edge heading into closings. Watching his mentor squirm, Tyler felt a swell of pride. *You've tried every trick, Professor, but you can't beat me.*

—

Jack Willistone was also about to burst. Once Yoda said he didn't have any further witnesses, all of Jack's actions would be rewarded. The fire. The deal with Wilma. Taking out Mule. Blackmailing Faith. Last night's game of *Fear Factor* with Willard. *It will all be worth it*, Jack thought as he closed his eyes and waited to hear the magic words.

—

The word "No" was almost out of Tom's mouth when a loud crashing sound broke through the silence, causing Tom to stop cold.

Tom, Rick, and everyone in the galley turned to look at the back of the courtroom, where the sound had rung out.

"Oh my God," Rick said.

A woman and two teenage boys stood just inside the double doors. The woman was dressed elegantly, wearing a black blouse over a crème-colored skirt.

"It's her," Rick said, his voice cracking with relief as he walked toward the woman.

Tom didn't have to ask who "her" was. He turned back to the bench.

"Your Honor, the plaintiff calls Ms. Faith Bulyard."

88

As the door slammed behind her, Faith just stood there a moment. Her entire body shook with nerves and exhaustion. She had not slept since her afternoon nap the day before. After dinner in Little Italy she had broken down and listened to her messages. Then she had understood why Jack had called. She knew exactly what she had to do. She would not live the rest of her life in fear of Jack Willistone. He was a bully. You couldn't negotiate with a bully and you couldn't just ignore one. *I have to fight back.* And the only way to fight was to go to Henshaw. But first she had to tell her boys the truth.

It had been the hardest thing she had ever done, but she did it. After two hours of anguishing over what to say and how to say it, Faith told Junior and Danny everything. That their father was gay, that he had cheated on her with other men, and that he had probably killed himself because Jack Willistone had threatened to reveal his sexuality. Now Jack was threatening Faith with the same stuff and it had to stop.

Both boys had cried, but Junior's sadness had turned to anger. It was as if he had aged a decade in fifteen minutes. "Nobody is ever going to threaten my momma," Junior had said, hugging her as tightly as he ever had in his life.

Now here they were, at the Henshaw County Courthouse, surrounded by hundreds of people, all of them staring at them.

Am I in the right place? Faith wondered. *Why are there so many people here?*

From the front of the courtroom, a young man walked hurriedly toward her. He wore a smile of relief, and Faith recognized him as the boy who came to her house.

"Ms. Bulyard," he said, grabbing her hand and shaking it. "Thanks so much for coming."

"I'm sorry I didn't call," she said. "It was all we could do just to get here."

"Don't worry about it," he said, his eyes moving past Faith to the boys.

"These are my two sons. Buck Jr. and Danny."

"Nice to meet you. My name is Rick Drake," Rick said, shaking their hands.

"Are you ready?" he asked, turning back to Faith.

"Right now?" she asked, feeling her heart rate jump.

"Yes. You're our last witness." He looked her in the eye. "Are you ready to testify?"

Faith didn't blink. "That's why we came."

—

Jack Willistone could not believe his eyes. He had sent this bitch to New York fucking City. *Why the hell would she come back?* Behind Faith were two teenaged boys. Jack had never seen the younger one, but he recognized the older one right off. Buck Bulyard Jr. Again, Jack couldn't believe his eyes. *What is this crazy bitch thinking?* Jack stood, wanting Faith to see him as she walked past. But she just stared straight ahead. He was helpless.

This cannot be happening.

—

Faith kept her eyes fixed straight ahead, walking tall with her boys at her heels. She knew Jack was somewhere watching her, but she'd deal with him later. When she got to the front, two men rose from their seats and let Danny and Junior sit down. Then a tall, stately looking man gestured toward the bench, and Faith stepped forward, seeing the judge for the first time.

"Raise your right hand," the judge ordered, and Faith did so. "Do you promise to tell the truth, the whole truth, and nothing but the truth, so help you God?"

Faith sucked in a deep breath. "I do."

—

"Ms. Bulyard," Tom began, forcing himself to ignore the shooting pain in his groin. *You can't pull up lame, old man,* he told himself. *Not at the finish line.* "On September 2, 2009, where were you employed?" Tom asked, looking at the jury, then to the back of the courtroom, where Powell Conrad and Bocephus Haynes stood side by side behind the members of the 1961 team. Powell and Bo had left their seats so that Faith Bulyard's sons could sit down. Tom wiped his forehead and met Bo's eye, then glanced down to Billy Neighbors. Another flare of pain nearly brought Tom to his knees, but he steadied himself by grabbing the counsel table.

"The Ultron Gasoline plant in Tuscaloosa, Alabama," Faith said.

Tom nodded and cleared his throat, and another shooting pain sent his hand to his knees.

"Professor McMurtrie, are you all right?" Cutler asked.

Tom blinked several times, trying to gather himself. His legs shook, and for a minute he thought he was going to fall. Feeling a hand on his arm, he looked up and saw Rick Drake's blurry face.

"Professor? Do you want me to take over?" Rick asked, and the words came out contorted, as if spoken through a piece of paper.

Tom almost nodded. He almost said yes. Then, forcing his eyes to move, he again looked to the back of the courtroom.

When he saw Neighbors, goose bumps broke out on his arm.

His old teammate on the defensive line was standing. As were Lee Roy and the rest of the team. They were all standing, and as if the voice were speaking right to him, Tom heard words from long ago: *Men, there's gonna come a day in your life when things aren't going too well. Your wife has left you or died, your house has burned down, you've lost your job, and you ain't feeling too good about nothing. When that day comes, what are you gonna do? You gonna quit?*

Tom blinked back tears of pain as the words of the Man came back to him. It had been summer workouts, 1960. Blistering heat that made you want to puke—and some did. Gassers followed by push-ups followed by more gassers. Some quit.

But not Thomas Jackson McMurtrie. Not then. Not now.

Not ever.

Tom removed his hands from his knees and straightened himself. He looked at Ruth Ann, and she too was standing, her face showing worry and strength. Turning, it appeared that half the courtroom was now standing. Rufus Cole, Bill Burbaker, every former student in the room and, finally, the Honorable Art Hancock.

Tom steadied himself and faced the bench. "I'm fine, Judge. Ms. Bulyard, what was your position at Ultron?"

On wobbly legs, Tom walked toward the back of the jury box, holding the bill of lading in his hand.

"Records custodian."

"And in your position as records custodian, did you keep bills of lading?"

"Yes, I did. When we received a bill, I would always sign at the bottom that I had received it and then I would file it away."

Tom approached the witness stand, handing the bill to Faith. "Ms. Bulyard, I'm showing you what's been marked as Plaintiff's Exhibit 2. Do you recognize this document?"

"Yes, I do."

"What is it?"

"It is a bill of lading for a delivery made by Willistone Trucking Company on September 2, 2009."

"Is that your signature at the bottom of the bill?"

"Yes, it is."

"Was this document made and kept in the normal course of business of Ultron Gasoline?"

"Yes, it was."

Almost there, Tom thought, squeezing his fists together as another stab of pain hit him.

"Your Honor, we would offer Plaintiff's Exhibit 2."

"Any objection?" Cutler asked, and Tom followed his eyes to Tyler, who to Tom's surprise remained seated.

"No, Your Honor."

"OK, the document is admitted," Cutler said.

Tom cut his eyes to Rick, but the boy was already moving, walking toward the defense table.

"Your Honor," Tom said. "We'd like to show this document to the jury. Would it be possible to use the defendant's laptop computer, as we do not have any of that equipment?"

Cutler shrugged and looked at the defense table. "Mr. Tyler?"

Tom turned also. "Jameson, could we please borrow your laptop for a few seconds?"

It was all Tom could do not to laugh. If Jameson refused the request, he would come off as a jerk, which in a case like this could be the difference between winning and losing.

"Certainly," Tyler replied, the voice of compassion and courtesy.

"Thank you," Tom said. Then he nodded at Rick, who inserted the flash drive in the laptop.

The bill of lading came to life on the screen to the right of the witness stand, in full view of the jury. Tom took a pointer and flashed the red light at the top of the bill. He had forgotten his pain in the adrenaline of the moment.

"What again is the date on this document?" Tom asked.

"September 2, 2009."

"And I see there's a blank for driver. What does that say?"

"Newton," Faith answered.

"And the blanks for loaders?"

"Morris and Carmichael."

"Can you tell on the bill where the load was going?"

"Yes, place of delivery is identified as Montgomery. Filling stations seven and eight."

Tom lowered his pointer to the next blank, feeling his heart pounding in his chest. "And delivery time—what does that mean?"

"That is the expected time that the load would be delivered."

"What was that time?"

"11:00 a.m."

Tom lowered the pointer and looked at the jury. "What does pickup time mean?"

"That is the time the load is picked up from the plant. The loaders are instructed to stamp the time in that blank right after they've loaded the truck."

Tom continued to gaze at the jury, all of whom were looking intently at the screen. "What is the time stamped in that blank, Ms. Bulyard?"

"9:57 a.m."

Tom paused, letting the answer sink in. *Time for the grand finale.*

"So, Ms. Bulyard, on September 2, 2009, driver Newton picked up a load of Ultron gasoline in Tuscaloosa at 9:57 a.m." Tom made sure his voice carried to the far reaches of the courtroom.

"Yes."

"And he was due in Montgomery by eleven?"

"Yes."

Yes. Tom looked at the jury, seeing several knowing nods. "No further questions."

—

"Cross-examination, Mr. Tyler?"

Jameson Tyler stood, smiling at the witness and trying to maintain his cool. For the first time since he was a pup lawyer, he didn't know what to do. His instincts said this witness was a landmine and that he shouldn't ask her any questions. *But that's not an option,* he thought. *I can't let the jury's last image of the trial be the bill of lading that shows we made Newton speed on the day of the accident. Even if I don't score any points with her, maybe I can at least muddy the water a little.*

"Yes, Your Honor," Tyler said, approaching the stand. "Ms. Bulyard, you don't have any personal knowledge of the schedule that Dewey Newton kept at Willistone Trucking Company, do you?"

"Well . . . the bill of lading"—Faith pointed to the screen, and Jameson tensed as he noticed that the bill still showed on the screen; his associate had forgotten to take it off—"shows his schedule for September 2 with us."

As calmly as he could manage, Jameson walked to his counsel table and leaned into his associate's ear. "Turn that damn thing off."

The screen went blank.

"OK, Ms. Bulyard, the document says what it says. But you don't know why Dewey Newton was late to your plant that day, do you?"

Faith shrugged. "I don't know he was late. For all I know, we may have been late."

Yes, Tyler thought, feeling relief flood his body as his eyes moved to the jury. *Did you hear that?* he tried to convey with his eyes. If the plant was late or slow loading the truck, then Willistone was in the clear. He could take all of the steam out of Tom's direct.

"That's right, Ms. Bulyard," Tyler said, keeping his voice measured. *Just one more question.* "So Mr. Newton's schedule with Willistone on September 2, 2009 could have been just fine, and for all you know it was Ultron's delay that caused the truck not to be loaded until 9:57, correct?"

Jameson held his breath for the answer, intending to sit down immediately after hearing "Yes" or "Correct." But the answer didn't immediately come. Faith Bulyard's face had reddened, and she looked angry, glaring not at Tyler but out in the galley.

"Ms. Bulyard, would you like me to repeat the question?" he asked, feeling a deep sense of dread come over him.

"No, I heard the question just fine," Faith said, still glaring past Tyler into the audience. He followed her gaze, and his chest constricted when he saw its intended target. *Oh, no . . .*

"Ms. Bulyard, let me—" he started, but Faith Bulyard's words cut through his like a knife.

"Shut up, Mr. Tyler," Faith said as her eyes burned into Jack Willistone's. The anger she'd built up for the past nine months pulsed in her veins. "I heard your question, and I'm going to answer it." Faith cut her eyes from Jack and looked directly at the jury. "The answer is, for that day I don't know exactly why the truck wasn't loaded until 9:57, but—"

"You answered my question," Tyler interrupted. "And I have nothing—"

"Let me finish," Faith said, her whole body trembling as she rose from the chair. She sensed that her time on the stand was almost over, and she still hadn't said what she came to say.

"Your Honor, if the witness says anything further, it will be unresponsive and irrelevant. We have no further questions."

Faith whirled around and looked at the judge, who was rubbing his eyebrows. "Your Honor, I have more to—"

"The witness will stop talking," Cutler interrupted, banging his gavel. "I agree with Mr. Tyler. You've answered his question."

"No," Faith said. "I—"

"Ms. Bulyard, if you don't stop talking I'm going to hold you in contempt," the judge said, again banging his gavel. "Now, will there be any redirect from the plaintiff?"

Faith continued to stand, moving her gaze to Rick Drake, whose eyes were as wide as her own. Behind Rick she saw her two sons. Junior's face was crimson with anger, but Danny was staring off into space, still in total shock.

What have I done? Faith thought. *Have I come all this way for nothing?*

"Ms. Bulyard."

Faith turned at the sound of the voice, and the older man—the Professor—was standing in front of her. His hand was on her shoulder.

"Please, ma'am, sit down and let me ask you a couple more questions."

Faith did as she was told.

"Ms. Bulyard, what were you about to say before Mr. Tyler cut you off?"

"Objection, Your Honor," Tyler cut in. He too had remained standing. "Ms. Bulyard answered my last question. Allowing her to give an unsolicited speech to this jury, which may include hearsay and other inadmissible material, would not be proper and could be highly prejudicial to the defendants."

"I agree," Cutler said. "The objection is sustained. Mr. McMurtrie, you'll need to ask a different question."

Tom looked at Faith's pleading face, thinking of the question that prompted her outburst. He had forgotten about the pain. He could sense that the entire trial might ride on what Faith Bulyard wanted to say.

"Ms. Bulyard, what do you know about the schedules Willistone Trucking Company put its drivers on?"

"Before he died, my husband, Buck, told me that—"

"Objection, Your Honor. Hearsay," Tyler said.

"Sustained," Cutler agreed.

Damnit, Tom thought. If there had been any time to talk with Faith prior to putting her on the stand, he would know exactly what to ask her. Now he was just winging it, trusting his instincts and forty years of experience.

"Ms. Bulyard, other than what Buck told you, what do you know about the schedules?"

Faith took a deep breath and tried to calm down. She could tell the Professor was trying to help her. "Well, there were bills of lading for all of Willistone's deliveries, and they all had the delivery and pickup times on them. On the night of this accident, there was a—"

"Objection, Your Honor. May I approach?" Tyler was already moving toward the bench. "The witness is clearly about to testify to the fire that destroyed the Ultron plant, which you specifically prohibited when you granted our pretrial motion in limine."

"The objection is sustained," Cutler said. "The witness is instructed not to mention the fire. Let's move on."

Tom glanced at Rick, who had joined Tom at the bench. "Any ideas, champ?" Tom asked.

"If I'd sued Ultron, Buck's statements would come in as a party admission, but—"

"Too late for that," Tom interrupted.

"She wants to help us," Rick whispered, the desperation evident in his voice. "There's gotta be something that's admissible."

Tom nodded, agreeing but unable to figure out what that was. The irony wasn't lost on him. He'd taught Evidence for forty years, and the whole trial hinged on getting Faith Bulyard's testimony into evidence.

"Professor, please continue," Cutler said.

Tom nodded at the judge, his eyes rotating to Faith Bulyard, who looked almost as desperate as Rick. Then to the jury, many of whom had confused, irritated expressions. Finally, Tom looked at Tyler, who was now sitting down, the picture of cool. *He thinks he's won.*

Tom's mind drifted to his book. *McMurtrie's Evidence.* The chapter on hearsay. There were twenty-three exceptions, and Tom had a subsection on each one. Then there were three types of statements that by definition were not hearsay. Tom felt a tickle in his brain. *What did Rick just say about Ultron? If he had sued Ultron . . .*

"Professor, if there are no further questions . . ." Cutler stopped, not needing to finish the thought.

Tom knew he was out of time. *Think . . .* With his back to the stand, Tom raised his eyes and looked to the galley. The courtroom was deathly quiet, all eyes on him. Adrenaline coursed through Tom, and as his eyes met Jack Willistone's he felt the tickle again. And then . . .

. . . it all clicked.

"Ms. Bulyard," Tom said, turning on a dime. "Have you had any conversations with anyone associated with Willistone Trucking Company regarding driver schedules, the bills of lading, or testifying at this trial?"

"Objection, Your Honor, the question clearly calls for—" Tyler started, but Tom was ready.

"Anything anyone from Willistone told her would be an admission by party opponent, which *by definition* is not hearsay. Rule 801 (d)(2) of the Alabama Rules of Evidence." Tom paused. "Chapter forty-seven, subpart five of my book."

Cutler opened his copy of *McMurtrie's Evidence* to the page, then shot Tyler a look. "Mr. Tyler?"

"It would have to be an officer or high-ranking official with Willistone for that section to apply," Tyler said, sounding weak.

"The objection is overruled," Cutler said. "Ms. Bulyard, please answer the question."

Faith cleared her throat and looked directly at Tom. "Yes. I've spoken with someone at Willistone."

"Who?" Tom asked, holding his breath.

"Jack Willistone. The *owner* of the company."

Tom's eyes shot to Tyler. *That high-ranking enough for you, Jamo?*

"Ms. Bulyard," Tom said, pausing and looking at the jury. *This is it*, he thought. "Tell the jury what Jack Willistone said to you."

—

Faith did not look at the jury. Instead, she glared at Jack Willistone. *How do you like me now, you bastard?* she tried to convey with her eyes. Then, clearing her throat, she began to speak.

"Jack Willistone threatened me and my family if I testified today."

"That is a goddamn lie!" Jack screamed, rising from his seat at the defense table and shaking his finger at Faith.

Loud banging came from the bench, and Judge Cutler stood. "Quiet! I'll have quiet in this courtroom. Mr. Willistone, another word from you and I will put you in jail for contempt. The jury will disregard this outburst. Mr. Tyler, you need to get control of your client."

Tyler turned toward Jack, but Jack waved him off, sat down, and crossed his arms. His face had turned beet red. Faith never blinked as she stared at the man who killed her husband.

"Ms. Bulyard." The Professor's calm voice broke through the tension like a gentle breeze. "How did Jack Willistone threaten you and your family?"

"He told me that if I testified or had any contact whatsoever with Mr. Drake, he would tell my sons that their father . . ." Faith's voice broke and she looked down at her hands. "That their father was a homosexual."

Several gasps rang out in the courtroom, and Faith looked up, this time turning her gaze to the jury.

"Jack had made videos and photographs of my husband with . . . other men. He sent them to me and told me he'd make them public if I testified in this case. He threatened me on the phone and in text messages. I never understood why he was so hot to keep me away. It wasn't until I saw that bill again that it clicked. He didn't want *you* to see that bill," Faith told the jury, and Jameson Tyler bolted out of his seat.

"Objection, Judge. She's just giving her opinion now. That's—"

"Sustained," Cutler said. "Just stick to what he told you, Ms. Bulyard. The jury will disregard that last comment."

"He paid me to go to New York City so I wouldn't be around this week, and he called me last night and *reminded* me what would happen if I came back. Well, *I don't care anymore*, Jack." Now it was Faith who was out of her seat. "My husband *was* gay and he cheated on me with other men. My sons know now because I told them." She paused. "So I don't care if you tell the whole world about it."

89

Tom let Faith's answer hang in the air for five seconds as silence filled the courtroom. He watched the jury, seeing outrage on some of their faces, while others appeared to be in shock. He toyed with introducing the text messages but decided against it. He didn't know what they said and, judging by the angry looks in the jury box, they would probably be overkill. *We can't end on a higher high than right now*, Tom thought, clearing his throat and looking at Cutler.

"We have no further questions, Your Honor."

"Recross, Mr. Tyler?"

Tom's eyes moved to the defense table, where Tyler was having a heated discussion with his associate and Jack Willistone.

"Mr. Tyler?" Cutler repeated.

Tyler rose from his seat, his red face a dead giveaway that he was frustrated. *Jamo is finally letting everyone see him sweat*, Tom thought.

"Your Honor, may we approach?"

Cutler motioned them all forward.

"Your Honor, we have not seen the text messages mentioned by Ms. Bulyard. Can we see those?"

Tom knew the defendant was entitled to see the texts, so he did not object. He only prayed they were as bad as Faith testified.

"Here," Faith said, leaning over the witness stand and handing her phone to Tyler. "Enjoy."

Tyler took the phone, and for at least a full minute they all watched his face as he reviewed the texts and their attachments. Slowly, he handed the phone back to Faith. Then he looked at Cutler.

"Your Honor, I move to withdraw myself and my law firm as counsel for Willistone Trucking Company."

"Denied," Cutler said, glaring at Tyler with unsympathetic eyes. "It's too late to be quitting, Mr. Tyler. It would be too prejudicial to your client, and I am not stopping this trial so it can get a new lawyer."

"Your Honor, Mr. Willistone's . . . actions have made it impossible for me to effectively represent his company—"

"No, Mr. Tyler," Cutler interrupted. "Mr. Willistone's actions may have made it impossible for you to win this case. Your motion is denied. Mr. McMurtrie, are you going to be offering any further rebuttal?"

"No, Your Honor," Tom said.

"Mr. Tyler. How about you? Any rebuttal witnesses?"

Tyler looked like a ten-year-old protesting a spanking. Gone was the aura of cool and invincibility.

"No, Your Honor."

"OK, unless there are other motions to take up, let's proceed with closing arguments."

90

Two hours later, at 4:00 p.m., the jury was given the case. There had been no motions. Tyler was so shocked by Faith Bulyard's testimony that he forgot to renew his motion for judgment as a matter of law. Not that it would have mattered—Faith Bulyard's testimony and the bill of lading killed any chance of Tyler getting the case thrown out.

Then came the closing arguments, which were predictably anticlimactic. Tom focused on Dewey Newton's speed and the bill of lading, while Tyler hammered home his expert's opinion that Bob Bradshaw should have seen Newton's rig prior to making his turn. Rick handled the rebuttal, where he stood before the jury—a jury he had grown up knowing—and asked that they render a verdict in the amount of nine million dollars: three million dollars for each death.

After closings, Judge Cutler read the jury instructions agreed upon by both sides earlier in the week. Then he adjourned the jury to their room, where they were to deliberate and decide the case.

Rick and Tom waited out in the hallway. Across from them Tyler sat alone, having sent his associate back to Birmingham. Jack Willistone remained glued to his chair in the courtroom, staring straight ahead.

Ruth Ann and Dawn had gone with Rick's parents to the farm. "Too nerve-racking to wait here," Ruth Ann had said, and she'd asked Dawn to keep her company. Rick had promised to call when the jury came back.

Faith Bulyard had taken her sons back home, though she had asked to be called after the verdict. Most of the crowd had dispersed, the only ones hanging around being reporters hoping that the verdict might come in before the end of the day.

After an hour Judge Cutler's bailiff came out and said the jury had asked to work late. They wanted to decide the case tonight without having to come back the next day. Tyler, Rick, and the Professor all grunted "OK," each with a half-dazed, fog-of-war look on his face. Rick called Ruth Ann and gave her the update. "Shouldn't be long now," Rick had lied. He didn't have a clue how long it would be.

Rick put the phone in his pocket and turned toward his partner, thinking of the long journey that had brought them to this point.

"Professor," Rick said, and Tom, who had his arms folded and was slumped in his chair, turned his head toward him.

"Yeah."

Rick paused, feeling emotion building in his chest. He was so tired. "I just wanted to thank you. I . . ." Rick wanted to say more but he couldn't find the words. "Thank you," he repeated.

Tom winced as he straightened himself in the chair. He couldn't move without feeling pain in his groin and abdomen, and he'd just pissed more blood in the bathroom. He too was exhausted, and badly needed to see a doctor. But he wouldn't leave Rick to wait for the jury alone. He'd come too far to abandon ship now. He looked into the boy's eyes, knowing what was on the line for him. Knowing this twenty-six-year-old kid, a year out of law school, had gone toe-to-toe with Jameson Tyler and had been willing to go the distance alone.

"No thanks necessary, Rick. You got guts, son," Tom said. "Guts and balls. What you have, a person can't teach. That's why I referred you this case. This case needed passion. It . . . needed you." Tom winced again.

"Are you OK, Professor? Do you feel—?"

"You boys gonna kiss?"

It was Tyler. He had walked over and now stood in front of them, smiling weakly. It was the first time he'd spoken or moved since they had come out in the hallway.

"Hell of a job, men. Hell of a job," Tyler said. "Not bad for your first trial, Rick. And Professor . . ." Tyler smiled, shaking his head. "Looks like the old bull still has a little gas in the tank."

"A little, Jamo. Enough to whip your ass."

For a moment the two men looked at each other. Then Tyler extended his hand.

"I know it doesn't matter now, but I'm sorry about what happened with the board."

Tom stood but did not extend his hand. "You're right, Jamo," he said, looking down on his former friend. "It doesn't matter now."

Tyler's face turned a bright shade of pink. It looked like he was about to say something else, but he never got a chance. At that moment the doors to the courtroom swung open and the bailiff stepped through, an anxious look on his face.

"They've reached a verdict."

91

The courtroom was again filled to capacity. Apparently, the people who had left when the jury was given the case had stuck around, hoping the case might be decided that evening. The courtroom was buzzing with electricity as the spectators talked amongst themselves. The excitement was palpable. Judge Cutler banged his gavel, and the buzz came to a halt. In seconds the courtroom was silent as a church.

"Mr. Foreman," Cutler bellowed. "Has the jury reached its verdict?"

In the back right corner of the jury box, Sam Roy Johnson stood holding a single piece of paper in his right hand. "Yes, we have, Your Honor."

"What says the jury?" the judge asked.

Tom placed his elbows on the table and watched Sam Roy. The last time Tom had heard a verdict read was June 20, 1969, three weeks before his breakfast with the Man. If anything, his adrenaline was pumping harder now that it had then. *There is no feeling in the world like this*, Tom thought, savoring it and knowing in his heart that they had done all they could do. *We left it on the field.*

Next to Tom, Rick leaned forward, gripping the photograph of the Bradshaw family in his pocket. *Please, God, give this family justice.* Taking the photograph out of his pocket, he placed it in Ruth Ann's hand and clasped hers with his. In this moment—the biggest moment of his life—Rick thought not of himself or his career. He thought only of the family in the picture. The young father and mother, not much older than Rick, who'd had their entire future and life shattered in the blink of an eye. The two-year-old little girl who should've had a long, wonderful life but instead burned to death in a Honda Accord. And finally, the grandmother who'd had the strength and courage to go the distance. Not for money or greed but for the truth. Tears burned Rick's eyes. All he could do now was pray . . . and listen.

Sam Roy Johnson cleared his throat. "We the jury of the Circuit Court of Henshaw County, Alabama, hereby find for the plaintiff, Ruth Ann Wilcox, as to all claims against the defendant, Willistone Trucking Company, and award her the total sum of . . .

"Ninety million dollars."

92

There were a lot of hugs. Once Judge Cutler dismissed the jury, Rick hugged Ruth Ann, and Tom joined in for a group hug, kissing Ruth Ann gently on the cheek.

Then Billy Drake came over and grabbed Rick in a bear hug. "I'm so proud of you, son."

Rick was in utter shock. *Ninety million dollars?*

When the verdict was read, there had been a collective, audible sigh from the courtroom. Sam Roy Johnson had gone on to read the jury's allocation—which was thirty million dollars for Bob Bradshaw's death, thirty million for Jeannie Bradshaw, and thirty million for little Nicole—but it was hard to hear due to the rustling in the courtroom. All of the reporters had headed for the double doors at the same time, each wanting to be the first to break the news.

Now it was a madhouse. People Rick didn't know were slapping him on the back, and the Professor was engulfed in a sea of the same. It was overwhelming and wonderful. But not complete. There was still someone else Rick wanted to see. *Where is she?* Rick stood on his toes and searched the crowd, still not seeing her. Then he felt a hand on his shoulder and he turned.

"Looking for someone?" Dawn smiled, though her eyes were red with tears. "Congratulations, Rick. You really deserve—"

But her words were drowned out by Rick's kiss. All of the energy, stress, and anguish of the past three days poured out of him. All he wanted to do now was be with Dawn. It took him a few seconds to realize that she was kissing him back.

"I love you," Dawn said. "I wish I had said it sooner, but—"

Rick interrupted her with another kiss. "No buts. I love you too."

"Damn, children, y'all need to get a room."

They both turned, and Bocephus Haynes was smiling at them. He handed Rick a cigar, hesitated for a second, and then gave Dawn one too. Then he put his arm around both of them and placed an even longer stogie in his own mouth.

"Bocephus loves a happy ending."

—

Jack Willistone grabbed Jameson Tyler by the throat.

"You better file an appeal tomorrow, you limp-dicked son of a bitch."

Jack started to say something else, but then all of a sudden the side of his face was being pressed into the mahogany counsel table and his hands were twisted behind him. Looking to his left, he saw a sandy-haired man standing next to a police officer.

Powell Conrad stepped forward. "Mr. Willistone, on behalf of the District Attorney's Office of Tuscaloosa County, it is my privilege to inform you that you are officially"—Powell leaned forward and lowered his voice so that only Jack could hear—"*fucked*."

Jack's eyes widened and Powell smiled. Then the police officer took cuffs out of his pocket and slapped them on Jack's wrists.

As Powell's smile widened, the officer spoke in a loud voice. "Mr. Willistone, you are under arrest for blackmail and witness tampering. You have the right to remain silent . . ."

—

A few minutes later the victorious party exited the courtroom, flashbulbs going off everywhere. Rick and Dawn came through first, with Rick's mom and dad in tow. Then came a procession of Tom's former students and colleagues, who had all shaken Tom's hand before leaving. Slinking through them like a snake was Dean Richard Lambert, who kept his head down and feet moving. But the one the reporters had been waiting for was Tom.

He held Ruth Ann's hand and slowly walked down the steps of the courthouse. Tom planned to make an appearance at Rick's farm—Rick's mother had invited everyone over to celebrate—and then head straight to Bill Davis's office. He doubted his urologist would deliver a verdict as good as the jury just had, but Tom wasn't going to think about that now. *It is what it is.*

Bocephus Haynes walked in front of Tom, serving as the lead blocker. At Tom's side was Judge Art Hancock, who seemed almost as happy as Tom about the result. And at Tom's flank were ten men wearing blue sport coats, all with the same ring on the third finger of their right hand. The same one Tom wore. The rings said "National Champions, 1961." They had stayed to the bitter end.

"Professor McMurtrie, how does it feel to have hit the largest verdict in Henshaw County history?"

"Professor, do you feel any vindication today for being forced to retire five months ago by the law school?"

"Professor, do you have any words for the law school or the university?"

The questions came from all directions, and Tom was blinded by the camera flashes. He was too tired for this.

Mercifully, Bocephus Haynes held up his hands and took over. "The Professor will be taking all of you good folks' questions in due time. As his attorney, however, I must tell you that I will be advising him not to answer questions about the law school as we plan on having a little chat with them."

Then Bo made a path through the crowd, and Tom and his entourage followed.

Just as Tom had almost made it past all of the onlookers, one last question reached his ears.

"Professor, how does a sixty-eight-year-old near-death law professor who hasn't tried a case in forty years hit the largest verdict in West Alabama history?"

Feeling one last tickle of adrenaline, Thomas Jackson McMurtrie turned and looked at them, moving his eyes past their greedy faces to the female reporter who'd raised the question. It was the same reporter who had accosted him immediately after he was forced to retire. The raucous mob turned silent in half a second.

Catching Judge Hancock's eye next to him, Tom said in a quiet voice, "What was Gus always saying in *Lonesome Dove*?"

The Cock smiled, and the Professor's mouth broke into a wide grin. He turned back to the reporter and spoke the words of Captain Augustus McCrae of the Texas Rangers.

"The older the violin, the sweeter the music."

EPILOGUE

On the northern tip of the Hazel Green farm, nestled between two cherry trees, is the McMurtrie family cemetery. In this twenty foot by twenty foot plot, there are three large headstones, and Tom took a minute with each one, running his fingers over the engraved letters.

Sutton Winslow McMurtrie. July 5, 1908–May 9, 1979.

Rene Graham McMurtrie. December 6, 1910–May 25, 1992.

Julie Lynn Rogers McMurtrie. March 16, 1943–April 17, 2007.

On his walk from the house, Tom had picked fresh wildflowers, Julie's favorite, and now he placed them on her grave as well as his momma's and daddy's. He stood back and gazed upward at the beautiful blue sky, taking in the fragrance of the flowers. Then he turned from them and walked to the edge of the plot, where the last headstone lay.

This one was small and it contained no dates or even a last name. Tom wiped a tear from his eye as he looked at the stone that so amply described the friend buried underneath.

MUSSO: "A Fighting Dog"

"First time I've ever been quoted on a monument."

Tom turned at the sound of the familiar voice. Bocephus Haynes approached and put his huge hand on Tom's shoulder.

"You want to tell me about it?" he said, his voice low.

Tom nodded, feeling the emotion in his chest as he thought back to the day when the world went white. "The day after my last treatment, when Rick came out here and asked me to try the Wilcox case with him"—Tom paused, wiping his eyes—"I refused at first. Didn't think I could do it. Too old. Too sick. I went for a long walk to think about it and didn't bring a gun. This farm is pretty tame but it's not without its wild animals. Remember hearing that bobcat squeal?"

"Yeah, dog. You said they were harmless."

"They normally are," Tom said, squinting at him. "Unless they're rabid . . ."

Bo's eyes widened.

"Took Musso with me," Tom continued. "It was too long a walk for him, and when I stopped at the creek I thought I might have to carry him back. Musso was so old." Tom's lip quivered but he continued. "He started limping halfway to the creek, but I wouldn't stop. Anyway, after he'd fallen asleep, I heard something behind me. It was that same high-pitched squeal that you heard, and I knew immediately it had to be a bobcat. I turned, and sure enough it was a yellow and black bobcat. Had to be at least fifty pounds, which is big for them." Tom paused. "When I saw the foam on its mouth, I knew I was screwed."

"Aw, shit," Bo whispered.

"I barely had time to move," Tom said. "The son of a bitch lunged for me, and I tripped over an uneven rock. Must have hit the back of my head on something, 'cause I was out cold for a while." Tom stopped, wiping his eyes and gazing down at the small headstone.

"Then what happened?" Bo asked.

"Well, damnedest thing. I woke up, and other than the back of my head hurting, I was fine. The damn thing hadn't touched me." Tom paused. "Which was *impossible*. He was coming right for me and he was rabid. I looked around and didn't see the bobcat. Then I noticed that Musso was gone too." Tom's heart hurt as he talked but he continued. "I walked around a little bit and saw them about thirty yards away, nestled against an oak tree."

"Them?" Bo raised an eyebrow.

"At first I wasn't sure what I was looking at. I could tell the bobcat was dead, 'cause I saw its tail underneath the red thing on top of him. When I got closer, I saw that . . . that the red thing was Musso. He was so scratched up, his white coat was almost solid red."

"But . . . but how—?" Bo tried to ask, but Tom interrupted.

"Musso had the bobcat's neck in his mouth and his eyes were shut. He had clamped down and held on."

Bo let out a low whistle. "Damn."

"He was thirteen years old and knocking on death's door and he killed a fifty-pound rabid bobcat."

"Was he still . . . ? I mean, when you found him . . ."

Tom felt the tears again but forced them back. "I spoke to him. I said, 'Musso, it's me. It's me . . .' and . . . he opened his eyes and let out the lowest, most ornery growl I've ever heard in my life. Then he finally let go. He had been holding on that whole time. Hours . . . He sank to the side of the bobcat but he didn't move. I put my hand down to his mouth and he licked it. Then . . ." Tom put his hand over his face and let the tears flow.

"He waited until he knew you were safe before he let himself die."

Tom nodded. "He fought, Bo. Just like you said he would."

"And so did you."

"Just like you said I would."

Bo smiled. "What can I say? I know a bulldog when I see one."

They walked back to the house, and the talk turned to the future.

"So what's the news from Tuscaloosa?" Tom asked.

Since the trial, Tom had finally given in to Bo's urging to strike back at the law school. Bo had written the board of directors a letter stating that Tom's retirement had been under duress and demanding that Tom be immediately reinstated to the faculty and that all of the conditions imposed by the board on his return be removed.

"As a matter of fact," Bo said, chuckling, "Rufus called me this morning. They've offered you your job back, Professor."

Tom cocked his head toward Bo and raised his eyebrows.

"Yep," Bo continued. "Evidence professor and trial team coach. They're throwing in a ten-thousand-dollar raise too."

"Jesus, Bo. How did you do it so fast?"

"Wasn't me," Bo said. "You saw the papers after the trial. The press may be annoying but they aren't stupid. The school suspended you for your actions toward Rick Drake and Dawn Murphy, both of whom helped you try and win the Wilcox case. The *Tuscaloosa News* and the local television stations called the board's decision fishy in light of Drake and Murphy's obvious allegiance to you. Anyway, after all the negative press, one of your supporters on the board was able to get a couple of the board members who had voted with Tyler to see the error of their ways."

"Rufus," Tom said, chuckling.

"Bingo," Bo said.

"What about Lambert?" Tom asked.

"Gone," Bo said, laughing. "Once Rufus got a majority of the board to vote you back in, that same majority voted to fire Lambert."

Tom shook his head. "And Tyler?"

Bo's laughter stopped and his face grew solemn. "That . . . is actually the best part. Rufus's majority asked the board of trustees of the university to remove Tyler as the law school attorney, and the president of the board of trustees issued a mandate that Jameson Tyler and the Jones & Butler firm never be allowed to do any legal work for the university ever again." Bo paused. "I believe you know the president of the board of trustees, don't you?"

Tom nodded, feeling goose bumps break out on his arm. "Paul Bryant Jr."

"Seems appropriate, doesn't it?" Bo said, but Tom was too moved by the gesture to speak. "Yeah . . ." Bo continued, nodding. "I think Coach would have loved that."

When they reached the driveway, Bo opened the door to the Lexus and then turned to look at Tom. "How did the surgery go?"

"Good," Tom said. "Bill said he got it all this time. I'll have to live with being scoped every three months for a while, but . . . I'm in pretty good shape."

Bo leaned against the open door and looked Tom in the eye. "So what are you gonna do now, dog? You've got your job back if you want it. Your health is good. And you just hit the largest verdict in West Alabama history. Sounds like the world is your oyster, Professor."

"I don't know yet, Bo. You've given me a lot to think about." He paused and looked back toward the farm. "But whatever it is, it'll be something. No more sitting around. I plan to live the rest of my life like Musso died."

"That's what I'm talking about," Bo said. "Now . . ." A low whine interrupted Bo's words, and Bo smiled. "Ah, hell, I almost forgot."

"Forgot what?" Tom asked, watching Bo walk around the car and open the back.

"Well, when you told me why I was coming up here today, I bought you a little present."

Bo stepped back and gestured at a small green crate.

"Well I'll be damned," Tom said.

Inside the crate was a tiny white and brown English bulldog puppy. Tom opened the crate and took the pup in his arms. Then he looked at his friend.

"You saved my life, Bo. I can't thank—"

"Save your thank-yous, Professor," Bo said, sliding into his car and turning the ignition.

"So, back to Pulaski?" Tom inquired once the automatic windows had come down.

"Home sweet home," Bo said.

"You ever gon' tell me why you practice in that town? You could make even more millions in a bigger city."

"I did tell you, remember?"

Tom's stomach tightened as the memory came back to him. "Because of what happened to your dad?"

Bo nodded, the smile leaving his face. "Unfinished business, dog."

"You ever gonna tell me the whole story?"

Bo shook his head. "Maybe, but not today. It's too long and I have to get home before Jazz tears me a new one."

Before Tom could say anything else, Bo eased the car forward. When it reached the end of the driveway, Tom remembered something Bo had said many moons ago.

"Bo!" Tom yelled, leaning back as his new puppy licked his face.

The car stopped, and Bo leaned his head out the window, waiting for Tom to speak.

But Tom didn't say anything. He simply held up the four fingers of his right hand.

Tuscaloosa, Alabama. Six months later

He arrived at the Waysider about 7:00 a.m. Hungry, both literally and figuratively. He ate eggs and bacon and read the newspaper, looking for new opportunities—an angle for the firm—but he didn't see any. Had he been less focused, he might have allowed himself to reminisce. To think back to that morning some forty years earlier in this same restaurant when the Man had asked him to come home. Instead, he drank coffee and thought about increasing the firm's caseload. He had by his count eaten at the Waysider at least once a week since he started. He had also eaten once a week at the City Café in Northport. Getting out and about and being noticed. Keeping his ear to the ground in the hopes of landing the home run case. That was the name of the game. The life of the plaintiff's lawyer.

Fifteen minutes later he was getting out of his car in the firm parking lot. Before going in, he stopped and looked at the sign that had replaced Rick's shingle a week ago.

McMurtrie & Drake, LLC.

Thomas Jackson McMurtrie breathed the cool Tuscaloosa air and allowed himself a second to smell the roses. He was sixty-nine years old. Last night he and Ruth Ann had eaten dinner at the Cypress Inn. They had been dating now for a few months, and Tom was happy, knowing in his heart that Julie would want him to keep living. This morning he had walked Lee Roy around the block. Though not as big as Musso at this age, Lee Roy Jordan McMurtrie had promise. And a hell of a lot of spirit. Sometimes Tom wasn't sure who was walking who.

Now Tom was about to practice his calling. After forty years of teaching—none of which he regretted—Thomas Jackson McMurtrie, the Professor, was a trial lawyer again.

Tom smiled, thinking of something Jameson Tyler had said a few months earlier, and then saying it out loud as he opened the door and ran up the stairs, not caring if anybody heard him.

"The old bull still has a little gas in the tank."

AUTHOR'S NOTE

In drawing the character of Tom McMurtrie, my aim was to create a legendary figure. A man of exceptional integrity, strength, and class. One of the ways I sought to achieve this purpose was to include Tom on Alabama's famed 1961 football team. Though Tom and the events of this novel are entirely fictional, the 1961 Alabama football team was very much real. As a lifelong Alabama football fan, I can say that all Alabama teams are in some way measured by the '61 team. This team formed the bedrock of Coach Paul "Bear" Bryant's Alabama football dynasty, and their names echo in crimson lore even today. Names like Billy Neighbors, Lee Roy Jordan, Pat Trammell, Darwin Holt, Mike Fracchia, Billy Richardson, Benny Nelson, Bill "Brother" Oliver, Mal Moore, Charley Pell, Bill Battle, and Cotton Clark, just to name a few.

Part of the historical significance of the '61 team is how far the football program had come since Coach Bryant's arrival. In 1958, Coach Bryant, an Alabama alumnus who played on the 1934 national champions, left Texas A&M to become the head coach of Alabama, famously proclaiming that "Mama called." Despite inheriting a program that had suffered four consecutive losing seasons, in his first meeting with the team in 1958 he promised them that they would win a national championship for Alabama.

Just three years later, the 1961 team fulfilled Coach Bryant's promise, going 11-0 and defeating Arkansas 10-3 in the Sugar Bowl to win the national championship. It was Coach Bryant's first of six national championships at Alabama and began an amazing run of excellence. From 1961 to 1966, the Crimson Tide went 60-5-1 and won three national championships (1961, 1964, and 1965) and four Southeastern Conference championships.

Perhaps an even bigger part of the legend of the 1961 team is the special bond that Coach Bryant shared with the players. Pat Trammell, the team's starting quarterback, is widely regarded as Bryant's favorite all-time player. At Trammel's funeral in 1968, after his untimely death from cancer, Bryant escorted Trammel's mother from the church with tears in his eyes. It is the only time Bryant is ever reported to have cried in public. Billy Neighbors, who started on the offensive *and* defensive line, became Bryant's stockbroker and close confidant. Bill "Brother" Oliver and Mal Moore both became assistant coaches for Bryant.

Even after Coach Bryant's death in 1982, players from the '61 team continued to have a dramatic impact on the university. Mal Moore, backup quarterback and defensive back on the '61 team, became athletic director in 1999 and held the position until 2013. In 2007, Coach Moore probably made the most significant coaching hire at Alabama since Bryant, luring Nick Saban away from the Miami Dolphins. After Moore's death in March 2013, Alabama suddenly had to replace the best athletic director in the country. It seems only appropriate that the university turned to Bill Battle, Moore's friend and teammate on the '61 team, to be his replacement.

Finally, the lasting legacy of the '61 team was its dominant defense. Even Coach Bryant, not prone to overstatement or hyperbole, proclaimed of the '61 defense, "We weren't just a good defensive team. We were a *great* defensive team." The '61 defense recorded six shutouts and allowed only three touchdowns to be scored against them. Indeed, opponents scored just twenty-five points against Alabama the entire '61 season.

The legend of the '61 team endures today. On January 9, 2012, I sat with my parents in the Superdome in New Orleans as Alabama won its fourteenth national championship, defeating LSU 21-0. The 2011 team was led by a defense that was first in every statistical defensive category. There were three NFL first round draft choices on the 2011 defense and one second rounder. But when I declared to my father that the 2011 defense had to be the greatest of all time, he just shook his head and with misty eyes said, "Not like '61. Hell, son, that team only gave up twenty-five points . . . the whole year."

ACKNOWLEDGMENTS

The Professor would not have happened without the love, support, and patience of my wonderful wife, Dixie. For eight years she put up with the alarm clock going off at 4:00 a.m. almost every morning, jarring her from sleep and many times waking up one of our three children. She read three different rewrites of the book, patiently wading through each one and offering encouragement and constructive criticism along the way. *The Professor* simply could not have happened without her, and I am so blessed to have her in my life.

My agent, Liza Fleissig, was my guardian angel on this trip, and her tenacity, enthusiasm, and persistence made my dream come true. A writer could not have a more loyal advocate than Liza.

Thanks to Emlyn Rees and everyone at Exhibit A and Angry Robot Publishing. Emlyn's ideas and careful editing improved my story, and I will be eternally grateful to Emlyn for giving me and my story a chance.

Thanks to Alan Turkus, Kjersti Egerdahl, Jacque Ben-Zekry, Tiffany Pokorny, and the entire team at Thomas & Mercer for discovering my story and helping me make it better.

I'd also like to send a huge thank you to Julie Schoerke, Marissa Curnutte, and everyone at JKS Communications for spreading the word about *The Professor* and helping the story find wings.

My parents, Randy and Beth Bailey, have taught me, inspired me, and encouraged me in everything I've tried to do in life, and they were there for me every step of the way during this process. I am so grateful for them.

My brother, Bo Bailey, was one of my earliest readers, and his constant encouragement has been a blessing.

Thanks to my father-in-law, Dr. Jim Davis, for his insights on urology and bladder cancer and for reading the book and being a lightning rod of positive energy.

I am eternally indebted to my wonderful friends Bill and Melanie Fowler, Rick Onkey, Mark Wittschen, Steve Shames, and Will Powell for reading the book and offering their ideas and encouragement.

Thanks to fellow authors Winston Groom, William Bernhardt, and Brian Haig for blurbing the book when it didn't even have a publisher.

Thanks to Davidson College, where my dream of being a writer first hatched, and to the University of Alabama School of Law, where so many of the ideas for this book were formed.

I am so blessed to have been born in the great state of Alabama and to have been raised on Alabama football and its legends. Coach Bryant passed away when I was nine years old, but his spirit lives on at the university and throughout the state.

Finally, my children—Jimmy, Bobby, and Allie—are my inspiration and the greatest joy in my life. I thank God for them . . . and for everything.

ABOUT THE AUTHOR

Photo © 2012 Dixie Bailey

Robert Bailey was born in Huntsville, Alabama. He earned a bachelor's degree in history from Davidson College in North Carolina before going to law school at the University of Alabama, where he made Law Review. For the past thirteen years, Bailey has been a civil defense trial lawyer in his hometown of Huntsville, where he lives with his wife and three children. *The Professor* is his first novel. For more information, please visit www.robertbaileybooks.com.